Strings Attached

Praise for Holly Stratimore

Arrested Hearts

"Holly Stratimore has written a wonderful book that ends up pulling the reader in and making them feel part of something very special…This is a remarkable story and I defy anyone to read it without a lump in their throat. A well deserved 5 stars."—*Kitty Kat's Book Review Blog*

Songs Unfinished

"Holly Stratimore does a wonderful job melding music and romance into a parallel narrative. As the characters' lives ebb and flow, so does their music…It's obvious the author has a deep knowledge of both music and relationships, and she blends them together into a beautiful chord of a novel."
—*Books and Movies and Stuff*

"*Songs Unfinished* is a tender and strong story, and I still smile when I think of it, over a week after finishing reading."
—*(un)Conventional Book Views*

"[A] romance with a flair for taking us in directions we never see coming. *Songs Unfinished* is a wonderful first offering that makes us hope for more stories for us to enjoy, from an author with great potential."—*Lambda Literary Review*

"*Songs Unfinished* is a sweet story about overcoming loss and shame and finding love. The two main characters are an endearing pair and the dialogue between them seemed realistic and natural. Over all, *Songs Unfinished* is a solid lesbian romance with a happy ending."—*Femlitica*

By the Author

Songs Unfinished

Arrested Hearts

Strings Attached

Strings Attached

by

Holly Stratimore

2019

STRINGS ATTACHED

ISBN 13: 978-1-63555-347-5

This Trade Paperback Original Is Published By
Bold Strokes Books, Inc.
P.O. Box 249
Valley Falls, NY 12185

First Edition: January 2019

Credits
Editors: Victoria Villaseñor and Barbara Ann Wright
Production Design: Stacia Seaman
Cover Design by Sheri (hindsightgraphics@gmail.com)

Acknowledgments

I never planned to write this story. The character Nikki Razer played a supporting role in my first two books, and she even appeared in the first book I'd ever written, which was never published. I was surprised when several of my readers asked me if Nikki would get her own book. Even more so, I was touched and flattered. Still, I had already started writing another story, so I simply tucked the idea away on the back burner—until Nikki started talking to me one day and wouldn't shut up.

So I abandoned the other story to write this one. About halfway through, my own life took a difficult turn, and my muse grew stubborn and, at times, went silent. How do you write about people falling in love when the future of your own relationship is up in the air? I had to put this story away more than once while I did my own soul searching. In the midst of all this, my company downsized and eliminated several positions—including mine. This derailed my manuscript again while I searched for employment and then had to focus my energies on learning a new job.

During Women's Week in Provincetown that year, I asked Rachel Spangler—one of my favorite authors—to talk about her process of developing characters. What stood out the most in her response was that she ultimately wanted the characters to become "better versions of themselves" by the end of the book. This resonated with me not only as a writer but as a person. It reminded me that people are flawed, and that's okay. What's important is that we always strive to learn and grow as human beings, and that it's a never-ending process. So thank you, Rachel. You continue to inspire me in more ways than I can count.

Thankfully, my wife and I worked through our issues and reconciled. Once my marriage was back on track, the creative juices flowed again. It was still a struggle at times, but I persevered. I need to thank my readers for your patience and encouragement. I am forever indebted and grateful for your support.

I have to express special thanks to my friend and fellow Bold Strokes Books author Jean Copeland, for hashing out ideas with me and helping me narrow down a central conflict. I also need to thank Senior Editor

Sandra Lowe for helping me strengthen that conflict and fill in gaps where I was struggling, and for the captivating blurb on the back of this book.

To Radclyffe and the entire Bold Strokes Books team, thank you for everything you do for the LGBT literary world. I am so proud and honored to be part of your amazing organization. For my editor, Vic, I cannot praise you enough. You have taught me so much, and I love working with you. Thank you, again, for bringing out the best in me. Thank you to my copy editor, Barbara, for your expertise in fine-tuning the final draft.

I couldn't write a story featuring a music teacher without acknowledging a few of my own. My eternal gratitude to: my first guitar teacher and hero, the late Chuck Mathena; guitar teacher Gerry Adams; my high school choir director, Tom Dugan, who taught me how to sing and the basics of music theory; and UMass-Lowell music theory professor Dr. Jacqueline Charette, who introduced me to the beauty of classical music. I also have to thank my mom, who wasn't a teacher but whose record collection expanded my ear and appreciation for early blues and jazz singers.

I wish I had room to acknowledge everyone by name for their love, support, and friendship, but please know that if you are in my life, you are a blessing that I never take for granted. I must share my heartfelt thanks to a few of you. Thanks to my dear friends Lorraine, Elaine, and the rest of our local gang, for always being there for me. Thanks to Teri for a lifetime of laughs, stories, and friendship. Thanks to my best BSB buds Cathy Frizzell, Lisa Moreau, and Jaycie Morrison for listening and lifting me up when I needed it most. I love you all.

Thanks to my family, for the unconditional love and support you've given me my entire life.

Most of all, thank you, Penny, for believing in me, for your faith in us, and for being my rock. I love you to the moon and back. As long as you're here with me, baby, this is home.

Dedication

This one’s for you, Penny.
For never giving up on me.
For never giving up on us.
I love you.

CHAPTER ONE

Even with protective earplugs, Nikki Razer thought her ears would bleed from the ungodly decibels generated by the roaring crowd. She stepped away from the piano. Her bandmates, Jaymi Del Harmon and Shawn Davies, had just finished singing a duet, a song that paid tribute to Jaymi's late mother. It had become their biggest hit since its debut three years ago. The cheers refused to diminish. The fans wanted what they came for: the scorching kiss between Jaymi and Shawn that always happened at least once in the show. They came together and locked lips. Nikki looked away as the noise level increased again.

There was a time when they cheered the loudest for me. She was the lead singer. She was the most popular member. She was the one who garnered the most attention. The one women chased and lusted after. The one who gladly obliged with a night of hot sex when she was so inclined. After Shawn joined the group, the Cinderella story that was Shawn and Jaymi's relationship took center stage, and Nikki had been pushed into the background to some degree.

Nikki couldn't blame the fans. They were fucking adorable, those two. Their love for each other was so obvious you could spot the glow from a fucking mile away. She didn't begrudge Jaymi her happiness. She'd never do that. She loved Jaymi with all her heart. She had to admit, she'd grown fond of Shawn, too.

It wasn't as if they didn't deserve the attention. They were both incredibly talented. Shawn kicked ass on rhythm guitar and had recently picked up mandolin and dabbled a bit on the piano. Jaymi could play anything she got her hands on. Lead or rhythm guitar. Fingerpicking classical guitar. Piano. Banjo. Bass. Sometimes she'd even kick Brian out from behind his drum kit to demonstrate how she wanted a part played in one of her songs. And she wrote amazing songs and sang like an angel.

Jaymi looked at her with her beautiful, deep blue eyes and raised an eyebrow. Oh yeah, they were doing a show. A guitar tech ran up to Nikki and slung a Gibson Les Paul over her shoulder. Next song was hers. Focus. She needed to focus. How the hell did Jaymi still do that to her? One look like that, with those soulful eyes so full of sincerity and passion, and anyone would come undone. *She's questioning if I'm okay.* Jaymi didn't need any words to show her concern. After almost a decade of friendship and practically living together 24/7 chasing their musical dreams, they knew each other that well.

She walked by Jaymi and gave her a reassuring smile. She stepped up to the microphone at center stage, flanked by Jaymi and Shawn to her right and Kay on bass to her left. Brian drove a steady beat on drums behind them all. She dove into the song and poured out her heart and soul. She couldn't let her fans down. She owed them everything.

Jaymi came to her side to play the guitar solo. She leaned against Nikki so they were back to back, and Nikki felt the softness of Jaymi's hair play over her neck. *God, don't do this to me, Jaymz.* It was Jaymi's way of letting her know she had her back if she wasn't feeling 100 percent. None of them were at this point. Despite how much fun it was to perform, touring was a bitch. One month to go and they would finally take a much-needed break. They fed off the crowd's energy, and the adrenaline pushed them onward.

Three songs to go until the encore. Nikki never thought she'd see the day when she would feel glad to be counting down till the end of a show.

An hour later, she stepped out of the shower in her dressing room. These larger venues had everything, and sinking into that couch for a few minutes alone to decompress was inviting, but she needed to hurry. They were heading back on the road, and the bus was waiting. She pulled on a pair of drawstring lounge pants and slipped on a T-shirt, not bothering with a bra. She'd be asleep on the bus in ten minutes, so she wanted to be comfortable. She brushed her teeth and slicked back her damp hair.

The mirror wasn't her friend tonight. Her normally olive complexion bordered on pale. Her eyes drooped and had dark circles beneath them. A lock of hair fell across her forehead. She needed a haircut, but there would be no time for that for God knew how long.

A knock on the door prompted her to throw her dirty clothes

into her suitcase and press it shut. It was probably Lance, the band's manager, telling her to get her ass in gear so they could get going.

"I'm coming already," she huffed as she swung open the door. *Wow*. Not Lance. Definitely not Lance.

It was a woman wearing a seductive smile and a low-cut dress so short it should be illegal. "Interesting choice of words, considering I haven't even touched you yet."

Nikki opened her mouth to respond, but the stranger swiftly covered it with her own. Her tongue found Nikki's as she scraped a finger beneath her waistband.

"I'm already late," Nikki whispered.

"That's okay. This won't take long." The woman pulled the string and slid a hand inside her pants.

Nikki gasped and pulled her lips away. The woman had long, flowing dark hair and striking blue eyes. Eyes like Jaymi's. Nikki kissed her hard and moved her own hand under the woman's dress. *Oh God, no underwear.*

The woman was right. It didn't take long. As she opened the door and let herself out, Nikki heard her say, "Unbelievable. I just fucked Nikki Razer."

Nikki snatched up her suitcase and caught her reflection in the mirror. "Yeah. Fuck me, all right. Fuck me."

She avoided everyone's eyes as she stumbled into the bus. They knew why she was late. They always knew. Brian was winding down by playing a video game on his tablet. Kay was texting. Probably with her girlfriend, LaKeisha. Lance shook his head in frustration. She caught Shawn's glare accompanied by a clenched jaw and what she guessed was a battle with her willpower to keep her mouth shut. Nikki said nothing. She begrudgingly took one more look back and locked eyes with Jaymi.

She wished Jaymi looked angry or disappointed or flustered. No. It was worse. Pity. That's what she saw in Jaymi's eyes. Fucking pity. Nikki looked away and ducked into her room. She shoved her luggage into a cubby and closed the door. The engine roared to life, and they were moving.

This was the first tour they'd done with this RV. It was like a hotel suite on wheels, complete with private sleeping quarters, a full bathroom, a kitchenette with a dining table and wraparound cushioned bench, and a lounge. It even had Wi-Fi, a flat screen TV, and a video game system. It still didn't feel like home.

Nikki crawled into her bunk. All she wanted was sleep. She tossed and turned, trying to find a comfortable position and a train of thought that would get tonight's sexual encounter out of her mind. She only let it happen because the woman's eyes reminded her of Jaymi. Right? Would she have continued if she'd had brown eyes? Or green?

Fuck yeah, you sleazebag. It hasn't stopped you before. Because all you ever have to do is close your eyes and imagine...

"Hey, you awake?"

That voice. Jaymi's sweet voice. She rolled onto her side and made room for Jaymi to sit down.

"What's up, Jaymz?"

"Are you okay?"

She knows. She always knows when I'm not okay.

"Yeah. Just tired, ya know?"

"Me too. It's been a long trip, huh? One month to go, though. Then we get to play a show at home and relax for a while. I can't wait."

"Me neither." Nikki propped up on one elbow and rested her head in her hand. She fiddled with a loose thread on the blanket. Better keep her hand busy so she wasn't tempted to caress Jaymi's cheek. Or anything else. "Any plans?"

Jaymi clearly knew she was trying to divert the conversation. But in true Jaymi form, she didn't press. "You know, the usual. Spend time with the family. Chill out with Devin and Sara. Catch up on sleep."

"Yeah. Sounds good."

Jaymi smiled, but the look in her eyes was still one of concern. "We're overdue for a movie night, just the two of us."

"What about Shawn?"

"We can have it at your place. It'll be good for us to get away from each other for a bit. I wouldn't want her to get sick of me."

Nikki smiled and shook her head. "That'll never happen."

"I hope not. Anyway, I'll let you get some sleep."

"Good night, Jaymi."

"Night." Jaymi hesitated at the door. "You deserve better, you know."

Yeah, sure. At least one person believed that. The one person she *didn't* deserve. "I'm fine, Jaymi. Now get outta here before Shawn misses you too much."

Jaymi gave her one more "I'm here if you need to talk" look before closing the door behind her.

If only she'd made her move years ago. If only Shawn hadn't come back from California.

If only if only if only…*shut the fuck up and go to sleep.* She slapped a hand over her eyes and gripped her temples. Her palm and face were soaked in no time flat. *You blew it, and you know it.*

CHAPTER TWO

Drew McNally beamed with pride at her student. Melissa smiled from ear to ear after flawlessly playing the Bach minuet she'd been practicing for a month. The final chord still resonated from her acoustic guitar.

"How about that? You nailed it! Great job, Melissa. I knew you could do it."

The sixteen-year-old wiped her palms on her jeans, and her cheeks grew pink. "I have a great teacher."

"Oh no, I can't take credit for that. All I do is demonstrate and guide. You're the one who puts in the hours of practice."

Melissa shrugged. Drew was pretty sure the teenager was gay, but Melissa hadn't indicated whether or not she'd acknowledged it yet. Drew didn't want to encourage the crush but couldn't help favoring her sometimes over her other pupils. She wanted to be a good role model and someone Melissa would trust if she ever needed someone to talk to. She'd been studying guitar with her since she was nine, and Melissa hadn't been shy around her until she'd hit puberty.

Melissa packed up her gear and headed out. Drew made her way down the short hall, past the other lesson rooms, the ensemble room, the office, and then on to the sales floor. She loved this place. Most of the time, anyway. Her dad had built the business from scratch, and since college, it had become her second home.

"I just need to close out the register and we're ready to go."

Drew turned to her father. "Okay. I'll get the lights and lock up."

He grinned. "Melissa seemed pretty excited when she left. How'd she do with that Bach piece?"

"She rocked it, Dad. I'm so proud of her."

"She's a talented kid. Reminds me of you when you were little."

"Don't insult her. She's way better than I ever was."

He finished counting the bills in his hands and looked at her thoughtfully. "Don't sell yourself short, kiddo. You could've made it big if you'd stuck it out."

"True. But I'm happy with what I'm doing." And she was, most of the time. She put away a few items that customers had left scattered around the store. "Besides, you know I couldn't have handled being around all those Hollywood phonies all the time."

He finalized the deposit and sealed the bag. "Just don't wanna see you have any regrets, that's all."

She saw the usual sadness pass over his eyes and again wondered if he'd settled for less. He thought she didn't notice, but she always did. Drew circled around the counter and kissed his cheek. "No regrets. I love teaching. The boss here is kind of a pain in the butt sometimes, though."

"So is the help. Good thing he's such a softie and keeps them on the payroll, eh?" He chuckled at her teasing.

"Good thing." *That payroll would be bigger with higher revenues, Dad. For all of us. If you'd only take my ideas seriously.*

They parted ways after they locked up the shop, and she made the short drive to her modest, one-bedroom apartment. She couldn't afford much, but it was home. Every picture or decoration she owned represented something she loved. Classical music. Paintings. Sculptures. The secondhand furniture was in good shape, and most importantly, it was comfortable.

Three cats greeted her and demanded to know why she was working late again instead of staying home to cater to their every need. She scooped up Vinnie, a black and white Maine Coon, who purred loudly and ate up the attention. Next it was Fret, a tiger, but she wasn't in the mood for lovin'—she wanted her supper. Andres, the oldest, sat aside watching and waiting. He was a big, round, fluffy orange tabby with soulful green eyes. She scratched his head and chin. She set down three bowls before heading to the bedroom to change.

She fixed a sandwich and curled up on the couch. Now Fret was her best friend. She hopped up next to Drew and began rubbing her cheek against her, all the while acting as if she wasn't trying to sneak a peek at what Drew was eating.

"Hey, you just ate. This is mine."

Fret didn't care. She tapped her arm repeatedly with her paw. Drew let her sniff the peanut butter sandwich, and she backed away.

She gave Drew a look as if to say, "Why aren't you eating something I like?" before settling in the opposite corner of the couch. Drew petted her. "Told ya you didn't want any."

Andres cuddled up beside her. Vinnie darted into the room and batted around several toys before taking his usual place on the back of the couch behind her. He stretched out, dangled his legs, and rested a paw on her shoulder. He purred contentedly and kneaded her intermittently.

She turned on the TV, but as usual, there was nothing that interested her, so she shut it off. Maybe she'd read for a while. She browsed her bookcase, but she'd read everything at least twice. She couldn't afford to buy anything new. She loved lesbian romances, but the selection at the library was limited. She usually opted for detective novels if she couldn't find anything else. Besides, sometimes the romance stories made her sad. It would be nice to have a girlfriend. She laughed at the thought. How was that ever going to happen when she never went anywhere? She closed her eyes and withdrew a book at random.

Being single wasn't so bad. It made life simple, which was the way she liked it. She had her freedom. Her cats kept her company. She loved her job, and she got to work with her dad—a big plus there. She smiled.

The holidays were right around the corner. Hopefully, the shop would do well enough in the fourth quarter to keep it going. Otherwise, she wasn't sure what she'd do. She sighed. Worrying about money right before bed was never a good idea. Worrying never solved anything anyway. What she needed was a plan to increase the bottom line. Her father had built a very successful store, but he was stubborn and resistant to change. He repeatedly rebuffed her suggestions to keep up with the new technology and the way things had changed in the retail world. The business needed an upgrade.

So much for not worrying. She reread the same page for the umpteenth time and gave up. She went to bed with her cats, her worries, and the ever-present niggle of loneliness she kept pushing away.

Chapter Three

A bright white light flashed through Nikki's eyelids. *What the hell was that?* Another one. *Damn it.* She opened her eyes and was blinded by another flash.

"Say cheese, hot shot."

"What the—"

The woman stuck a smartphone in her face again and snapped off another picture. "I just wanted a little souvenir of our night together."

Nikki pulled the covers up over her naked body, realizing her upper half had been completely exposed. And now this stranger had pictures of it. Great. Just great. "Is it morning already?"

"Six o'clock. I need to get to work." She bent and placed a kiss on Nikki's lips. "Thank you for a *very* memorable evening." She tossed back her blond hair and smiled. "Even if you did call me Jaymi three times."

Oh shit. "You said that was your name."

"*Amy*. My name's Amy. Don't worry. I'll remember *your* name. And our night together." She scribbled on the notepad on the bedside table. "My number. In case you'd like company again next time you're in town." She smiled. "So, what's the deal with Jaymi and Shawn, then? Is that all just an act, or do you and Shawn take turns with her?"

Nikki bolted upright, clutching the sheet to her chest. "You watch what you say about Jaymi."

Amy stepped back, obviously alarmed by the ire in Nikki's tone. She quickly recovered and winked. "Wow. Somebody's jealous. Does Shawn know you're imagining her girlfriend while you're—"

"Get out."

Amy grinned. "Glad I could uh…*fill in.* Jaymi's a doll. I can see why you'd want to fuck her. See you later, stud." She left.

Nikki fell back onto the bed and let out a growl. "I'm done. I'm so fucking done."

She didn't realize she'd fallen back asleep until a knock on her door woke her up. She checked the clock. *Shit.*

She scurried to the bathroom, threw on a hotel robe, and answered the door. Jaymi was red in the face.

"You're not even dressed? We're leaving in fifteen minutes."

"Give me ten to shower, and I'll meet you down there."

Jaymi took in a deep breath and let it out slowly. She was most definitely pissed. "Don't worry about checking out. Lance is taking care of it."

Nikki nodded, just wanting Jaymi to leave her alone.

"Nik, what's going on with you?"

"Nothing. I'll see you in a few minutes, all right?" Jaymi stared at her and didn't move. "Don't worry, Jaymi. You know better than anybody how quickly I can get ready."

"Unfortunately, yes I do. It's a miracle I don't have high blood pressure."

Nikki grinned at her. "If you grab me a coffee on your way out, I'll beg for your forgiveness and be your servant for life."

Jaymi gave her a playful shove. "Like you haven't promised that before."

"Yeah, but this time I mean it."

"You're wasting time, Nikki."

She spun and dropped her robe just before she entered the bathroom—in Jaymi's full view. She probably wouldn't even notice, but just in case…

Jaymi's words echoed in her head as she showered. Wasting time. *Ain't that the truth.*

She should have told Jaymi a long time ago she was in love with her. If it weren't for that damn rule they had about not dating bandmates, she might have. Then again, those boundaries probably saved the group on more than one occasion. Nikki knew in her heart she could never be the kind of partner Jaymi needed. Then Jaymi fell in love with Shawn, and it was clear as day they were meant to be together. Nikki never had a chance.

Wasted time. By the time Nikki told Jaymi the truth about how she felt, it was too late. And now, things were awkward. Not all the time, but sometimes when they were alone, it was all Nikki could do not to reach out and take Jaymi in her arms and…

Shut the hell up. It's never going to happen, so just forget it. She shut off the water and dressed quickly, with only minutes to spare. She raced onto the bus and slouched into a seat. No one even glanced up to see she was there.

Nikki fumbled with her phone and considered calling her friend Randi, who used to be her favorite "friend with benefits." Not anymore. Randi had a steady girl now, too, and a new career training police dogs. She was probably busy.

She aimed the remote at the TV and searched for a distraction. She found a football game and muted the sound so she wouldn't disturb the others. At least they were headed east and would be home in a few hours. She hoped the falling snow wouldn't slow them down too much.

Home. Where she could spend more time alone with her thoughts.

Great.

❖

Nikki hauled her luggage up the stairs and left it in the laundry room. Her luxury condo had all the modern conveniences, including a two-car garage where she housed her Mustang and motorcycle. Not the best set of wheels for New Hampshire winters, but she would be taking care of that problem soon at the Jeep dealership. She had plenty of money now, so why not spoil herself? She'd moved into this place last summer during the band's break. It had state-of-the-art appliances, four TVs, the best stereo system money could buy with wireless speakers in every room, a spare bedroom where she kept her instruments, and expensive art on the walls. The works.

It was nothing new to have an abundance of possessions, but it felt better now knowing she'd bought them all with her own hard-earned money. Still, they were merely *things*. She had no one to share them with...yet.

She stripped and settled into the Jacuzzi with a glass and bottle of wine. She sipped and closed her eyes. The tension melted away. She couldn't wait to sleep in her own bed tonight. Away from the band.

Away from Jaymi.

Away from the fans that followed her and always wanted something from her. An autograph or photo was fine. That kind of attention never bothered her. But for some, it wasn't enough. For some fans, it seemed as though all they wanted was to get into her pants. It was flattering, and she couldn't deny that she enjoyed sleeping with all those women, but it was nothing more than sex. They never wanted anything else. No one cared about getting to know her. No one asked what her favorite color was or what she liked to eat or what her hobbies were or what other interests she had besides music. Lately, the sheer emptiness of their adoration was smothering her.

Half the bottle was gone by the time she got out of the tub. She walked to the window and watched the snow continue to fall. She finished off another glass. She turned and looked around. She was surrounded by every possible material thing she'd ever wanted.

She'd never felt so empty in all her life.

CHAPTER FOUR

Come on, Dad. Please think about it. If we're going to keep up with the competition, we're going to have to make these investments soon." Drew hated putting her father on the spot. She'd been reluctant to step on his toes—and his pride—by pushing him out of his comfort zone, but she needed to convince him that their livelihood depended on it.

Her dad's laugh lines creased his handsome face. His body had grown soft. His thick, sandy hair hid his grays well, but they were there. Drew's would probably look the same when she was his age. She hoped she'd be that lucky.

"It's not that I'm putting down your ideas, Doodlebug, but we just don't have the money right now. Even if we did, we're a small business, and I intend to keep it that way." He spoke gently, with kindness in his eyes and a patience she'd gratefully inherited. A trait that she knew made her a successful teacher, but one she found increasingly frustrating at the moment.

"I'm proud that we don't have corporate micromanagers dictating our pricing or policies or highfalutin stockholders telling me how to run my business. That's why our customers shop here instead of the big chain stores."

It was hard to stay upset with him when he used her childhood nickname and said things like "highfalutin." *Mom should have appreciated those little things instead of putting him down all the time.*

The bells on the door chimed. The rest of the conversation would have to wait while she took care of the customers. "Welcome to DJ's. I'm Drew, and this is Jerry. Let us know if we can help you with anything."

The two women said hello, and then the rusty-haired one said, "Thanks. We're here to check out some guitars."

They looked familiar, and it only took a second or two for her to place them. Jaymi Del Harmon and Shawn Davies of the local band Passion Play were in her store shopping for guitars. She reined in her excitement—*this could be good for business*. She liked their music, but she didn't really consider herself a huge fan. She wondered if their success had turned them into snobs like the people her mother associated with.

"Are you looking for acoustic or electric?"

"Both, actually," said Jaymi.

"Our equipment truck was in an accident last night," explained Shawn. "Wiped out in the snowstorm and tipped over. Then someone slammed into it, and the whole thing caught fire."

"Oh my God. Was anyone hurt?"

"Nothing serious, thank goodness," Jaymi said. "But we lost all our instruments, so we need to replace everything."

"Wow. I'm so sorry. I'll do whatever I can to help. What would you like to see first?"

Shawn smiled. "I remember you. You sold me a Gibson SG a few years ago."

"Yes, I remember. Was that lost, too?" How sweet was that? *Shawn's the one who's famous, yet she remembered me.* How refreshing. Maybe they hadn't changed at all.

"Afraid so. That was a great axe, too. I'm gonna miss it."

"You're in luck. I have three in stock if you want another one."

"Cool."

"I'm happy to see Passion Play doing so well. You've done New Hampshire proud." She didn't need to be a fan to know how to treat her customers. Especially when she knew they could afford to spend a lot.

Jaymi said, "Well, thank you, Drew."

Jaymi's sincerity melted her heart. She was sure she was blushing. Drew handed Shawn a cable and told her to plug into any amp she wanted. She took down the first guitar Shawn selected. Jaymi said she'd be in the acoustic room.

They were in the store for almost three hours. While they tried out guitar after guitar, they stopped and politely chatted with other customers and gave autographs to everyone who asked for one. At one point, they played an entire song together. It was like being at a private jam session. Their enthusiasm was contagious, and their presence breathed new life into the place.

They left with seven instruments that came to almost twenty thousand dollars in sales. The minute they were out the door, she and her dad hooted and hollered with joy.

The next day, their drummer Brian came in and spent a small fortune on a drum set and several accessories. He said his cousin Jaymi raved about the place, and he was a big believer in supporting small local businesses. The day after that, she sold three bass guitars to their bassist, Kay Burnes. Jaymi and Shawn came in again and stocked up on strings, effects pedals, two amps, and a few other odds and ends. Her dad waited on them this time. Drew was busy teaching, but she couldn't help but be distracted knowing who was in the shop.

When Melissa came out of her lesson, she got the surprise of her life. Jaymi sat with her and showed her how to play a song. Shawn helped her out with her fingering, and then the three of them played a song together. Melissa floated out of the store on cloud nine. Drew was beyond touched that they'd spent so much quality time with one of her students.

They were now close to making their annual sales goal with two months left in the quarter. She wasn't about to count her chickens, but now she was anxious to keep the momentum going and find ways to sustain it.

She sailed home with her business wheels spinning. If she could get Passion Play to do regular appearances when they were home, imagine what it could do for sales. Having all of them together might be too much for their shop to handle. She didn't want to cause mayhem, but one or two of them at a time?

"What do you think, Fret?"

Fret was a music lover. She'd named her that because as a kitten, she would bat at Drew's fingers while she was playing her guitar.

The juices were flowing now. She'd always wanted to start an after-school ensemble program for kids. Maybe even a scholarship fund so that kids could afford instruments and lessons. The store hadn't been making enough profit for those things or for the additional employees they'd need. They had two part-timers and a part-time assistant manager, but otherwise, it was just her and Dad. She loved her job, but if things didn't turn around soon, the shrinking budget might force her into a career change. He was paying her twenty-five percent below her market value. He'd never find a replacement manager at that salary. No one with her level of expertise would accept such a measly offer.

She shook her head. It wasn't her responsibility to save the business, but DJ's was her dad's baby. And there was no one on earth she loved more than her dad. *Dad would be crushed if I left.* There had to be a way to meet in the middle and move DJ's into the modern age.

She put on a Brahms record and sat down with a pen and notebook. She spent an hour brainstorming. Too keyed up to sleep, she made some instant cocoa and relaxed into her comfy couch. As her mind relaxed, one thing occurred to her. Why hadn't the lead singer Nikki Razer come in for new guitars? Surely Jaymi would have recommended DJ's to her, too.

She shrugged. Maybe Nikki didn't live locally like the rest of the band. She wasn't so sure she'd like Nikki anyway. She had a reputation as a player with a big ego. Just the kind of person she preferred to avoid. Probably a partier, too. *Just like Mom.*

All her mother cared about was her acting career and everything that went with it. The fame and fortune. The celebrity status. The Hollywood parties. The fanfare. She wanted it so badly, she put on an act to attract attention wherever she went. Drew never knew if it was her mother or the actress in her presence.

Poor Dad. He was nothing more than arm candy to her. She could remember her telling him to behave a certain way so she could make an impression on some big-time movie producer or casting director. He just wanted to play in his band and write songs. She wouldn't even take his name when they got married for fear it would confuse her fans, and she'd have to start over making a name for herself. Margo Hollister was the name on every headline, and she wanted to make damn sure it stayed that way.

No wonder their marriage hadn't lasted. Her own relationship with her mother had dwindled down to obligatory niceties exchanged during holidays, special occasions, or otherwise "big deals" in their lives. Their definitions of what qualified as "special" or "big" differed drastically, something that was clear as day when a last minute "big" audition trumped a flight east for Drew's college graduation. It wasn't that she didn't love her mother, but the bond between them barely scratched the surface of Drew's heart.

She readied herself for bed and paused at her dresser, picking up the framed photo of what used to be a happy family. She was five. Her parents were still young and in love, with their whole lives and dreams ahead of them.

Different dreams, it turned out. Different means. Different directions. Different motivators. Just…different.

She set down the picture and crawled into bed. How frustrating that a picture could last forever, but a moment could not.

CHAPTER FIVE

Drew went over the figures again. Even with their recent big sales, it wasn't enough. They'd been struggling for so long and were so far in the red that the money had simply allowed them to get back into the black but only just. She needed to do something and fast. She had a few special promotions in mind for the month of December. Most of her Christmas shoppers were parents buying starter kits for their kids. Although they always did well with those deals, it didn't generate the profits that the more expensive gear did. Musicians were fussy shoppers when it came to buying instruments, and rightfully so. A guitar not only had to have the sound they were looking for, it had to feel right in their hands. Looks and brand name mattered, too. Finding that perfect combination could be difficult. That was where she came in—to make sure their customers didn't leave without finding what they needed.

She crunched the numbers again. She'd already cut every expense she could possibly cut. She loved her father dearly, but he'd relied too much on his old-school approach when it came to advertising and marketing. He barely knew how to use a computer, much less the internet.

She slammed the accounts register closed and blew out an exasperated breath. The office walls were closing in. It should've been neat as a pin with all the spare time she'd had this year with the slow business. She'd lost interest in her annual spring-cleaning, and here it was November, and it was still a dump.

A light knock on the door interrupted her misery. Dad knew he didn't have to knock, but he always did anyway.

"Yes?"

The door opened, and he poked his head through. "There's a

customer in here asking for you. Said her friends recommended you personally." He smiled wryly. "She's quite a looker, too."

Drew knew what that meant. He was always keeping an eye out for "a nice girl" for her to go out with, even though she'd told him a thousand times she hated fix-ups.

"Okay. Be there in a sec."

She followed him down the hall and saw a black-haired woman with her back to them, looking at a guitar on a stand. Her dad slinked away and made a fuss over straightening some merchandise.

"Hello. What can I do for you?"

The woman turned around slowly, and Drew's jaw dropped. Nikki Razer, in the flesh. Not ordinary gorgeous but *holy shit* gorgeous. In fact, she may have been the sexiest thing she'd ever laid eyes on. In the dead of winter, she wore a waist-length black leather jacket, tight blue jeans, and black leather boots. Not very sensible attire for this time of year. *She must be more interested in attracting attention than staying warm. A bit of a turnoff, but nonetheless, she's definitely easy on the eyes.*

Drew quickly collected herself and hated that she was nervous. Nikki was just a person. A human being who was no better than anyone else.

Nikki smiled, and Drew saw a twinkle in her large, dark eyes. *Get a grip!*

"Drew?"

"Yes. What can I do for you?" Idiot. She'd already said that once. Nikki was probably used to people being nervous around her. Drew didn't want to be one of them.

Nikki continued to look her in the eye, making her even more uneasy. "Wow," Nikki said softly.

"Excuse me?"

"I'm sorry for staring, but you have the most beautiful eyes I've ever seen."

They hadn't even exchanged names yet, and the woman was already flirting and smiling at her as if she were used to getting whatever she wanted with her looks and fame alone. *Just like Mother.*

"Do you use that line on everyone?" She hoped her smile and the raised pitch in her voice would come across light-hearted even as she was fighting the impression that Nikki thought she was God's gift to women. Nikki was a customer, after all—one who could potentially spend a lot of money in her shop. She should be playing along to generate more sales, but doing so would just make her feel like a greedy, ass-kissing salesperson who only cared about landing a sale.

Nikki smiled widely. "If I have, I'll never have to use it again."

Drew stepped back, shaking her head. No chance in hell was she falling for something like that.

"What? You think I don't mean it?"

It's kind of hard to think so with your reputation, Ms. Razer. She almost said it out loud and realized how rude it would sound. Instead, she just shrugged.

Nikki looked down momentarily. "Whether you believe me or not, it's the truth."

Drew wasn't sure if she was sincere or if this was just another method she used to charm her way into someone's bed. Either way, she needed to do something to ease the tension so she wouldn't lose her as a customer. "I'm sorry. I shouldn't assume things about you when I don't know you."

"No, you don't. But I don't know you, either. I shouldn't have assumed you would enjoy being complimented."

Ouch. Okay, maybe she deserved that.

"So, how about we forget about all this and start over?" Nikki extended her hand and smiled. "Hello, Drew. It's nice to meet you. I'm Nikki," she said with exaggerated dramatic flair. "You were highly recommended by the most talented musician I know, Jaymi Del Harmon. I need two guitars, one acoustic and one electric. I would be forever indebted to you if you could help me with that."

Nikki hadn't let go of her hand. It was warm and soft. Strong. Long, nimble musician's fingers enclosed her hand. Fingers that she was sure held talents beyond tickling the ivories. *I'm pathetic.*

Drew pulled away. "I can definitely help you with that. What would you like to see first?"

"Acoustics."

"Follow me." Drew led the way to the soundproof acoustic guitar room, hoping its construction didn't amplify her out of control heartbeat. "Any particular brand?"

"I've been playing Ovations mostly, but I was thinking of changing things up and going with something with a richer tone."

Drew pulled open the glass door and gestured for Nikki to go through ahead of her. "I have several I can recommend. These Martins and Takamines have warm tones." She pointed to them as she mentioned them. "I also have a few Taylors that sound really nice."

Nikki grinned and made no effort to hide a look that traveled the entire length of Drew's body and back up again. She slipped off her jacket, revealing a beautifully shaped body in a heather-black quarter-zip sweater. "Okay."

"Okay, what?" Drew barely hid her contempt, which was as strong for Nikki as it was for herself at the moment.

"Okay, I'll try them all." She withdrew a guitar pick from her hip pocket, held it up, and smiled crookedly. "I came prepared."

I bet you did. She took down a guitar with a black finish and handed it to her.

Nikki thanked her and sat down on the padded bench in the middle of the room. She looked it over and strummed a few chords. "How'd you know I'd like the black one?"

Drew shrugged. "Other than your jeans, it's all you're wearing. I doubt you'd wear a color you don't like."

"Smart sales technique. I'm impressed."

"I don't think of it that way. I'm just observant."

"Either way, I'm impressed. I like this one, but I'm thinking I need a change. What else do you have?"

Drew rehung the Takamine and perused the wall. "Take your pick."

Nikki stood and looked over the selection. "This one's beautiful." She lifted a deep brown and gold sunburst Gibson off its hook. "The colors remind me of your eyes." She sat down with it and began to strum. "Warm. Soulful. Pure." She locked eyes with Drew. "Just like it sounds."

And then, Nikki began to sing. Her alto voice was smooth and clear and without the edge and occasional rasp that Drew knew from the few Passion Play songs she'd heard on the radio. The rich acoustics of the room only enhanced how beautifully it blended with the tones of the guitar. *That's the one she should buy.*

The enclosed space suddenly felt too small. Drew pulled her gaze away. The woman's ego perturbed her, but she couldn't deny that Nikki was as talented as she was beautiful. She looked out into the store. Her dad was busy signing for a delivery. Perfect. "Listen, I need to check on that shipment. Try anything you like, and I'll be back shortly. Just holler if you need anything."

She slipped out the door before Nikki could reply. After a few minutes of assisting with sorting out the merchandise, she saw Nikki step out of the room with the Gibson.

"I'll take it."

"Good choice. I'll go grab the hard-shell case that comes with it and hold it for you behind the counter. Jerry will keep an eye on it."

"Thanks, Jerry." They exchanged smiles, and Nikki turned her attention back to her. "Now, I'm going to check out your electrics. Are you free to assist me, or do you trust me to help myself?"

"Whatever you'd like. I don't want to crowd you." She hoped Nikki preferred to be left alone. "There are cables in there so you can plug into any of the amps, but if you want to try anything that's hung up high, I'll have to help you with that."

"What if I want your professional opinion?"

"Don't worry about this stuff, dear," said her father. He smiled at Nikki. "She's at your service, miss, for as long as you need her."

Drew gave him a scolding look and escorted Nikki to the electric guitar area.

"Dear?"

"He's my father."

"Ah. That explains the matching hair color and striking good looks."

Drew fumed. Nikki was a relentless flirt. She knew what she was doing, and she was shameless in doing so. Her confidence bordered on arrogance. Yet she was so goddamned beautiful it was no wonder women fell all over her. Drew supposed being a rich and famous rock star didn't hurt, but there was no way she was going to let herself become another notch on Nikki Razer's bedpost.

"Your mother must be stunning."

Drew cringed. Nikki and her mother would probably get along splendidly. Nonstop flirtation with an endless supply of charming compliments designed to get whatever they wanted from people. It was sickening how well it worked. It wasn't going to work on her. She'd appease her while she was here—she couldn't very well be rude to a paying customer—and then she could go back to her normal life.

"I'm sorry. I said something that upset you," Nikki said softly, tilting her head.

Drew tightened her jaw and stared at the wall of guitars. "You didn't upset me. My mother is…well, it's…never mind." Her mother was none of her business. "So, what other colors do you like besides black?"

Nikki followed her line of sight. "Whatever you call that shade of blue." She took down a Paul Reed Smith solid-body with dual humbucking pickups. It was a brilliant cobalt blue with black tiger-stripe streaks through it. Nikki held it up by the neck and scanned it over. An unreadable expression crossed her face. "On second thought, I think I'll try the dark red one instead. It's the same model, right?"

"Yes, identical other than the color."

Nikki tried out five other guitars but kept going back to the red PRS. "I think this is the one—oh boy." She looked over Drew's shoulder.

The hysterical voices behind her told Drew all she needed to know.

"My God, it's true! Are you…"

"Ahh! It's her!" the other teen squealed, then more quietly said, "It's Nikki Razer!"

Nikki handed Drew the guitar. "Excuse me a minute." The gaggle of girls swarmed her before Nikki could approach them first. "How's it going, ladies?"

Amidst the spouts of praise and "we're your biggest fans" were requests for autographs.

Nikki looked at Drew. "Drew, keep these darlings entertained for a moment, will you?" She stepped around them and added, "I'll be right back, I promise." Nikki winked at them and dashed out of the store.

The groupies' faces fell harder than boulders to the floor. "You think she ditched us?"

If she did, it was a rotten thing to do. Although she doubted it. Celebrities thrived on this kind of thing. She'd seen her mother soak it up a million times. They got their answer when Nikki raced back in with a stack of photos in her hand.

"Who's first?" Nikki asked as she uncapped a black Sharpie. "What's your name?" She personalized each message, taking time with each fan, asking their favorite Passion Play song, joking that it had better be one of hers, and none of them let her down.

How convenient that she carries photos with her wherever she goes, as if she knows she'll need them. The other members of Passion Play hadn't done that when they were there. They'd simply signed whatever was available.

The mob finally left—without making a single purchase, of course. Drew crossed her arms and waited. Perhaps *now* she could get back to selling the egomaniac her damn guitar.

Nikki spun around with a smile. "Now, where were we?"

Drew pasted a smile on her face and retrieved the guitar.

"Oh yeah. Sorry about the interruption. I guess word got out we were all shopping here."

"Don't worry about it."

"You know." Nikki leaned in and spoke quietly. "Believe it or not, sometimes I wish people didn't recognize me."

What a bunch of malarkey. Drew tried to smile sympathetically.

She sighed. "But I can't complain. I wanted success, I got it, so it goes with the territory, right?"

There are other ways to measure success, Ms. Razer. Fame wasn't at the top of that scale. Not by a long shot. "So, have you decided?" She needed to get back to business.

Nikki gave her a questioning look, probably for not answering her question. "I'll take it." She handed the guitar back to Drew. "Where can I find your straps?"

"My…straps?"

"Yes. New guitars deserve new straps to go with them, don't you agree?"

Good Lord. Of course Nikki meant guitar straps. They weren't in a lingerie shop, for crying out loud. She shook off the brief curiosity about what kind of bra Nikki was wearing beneath that tight sweater and led her to the accessories department.

Trying to ignore the way her legs felt like jelly, she walked to the stock room and found the case for the PRS. Nikki was at the checkout when she returned.

Her dad rang up the sale and placed both guitars in the cases. "Thank you for the autographed pictures. That's a great idea to give them away with purchases over fifty dollars."

"It's the least I can do," Nikki responded.

Actually, that *was* a good idea. She might as well capitalize on Nikki's popularity. The business needed all the help it could get these days.

"Thank you both for all your help today. This was fun. I haven't shopped for guitars in years."

"Drew, help this young lady out with those, will you?" He rushed out from behind the counter and held the door open for them.

"Of course." She picked up the electric and followed Nikki out the front door.

Jerry said, "Be careful out here. It might be a little slick. It's been snowing for the last hour or so."

Oh shit. At least three inches of snow covered the only customer car in the lot. Judging by the shape, it was some sort of sports car that sat very low to the ground.

Nikki pressed the remote on her key and pried open the passenger door. A pile of wet, heavy snow slid off and dusted the interior. Nikki released the seat forward and placed the guitar she was carrying into the rear.

"Let me take that from you," Nikki said, reaching for the other instrument in Drew's hands. After she had them situated the way she liked, she emerged with a snowbrush in her hand. "Thank you again for your help today."

She trudged around the front end of the car and disappeared inside. The engine roared to life. A few measures of rock music blared from the stereo before she cut the volume. She hopped back out and began clearing off the snow. It was a gorgeous red Mustang. Great for summer cruising. The worst thing to be driving in this weather.

"Will you be able to get home okay?"

"I grew up in Massachusetts. I know how to drive in the snow."

"Yeah but…are you saying you grew up in New England, and you don't know any better than to drive a sports car in the winter?"

Nikki stopped brushing and glared at her. "For your information, wise guy, I bought a Jeep Wrangler yesterday."

Drew choked down a laugh. "So, where is it?"

"They didn't have the model I wanted in stock. It's being delivered from another dealer on Monday."

"Maybe you should have waited to go guitar shopping after you picked it up."

Nikki leaned toward her. "I couldn't wait. We have a show tomorrow night. Besides, I wouldn't have had such an enjoyable afternoon today."

Drew felt her face grow hot. Nikki was flirting again. If it was anybody else, she might've been flattered.

"Glad we could help."

"I better get going before the roads get any worse."

"Be careful."

"I will." Nikki climbed in and lowered the window. "I'll be back again. I may need to pick up something else." She winked and pulled away.

Drew knew exactly what Nikki wanted to pick up, and it wasn't something she could buy.

CHAPTER SIX

Nikki fishtailed when she pulled out of DJ's parking lot. The slippery roads weren't her only worry. She could barely see. The wind was pushing her car around at will, and the snow flying sideways limited visibility. A large truck blinded her momentarily with its headlights, and she felt the back end swerve again. She lifted her foot off the gas and let the car coast to a slower speed. She was crawling, but even at this speed, she was nervous. She hadn't wanted to let Drew see it, though.

That's what she got for not checking the forecast. She should have gone guitar shopping earlier in the week with everyone else, but she couldn't bear to spend another day with Jaymi and Shawn together.

She thought about Drew. When she'd first seen that her hair color was similar to Jaymi's, she'd expected the same shade of blue eyes that crushed her every time. Instead, Drew's eyes were brown. Not an ordinary brown. They were something in between caramel and milk chocolate. Maybe a speckling of both. Anyway, all she knew was that they were the most beautiful eyes she'd ever seen. She wasn't feeding Drew a line. It was the truth.

Except for the players that came after her looking for sex, most women got nervous and tongue-tied around her. Nikki tried her best to put them at ease, but sometimes, it made the situation more awkward. Why couldn't people just treat her like a person?

That's exactly how Drew had treated her, even though she sensed that Drew wasn't 100 percent comfortable around her. In fact, there were moments when she thought Drew didn't like her at all and that she was just showing her the same courtesy and manners she would any customer. It was a novel experience, and instead of putting her off, she found it intriguing.

She wondered how Drew had been around the rest of the band. She'd have to ask. Then again, it didn't matter. Nikki had more to buy. She had what she needed for this weekend's show, but she hadn't replaced everything. Her heart did a little happy dance. *I hope Drew's working again when I go back next week.*

The Mustang's nose suddenly slid toward the center line. "Shit!"

There was an oncoming vehicle. She yanked the wheel and got back in her own lane just in time, but the overcompensation caused the tail end to skid. She cursed again and cranked the wheel again in the opposite direction, but it wouldn't turn. She hit the brake—a little harder than she intended to—and it started to spin. The combination of the darkness and whiteout conditions made it impossible to see where the lane was. The car veered off the road and jerked to a stop.

She slammed her palms on the wheel and cursed some more. She felt like a fool. She'd never had a problem driving in the snow before. If she hadn't been distracted by a beautiful woman…

She took a deep breath and shifted into reverse. She carefully pressed on the gas and slightly let up the clutch. The rear tires made a whirring noise as they spun. The car moved about an inch. She shoved it into first and tried the same thing going forward. Nothing. She didn't have enough room to rock it and gain traction.

"Fuckin' A!" She got out and assessed the situation. She shivered and swore again at her lack of sense to wear a winter coat. Why did she always have to be more concerned with appearance than comfort?

All four wheels were buried in the snowbank along the side of the road. Fortunately, she hadn't hit a tree or utility pole. She popped her trunk. She had a small emergency shovel and a pair of shitty old gloves. They'd have to do.

She extended the telescopic handle and started scooping snow out from around the tires. The entire right side of the car was buried above the wheel wells. She'd have to squeeze herself in to clear it out. As she moved around to the front end, she saw approaching headlights. The vehicle slowed and pulled up behind her car. She could either be relieved or afraid of being in danger. *You never know these days.*

A figure dropped out of the SUV and took a step toward her. The size suggested a woman. Good. She was in a parka and stocking cap with a big pom-pom. As she came closer, Nikki couldn't believe her luck.

"Hey, are you okay?" Drew called out.

"Yeah. But if you give me any shit about driving my Mustang in the snow again, I'm never buying another guitar from you."

Drew came up next to her and shrugged. "I'll just have to sell you something else. Can I interest you in a keyboard? A saxophone? New harmonica set?"

"Wow. You know every instrument I play. And here I thought you weren't a fan."

"It's my business to know my customers. That includes being familiar with all kinds of music, whether I'm a fan or not. If someone's shopping for an instrument and they like Passion Play's sound, I know what to show them. And you're making assumptions again."

Nikki grinned. "Shame on me. Well then, did you stop to chat or are you here to rescue me? I have to ask. I don't want to assume one way or the other."

"Go get in my truck and get warm. I'll call for a tow. There's no way you're digging that out."

"All righty then. Rescue it is." She *was* freezing her ass off.

They climbed into Drew's truck. Nikki rubbed her hands together and then held them in front of the heat vents. It was an old truck but clean. Drew called AAA and gave them her membership number and location. She looked adorable in her smoky-blue coat. She removed her cap, and strands of her static-infused hair reached toward the roof.

"They said it could be at least forty-five minutes," Drew said when she disconnected. She glanced at the dash. "I don't have much gas, so I don't think I can keep the engine running the whole time."

"That's okay. I can think of a few ways we can keep warm." Nikki smiled at her and loved the blush that spread across Drew's cheeks, but the frown suggested she was pissed, not flattered.

"You must be frozen in that jacket. Hold on a sec."

Drew got out and opened the rear gate. A gust of wind blasted through the interior, and tiny wet flakes stung the back of Nikki's neck. Drew slammed it shut and returned with two blankets. "Here. This'll help."

She reached over and placed the blanket over her, bringing their faces close together. Nikki felt as if she was being tucked into bed. It would've been so easy to kiss her right then. Drew kept her gaze down as if refusing to look her in the eye.

"You do know I'll have to do something to thank you for all this," Nikki said as Drew retreated to her own seat, wrapping herself within the other blanket.

Drew shook her head. "No thanks necessary. What was I supposed to do? Drive by and leave you stranded?"

"I have a cell phone. I could've called for help."

"Still, I wouldn't have felt right just going by. Really, it's no trouble. I would've done the same for anybody."

Nikki grinned at her again. "Anybody? So you're saying I'm not special?" Nikki took Drew's standoffishness as a challenge and just had to push.

"I, uh, no that's not what I'm saying at all. I mean—"

"Relax. I'm just messing with you."

Drew's eyebrows furrowed. She shifted away and leaned back against the door. "I don't appreciate being toyed with."

Nikki couldn't help but laugh. Drew seemed to be trying awfully hard to not like her. Nikki would have to work a bit harder to win her over, then. Not something she was used to doing, but no sweat. She was up for it.

"Sorry. I'm just an idiot who doesn't have the sense to check the forecast in November before I venture out in anything other than a four-by-four. You had the decency to help me out. The truth is, you're the one who's special here, not me."

Drew's soft brown eyes grew darker. "You never stop, do you?"

"What do you mean?"

"Every other sentence out of your mouth is some kind of flirtatious comment. Is that all you care about, getting women into bed? Because I, for one, will not be one of them."

Nikki almost cowered under Drew's glare. It probably didn't show on her face, but inside, she felt an inch tall. She'd done it again. She'd failed to rein in her habitual ways and respect a woman's boundaries. For the first time she could remember, instead of giving a woman what she wanted, she'd offended her.

She slinked down in her seat and pulled the blanket up to her chin. She couldn't even look her in the eye now. "I'm sorry. I find it hard to hold back compliments when it comes to beautiful women. If you find that offensive, then I apologize."

"Oh, for God's sake. You just did it again." Drew's tone wasn't angry this time. She sounded amused.

"Told ya."

Drew shook her head and looked out her window. Nikki swore she was fighting a smile. She thought the long wait would end up feeling awkward, but when she got Drew talking about guitars, the tension all but disappeared. When the tow truck arrived, she thanked Drew again and watched the SUV take off as she climbed back into her car. There was no doubt in her mind that Drew would occupy her thoughts tonight. She wondered what she was going to do about it.

❖

Drew finished taking care of the cats and opened the fridge. She wasn't hungry, though she should be. It was after ten o'clock, and she hadn't eaten since her late afternoon lunch. Normally, she would have grabbed a snack during her evening break, but she'd been so caught up in taking care of Nikki, she'd forgotten all about it. She emptied a can of vegetable soup into a bowl and threw it in the microwave.

She perused a month-old *Musician* magazine as she ate—an unsold return the vendor had written off and let her keep—and then picked up her phone to check the weather and her bank account.

Perhaps if she'd listened to her friends at Berklee, she would have become a filthy rich recording artist, too. Then *she* could throw down hundred-dollar bills for instruments without thinking twice, as Nikki Razer had today.

It always felt as if everyone else's dreams were grander than hers. Her college friends thought she was wasting her talent on teaching. They'd say things like, *Let's form a band. We'll be the next big thing.*

Drew didn't want to be the next big thing. She wanted to teach. She'd always wanted to teach. That's where her true passion was, and no one could convince her otherwise.

She put on Beethoven's Symphony No. 7 on vinyl and skipped to the second movement. She slumped into her recliner, closing her eyes and focusing on the beautiful yet simple melody that gradually grew stronger. She loved this piece. Fret curled up on her lap. Andres rubbed his body across her leg as he passed by, and Vinnie pounced onto the back of the chair behind her and draped a paw on her shoulder.

The music was soothing, but it didn't stop her mind from playing back her day with Nikki. One minute she was sweet and naturally charming, the next an infuriating, flirtatious egomaniac. Nikki reminded her too much of her mother.

The more successful her mother became, the more she expected people to cater to her every whim. Drew hated the way men tried to get her mother's attention just because she was beautiful and famous. She didn't hesitate to stroke their precious male egos either, leading them on, knowing she had her pick of whom she brought home to bed. After Dad left, there were plenty of them. Nikki Razer seemed just like her.

The lively sounds of the third movement began, and it almost made her jump. Fret protested when she got up and pulled Vinnie into her arms. She extended his front leg with his paw in her hand as if they were waltzing, and she danced around the living room with him. Fret meowed and pranced around her feet as Andres looked on from his bed with a bored expression on his face. A minute or so later, she put Vinnie down. She engaged the two younger kitties in a game of chase with a long, felt ribbon at the end of a plastic wand. Andres snatched at it when it came close to him, but he didn't bother getting up.

She went to bed after they all ran out of energy. Nikki consumed her thoughts again as she tried in vain to sleep. The more she tried to get Nikki out of her head, the harder it was to fall asleep. What was it about her that got under her skin?

CHAPTER SEVEN

Nikki strolled into DJ's Saturday morning soon after they opened. She couldn't believe what she was hearing. The jazzy, warm tones of a semi-solid Gibson swarmed around her. If B.B. King hadn't passed away, she'd swear it was him playing. There was no one at the front counter, so she followed the sounds around the corner into the electric guitar part of the shop. It was Jerry. His eyes were closed, and his face contorted with emotion as he plucked out blues riffs as if they were an extension of his soul. Mesmerized, she didn't notice Drew walk up next to her.

"He's incredible!" Nikki whispered.

Drew's face lit up. "He is."

"Where can I see him perform?"

"You just did."

They quietly walked out of the area, neither wanting to disturb him.

"Are you serious? He doesn't perform professionally anywhere?" Nikki shook her head in disbelief.

"Not anymore. He used to play in a band when I was a kid. He did a few jobs as a studio musician, too."

"I can't believe it. You could charge admission right here. Seriously. You'd make a killing."

"He loves to play, but he hates being the center of attention. Besides, he wouldn't want the commitment and all the pressure that goes along with a gig schedule."

"Wow. What about just recording it? Hell, I'd pay for that CD a thousand times over. We have our own rehearsal studio with recording equipment. He could—"

"Nikki, stop. He's happy. Leave him alone."

"But—"

"But nothing. Not everyone wants fame and fortune. Why can't people accept that?"

Nikki got the impression Drew had made this argument before. She wasn't even sure if Drew was speaking to her or was thinking of someone else. Once again, she'd unintentionally hit a nerve.

The music stopped for a minute. A different guitar took its place. He quickly tuned it, then started playing with the unmistakable tone of a Fender Stratocaster. Now it sounded as if Stevie Ray Vaughan was there. What a waste. The world was missing out on all this talent.

"What about you?" Nikki asked. Maybe she could make things right.

"What about me?"

Another guitar took the Strat's place. Nikki figured out what he was doing. He was taking down each instrument and tuning them all.

"Do you play?"

"I teach."

"So, you play."

"Yes. I play."

"Which instruments?"

Drew shrugged modestly. "Just about all of them. I studied a little of everything in college. I have a degree in music education."

"I'm impressed. Again."

"Thanks."

"So, is there someplace I can see *you* perform?" Nikki smiled at her, hoping Drew didn't interpret her question as a double entendre. Though it was tempting to add *or do I need to take lessons from you*, knowing it would probably get her kicked out of the store for good. Drew was so fucking cute, and so unavailable, it was making her head spin.

"Not everyone has to be a performer to enjoy making music. I'm happy with what I do here. It's very fulfilling."

Madness. Complete and utter madness. She couldn't grasp how someone could have all that music inside them and not feel the need to perform it. She couldn't do it. Not in a zillion years. Jaymi would probably be content teaching, but she loved writing songs and playing so much, Nikki doubted she'd feel complete if she didn't share it even on a small scale. And Shawn, forget it. She'd rather kill herself than give it up.

"So, what can I help you with? Did you forget something yesterday?"

Drew's questions lured her out of her musings. "No, I'm good for now." She reached into her back pocket and withdrew an envelope. "I brought you a little thank-you gift for rescuing me and my car last night. My 'stang appreciated it. And, well, also for your help in the store yesterday. Thanks to you, the show will go on tonight without me having to borrow guitars from my mates."

Drew looked at her suspiciously as she took it from her. Her eyes widened when she saw the contents. "Concert tickets?"

Nikki nodded. "Sorry there are only two. It's all I could scrounge up for comps. The rest of the band scoffed up the rest of 'em."

"I, uh…this really wasn't necessary."

"I know, but I wanted to do it. You must have someone you can bring. Your dad, a friend." Nikki was suddenly nervous. "A date?" She hoped Drew didn't opt for a date. *Shit.* For all she knew, she had a girlfriend. Or worse—a boyfriend. What a slime she was. She hadn't even considered that. Drew was sweet and gorgeous. Why wouldn't she have someone?

"I appreciate the gesture, but I can't get coverage on such short notice. But I do know a couple of people I could give them to."

Was she serious? She would give them away? The whole idea was to thank *Drew* and to have *Drew* at the show. And maybe, score a few points with her. "Look, if you don't care so much about seeing Passion Play, then at least come to support the opening act." She pointed out the name on the ticket. "They're local and they won a Battle of the Bands competition sponsored by the same radio station that gave Passion Play its start. They're a fantastic group."

Drew studied the tickets again, and her face showed signs of recognition. She smiled. "Hey, they shop here. Good for them!"

"So, you'll go?"

"I don't know. It's in Boston. I'm not crazy about driving in the city at night. When I went to school there, I always used public transportation. I'd be too afraid of getting lost or in an accident—"

"Then you'll ride with us in the limo." They'd already booked the extra car so Brian and Kay could each bring one guest, so she knew it wouldn't be an issue. She wanted her to say yes so badly. She wanted an excuse to see her again and not as a customer. "Please? It would mean a lot to me to have you there. You know…as a thank you—you really saved my ass last night. And the rest of the band owes you, too."

Am I begging? It sounds like I'm begging. I've never begged a woman for anything in my life. What the hell was going on?

Before Drew could answer, Jerry walked over. "Good morning, Miss Razer. Back again? Everything okay with your new guitars?"

"Hi, Jerry. They're great. I love them."

"Dad, she's giving me tickets for tonight's Passion Play show in Boston."

"We-he-hell! That's awful generous of you, Nikki."

"I think she's afraid I'll ask her to join us onstage." Nikki lightly elbowed Drew in the ribs.

Jerry smiled proudly. "She wouldn't disappoint you if you did. She's one heck of a musician."

"Dad, stop." Drew blushed.

"If she takes after you, she must be amazing."

Jerry gave her a dismissive wave. "Ah, that's just me foolin' around. Nope. She's the prodigy. I'm just an old-timer. I've had my day in the sun, and that's fine with me."

"I'd love to hear her play sometime."

"You know, I am in the room."

Drew looked as if she was getting mad again. Nikki wished she had that kind of relationship with her own father. Mom said he was proud of her, but it wouldn't kill him to say so himself.

"I appreciate the gesture, but I can't leave work early."

"Honey, we have coverage today. Geena will be in at one, and you never get out and have any fun. Go and enjoy yourself. We can handle things here."

"Dad—"

Jerry folded his arms and gave her a stern look. "I'm still the boss around here, kiddo. And I say take the rest of the day off." He smiled at Nikki and said, "Thank you. She needs a break from this place, whether she admits it or not."

Drew seemed to realize she was outnumbered. She let out a huff and said, "Okay. I'll go." She turned to Nikki. "I'm sorry, but I need to ask this. I don't have to worry about being around drugs or alcohol, do I?"

The question surprised her, but Nikki respected her for having the guts to ask. "Not at all."

Drew still looked skeptical. "I don't mean just you, I mean anyone who'll be with us. Because if I see any signs of drugs—"

"Hey, I mean it. We have a few social drinks once in a while, but I promise you, that's it. We don't touch drugs."

"Okay, good. I just need to make a phone call. I know exactly who I'd like to take with me."

Nikki's heart rose and sank within the same heartbeat. Damn. She hadn't thought this through.

Drew went behind the counter. Nikki tried not to look as if she was eavesdropping when Drew picked up the phone and asked for Melissa. A customer entered the store, and Jerry excused himself to wait on him.

Drew hung up and walked back over. "All set. Where should we meet you and at what time?"

"Right here is fine, if that works for you. Can you be ready by three? I hope you don't mind getting there a little early. We'll have to set up and do sound checks. Then we'll grab a bite to eat and warm up. You can go to all of it, of course, and you won't have to pay for a thing."

Drew nodded. "Yeah, that'll be fine."

"So, this Melissa. She someone special?"

Drew smiled thoughtfully. "Yeah. She's someone very special. I can't wait for you to meet her."

Nikki forced a smile. Maybe this wasn't such a good idea after all. She could've kept it simple. A CD autographed by the whole band or something. *But no, as usual, you had to go over the top.*

Her stomach churned. Jealousy had become an all too familiar feeling. It didn't agree with her one bit.

Chapter Eight

"I can't believe we're going to a Passion Play concert, and we get to ride in a limo with them! Are you sure I look all right?" Melissa was going to trigger an earthquake if she didn't stand still.

They were just inside the front door of DJ's, waiting for Nikki and the band to pick them up. Melissa wore faded blue jeans with intentional rips in them, a pair of high-top cross-trainer sneakers, and a waist-length navy blue nylon winter coat. Her long brown hair was down, with one pencil-thick braid tied alongside one ear. A long silver earring shaped like an electric guitar dangled from her left ear. A row of studs adorned the other.

"Relax. You look great."

She was glad Melissa was such a big fan. Otherwise, she wasn't sure how she was going to get out of accepting the tickets without looking like a total asshole. She'd have no trouble turning Nikki down, but she didn't want to lose her business. And she had to admit she felt a certain pride in knowing that the opening act's band members were customers of hers, and she was curious to see them in action.

Melissa fiddled with her cell phone and held it out in front of them. She scrolled through Passion Play's Facebook page, pointing out her favorite pictures and gushing about this and that. She said she'd "liked" the members' individual pages, too, and proceeded to show those to Drew as well. Drew feigned interest. She'd created her own Facebook page a few years ago but hardly ever logged on. She didn't keep in touch with enough people to get much out of it. She mentally kicked herself for forgetting to add this week's post on DJ's page.

A few minutes later, two white limousines pulled in and made wide semicircle turns in front of the store. Nikki emerged from the back door of one of them dressed in a black pea coat and blue jeans.

"OhmyGodohmyGodohmyGod. Here comes Nikki." Melissa bounced up and down on the balls of her feet. "She's even more gorgeous than in the pictures."

Drew couldn't agree more, but no way in hell was she going to let Nikki know that. At least with Melissa with her, she shouldn't have to worry about Nikki making passes at her.

Melissa grabbed Drew's sleeve as if she were trying to steady herself.

Nikki swung the door open and looked first at Drew, then Melissa. For a moment she looked perplexed, then smiled crookedly. "Hi."

"Hi, Nikki."

Nikki extended a hand to Melissa. "And you must be Melissa?" Melissa's hand was visibly shaking, but Nikki gave it a squeeze and said, "It's okay. I was nervous to meet you, too. I'm Nikki."

Nikki was nervous? Yeah right. *Back off. She's just a kid.*

Melissa nodded. "I know. Uh, I mean, yeah. I'm Melissa."

Nikki released her hand and smiled sweetly at the two of them.

Drew said, "Melissa's one of my star pupils."

"Oh yeah? What do you play?"

The teen blushed and shrugged. "Guitar mainly. I've been teaching myself piano, too."

"Cool, very cool."

"I even jammed with Jaymi and Shawn here the other day."

Nikki quirked an eyebrow. "No kidding? Were they any good?"

Melissa grinned. "They were all right," she deadpanned.

Awesome. The kid was loosening up a little. Drew sensed someone beside her. Geena nudged her arm and cleared her throat. *Subtle, Geena. Real subtle.*

"Nikki, this is Geena, my assistant manager and drum teacher."

It took another fifteen minutes to leave when the few customers in the store realized who was there. Nikki again politely signed autographs, pronounced DJ's as the greatest music store north of Boston, and declared she'd never shop anywhere else. Thankfully, the other members of the band stayed in the limo; otherwise, they'd have never gotten out of there. Nikki excused herself when the limo driver honked the horn.

The driver swung open the door and ushered Drew and Melissa inside. Nikki slid in afterward, sandwiching Drew between them. Jaymi and Shawn sat cuddled together opposite them.

Shawn lit up when she saw Melissa. "Hey, look who it is! Our new jammin' buddy!"

Everyone exchanged hellos, then Nikki said, "What's with the hat, Shawn?"

Shawn shifted a black fedora forward on her head. "I'm trying a new look. Whadda you think?"

"I think it's totally rad," piped up Melissa, who immediately blushed.

"We picked it up at Macy's yesterday," said Jaymi, an adoring smile on her face. "She was just playing around, but she looked so damn cute in it, I had to get it for her."

"I got a cool blazer to wear with it for the show tonight, along with a new shirt and tie."

Drew said, "I like it."

Jaymi was right. Shawn was cute and cool all rolled into one. She was petite but rugged-looking with shaggy, reddish-brown hair, ripped jeans, and a navy plaid flannel shirt. It was refreshing how down-to-earth and casual Jaymi and Shawn were. Not like the Hollywood crowd she was used to at her mother's house. Then again, in her experience, musicians were a different breed of entertainer.

"That outfit's gonna look way cool," Melissa added.

Shawn tipped the hat at Melissa and made her blush again. Drew knew that Jaymi was Melissa's guitar idol, but she was sensing that she might be developing a crush on Shawn.

"Smart move, cute stuff," Nikki said to Shawn. "Because girls don't drool over you enough already."

Shawn shot Nikki an annoyed look, but Drew couldn't tell if it was serious or not.

Nikki fidgeted beside her and whispered into Drew's ear. "She hates when I call her that."

If that was the case, why had Nikki intentionally provoked her?

Jaymi quickly changed the subject. "I can't wait to see how the new instruments sound tonight. We owe you a big thanks for saving our skins this week."

Nikki tucked one leg under her and swiveled so that she faced Drew. "Drew's good at playing the hero, aren't you?"

"I'd hardly call myself a hero." *Here we go again.* It seemed that Nikki liked provoking everyone around her.

"Did I tell you Drew rescued me after I went off the road last night?" Nikki proceeded to tell everyone about the incident. "She saved my ass."

"It was nothing, really."

"You don't think saving my ass is a big deal?" She got up and shook her butt in the air and slapped it. "This thing's one of my best moneymakers. Don't you think so, Jaymi?"

"I think it's a good thing you can sing."

Nikki grinned and high-fived Melissa, who was quietly snickering at the whole exchange. "Ha! Jaymi's right. Take my advice, kid: always listen to Jaymi. She's one smart cookie."

Jaymi rolled her eyes. Nikki looked at Jaymi and held her gaze for a long moment. The group fell quiet, and subtle tension filled the space. Nikki settled back into her seat, much closer to Drew this time. Their thighs were touching. She could smell Nikki's cologne and feel the heat radiating off her body. Nikki stretched and nonchalantly placed her arm along the back of the seat behind her. How many other women had she practiced this move on? Was she about to lower her arm around her shoulders?

She didn't want to make a scene if she did, but at the same time, she couldn't let Nikki think she could do whatever she pleased just because she'd invited her to the concert tonight. She was sure Nikki had planned this seating arrangement on purpose. She tried not to think about it—she didn't want to ruin Melissa's night.

She didn't quite know what to think of the group's dynamic. Drew was surprised to find that Nikki didn't take herself too seriously. She had no problem being the butt of Jaymi's joke—no pun intended. She could also tell that Nikki's admiration for Jaymi was sincere. Maybe it was more than admiration. She wondered if there was any romantic history between them. If so, that would explain the tension between Nikki and Shawn.

"How long have you worked at the music store, Drew?" Shawn's question pulled Drew out of her thoughts.

"Oh, uh, since college. My dad owns the store. He even named it using our initials. I worked as a salesperson during the summers, and after I graduated, he told me I had to work there at least a year to pay my dues before he moved me up to manager."

"Her father's an amazing guitarist," Nikki said. "You should hear him play." She lightly tugged on Drew's shoulder. "Maybe one of these days I can get this shy one to play for me."

Melissa said, "Oh yeah, she's, like, freaking awesome! She's a great teacher, too. You have no idea."

Now it was Drew's turn to blush.

"Well, she's doing something right," said Jaymi, looking from Drew to Melissa. "You've got some serious chops yourself. I wouldn't be surprised if we'll all be going to your concerts someday."

"I hope so."

"Just keep practicing. We'll have to keep in touch so we can give you some pointers."

"Really? You mean it?"

"Of course I do. You can never have enough support getting a music career off the ground."

Wow. That's really sweet of Jaymi. She was sure Melissa was beside herself with awe right now.

Shawn said, "I really love your store, Drew."

"Yeah. And you can't beat the personal attention you give your customers." Nikki smiled. She could have easily used a flirtatious tone, but she sounded completely serious this time. "That makes a big difference. I wasn't kidding when I said I won't go anywhere else now."

"I agree," said Jaymi. "Do you know how many music stores I've gone into and been ignored? They don't take female musicians seriously. Your place is the first where I've even seen female employees."

"Well, thanks, you guys. That's exactly how I always felt. That's one of the reasons I love my job. I really do appreciate your business. It's been a little rough with the struggling economy the last few years. We've been steady with the little stuff, like strings and drumsticks and accessories, but people just aren't making as many major purchases these days." Shit. She hadn't meant to whine about the sorry state of the business. Not with them.

"You know, maybe we can help promote the store for you," Jaymi said.

"I didn't mean to sound like I was dropping hints or anything."

"We know that." Nikki tapped her shoulder again. "Listen, we have a strict policy of only endorsing things we actually use or agree with. We all love your store and the one-on-one attention."

Her heart rate picked up. She didn't want to feel as if she was capitalizing on their success for her own benefit, but if they were offering, she was in no position to refuse. Free publicity for the store was a smart business move. It wasn't as if she was selling out. And if the offer was coming from Jaymi, at least she knew it wasn't because Jaymi wanted something in return. Had it been Nikki's suggestion…

"You don't have to do that, but honestly, I'd appreciate anything you can do for me. We could use all the help we can get."

"We'll put our heads together at our next group meeting and see what we can come up with," said Jaymi. "How's that sound?"

"That…wow. That would be fantastic."

Nikki said, "The band always makes decisions together, so yeah. We'll talk to Brian and Kay and then run it by our manager to see what we can do. It's good publicity for the band, too."

Drew relaxed for the rest of the ride. Maybe accepting the tickets was a smart move after all.

Chapter Nine

When Nikki had walked into DJ's and seen that Drew's "date" was a teenager, her gut reacted with relief, then confusion. Drew barely looked old enough to have a daughter that age. Although if she did have a kid, that was okay with her. It would explain why Drew had seemed flattered by her flirting but reluctant to flirt back. Single mothers were cautious about who they dated and rightfully so.

Then again, maybe Drew just wasn't interested. That bothered her. It had been ages since she'd felt attracted to someone for more than just sex. There was something about Drew that intrigued her. And she didn't think it had anything to do with the thrill of the chase, either.

The band was about halfway through the concert, a point when they slowed things down a bit and played a few love songs in a row. Fans were tossing flowers and other gifts onto the stage. Nikki picked up a rose, put it between her teeth during the solo, and danced around the stage. She looked out into the audience and saw her guests in the front row.

Then she did something she hadn't done since they scored their recording contract. She sauntered down the steps and off the side of the stage and made her way up and down the aisles. Lance was going to kill her, but she could handle Lance. Two security guards swiftly showed up to accompany her, one scooting ahead to control the crowd, the other following her every move from behind. Holding the rose and mike in one hand, she reached out to touch fans' hands as she passed them. After going full circuit, she walked along the front row and handed Drew the rose. The crowd went nuts.

The group improvised into an interlude. Nikki lowered her mike and asked Drew, "Dance with me?"

Drew looked at her as though she hadn't heard her correctly. Nikki took a quick bow and held out her hand. She brought the microphone to her lips. "Will you please honor me with a dance?"

The invitation boomed out into the auditorium. Drew glared at her and sat back in her seat. And then, the worst thing that could've happened, happened. The fans started booing.

"What an idiot!" she heard someone say. Then, "I'll dance with you, Nikki!" And "What's wrong with that girl? Is she fucking crazy?"

She had to fix this and fast. If Drew wanted to humiliate her, fine, but she wasn't going to stand for Drew being insulted and ridiculed. "I don't blame her," she announced into the mike. "The most beautiful woman in the room deserves better. But Jaymi's already taken, so you'll have to settle for me."

That got a smile from Drew and a chuckle from the crowd. Drew shook her head and took her hand. The people cheered. She led Drew to the stage and pulled her close, singing the rest of the song while they danced. She felt perfect in her arms. They moved easily, with Nikki leading. Drew couldn't seem to wipe the smile off her face, but Nikki didn't miss the fire in her eyes. When the song was over, Nikki gave her a kiss on the cheek and summoned security to escort her back to her seat.

She looked at Jaymi, who was smiling from ear to ear. Nikki thanked her with a wink. Hey, if Jaymi and Shawn could have their onstage kiss, then what the hell, maybe she'd make dancing with a fan her thing.

They were all still wound up when they climbed into the town car for the ride home. She thought Melissa would be tired, but she was more energized than anyone. After being quiet and reserved on the ride down, this time, she wouldn't shut up. The kid was going somewhere. With the passion she was expressing about music, Nikki knew that with the right training and encouragement, she'd be something special.

About halfway home, fatigue kicked in, and the gang gradually came down from their highs. She looked across the way at Jaymi and Shawn. Jaymi had her wrapped snugly in her arms, her cheek resting on Shawn's head. Sharing their love for each other without having to speak. Content. Happy.

It used to rip her heart apart when she saw them together. Now her heart filled with warmth and a sense of gratitude. It was what Jaymi deserved. Shawn gave her what she needed, and Nikki loved Shawn for that. Shawn would never believe it, but it was true. After the pain Jaymi had gone through a few years ago, with Peach cheating on her and then losing her mother, Nikki couldn't have wished for a happier ending. *Even though she didn't end up with me.*

Melissa's thumbs were dancing on her phone, probably texting her friends about her night. Nikki took a peek at Drew, who hadn't said anything for a while. Her eyes were closed. Shit, she'd forgotten that Drew had worked this morning. No wonder she was tired. She caught Melissa's eye and pointed to Drew. Melissa shrugged, grinned, and went back to playing with her phone.

They hit a bump, and Drew slumped against Nikki's body. Startled, she straightened quickly, but in a matter of minutes, fell back into her as she drifted to sleep again. Nikki carefully extracted her arm and put it around her. Drew snuggled against her, and Nikki knew she was really asleep now. No way would she be doing this consciously. Sometimes, Drew acted as if she didn't even like her. But hot damn, did she feel good. As if she belonged there. It had felt that way when they were dancing onstage, too.

She about died when Drew began snoring. Though they weren't really snores. More like quiet purrs. It was the cutest thing she'd ever heard. She rested her head against Drew's and smiled. She breathed in her scent and closed her eyes. She could get used to this.

She wondered what Drew thought of her night with the band. And their dance. Did she know that she was the envy of the whole crowd? Yeah, maybe that sounded conceited, but Nikki had enough experience with this rock star stuff to know what women thought of her. She was a heartthrob. A sexual fantasy.

And Nikki had no real interest in any of them. None of them knew that for years, her heart had belonged to Jaymi, and Jaymi never had a clue. She'd kept her feelings to herself. Until that drunken night at Jaymi's place during that temporary breakup with Shawn. She hadn't intended to tell her. But Nikki's defenses were down, and when Jaymi pressed her for what was on her mind, she lost control. Nikki caught her totally off guard and kissed her for all it was worth.

I'm such a shmuck. She'd known Jaymi didn't feel the same way, but in that moment, her emotions had taken over like a runaway train. By then it was too late. Jaymi was in love with Shawn. Everyone knew they'd work things out. And they had.

Drew shifted slightly, and her arm slid across Nikki's stomach. Her breath hitched, and for a second, she was afraid Drew would wake up. She didn't want her to wake up. It felt so nice to cuddle with her, even if Drew didn't know what she was doing. Or did she?

Drew's hair fell across her face. Nikki gently brushed it back and resisted the urge to caress her cheek. It was dark, but Nikki took advantage of every streetlight they rushed past to look at her. She had long lashes. Her dark brows looked sexy behind her blond hair. There were faint freckles on her soft cheekbones. Her lips looked soft and oh so kissable.

The world slipped away. She couldn't take her eyes off her. She was still staring at her when they pulled into DJ's parking lot. The ceased motion awoke Drew, and her eyes shot open when she realized she was nestled in her arms. Neither of them moved. Melissa sat nervously beside them as if she didn't dare disturb them.

"Time to get up, sleeping beauty," Nikki said softly. She released her as she withdrew.

"I…oh man, I fell asleep?" Drew suddenly pushed off her as if she'd been burned. "How did I…we—"

"It's okay. You didn't snore much."

Drew's brows shot up in horror.

"I'm kidding. You didn't snore at all."

Nikki caught Melissa's eye and winked. Melissa put a finger to her lips, indicating she wouldn't snitch.

"You've had a long day. I'm sure you're ready to get home to bed."

The driver opened the door. There was a burst of cold air, and Nikki quickly got out and extended Drew her hand. Drew hesitated long enough to say thanks and good night to Shawn and Jaymi before letting Nikki guide her out of the car. She still looked half asleep and was so freakin' adorable when she swayed like a toddler who was resisting bedtime.

Melissa climbed out behind her. "I can start the truck if you want to give me the keys. Get it warmed up."

Smart kid. She must have sensed that Nikki wanted a moment alone with her.

"Huh?" Drew said. She rubbed her eyes and shook her head as if trying to force herself awake.

Melissa held out her hand. "Keys?"

Drew handed them to her. "Call your mom and let her know I'll have you home in a few minutes. I'm sure she's waiting up."

Melissa agreed and then turned to Nikki. "Thanks, Nikki. For everything. I had a blast."

"Anytime."

"Will I get to see you guys again? I mean, it doesn't have to be a concert, but just...you know, around here maybe?"

"You bet."

"Cool. Thanks again." She ran across the lot to Drew's truck.

Drew said, "She's going to be on cloud nine for months."

Nikki shrugged. "Are you okay to drive home? You're not too tired, are you?"

"This cold air is waking me up, and it's a short ride. I'll be fine." She gestured to Melissa. "I better get her home."

"She's a great kid."

Drew smiled. "She has a great attitude considering everything she's been through. I don't know the whole story, but I know her father's never been around. Her mother works two jobs to support them, and she'll do anything for her daughter."

"And she's got you."

"She's like the little sister I never had." Drew shivered and hugged herself. She looked up into Nikki's eyes.

Nikki wanted nothing more than to pull her close and give her a good-night kiss, but that would be totally out of line. She wasn't picking up some fan for a one-night stand. She didn't want to make the wrong move, and she wanted to see Drew again. Not as a customer. Not as a fan. As what? A love interest? What was that exactly?

"Nikki?"

She wasn't sure how long she'd been standing there with thoughts galloping through her head, but it was probably too long.

"Hmm?"

"If you guys really do plan to share advice with Melissa, then you'd better not leave anything out."

"What do you mean?"

"Tonight was fun, but you only showed her the exciting side of what you do. She's just a kid. She has no idea what she'd be sacrificing if she follows in your footsteps and makes it big."

Nikki stepped back. "If you mean paying your dues and working hard, then yes, there are sacrifices. But if you get what you want, it's worth it, don't you think?"

"Not when those sacrifices are people. People that should matter more than strangers in an audience."

Where is this coming from? "For your information, Drew, I didn't sacrifice any *people* to get what I wanted, and neither did anyone else in the band. If anything, the sacrifices we made were our own. We could've taken the fast track to where we are now by staying in California, but did we? No. We left so that Jaymi could be with her mother. And those *strangers* in the audience happen to be the reason we're successful. They're not sacrifices—they're our inspiration."

Drew dropped her gaze and shoved her hands in her coat pockets. "Well, I guess you were one of the lucky ones, then."

Obviously, there was more to this than Drew was letting on. Whatever pain she was transferring had left scars, but now was not the time or place to ask her about it. Hell, they barely knew each other.

"Hey, Nikki?"

She turned at the sound of Jaymi's voice coming from the limo. *Jaymi. I sacrificed Jaymi for our careers. Is that what Drew's talking about?*

"I don't mean to interrupt, but we have to get going."

Drew moved away. "Sorry for holding you up."

Nikki took a step toward her, but Drew was already walking away. "Drew?"

"I'll see you at the store." Drew disappeared into her truck and took off as if she couldn't get away fast enough.

Nikki got back in the car and slouched in her seat. When Jaymi gave her a questioning look, she just shook her head and closed her eyes. This emotion shit was exhausting.

CHAPTER TEN

Drew slept late and woke up exhausted. By the time she'd dropped off Melissa, driven home, and crawled into bed with her three furry roommates, it was after two in the morning. She'd tossed and turned as the night replayed in her mind. What little sleep she did get was sporadic. The last time she looked at the clock, it was closing in on four.

She hated to admit it, but she hadn't had such a good time in ages—which was why she was so angry. It could have ended on a pleasant note if she'd handled things differently. Maybe she shouldn't have taken Melissa. She'd have to have a talk with her to make sure she knew what she'd be getting herself into if she ever became famous. No matter what Nikki said, Drew knew full well the cost that could come with success.

Yet she was having the hardest time reconciling the difference between what she expected last night and what it was actually like. She'd had so much anxiety about how the evening would go, and none of it came to fruition. Although Nikki had assured her there would be no drugs or drinking, Drew hadn't really believed her. She'd still expected an atmosphere of rowdy partiers, egomaniacs, and mayhem. It couldn't have been more opposite.

From hanging out during sound check, to the catered meal, to the introductions to the crew, to the backstage tour, and to the concert itself, Nikki and the rest of the band had been the most gracious of hosts. Each band member took a turn spending time with Melissa. They patiently answered her endless questions. They gave her advice. They let her play their instruments. She jammed with Shawn. Was all that for their benefit, or was that how they were all the time? She didn't trust it. It seemed too good to be true, and Melissa was too young to know any better.

As easily as Melissa had hit it off with Nikki, Shawn, and Jaymi, it was Jaymi's cousin Brian whom she'd relaxed with immediately. He played drums and was a total jokester. He had a boyish face, dark hair with loose curls that landed just above the shoulder, and the same blue eyes as Jaymi. He and Jaymi tossed puns and wisecracks back and forth that had everyone either groaning or laughing their asses off. Kay, the bass player, was also as laid back as the rest of them, and despite a more serious demeanor, she was sweet as pie in every interaction.

This band was clearly more than a group of coworkers who happened to click musically. They were a family. The love and mutual respect and camaraderie between them was magical. They'd been together for almost a decade, and they still exhibited an enthusiasm for their craft that was typically seen in musicians just starting out. She'd seen that passion in her dad when he was young. Until her mother had chipped away at it, forcing his dreams aside as she became more obsessed with her own career. Drew missed seeing him like that.

When the time came to get serious, Passion Play seamlessly put the jokes aside and became consummate professionals. The show was fantastic. She hadn't been a fan before, but she couldn't deny that she was now. It was the last concert of the tour, and though she knew they were all tired, it seemed to have lifted a burden from their shoulders. They were sharp, yet relaxed and loose, typical of someone on a last day of work before starting a vacation.

Among all the other thoughts that had kept her awake, Nikki had dominated them all.

Drew had trouble taking her eyes off her all night. Not only because she was beautiful, but her charisma was off the charts. And sexy…*don't even get me started on how sexy she is without even trying.*

Shit. She needed to derail that train of thought and fast. It was one thing to find her attractive, but getting involved with her was out of the question. *What could Nikki Razer possibly want with me, anyway?*

Sex, of course. People like Nikki were always after sex. It was about conquest. *They think that just because they're famous and gorgeous, they can sleep with whomever they want.* She could've killed her for putting her on the spot with that dance. What was she supposed to do? Say no? Especially when they started booing her? She'd never been so embarrassed in her life. Well, that wasn't entirely true, but it was close. Her mother had humiliated her more times than she could count. Flaunting her sex appeal to land an audition. Displaying her cleavage to anyone she thought might give her a shot at a leading role. Sleeping with anyone who came on to her because it fed her precious ego—it made her sick just thinking about it.

No wonder Nikki had been attentive to her every need throughout the evening.

And though she was pissed off, she had to admit that Nikki's invitation to dance was the most romantic thing she'd ever experienced. It had taken her so off guard, she hadn't been able to answer right away. It was possible that only Drew caught it, but for a moment, Nikki had looked dejected. She'd accepted Nikki's hand, and it transformed Nikki's expression to one of joy. Nikki looked dashing in black pants and boots, a black leather vest, and a red dress shirt with pirate sleeves. Her black hair came just to her shoulders and shone brightly under the colorful stage lights. She'd kept her deep brown eyes locked on Drew's throughout the whole song, and she didn't just *sing* the song. She sang the song *to* her.

It was a strange feeling. She knew they were the center of attention for that three or four minutes, yet the entire world had disappeared. It was just her and Nikki.

She didn't remember falling asleep during the ride home. The long day must've caught up to her. At first, it had felt nice to wake up with Nikki's arm draped around her. It felt as if it belonged there. It'd been a very long time since she'd woken up in a woman's arms. Why did it have to be Nikki? And why did it have to feel so damn good?

Even if she wanted to date Nikki, she couldn't forget that Nikki was a celebrity. She knew the lifestyle that went along with that. Malicious scrutiny by a judgmental public. Surrendered privacy. Cameras in your face. Constant expectations to uphold a certain image. The pressure to repeat success with every new album. Months away from home and loved ones. The unfair standards of having to stay looking young and beautiful as you aged. The list went on and on, and Drew would never put herself in that position again.

Nikki would always have women throwing themselves at her. *Oh God, I hope Nikki didn't think that's what I was doing last night.* What would have happened if Melissa hadn't been with them? Would Nikki have sent the limo on its way and tried to charm a ride home with her?

Drew grunted and got up from the table. She had no use for analyzing this any further. She had housework to do and a business to keep afloat. Nikki Razer had occupied enough of her mind for one day.

CHAPTER ELEVEN

What a great feeling to sleep in and have no place to go. No rehearsal. No playlists to compile. No endless boring bus rides. No wondering what damn city you were in. No audience to please—although that was always the fun part.

No nameless girl in bed with you. The only girl on Nikki's mind was a small-town music store manager. She'd seen glimpses of interest from Drew last night but also apprehension. She wondered what was holding Drew back. It wasn't how women usually treated her—as if Drew wanted to keep her distance but was fighting an attraction. They barely knew each other, but if there was one thing she was sure of, it was that Drew was nothing like the women she usually seduced.

She didn't like to think of herself as a player, but that was exactly what she'd become. In her desperation to bury her feelings for Jaymi, she'd lost a sense of who she was and what she needed. She didn't want any of those women for anything other than sex. She didn't want to fall in love with them. She didn't want a relationship with them.

But…she did want someone to love her. Simple.

No. Nothing about love is simple.

She got out of bed at one in the afternoon feeling more rested and refreshed than she had in months. She and the band would have nearly two and a half months off to relax, spend time with family and friends, and enjoy the holidays before starting work on their next album.

Nikki soaped up in the shower. It was heaven to be home. She loved touring and doing shows, but she hated living out of a suitcase. She lingered under the hot stream and savored the familiarity of finding the shampoo without having to open her eyes.

The upcoming holidays didn't bring happy thoughts. She dreaded calling her mom to discuss Thanksgiving. It was still two weeks away, but she might as well get the call over with today. Better chance of catching her at home on a Sunday. During the week, she was more likely to be with her father, helping him schmooze his next potential campaign contributors.

She had no food in the house, so she drove to Dunkin' Donuts for a breakfast sandwich and coffee, then headed to the grocery store with a long list. It would be nice to do something ordinary for a change, but when she pulled into the parking lot, she decided she wasn't in the mood to shop. It wasn't like her to procrastinate, but what the hell. It could wait an hour or so. She pulled back onto the road and wondered if it was still okay to show up unannounced. Of course, she couldn't take her to bed today. Or any day anymore. Randi Hartwell had a girlfriend now. A very beautiful catch of a girlfriend named Jule.

She pulled into the driveway of Jule's New Englander house. Both cars were there, so they were home. Good sign. She gave the horn two staccato honks and grinned when she heard an eruption of barking dogs. Followed by two German shepherds, Randi bolted out the front door without a coat and bounded down the front porch steps. Nikki got out of the car, and Randi caught her in a big hug. Nikki caught Jule's watchful eye through the kitchen window and waved. Jule put her hand up just long enough to acknowledge her, then disappeared. Oh well. She couldn't blame her after Jule had learned that she and Randi used to sleep together. Not to mention the time Nikki suggested a threesome, and Jule turned her down flat. Nikki loved her for that. Well, and also because she made Randi happy.

They gathered in the living room. It took a few minutes for the dogs to settle down, but they did so immediately when Jule and Randi commanded them to do so. That was a given, since Randi now made a living as a police dog trainer.

Randi sat on the couch next to Jule. "How was the tour?" Her dog leaned against her leg and plopped his chin on her thigh. Randi fussed over him and scrubbed his neck.

"It went well, but I'm relieved it's over. Tucker's getting big."

"Yeah, he's over sixty pounds now."

Jule stood. "It sounds like the coffee's ready. Be back in a minute."

It was odd how awkward things felt now. She and Randi had had great chemistry in the bedroom, but their relationship as friends had drifted when Randi fell in love with Jule. Before Jule, they'd go to the club or a party and feel at home with each other. She guessed because they knew there were no strings attached. It was all about having fun and having someone to go out with. Although they'd grown to care about each other, the sex they'd shared seemed to have defined their bond more than anything else. Maybe coming here had been a mistake.

Randi crossed an ankle over her knee and looked at her with a furrowed brow. "What's wrong, Nik?"

But then, maybe she just had to learn how to be a friend. "Randi, what would you say if I told you I met someone I really think I could fall for?"

Randi dropped her foot to the floor and leaned forward, gazing at her with those dark, sensuous eyes. "I think there will be millions of Passion Play fans with broken hearts out there when they find out the sexiest woman alive is no longer available."

Jule walked in with a mug in each hand. "Excuse me?"

Randi grinned at Jule and loudly cleared her throat. "I mean the *second* sexiest woman alive."

Jule put the drinks on the coffee table and smiled first at Randi and then Nikki. "Is that threesome offer still on the table, Nikki? 'Cause I think maybe Randi's getting bored with me."

Nikki's face grew hot. Jule was the one person who could make her blush. She loved how fiery Jule was, and it was such a turn-on. She had long, beautiful gold-streaked brown hair and a rugged full figure that filled out her jeans and sweater nicely. She was an independent do-it-yourselfer who had done most of the renovations on her house by herself. If Nikki thought for one second Jule was serious, she'd have half her clothes off already.

"Not a chance, angel." Randi pulled Jule down onto the couch next to her, and they laughed and kissed like teenagers.

Sheesh. It was hard enough being around all the happy couples affiliated with the band right now. She didn't need this, too.

Jule pried herself away and headed back toward the kitchen. She winked at Nikki on her way. "I'll give you two a chance to catch up." She patted her leg and said, "Come on, boys. Time to go out." The dogs trotted after her, and they heard the back door open and close.

"Sorry about that," Randi said.

She wasn't sorry. She was in love. A Brillo pad couldn't wipe the smile off her face. "No need to be sorry, my friend. It's good to see you happy."

"Yeah. It is." They sipped their coffee, and Randi's dreamy look finally dissipated. "Tell me about this girl."

"I don't even know if she's interested."

"Bullshit. Tell me about her."

Nikki laughed. Without Jule in the room, they both relaxed. "She manages the music store downtown. I bought some new guitars there on Friday."

"You mean DJ's?"

"You know her?"

"No. I know the store. I used to be a cop, remember? I know every place in this town."

"Right."

"What's her name?"

"Drew."

"And?"

"And she's beautiful and smart and kind of quiet. She teaches music there, too. You should see her with this one student. She's amazing."

Nikki filled her in from their first meeting at the store to Drew's weird warning when they parted last night and everything in between.

Randi nodded and held her gaze. "So, what's she got that Jaymi doesn't have?"

"Don't be an asshole."

Randi didn't budge. "Answer the question, Nikki. There's gotta be something to make her measure up to Jaymi and then some. Otherwise, you'll go on tormenting yourself forever. What does she have that Jaymi doesn't?"

She blew out a breath. "I'll tell you what she doesn't have. A girlfriend."

"And?"

She shook her head and shrugged, unsure of Randi's line of questioning.

Randi walked over and brushed back Nikki's hair. The soft caress of her hand on her face was intoxicating, a torturous reminder of the heat they used to share and of what they could never share again. Randi touched her lips to her cheek, lingering just a bit longer than she probably should. They'd both be in deep shit if Jule walked in on them right now. Yet she knew without a doubt that Randi would never cheat on Jule.

Randi drew back and gave her a serious look. "I'll tell you *one* thing she doesn't have," she said softly. "She doesn't have *you*, Nikki. If she deserves your heart, then what are you waiting for? Spend some time with her and figure it out. At the very least, maybe you'll become friends." She smiled. "Look at what I've got now. You never know if you don't try. Isn't that what you told me?"

Yes, it was. It was exactly what she'd told her.

Maybe it was time she took her own advice.

Chapter Twelve

Drew retreated to the office to eat her bagged lunch. Mondays were typically slow, and today was no exception. Only one customer so far and two lessons. There was only one lesson this afternoon, so the rest of the day would drag, too. It was discouraging that the holidays were closing in, and she'd only seen a slight increase in sales. Maybe after Thanksgiving, things would pick up. She'd already remerchandised the whole store, bumped up her inventory, determined her specials, and submitted the store's Black Friday ads. That should help. She just hoped the investment in the glossy quarter-page-sized sales flyers and sponsored ads on social media would pay off.

Her dad knocked on the open door and poked his head in. "Looks like you made quite an impression the other night."

"What do you mean?"

"Hold on." He ducked out and reappeared a minute later with a huge bouquet of flowers cradled in his hands. "This just came for you." He set them on the desk and winked before slipping out again.

Her heart kicked into a drum roll as she wedged the tiny envelope from the plastic card holder. She knew whom they were from. On the one hand, she was flattered beyond words. On the other, she hated to admit she was tempted to let herself be swept up by a rock star who most likely saw her as just another fling.

She lifted the flap and pulled out the card. She smiled at the simple sentiment.

Thank you for the dance—Nikki

She held the card to her heart as she remembered their dance. She couldn't help it. She loved the way Nikki had looked into her eyes as she sang to her. The way they moved so easily together. The safe feeling she had when she woke up in the limo with Nikki's arm around her.

Just because she'd never get involved with her didn't mean she couldn't at least appreciate the experience while it lasted. Face it, Nikki Razer was hot. Her reverie dissipated when she realized she had no way to call Nikki and thank her. She had no idea if or when she'd see her again. Maybe this thank-you was simply a thank-you. Nothing more, nothing less.

Still, as the afternoon dragged on, she felt anxious with the hope that Nikki would stop by. Although she was sure Nikki must have better things to do than shop at DJ's.

"Any big plans for tonight?"

Geena's voice snapped her out of her daze. Drew was ready to leave for the day and was in the office debating if she should leave the flowers there or bring them home and risk the cats getting into them.

"Yes." Geena didn't need to know her big plans involved frozen pizza and a movie rental.

Geena looked at her curiously. "Hot date with a rock star, maybe?"

She guffawed. "Please. She is *so* not my type."

"A rich, gorgeous sex goddess rock star isn't your type?"

"You forgot conceited."

"She didn't seem conceited to me."

"You didn't spend as much time with her as I did."

Geena rolled her eyes. "Sheez, loosen up, dude. You don't have to marry her; just have a little fun with her. I get the impression she wouldn't mind."

"Not my thing, *dude*, and you know it."

"Maybe it should be. A little fling is probably just what you need. And shit, if it's with Nikki Razer—"

"Good night, Geena." She shrugged into her coat and decided the bouquet could stay on her desk. Taking it home might give Geena the impression that she attached more meaning to it than accepting a simple gesture of thanks.

Tuesday was a little busier than Monday, and it was their biggest delivery day, which helped pass the time. It also meant she had both her dad and Geena on with her. They spent the morning unpacking cases of merchandise and taking pleasure in what they'd received as if they were opening gifts. No new instruments today, though. Those were always the most fun.

She left them to watch the storefront so she could straighten the lesson rooms. She had students coming in later today. She walked into the strings room and looked at the cello on a stand in the corner. It needed a polish. It needed more than that. It begged to be played. Most of her students studied the usual instruments: guitar, bass, piano, drums. She taught all of them except for drums, which Geena handled. It had been a while since she'd had anyone ask for violin or cello lessons.

She ran a carpet sweep over the floor and a duster over the room. She wasn't sure why she was compelled to arrange four chairs and music stands in a semicircle. Maybe the universe would pick up on her hint that she'd love a string quartet to walk in and rent the space for rehearsals.

She cast another look at the cello. It was calling her. She took a bow from its case on a shelf, carefully applied rosin, and settled the cello between her knees.

After tuning, she gently slid the bow across the strings. Instantly, her heart rate slowed, and she closed her eyes. She hadn't played this piece by Haydn in years, but as soon as she got through the first sixteen bars, it flowed with perfection. The soulful sound of the instrument always transported her, like the soothing voice of a lover, to a place of peace and tranquility.

As she played the last few measures, she reveled in the joy of playing simply for pleasure. She flexed her fingers and ran her palm over the smooth wood of the neck. She found her place and began a Beethoven sonata. She slowly drew the bow across for the final note and savored its ring as it faded into the air. She opened her eyes and gasped.

Nikki was leaning against the doorjamb, her thumbs hooked in her jeans pockets and a content smile on her face. She was in her leather jacket again today but had opted for more practical footwear in a pair of high-top suede hikers. She looked perfect.

"That had to be one of the most beautiful things I've ever heard in my life."

"I find that hard to believe. I'm rusty as hell."

Nikki raised her eyebrows. "If that's how you sound when you're rusty, I'd love to oil you up, because that was amazing."

Okay. Nikki was flirting again. *Say something clever, you idiot.* She must have waited too long to reply because Nikki was walking toward her with a killer smile on her face.

She stopped beside her. "Are you hungry?"

Drew was sure her face was as red as Nikki's Mustang with the inappropriate answers that flooded her mind. She was starving. But not for food. God, what was happening to her?

"You do get a lunch break, don't you?"

"Yes. Of course."

"Would you care to check out my new ride and join me for a bite, then?"

Drew's thoughts shifted as she pictured how much money she had in her wallet. She hated that she had to watch every penny she spent, and a simple decision of whether or not she could afford to eat out for lunch irritated her no end. Nikki seemed to sense she was struggling with her answer, which only made it worse.

"A little fling is just what you need." Now she was even more irritated that she was considering going. *Damn you, Geena.* No. A fling with a celebrity was exactly the opposite of what she needed.

"I really can't. I'm sorry."

Nikki's face fell. "Oh. Well, would you at least like to come out and see it?"

Geena appeared in the doorway. "Go ahead, Drew. Store's slow right now. We can handle it."

Great. First Dad, now Geena. "Okay, okay. I'll come look at your Jeep. But I—"

Nikki swiftly looped her arm through hers. "See? Geena has it under control. Nothing to worry about."

She felt a jolt when Nikki's face lit up, as if she'd expected Drew to turn her down. Could she have really been anxious about Drew's answer? The thought that Nikki might have a vulnerable side only made her like her more. *Damn it.*

Drew yanked her coat out of Geena's hands—how convenient that she'd gotten it for her—and they stepped outside. Drew stopped and stared at the black four-door Jeep Wrangler parked in front of her shop. With the bright sunlight, the luster was nearly blinding. It had oversized tires with black sport rims and tinted windows.

"You like it?"

"Wow, Nikki. That's really sharp." She gave Nikki a sideways glance. "Black again?"

Nikki threw her a disarming smile. "What can I say—I look good in black."

Yes, you do. She caught herself before she said it out loud. Instead, she returned the smile and said, "It *is* your trademark color. Good choice."

"Want to sit in it?"

"Sure." No harm in appeasing her a bit more, was there?

Nikki opened the passenger side door and closed it behind her. She sighed. It was pathetic that the black leather seat was more comfortable than her living room furniture.

Nikki climbed in and buckled up. She turned the key and shifted into gear.

Drew grabbed her arm. "What are you doing?"

Nikki stepped on the gas and pulled out of the parking space. "You can't just sit in a brand-new car and not go for a little spin! Can you believe how smooth this rides for a Jeep?"

"I don't have time for a ride—"

"Yes, you do. I already cleared it with your father. The store's covered."

"You…you *cleared it* with my father? When did you—wait, that's not the point. You tricked me!" An annoying beeping sounded from the dash, as if it knew it needed to bleep out the expletives about to escape her lips.

"Hey, you admitted you had a lunch break and that you're hungry. So I'm making sure you eat." She turned at a light. "And fasten your seat belt. That alarm is driving me crazy."

She yanked on the belt and clicked it. "So I don't have a choice? You're kidnapping me for lunch whether I like or not?"

"Kidnapping is a rather strong word. I prefer to think of it as whisking you away for a much-needed break."

She exhaled, resigned. She supposed being whisked away by a beautiful woman did have a nicer ring to it. Fine. She'd swallow defeat this time. She couldn't very well jump out of a moving vehicle.

"If you relax and stop worrying about work, you might actually enjoy yourself." Nikki negotiated another turn.

"You just caught me off guard, that's all." Nikki seemed to have a knack for doing that. Her heartbeat gradually fell back into its normal rhythm. She might as well make the most of the situation.

"And lunch is on me, so don't worry about that, either."

"I can pay my own way."

Nikki took advantage of a stop at a red light to look at her. "I'm not implying that you can't—no assumptions, remember? I figured if I'm going to whisk you away against your will, the least I can do is treat."

Sure. Flaunt your riches in my face a little more, why don't you? "Either I pay my own way, or I'm not ordering anything."

"Suit yourself. But I better not catch you stealing fries off my plate."

"I'm not that desperate."

"I hope not. I'd hate to have to fight you off with the ketchup bottle."

Drew laughed in spite of herself. She had to give Nikki credit. She was being a total killjoy, and Nikki was cracking jokes. "I just don't want you to think I'm a freeloader. I'd feel better if we go Dutch."

"Then that's what we'll do." Nikki smiled as she cruised through the intersection. "So, if you could eat anywhere, where would you go?"

Drew thought of the local restaurants, many of which were priced beyond her modest budget. "I'm not fussy. Wherever you want to go is fine with me."

"Okay, but that wasn't what I asked you. Have you ever been to Italy?"

Whoa. What? Surely she was joking. "No, I haven't. But I don't think we can get to Rome and back in an hour. I do have to go back to work this afternoon, you know."

Nikki laughed. "Okay, then. We'll stay local today and save Rome for another day." She cranked up the stereo, and the Jeep filled with an unexpected sound.

"You listen to opera?"

"This is my favorite Mozart aria. Can you believe I used to be able to sing this piece?"

Wow. Nikki Razer could sing opera? She was full of surprises. "My God, Nikki. That's…incredible. But this is for a soprano. You sing alto. I'm impressed."

"Four octave range on a good day. My parents put me into opera lessons when I was eight. I rarely hit those high notes now, unless we do a Heart cover. I could never be Ann Wilson, though. She's untouchable. Most of our songs are in guitar keys, so we stick to our lower registers for most of our stuff. I do expand a bit when I write on the piano, but for the most part, Jaymi's the prolific one when it comes to writing songs. And Shawn, she's cranking out new tunes like a madwoman these days."

"I would've never believed you were into opera."

Nikki pulled into a parking space in the downtown garage. "Don't tell anyone. You'll spoil my reputation."

"Your secret's safe with me."

They began walking through the old town, carefully avoiding the smattering of ice and snow on the sidewalks.

"I missed this place," said Nikki. "Portsmouth is so quaint. They have the most interesting little shops down here. Do they still have that blown glass shop down on Bow Street?"

"Yeah. I love browsing in there, but it's so expensive, I've never bought anything. And I'm always afraid I'll turn into a bull in a china shop and knock something over and have to pay for it."

"I know what you mean."

Drew had a hard time picturing Nikki being clumsy in any setting. They walked on in a steady rhythm, and a comfortable easiness settled between them. She had to admit, Nikki was right. Now that she was relaxed, she was enjoying herself.

And then she slipped. Her foot shot forward, and her body went backward, right into Nikki's arms. Nikki caught her just before she hit the ground. She looked up into Nikki's face—which was upside down because she was leaning over her from behind—and cursed the heat flooding her face. She should have been feeling grateful that Nikki had broken her fall, but the rush of other emotions she felt at the same time pissed her off.

"You okay?" Nikki lifted her and held on until Drew found her footing again.

"Yeah. Thank you." She brushed herself off, more so than necessary, until she could collect herself and make eye contact again without feeling like a total fool.

"You sure? You look a little flushed."

"Yeah, I'm fine. Really."

They reached the restaurant a few minutes later, and Nikki opened the door for her. "After you, m'lady."

❖

Nikki slid into a booth across from Drew. They ordered drinks and picked up their menus. She had a hard time concentrating on her choices. The serious expression on Drew's face as she studied the menu was so sexy. Those beautiful eyes of hers had a dizzying effect.

She couldn't get enough of them. She hadn't been this excited to be in another woman's company since…since ever. Well, other than Jaymi.

"Good afternoon, ladies. What can I get you today?"

Nikki silently thanked the server for interrupting her thoughts. They each ordered a soup and half-sandwich meal deal and then awkwardly took long sips on their straws.

Drew asked, "So, whose idea was it for you to study opera?"

"My parents'. They say I started singing before I started talking. They thought I was some sort of prodigy."

"Why opera, though? Why not just regular singing lessons?"

"Oh no. There's no such thing as regular in my family. You either shoot for the top or nothing."

Drew looked at her as if waiting further explanation.

Nikki sighed heavily. "My father was climbing the corporate ladder. He worked his way up to CEO and then got into politics. He wasn't about to let me be some ordinary garage band singer slamming out barre chords on an electric guitar. Too uncivilized for his taste. Or his reputation."

"Politics, huh?"

Nikki cringed. "He's a Massachusetts state senator. Ever heard of Nicholas Rozelli?"

"Your father is Senator Rozelli? Is that your real name?"

"Yeah. Razer is my stage name." She didn't bother explaining that she'd changed it more to spite her father than to make herself more marketable. Then again, he wouldn't have wanted the press to know his daughter was in a lesbian rock group.

"So, what changed? How'd you end up in a rock band?"

"I came out to him during my senior year of high school."

Drew tipped her head in a sympathetic gesture. "I'm guessing he didn't take the news well."

Nikki drew a long sip. "He threatened to cut me off financially. I didn't want his money, but I wanted to go to school. Not only because I wanted to study music, but I wanted out from under his roof."

Their food arrived, and Nikki appreciated that Drew gave them a minute to dig into their meals.

"So, what happened?"

"I lied and told him it was just a phase. It only made me more determined to make it as a rock singer. He agreed to pay my tuition and school expenses, but I never took another dime from him for anything else. I worked part-time as a bartender during college for spending money. After our first album went gold, I paid him back every stinking cent."

Nikki tore off a huge bite of her sandwich. Talking about her father always put a damper on her mood. But it felt good that Drew was actually interested enough to ask about her life, even if it wasn't her favorite topic of conversation.

"That's definitely something to be proud of."

"You'd think so, wouldn't you? But he isn't." Her food suddenly had a foul aftertaste.

Drew reached across the table and covered her hand. "I meant that you must be proud of yourself. If he's not proud of you, then there's something very wrong with him—and I hope I'm not out of line saying that."

Nikki looked down at their joined hands. Drew's palm was soft, and smooth calluses on her fingertips gave her an immediate feeling of familiarity. A musician's touch. Strong. Sure. Capable. Gifted. It was unlikely that Drew would be offended by her own protective layer of skin and closely cropped fingernails. She had a sudden urge to cry. *How did she just do that?*

"You're not out of line," she said quietly. She swallowed hard and forced herself to look up. "The crazy part is, he's come around about my sexuality. We just don't see eye to eye on my career choices." She relaxed in the warm scrutiny of Drew's unwavering attention. *I could drown in those beautiful eyes.* "He's never been one to dish out compliments or put his heart on his sleeve either, if you know what I mean."

"I know exactly what you mean, when it comes to my mother, anyway." Drew repeatedly doused a French fry in ketchup but didn't eat it.

"You're not close?"

"No. Emotionally or geographically. Which is fine with me." Drew's tone suggested otherwise. "My dad more than makes up for it, though." She ate the fry. "I'm sorry you had a rough time with your dad."

She mentally noted Drew's quick deflection back to fathers and didn't dare force the subject. "It's not all on him. I know I was a handful growing up. Sometimes I think if he hadn't been such a pain in my ass, I wouldn't have had as strong a drive to succeed. Guess I should be thankful."

Drew smiled and withdrew her hand. Nikki missed the physical touch immediately, but the emotional connection she was feeling made up for it big-time.

Drew tipped her soup bowl and scooped up the last of its contents. "I'm sure your fans are thankful."

"You're very sweet, you know that?"

Drew blushed, and it took Nikki every ounce of energy not to grab her hand and pull her up out of the seat so she could kiss her senseless.

"I'll be even sweeter if you let me order dessert," Drew said, her cheeks growing even redder.

Nikki got the impression she wasn't used to flirting. It was endearing.

"You can order anything you want. Dutch, remember?" Nikki checked her watch. "Do we have time?" God, she hoped they had time. Right now, she couldn't get enough time with her.

"What the hell. I rarely take my full hour lunch." She pulled out her phone and dialed. "Hey Geena? What time's my next lesson this afternoon?"

Nikki grinned. She liked the sound of this.

"I know Jerry's leaving for the day right about now, but are you okay if I'm not back until then? Okay, then. I'll see you at three." Drew released a smile and picked up the dessert menu. "Wanna share something?"

Did she ever. They placed their order.

"By the way, Nikki, you're welcome and thank you."

"For what?"

"You're welcome for the dance," Drew explained. "And thank you for the flowers." Nikki smiled and shrugged.

"I wanted to thank you yesterday, but I had no way to call you."

Nikki held out her hand. "I can fix that. Let me see your phone."

Drew slipped it out of the holster on her hip and gave it to her. Nikki found the contacts page and added her number.

"Seriously?" Drew said. "You're giving me your number?"

"Can I trust you not to sell it on eBay or share it on your Facebook page?"

"I don't know. I could make a lot of money with this."

"What if I make it worth your while to keep it to yourself?"

"How so?"

Nikki handed Drew her own phone. "I promise I won't sell your number either. And next time, lunch is on me."

"That's it? Nikki Razer's number is only worth one lunch?"

"Hey, you're also the first one to get a ride in my new Jeep, and…"

"And what?"

Nikki grinned. "You don't think I'm going to show all my cards at once, do you?"

Drew toyed with the phone for a minute and then gave it back to her. "You're assuming you'll have another opportunity to show me more cards."

"Ah, we're back to that, are we?"

The server showed up with their chocolate mousse pie. Nikki's attention was torn between the succulent flavors on her tongue and the fantasies of licking it off Drew's body instead. They had no problem polishing it off. Nikki left a generous tip, and they walked quietly back to the parking garage.

"I feel bad that we spent our whole time talking about me," Nikki said when they got to the Jeep. "That wasn't why I asked you to lunch."

"*Kidnapped* me for lunch. You kidnapped me, remember?"

"I thought we agreed on whisking?"

"Tomato, tomahto. Either way, it's fine. I don't have much to talk about. I love my job, but other than that, my life isn't all that interesting."

"I don't believe that for a second. I see the way you light up when you talk about teaching. It's obvious you enjoy what you do. You're close enough to your father that you guys can work together. That alone makes me jealous."

Drew laughed. "Yeah, right. You're jealous of *me*."

"Hey, you think just because I'm famous my life is perfect? Trust me. It isn't."

Drew looked away and shoved her hands into her coat pockets. "I *do* know. Far too well."

Nikki had hit a nerve, but she didn't know what it was. "Drew? What is it? What'd I say?" She saw Drew check her watch and knew she didn't have much time to turn this around. She lifted Drew's chin and looked into sad eyes. Someone had hurt her. "Who are you thinking about?"

"It doesn't matter. I'm sorry. Forget I said anything, okay?"

"Okay." Damn. After having such a good time, this wasn't how she pictured they'd part. She wanted another chance. She wanted more time with her. That had to mean something. It was a long five-minute drive back to DJ's.

"I think your student is here." Nikki pointed to a teenage boy who'd just been dropped off in front of the store carrying a guitar in a vinyl gig bag. Drew made no move to get out and sighed heavily. Nikki poked her in the shoulder. "Get going, you slacker. Who do you think you are taking off for an extended lunch with a crazy-ass rock star?"

Drew's smile seemed forced, but she was glad her attempt at humor lightened the mood a little. "I have to get back to work." Drew opened the door, and Nikki caught her arm before she jumped out.

"Hey, can I take you out again?" Nikki flashed her best smile. "Please?"

"I don't think that's a good idea." She got out and closed the door without another word.

She watched Drew jog into the store and disappear. *Wow. Either I'm losing my touch or she's...she's what?* What the hell was the rest of that sentence? Not interested? Gun-shy from being burned in the past?

Confused?

Because I certainly am.

❖

"I can't believe you're dating Nikki Razer." Geena sounded even more excited than Drew was feeling. She was helping Drew organize the books and sheet music racks so the night person wouldn't have to worry about it when he came in at five.

"We're not dating. It was just lunch."

"Yeah, a two-hour lunch and then some. You never take more than a half-hour."

Drew shrugged as if it were no big deal. She didn't know how she felt about it, and she wasn't ready to dive into analysis.

Geena said, "So, let's review: she spent half the day in here shopping and flirted with you the whole time. Then she takes you to her concert in her limo. She sends you flowers, and then today, she takes you to lunch? Sounds like dating to me."

Geena was on Drew's heels as she retreated to the office to get her things.

"She's been on tour for months. She's probably having withdrawal from the excitement and needs something to do to keep from getting bored. She probably has a fling with some lonely chick every time she comes off tour, one who'll fall all over her because of who she is."

She hated the words as soon as they came out of her mouth. Nikki acted cocky at times, but when she wasn't, she had been nothing but sweet. Yet Drew still managed to push her away. Anyway, it didn't matter. It wasn't as if this thing between them was going to lead to anything. Before long, Nikki would be busy writing and recording again, and then she'd be back on the road to who knew where for who knew how long. Drew would be left behind and forgotten. Again.

"Drew, you're nuts. Haven't you seen the way she looks at you? Have you guys kissed yet?"

"What? No, we haven't kissed because we're *not* dating. Not that it's any of your business."

Drew shrugged into her coat, and they headed down the hall. Mario was helping a customer with guitar amps. She made sure he was all set for the evening and told him they were leaving.

Once outside, Geena gave her a playful shove.

"Hey, you behave," Drew said with a laugh. "I'm still your boss, you know. There are boundaries that say I don't have to share details about my private life with you."

"I know that. Which is why I have no problem with you taking two-hour lunches."

"Good to hear."

Geena tucked her straight, sandy-brown hair under a University of New Hampshire Women's Hockey cap and zipped up her heavyweight Army jacket. She had a girlfriend on campus who played on the team, but Drew knew she turned a lot of heads and enjoyed the attention. And why not? She was twenty-one and would be graduating top of her class with a business degree in the spring. She was attractive and smart and had her shit together. She had no interest in the college party life and rarely drank, which was another reason why Drew trusted her with the store.

She knew that Geena's studies came first, and she wouldn't stick around forever. Once she had her bachelor's, she could write her own ticket and go to work for a company that could pay her what she was worth. *And we'll probably have to hire two people to replace her because what are the chances I can find a new assistant manager who can double as a drum teacher?*

"Good job today keeping an eye on things for me. I appreciate it." She unlocked her truck.

"Anytime. You know you can count on me."

"Have a good night, Geena."

"You too." Geena sank into her own car. "Hey, Drew?"

"What?"

Geena's expression was gentle. "Even if Nikki is just looking for something casual, there's no reason why you can't do the same, you know." She smiled. "That way, when she takes off on tour again, it won't break your heart. You hear what I'm sayin', girlfriend?"

Except Drew didn't do casual. Not with a local yokel, and most certainly not with someone in show business.

Even if it was someone as gorgeous and charming as Nikki.

Chapter Thirteen

Nikki didn't know what to do with herself. It had been so long since she'd had no commitments, she was restless. Not to mention all the pent-up sexual energy she had and no one to relieve it for her. She couldn't hook up with Randi anymore, and picking up someone at a bar on a Tuesday afternoon held no appeal whatsoever. She didn't want them anyway, today or any other day. And for once, she didn't even want Jaymi. She wanted Drew.

Trouble was, she wasn't sure if Drew wanted her. She'd definitely felt a vibe there, but something was holding Drew back. *Maybe I'm reading too much into that vibe. I'm only seeing what I want to see, not something that's actually there.* Vibe or no vibe, Drew had made it clear she didn't want to see her again.

Drew's mood had turned as soon as she'd said something about her fame. If her reservations had to do with her profession, why were those objections so strong? Had word really gone that widespread about her one-nighters with strangers? If that was her reputation, how the hell was she supposed to change it? Did she have to become celibate for some crazy length of time or something? Make a public announcement?

She chuckled. As if people really cared about her promiscuity. *People that matter would care.* And she wanted Drew to be someone who mattered. If Drew *was* aware of her old habits, she'd have good reason to keep her distance.

She needed to get her mind off Drew and all the other crazy feelings that were shocking her system. *Do something mundane. That ought to help.* She decided to swing by the town hall and register the Jeep. Once that was done, she headed home, again at a loss. She slumped onto the couch and stared at her cell phone. She scrolled through her contacts and pulled up Drew's profile. So much for not thinking about her. Was it too soon to call her? They'd only parted two hours ago, and she already wanted to see her again. *I'm pathetic.*

She jumped when the phone rang in her hand. Jaymi's name and picture filled the screen.

"Nikki Razer here, your one-stop shop for all things rock and roll, trouble, and everything in between."

"I wasn't looking for trouble, but I'll take one rock and two rolls to go."

"Comin' right up, toots."

"How's it going?"

"All right." She should ask Jaymi the same question, but she already knew the answer. Jaymi was great. Shawn was great. Life was great. Everything was great, great, great. "What's up?"

"Shawn and I have been brainstorming ideas with ways we can help Drew promote her shop. We thought maybe you could call her and arrange a time we could all meet."

Nikki's stomach flipped. She had an excuse to call Drew. *Yessaah.* "Good idea. Give me some days and times, and I'll see what I can do." Nikki grabbed a notepad off the kitchen counter and wrote down Jaymi's availability.

"The sooner the better, don't you think?" Jaymi asked. "I'm thinking if we can do a couple of things between now and Thanksgiving, we could boost her holiday sales a bit."

"Exactly what I was thinking. Let's hope she can see us tomorrow."

"Yeah."

Nikki heard Shawn's voice in the background and couldn't help but sigh internally.

"Nikki?"

"Yeah?" Nikki dropped into her easy chair and rubbed her forehead.

"Are you okay?"

And here she was again, back in *Jaymiland.* Jaymi's sweet, concerned voice did her in every time. "Yeah, I'm fine."

"No, you're not. I know you better than that. You should know that by now."

"Jaymi, I'm fine. I'll call Drew and see what I can arrange and get back to you, okay?" She didn't mean to sound so abrupt, but she needed to get off the phone and away from the emotions Jaymi still brought up in her.

"Okay." She could tell by Jaymi's tone that she didn't believe her. "Drew's really sweet, don't you think?"

Nikki almost laughed. *Jaymi, you know me too well.* "I took her to lunch today."

"Oh really?" There was a smile in Jaymi's voice. "As in a date?"

"Well, I don't think I can technically call it a date. We didn't plan it. I showed up at the store and offered to take her for a ride in my new Jeep on her lunch break."

"Well, that's a start, but you're right. I'm not sure I would count that as a date, especially if she only thought of it as a friendly gesture. Still, how'd it go?"

"I'm not sure."

"What do you mean?"

Might as well pick Jaymi's brain. *Who else you gonna ask?* She wasn't exactly being smothered by friends. "I'm not sure how she feels about me. And she turned down my offer to take her out again."

"I'm sorry."

"No shit. And she seems to have a thing against famous people."

"Well, it is a lot to consider. Famous people don't always have the best reputations when it comes to romantic relationships."

Nikki sank deeper into the chair. "My reputation's going to come back and bite me in the ass, isn't it?"

"You said it, not me." She couldn't tell if Jaymi was serious or if she was teasing her.

Nikki smiled. "You're not helping, wiseass."

"Hey, I keep telling you that you deserve better. It's about time you listened to me."

She picked at the fabric of the chair's arm. "You are the wisest person I know. Even when you're being a wiseass."

"Leave my ass out of it. I mean it, Nikki. I think Drew likes you. Give it a chance."

She sighed heavily. "I have no idea what I'm doing."

"Then follow your heart and play it by ear. You've always been good at improvising. Love and music aren't all that different, you know. Once a melody speaks to you, you can't ignore it."

"Music's one thing, but you know me and relationships—or lack thereof. I'm not so sure I should be improvising when Drew's feelings are on the line. She's not like a normal groupie, you know? I'll probably screw things up before we even get past the first verse. I can see it now:

we'll get cozy, I'll kiss her once, and then I won't want to stop at that. You know what a horndog I am. I got the impression she doesn't go out with just anyone."

"Then don't be 'just anyone.'"

"I'm *no one* if she won't even go out with me again."

"Well, if she does, take your time with her. Don't try to force anything."

"You mean, don't even kiss her?"

Jaymi chuckled. "You're getting ahead of yourself again. Have you considered that just becoming friends would be a good place to start?"

Friends? Randi had mentioned that, too. Would she be able to keep her attraction in check if that's all they ever became, or would it lead to the same torture of wanting something she couldn't have, like it had with Jaymi?

"I don't know what the hell I'm doing, do I?"

"Exactly why you should listen to me. Attraction is great, but if you don't build a friendship as a foundation, attraction alone amounts to nothing meaningful."

"You're right, I should listen to you. After all, the 'friends first' bit worked for you and Shawn."

"You got that right. My parents, too. People used to ask them what their secret was, and they'd always say, 'we just get along.'"

Nikki smiled as she recalled the ease with which Jaymi's mom and dad had interacted with each other. "Now, that's setting the bar high. You can't get much better than what they had."

"That's for sure."

Jaymi paused, and Nikki knew she was probably lost in a memory, fighting off the sadness that always accompanied thoughts of her mother.

"You want to see if Drew's someone special? Promise yourself that you won't make a move on her, and take the time to get to know her. I mean *really* know her. Who she is. What she wants out of life. Find out as much as you can about her. You know what I'm getting at?"

"You know, I always thought I was the toughest one in the group. I was wrong. You're a badass when you want to be."

"There you go, talking smack about my ass again. Come on, Nik, this is me you're talking to. I happen to know you're not so tough. You need to let her in, too. It has to work both ways. If you let her see the real you, she'll find you irresistible in no time." Jaymi paused. "And even if she's not the one, maybe it will start you on the path to letting people in."

"I don't know if I can wait that long to kiss her."

"Trust me, it'll be worth the wait."

"What if Drew makes the first move?"

"It's your call. I think you'll have it figured out by then. But only a kiss. No sex. In fact, the longer you wait for that, the better. Take things slowly. Trust me."

"Sheesh, you really are tough. I'm hanging up before you volunteer to chaperone, too."

"Ooh, that's not a bad idea."

"Good night, Jaymi."

"Night."

"Hey, Jaymi? Thanks."

"Anytime."

Her heart hurt for only a moment. She felt strangely close to Jaymi right now, which was weird considering their conversation revolved around her interest in someone else. Maybe it was just weird that she actually *was* interested in someone else.

Jaymi's advice seemed solid enough. She reached under her shirt and rubbed her stomach as if it would calm its sudden dance. What if she and Drew did end up dating? What if she took things *too* slowly? How long *should* they wait to have sex? Would Drew grow impatient and lose interest? She'd already lost Jaymi to Shawn because she hadn't made a move soon enough. And what if Drew wasn't interested at all?

But that wasn't even the burning question, was it? *Can I offer her a meaningful relationship if she* is *interested? What if I really am only good for one thing?* Drew had already given Nikki strong vibes that if that was the case, she wanted nothing to do with her. She respected Drew for that, but how could she possibly earn Drew's respect in return if she sucked at the whole "friends leading to more" thing?

She knew she was good at a lot of things, but none of them were remotely related to being someone's girlfriend. *Maybe I should just forget the whole thing.* Drew wasn't a career move or an instrument she was learning to play or a song arrangement. She was a human being that deserved companionship and devotion. *And emotional intimacy.* Things she wasn't sure she could give. She wasn't sure she even knew how.

Jaymi's advice spoke loudly through her musings. She brightened. *Friendship*. Now *that* was something she was good at. There were no guarantees, but if that's all they were destined for, having another friend in her life wouldn't be a bad thing.

CHAPTER FOURTEEN

After the filling lunch she'd had, Drew skipped making dinner and instead munched on a tossed salad. The cats weren't happy about it. No meat scraps for them tonight. They got over it once she sidetracked them with a few treats and a game of spongy bouncy ball. She curled up with them on the couch and turned on the TV. She enjoyed a humbling episode of *Jeopardy* and then tried unsuccessfully to get into a documentary about climate change. She knew it was important to stay informed and educated, but it was impossible to absorb all those scientific facts when her thoughts kept wandering to Nikki.

With all the people in this town, why did she have to be drawn to a damn musician? And a famous one to boot? *Well, duh. You work in a music store and spend very little time anywhere else. What do you expect?*

She shifted Fret off her lap and went to the refrigerator. She found two wine coolers in the back corner that had been there so long they were probably flat. She popped one open and took a tentative sip. Still good. She drank down about a third of the bottle before she started to relax.

Once her body calmed down, her mind followed by drifting back to her afternoon with Nikki. As she replayed their time together so far, she had to admit she'd been tempted to give in to her attraction to Nikki, especially at the restaurant, when they'd begun to open up to each other. She still didn't trust Nikki's intentions.

She finished off the bottle and then dug out the other one. What the hell. She hadn't had a drink in ages. Two wine coolers weren't going to kill her. Maybe it'd do her some good.

She picked up her phone. Maybe she should call and apologize for how she ended things. That was it, though. A quick call to say she was sorry and nothing more. She needed to make it clear she had no interest in going out again, but she also wanted to eliminate any awkwardness between them. She couldn't afford to lose Passion Play as customers—especially after they were kind enough to offer free publicity.

Should she, or shouldn't she? Suddenly, her belly buzzed with nerves. She scrolled to the Ns. Nikki's name wasn't there. What the hell? She'd watched Nikki enter the number. Did she put it in under her last name? Nope. Not in the Rs either. She started over at the top and went slowly down the list. She reached the Ms. *You've got to be kidding me.*

Her phone chimed in her hand, and she nearly vaulted off the couch. *My Favorite Customer* lit up the text display.

Hey it's Nikki. Are you home right now?

Yes. Why?

I didn't want to disturb you at work.

Wow. Nikki was being respectful. Before she could answer, Nikki sent a follow-up.

Can you spare some time for me tomorrow?

Either Nikki didn't know how to take a hint, or she was maddeningly persistent. Or both. She had to nip this in the bud. Now.

I told you I didn't think we should see each other.

What if it's a business meeting?

The phone rang. She checked the readout and answered. "Hi, Nikki."

"I'd rather hear your voice than spend the night typing. Is that okay?"

"I suppose it would be easier. Actually, I'm glad you called." If she wanted to clear the air, she might as well get it over with now.

"Oh really?"

She ignored the flirtatious lilt in Nikki's voice. "I want to apologize for how I left things. I still don't think we should see each other socially, but I don't want to jeopardize our business relationship, so let's just leave it at that. I had a great time at the concert, and I appreciate the gesture. But I can't offer anything more."

The line went dead. Or did it? She heard breathing and…was that Sarah Vaughan singing in the background? The blues-jazz singer from the 50s? She'd never met anyone her age who listened to Sarah Vaughan.

"That's okay."

Nikki's voice made her jump. She was desperate to ask about

Nikki's musical choice, but disclosing a commonality so rare would only encourage her.

"So, are you free for a business meeting tomorrow or not?"

"I…sure. What kind of business meeting?"

"With me and the band. We have some promo ideas for your store and want to see what you think of them."

She sighed with relief. That would be a perfect way to smooth the waters. Having others around should make it harder for Nikki to hit on her, too. "I'd like that. How does one o'clock sound?"

"Sounds like a plan, Stan."

She chuckled at the variation on the Paul Simon lyric. "See you when you hop off the bus, Gus."

"See you later, alligator."

"That's not the next line."

"No shit, Sherlock."

"Indeed, Watson. Indeed."

"So, we're quoting literature now?"

They both laughed. If she wasn't careful, she'd let herself enjoy this. "Apparently. I'll see you tomorrow, Nikki."

"Parting is such sweet sorrow."

Now that was more appropriate. *Sorrow* was exactly why she needed to stay away from this Romeo and keep things strictly business. "How about we just say good night?"

"If you insist. Good night, Drew."

"Good night."

CHAPTER FIFTEEN

They had barely exchanged hellos when two customers burst into DJ's and went directly to the band members. They humbly signed autographs and chatted with them briefly. When the women turned to leave, it was obvious they had only come in to see the celebrities. That was all fine and good, but Drew needed them to shop, too. They probably weren't even musicians. Oh well. Maybe if word got out that Passion Play members were regular customers it would still boost business.

Surprisingly, Nikki seemed unhappy with the interruption. She hid it well and gave them what they wanted, but Drew sensed she just wanted to be left alone. *Odd.* She took a deep breath. *Now, remember, put your damn crush aside and focus on business and your livelihood.*

"Good to see you again, Drew," Jaymi said after the fans left. She gave Nikki the kind of knowing smile you share with an old friend. "You're on time. What's the occasion?" She nudged Nikki playfully.

Drew bet that Jaymi might be the only person who got away with teasing her. It was good to see that someone could knock her down a peg.

Nikki turned to Drew and smiled. "I had good reason to be punctual."

Crap. Here we go with the flirting again. Just ignore it.

Jaymi smiled crookedly and raised an eyebrow. "I see. I love the new Jeep, by the way. I might be tempted to trade in my truck for one myself."

Shawn straightened and shoved her hands into her coat pockets. "What gives, Nikki? No vanity plates?" There it was again. That unspoken tension between Shawn and Nikki.

Nikki smiled and cocked her chin in Shawn's direction. "Don't you think I have enough vanity already?"

"You said it, not me," Jaymi said dryly. "Now come on, you guys, behave."

"How about we get this meeting under way?" Drew asked. She couldn't afford to waste time, and she was irked with this side of Nikki that seemed to show itself whenever she was with these two.

Once they settled down and started tossing ideas around, Drew was thrilled with their enthusiasm and even more excited about the plans they put together. Shawn was all about giveaways. Jaymi's focus was on teaching. Kay and Brian hashed out advertising ideas.

Considering what she'd disclosed about her father, it wasn't surprising that it was Nikki who'd put a profitable twist on every promo. Weekly raffle entries with every purchase, in which the recipient won a one-hour jam session with the band. Sign-ups for kids seventeen and under to participate in a music workshop with them. Autographed photos for purchases over fifty dollars and autographed CDs for purchases over one hundred dollars. Anyone who signed up for lessons could enter for a chance to win a one-on-one session with one of the band members. Any single purchase over one thousand dollars earned an entry for the grand prize of four tickets and backstage passes to a concert on their next tour.

Everything would be on a limited-time basis, since the band's break would end in about six weeks, but the holiday season was the perfect time to add purchase incentives. In addition to printed materials, Brian offered to have the group do a YouTube video to publicly endorse the store.

Nikki spoke with such passion that Drew couldn't take her eyes off her. Not only did Nikki have great business sense, but she seemed to genuinely care about the success of her store. Her sincerity tugged at her heart. Nikki's beauty tugged at another, much lower, place. Damn it. She needed to keep her feelings in check. She was relieved whenever someone else picked up the conversation, and she could turn her attention elsewhere.

The meeting broke up just as Melissa arrived for her lesson. She got a fist bump from Shawn, and they all treated her as if they'd been pals forever.

"Go get set up, Melissa," Drew said. "I'll be right in." She turned to her guests and said, "I don't know how to thank you for all this. It's amazing. I'll start putting together advertising materials this weekend, and we'll kick it off on Monday."

"I can't wait," Jaymi said. "This'll be a real treat for me. If the band hadn't taken off, I'd be a music teacher, too."

Shawn added, "Yeah, and those jam sessions and workshops will be a blast."

"Well, we better get going," Jaymi said. "We don't want to keep your star pupil waiting. We might want her as our opening act someday."

Drew's heart swelled, and she thanked them again. Nikki lingered behind, standing with her thumbs hooked in her jeans pockets and with a giant grin on her face. She braced herself for the predictable come-on that she knew was coming. *Be strong.*

"Do you need to shop for something today, too?"

Nikki shook her head. "You really do have the most beautiful eyes. I love seeing them all lit up when you're happy."

"I'm ready." Melissa called from the doorway of the lesson room.

Saved by the bell. Or something like that. "Okay. Be right there."

"There it is again." Nikki walked to the store entrance and stopped. She pointed in Melissa's direction. "Showtime, Professor." She flashed a smile and was gone.

Drew let out a long breath, relieved. Or was she? Of course she was relieved. She'd told Nikki she didn't want to go out with her again, and Nikki hadn't asked her out. She got what she'd asked for. She wasn't disappointed. Not at all. So what if it was the first time since they'd met that Nikki hadn't hit on her? Flirted a little, but she'd already spent enough time with Nikki to know that that was just how she was. Flirtatious.

All she had to do was continue to ignore the flirting, then Nikki would grow tired of trying and give up. She would eventually see that keeping their relationship strictly business was definitely the right way to go.

She nodded resolutely and headed to Melissa's lesson room.

❖

Nikki found Jaymi with her face pressed to the Jeep's driver's side window, shielding her eyes from the glare of the sun-drenched snow. Shawn was crouched on the ground at the front end, looking at the underneath.

"You want me to pop the hood, Shawn?"

Shawn craned her neck and smiled. "How'd you know?"

She gladly obliged, and while Shawn inspected the engine, marveling at this and that, Jaymi motioned Nikki aside. "So, that went well, don't you think?"

"I didn't ask her out again, if that's what you mean. She made it clear she's not interested, believe me."

Jaymi frowned and placed the back of her hand on Nikki's forehead. "Hmm. No fever." She took her by the wrist. "Maybe I should check your pulse."

Nikki pulled away. "Very funny."

"I'm just giving you shit. I'm proud of you." Jaymi zipped her coat and flipped up the collar. "Don't forget what I said about patience and feeling out a possible friendship."

"I'm not sure she's even interested in friendship. Didn't you notice how she was all business today? I should just cut my losses and move on."

"Of course she was all business. It was a *business* meeting, you knucklehead. And she's at work. What do you expect?"

She paced for a moment, trying to formulate words for what she was feeling.

Jaymi's eyebrows knitted together. "Put yourself in her shoes, Nik. You've been hitting on her since you met, and she's been turning you down. I know it goes against your nature, but quit trying so hard, and let the pieces fall where they may."

"We got along well on the phone last night. We even joked around a bit."

Jaymi smiled. "There you go. I was watching her during the meeting today. She had her eyes glued to you every chance she got. I think she likes you."

"Jaymi's right." Shawn carefully closed the Jeep's hood, pressing it down with a click. She gave Nikki's shoulder a little shove and grinned. "Not sure why, but she does seem to have the hots for you. Poor fool." She ducked and scampered away as if Nikki would chase her for the tease.

"Yeah, laugh all you want, you spoiled brat," Nikki shouted at Shawn. "You were one sorry sap drooling over Jaymi not too long ago."

Shawn made a show of wiping her chin and continued her exploration of the new vehicle. Normally, she would've found Shawn's antics amusing, but today, they only served to make her feel totally inadequate. How could Jaymi and Shawn see something in Drew that she couldn't? Were her instincts that far off?

Jaymi waved a hand in front of her face. "Hello?"

"How do you put up with her?"

Jaymi just smiled.

"Never mind. Are you sure, Jaymi? You think Drew likes me?"

"Yes, but for some reason, she doesn't want to."

"Thanks. That really helps."

Jaymi smiled her trademark crooked smile. "Listen to me. You said she seemed to have a problem with you being famous. Do you know why? See, this is what I meant about taking time to get to know each other. She seems to be attracted to you. There might be a specific reason why she's hesitant to get involved with you."

Nikki folded her arms, the cold seeping into her bones, but the small glimmer of hope Jaymi was giving her kept the shivers at bay. "How do I get to know her if she won't give me the time of day?"

Jaymi must have heard the desperation in her voice. She pulled Nikki into a hug. "Let her see you for you, and who knows? Maybe she'll let down her guard."

"This isn't going to be easy."

Jaymi took a few steps backward. "That's never stopped you before. In anything."

She chuckled. "Good point."

"So, are you going to take us for a spin in your fancy new four-by-four or what?" Jaymi gave Shawn a quick glance. "Look at my poor girlfriend over there. She's champing at the bit worse than a dog who loves going for rides."

Nikki grinned in Shawn's direction. "She's gonna ask to drive, isn't she?"

"You might as well hand over the keys now."

Forty-five minutes later, after Shawn and Jaymi had each had a turn at the wheel, Nikki dropped them off at Jaymi's truck. She watched Jaymi drive away. She was beginning to like this new development in their friendship. Who knew Jaymi was so good at relationship advice?

Maybe if she'd had a friend like this before Shawn came along, she could've used the advice to win Jaymi over. Then again, Jaymi's relationship with Shawn was probably the reason Jaymi had such good advice.

Nice fucking irony.

The front door of DJ's opened. Drew held the door open while Melissa stepped out with her guitar. Drew's fondness and protectiveness was obvious as she watched her student get into a bronze-colored sedan that was well past its prime.

Drew suddenly looked her way as if startled by her presence. She was too far away for Nikki to read her expression, but she stood there unmoving for much longer than necessary.

Did Drew think she'd been out here this whole time and was stalking her now? Not exactly the impression she wanted to give.

She drove toward the front of the store and lowered her window, but it was too late. Drew slipped back inside. What to do now? Chase her inside? Would that make things worse? At least she could explain herself. Or maybe she should just give Drew her space.

Damn it all. This seemed a whole lot easier with Jaymi by her side telling her what to do. *When did I become such a bumbling idiot when it comes to women?* She stared at the glass storefront, hoping for another glimpse of Drew, when she heard the sputtering engine of Melissa's car stall and go silent. She pulled into the neighboring space. Melissa cranked the ignition, and it started again, but its revival was short-lived. Melissa noticed her then and seemed to shrink with embarrassment. Poor kid.

She hopped out of the Jeep and motioned for Melissa to open her window. "Too bad cars aren't as easy to keep in tune as guitars, huh?"

"Especially when you run out of gas. I was supposed to get some before school this morning and forgot."

"I don't know much about cars, but I do know they don't work without fuel." She tapped her temple. "See this? It's more than a hat rack. My Jeep came with a gas can, so I can run down the street and get you some. You'll freeze if you stay in the car. Would you like to come with me, or would you rather wait inside with Drew?"

Melissa checked her watch. "We gotta hurry. I'm supposed to pick my mom up from work at four and get us home for supper in time for her to get to her other job by six." Her head dropped back against the seat. "I can't believe I forgot. She gave me money for it and everything."

"Then quit wasting time and let's go."

Melissa hopped in and buckled up. "She let me take the car today so I could go to my lesson after school." She checked out the interior of the Jeep. "Man, someday I'd love to have the money to buy something like this."

Nikki recalled Drew's comments about being up front with

Melissa about the downfalls of life on the road. She'd just walked into a perfect opportunity to share them.

"It took a lot of hard work and sacrifice to get this far. Fame isn't all it's cracked up to be, you know. I'm not saying it isn't nice that people admire us for what we do, but it's tough having your personal space invaded every time you turn around."

Melissa was quiet for a few minutes. "I don't care. I'm sick of my mom having to work herself to death, and we still barely scrape by. I'm gonna make sure she doesn't have to do that anymore. I don't care what it takes."

Nikki was tempted to ask about the girl's absent father, but it was none of her business. She pulled in next to the gas pump and shivered in the energy emitting from the frustrated adolescent beside her. A father's physical presence didn't guarantee him being present in other ways. There were times she would have been better off if her father *hadn't* been around. Still, she'd somehow found a way to steer away that bitterness when she needed to. Most of the time.

"That determination will take you far, but don't make the mistake of not caring. There's a right way and a wrong way to break into this business. The wrong way ends up with a lot of people getting hurt." She jumped out and added, "Including yourself."

She grabbed the plastic gas can from the back of the Jeep, one of the many accessories included in an options package she'd added to the deal as an afterthought. Was she taking those types of purchases for granted now? Had she become that spoiled and out of touch that she'd grown insensitive to those who couldn't afford such luxuries? Maybe it was time to follow Jaymi's example and start sharing more of her wealth. She made a mental note to research some worthy causes.

She was about to swipe her debit card through the reader when Melissa rushed to her side. "I can pay for it. I have the money she gave me." She held up a ten-dollar bill as proof.

Nikki slid the card back into her wallet and held out a ten of her own. "Suit yourself. But do me a favor and get me a hot chocolate while you're in there." Melissa stared at the bill for a moment and then took it. "Get yourself one, too. And that's not charity. It's a bribe so you won't forget about me when you're rich and famous."

Melissa shook her head and finally smiled. "Okay."

She loved the kid's spirit, but Melissa's pride was going to be a hindrance if she wasn't careful.

The return trip to DJ's was quiet as they sipped their drinks. As

Melissa poured the gas into her car, Nikki couldn't help watching for glimpses of Drew. Nothing. Maybe she was with another student. Drew was right about one thing, though. Melissa needed guidance. Maybe she wasn't the only one to give it to her.

"Hey, if you want to learn how to take care of your car, I know someone who'd love to show you." Two people, actually, if she counted Randi. But there was a more logical choice.

"Who?" Melissa replaced the gas cap and handed Nikki the empty can.

"Shawn. She's almost as good at playing guitar as she is at fixing cars."

Melissa's face flushed pink. There was definitely a crush there. Her shoulders dropped along with her head. "Nah, I don't wanna bother her with this stuff—"

"Are you kidding me? She'd be in her glory showing off all her expertise of automobile doohickeys and whosie-whats-its."

Melissa held back a smirk. "Whosie-whats-its?"

"I believe that's the technical term for some wingy dingy thingie under the hood." She mirrored Melissa's grin and winked. "Now you know who writes all the best rhymes in our songs. A secret we only let insiders like you know."

Melissa laughed. "You're kind of a dork, you know that?"

She gave Melissa a friendly shake and laughed with her. "Another insider secret." She secured the gas can in the back and closed the hatch. "You don't have any ambitions of becoming a tabloid journalist, do you?"

"No way. Those people are wacked."

"Agreed. There are some crazy fans out there, too. You need to be very careful. Something else to keep in mind."

"That's for sure."

"What's going on out here? Melissa, don't you have to pick up your mother?"

They both turned at the sound of Drew's voice.

"Shit! Oops, sorry. I mean shoot," Melissa added sheepishly. "I gotta go. Thanks, Nikki."

"No problem, bud. I'll talk to Shawn, okay?"

"Yeah. That'll be good because as soon as I get a job, I'm gonna save for my own car so my mom won't have to share hers." She climbed in and started the engine.

"You do that," Nikki said. "Be careful driving."

"I will. Thanks again." She waved and drove off.

Nikki turned in Drew's direction. She wanted to step closer, but Drew's body language told her to maintain the five-foot gap between them, and her expression begged for an explanation. It didn't matter what kind of look she had on her face. Drew's beautiful eyes took her breath away. Every time.

"You'll freeze out here without a coat."

Drew kept her stance, arms folded, feet apart. If Drew had any idea of how her confidence was affecting Nikki's insides, she didn't show it. "I'm fine, but I need to know that Melissa's okay. Her mother trusts me to look out for her while she's here."

"And you don't think she's safe with me?"

"I don't know. Is she? You do know she's sixteen, right? She's at a very impressionable age—"

"Why don't you ask Melissa?" She couldn't believe Drew would think she'd have anything other than Melissa's best interests at heart. Her thrashing heartbeat now simmered in anger. "That'll save you the trouble of deciphering which story to believe. You obviously trust Melissa to tell you the truth, even if you don't think I will."

She climbed into the Jeep and cranked the key. She watched Drew's shocked expression shrink in her rearview mirror as she sped out of the parking lot. Minutes later, she turned into the same gas station she'd just visited and pulled off to the side.

She left the engine running, hugged the steering wheel, and dropped her head onto her arms. Why did people always assume the worst about her? More importantly, why did *Drew* have to be one of those people? Why didn't anyone take the time to get to know her?

Maybe she was wasting her time. Drew didn't like her; she was just being nice to her because she was a customer.

No. Her instincts weren't *that* bad. If there was one thing she was sure of about Drew, it was that she wasn't a phony. She'd seen glimpses of interest.

She switched off the stereo and headed home. As she drove, an uneasy prickling teased her thoughts. Maybe Drew was the one with the good instincts. *Maybe Drew's gut is telling her that I have no experience with relationships—romantic or otherwise.*

Dad was wrong. There were times when taking no for an answer was not only okay, but it was the right thing to do.

She wanted to do better. She wanted to *be* better. She wanted to prove that she had it in her to change. Not to Drew. Not to Jaymi. Not even to her father. She needed to prove it to herself.

She pressed the button on the garage door opener and put the Jeep to bed for the night. Once inside, she poured a glass of wine, put on some classical music, and turned on the gas fireplace. She stared at the flames as they flickered and danced, mesmerized by their ability to clarify her jumbled musings as she sank onto the couch. She imagined hanging out with Drew as friends. She bet it'd be fun.

She sipped her wine. Could she overcome her crush and handle just a friendship with Drew? Maybe if Drew was willing to spend a little more time with her…

How was that going to happen?

A string quartet played at a slow tempo through the six wall-mounted speakers. The beautiful blend of sounds was soothing, but instead of slowing down, her pulse quickened. She sat up, excited. If they were on Drew's turf, in Drew's comfort zone, focused on a common interest that had nothing to do with dating…

She grinned as the idea formulated. *I think I'm on to something.*

CHAPTER SIXTEEN

It's official. I'm an ass. Drew stared at Melissa's phone number on her cell. The brief conversation with Melissa had confirmed it. She'd assumed the worst when Nikki had not only done Melissa a huge favor, but she'd also given her some sound advice. Just like she'd asked Nikki to do. Hell, if she hadn't rushed out of the store and barged in on them, she wouldn't have even known about it unless Melissa mentioned it.

Yep. I'm an ass. She burrowed deeper into the couch and wrapped her arms around Fret, who was napping on her chest. Her purrs relaxed her body, but they did nothing for her warring mind. The Segovia record had ended almost an hour ago, and she hadn't noticed the silence until now. Maybe the yelling she'd been doing at herself in her head had been too loud.

"What am I going to do?" she asked her feline friends. "One minute I hate her guts. The next, I think she's the sweetest thing ever. And why does she have to be so friggin' gorgeous? Answer me that, will you?" They offered nothing. Not even Vinnie, who pawed her shoulder from his perch on the back of the couch. She reached up and scratched his head. Fret stirred and let out a tiny, annoyed mew at the movement. "Aw, poor Fretty. Am I disrupting your eighteen hours of sleep? You poor thing." She kissed her nose and gave her a little squeeze.

Fret stretched and settled back in. Drew got up, much to Fret's dismay, and powered off the stereo. She didn't even bother putting away the record. What was wrong with her? It would collect dust if she left it there too long. She headed to bed. She'd take care of it in the morning. She needed to take care of her heart tonight.

No woman had ever had such a strong effect on her. Of the few girlfriends she'd had, none of them had taken over her thoughts the way Nikki had. Not before they'd dated, not during, and most certainly not after they'd broken up. She'd gone to lunch with Nikki once. And that wasn't even a date.

But it felt like a date. Until she'd put Nikki in her place and told her they couldn't see each other anymore. She looked in the mirror as she brushed her teeth. She told her reflection it was the right thing to do. Right? Right. No matter how sweet and charming Nikki could be, it didn't change the fact that she spent half her life on the road in the limelight.

Sure, she could take Geena's advice and have fun with Nikki when she was home, but then what? Sit home alone while Nikki did whatever she wanted with whomever she wanted?

She spat and rinsed. *Then again, there'd be nothing stopping me from doing whatever* I *wanted while she's away.* Huh. She'd never thought of that before. *Not only am I an ass, I'm an ass with double standards.* Trust worked both ways. Should she continue her assuming ways and label Nikki as untrustworthy? Based on what? Her reputation in the media? Or her personal observations?

She hated the way they'd left things today. That was twice now they'd parted on a sour note. At the very least, she needed to apologize. Before she could talk herself out of it, she picked up her phone and sent Nikki a text.

I'm sorry I misjudged you.

Simple. Short and to the point. Just a little olive branch so things wouldn't be awkward next time Nikki came in shopping. Because really, she needed Nikki the wealthy customer more than she needed Nikki the potential love interest. Right? Right.

She waited for a reply. Nothing.

She crawled into bed. Vinnie curled up on the pillow by her head. Andres nudged his way under the covers behind her knees. Fret, now wide awake, began her nightly prowl.

One observation was making itself crystal clear. Nikki was occupying her thoughts more and more often. And more and more often, those thoughts weren't unpleasant. Not unpleasant at all. Quite the opposite, actually.

Damn it.

❖

Drew dropped her head onto the desk. Maybe no one would notice if she took a five-minute snooze. The way she was feeling, it would turn into five hours. She'd flip-flopped in bed so many times last night it almost qualified as exercise. Even the cats had gotten fed up and found other places to sleep. Obsessively checking the phone on an hourly basis didn't help.

Payroll wasn't going to finish itself. She pushed off the cool, hard wood and tried to make her eyes as big as silver dollars. Dollars. Yes, focus on dollars. She glanced at the clock. She had less than an hour to send in the figures to their paycheck vendor. Pissing off your employees by screwing with their pay was not an option. She stood, stretched, and went across the hall to the break room to pour another cup of coffee, her fourth of the day. The acid was already burning a hole through her stomach, but she ignored it. She already felt like shit, so what difference did it make?

Nikki still hadn't replied to her text. Fine. Text or no text, Drew got the message, loud and clear. Screw Nikki Razer. The caffeine jolt boosted her resolve. It was easier than she thought. All she had to do was think about her mother.

"Hey, Drew?"

She flinched when Geena peeked around the doorway into her office. "Yes?"

"I need your help with a customer. Can you spare a minute?"

She groaned. Normally, that made her day. Today? Not so much. Despite her pep talk, she hadn't the time or energy to be a perky saleswoman.

"Are you all right?"

"Yes. Just tired. Can you handle it? Do you mind?"

"I can try, but cellos aren't really up my alley. I need your expertise. How close are you to finishing payroll?"

Drew narrowed her eyes. "How'd you know?"

She tossed her hands up as if it was obvious. "I do pay attention when you teach me stuff, you know."

"I know you do."

"So, how close?"

"Ten, maybe fifteen minutes."

"Well, okay then. I wanna get paid, so I can stall her while you finish payroll, and I'll see you out there in ten or fifteen minutes." Geena left before she could reply.

She's gonna make a great manager someday. Too bad it probably won't be here. She wrapped up payroll in record time. A cello sale was a huge deal. Depending on how much the customer was willing to spend, she could hit today's numbers in one sale. She hit send and hurried to the orchestral strings room.

"Good afternoon, Professor."

She screeched to a stop. Nikki sat before her with an eight-thousand-dollar cello between her knees and a smile as wide as the bow was long.

"Careful, Drew. If your jaw drops any lower, you'll scrape your chin on the floor."

She closed her mouth. "Hi," was all she could get out. She was going to kill Geena. Her matchmaking skills were getting as savvy as her business acumen.

"Could you play something on this so I can hear how it sounds before I buy it?"

"Sure, but…" Did Nikki think buying her a cello was going to change her mind about dating her? This was definitely going too far. She couldn't be bought—big fat potential sale or not. "I'm quite attached to the sound of my own, thank you."

Nikki's gorgeous smile vanished, and her eyebrows crinkled. "That's great, but that doesn't help me unless you want to sell me yours."

Don't play coy with me, Nikki Razer. Still, the look on Nikki's face said she was genuinely confused. What was she up to?

"Drew, are you all right?" Nikki adjusted her position on the stool and set down the bow. "I never thought I'd say this, but you don't look so good today."

Thanks to you. Or me. However you want to look at it. "Gee, thanks. Your charm is off its game today, too, I see."

Nikki's grin grew slowly. She got up and handed Drew the cello. "So, you *do* think I'm charming."

"That's not what I said."

Nikki shook her head slightly and pursed her lips. "I'm sorry, that was uncalled for. I didn't mean to put words in your mouth." Her tone sounded sincere.

"Apology accepted."

Nikki's smile returned, and she stepped closer. "I appreciate that. I'm relying on your expertise here, so play me something sweet so I can make a wise decision. I'm very selective about my instruments." She stepped away and motioned for Drew to sit. "You must at least know *that* about me by now."

Way to charm me and make me feel like an ass at the same time.

She stumbled over her own feet reaching for the bow and planted her butt on the stool. She seethed at how off balance Nikki made her feel and then quickly blamed it on sleep deprivation.

Nikki sat across from her on the wooden bench. She extended her legs out in front of her, crossed her ankles, and folded her arms. Her shit-eating grin was about to break her face. "I'm waiting."

Drew positioned her bow. "Whomever you're buying this for must be very special to you."

"It's not a gift."

Drew froze. "You're buying it for yourself?"

"Yes. Who'd you think it was for?"

Heat flooded her cheeks. She wasn't about to answer *that* question honestly. "But you don't play the cello." *Good sidestep there, ass.* "Do you?"

"Not yet." Nikki leaned forward. "I just signed up for lessons."

Comprehension swiftly replaced her private embarrassment. Nikki was going to spend an hour with her once a week. An hour alone. As a student. As *her* student. Did Nikki really want to play the cello? Or had her rejection bruised her ego so badly that she was willing to spend thousands of dollars and take cello lessons just so she could keep trying to win her over?

She couldn't help herself. She started laughing. It was utterly ridiculous. Either Nikki couldn't handle people telling her no, which was pathetic, or...*or she really likes me.*

Nikki leaned back. "Well, you sure know how to instill confidence in a new student."

Drew wiped her eyes with the back of her hand. "I'm sorry. I just can't believe—never mind."

"Never mind what?" Nikki was dead serious now.

"Nothing. I'm overtired, so I'm feeling a bit silly. Anyway, I'd strongly suggest renting a cello for now. See if you like playing it first before you invest so much money buying one."

Nikki straightened. "Let me tell you something, Drew. Once I commit to something, I see it through. Renting is not an option." She settled back and crossed her arms again. "Now, play me something, damn it, because come hell or high water, I'm going to learn to play the fucking cello."

Drew returned her glare and drew the bow across the strings. Loudly. If Nikki wanted a challenge, then she'd get one. Both musically and personally. Getting romantically involved with a student was strictly against DJ's policies. It was a matter of professional ethics. If Nikki thought that taking lessons was going to get her into Drew's pants, her plan was going to backfire.

That thought wasn't as gratifying as she wanted it to be. Luckily, she didn't have time to ruminate. Nikki was up and presenting her with another cello. They made the exchange and resumed their positions.

A half hour later, Drew had played DJ's entire cello inventory twice, and Nikki was walking out the door with the most expensive one. She'd not only exceeded today's sales goal, she'd made a dent in tomorrow's threshold as well.

"Now you see why I needed you?" Geena teased. They were behind the counter together running the five o'clock register tally.

"Shut up."

"Oh, methinks someone has a crush," Geena singsonged. She flipped the spring-loaded bill holders down and shut the drawer.

"Shut up."

"Nice way to talk to your favorite employee."

"You could've told me it was her."

Geena smiled. "And miss the fun of seeing you all hot and bothered? No way. What happened in there?"

"Nothing." Drew "accidentally" shoved into her as she squeezed behind her on the way back to the floor. "Get back to work."

Geena's smile widened. "I'm off now. Hockey game tonight, remember?"

"Then get out of here. I'm not paying you overtime."

"Hey, after that sale, you can afford it."

Drew hooked elbows with her and dragged her toward the break room. She tossed Geena's Army jacket at her, and she donned it proudly. It was her mother's.

"You could at least split the commission with me."

"Go."

Geena stiffened her posture and saluted. "Yes, ma'am." She marched out.

A few minutes later, Drew's phone dinged. Nikki.

I'm sorry I lost my temper about the Melissa thing. Truce?

She smiled and typed one word.

Truce.

At least tonight she'd sleep.

CHAPTER SEVENTEEN

Drew hit the snooze button for the third time. Another sleepless night was the last thing she needed. She couldn't call in sick. Her dad had a dentist appointment, and Geena had classes this morning, so it was up to her to get the store open. She wished they could hire one more person.

She'd never needed to worry about it before because she never took an unscheduled day off. She wasn't sick. Not physically. Frustrated. Confused. Angry. She'd been content with her single, uncomplicated life for years. With the lousy example of marriage her mother had exposed her to, it was no wonder she'd shied away from relationships.

Four failed marriages. What a joke. Granted, she was nothing like her mother. Her father hadn't dated much since the divorce. He was still single and doing just fine. Anytime she asked him if he was lonely or had a longing for a girlfriend, he always said if the right person came along, he'd know it, and there was no sense forcing something.

His philosophy had apparently rubbed off on her.

So why couldn't she stop thinking about Nikki? Why did the sight of her gorgeous face, smoking hot body, and endless charm have to affect her so intensely? Not to mention what it was doing to her libido.

The alarm went off again. Good thing, or she'd be late to work because she needed to satisfy a sexual craving more than she cared to admit. Geena was right. It had been far too long since she'd dated or had sex.

She begrudgingly fumbled out of bed and readied herself for work. At least Nikki's first cello lesson wasn't until next week. Although at the rate she was going, she would need more time than that to work Nikki out of her system. At least she wasn't obligated to see her any more than once a week in a working capacity.

By the time she got to work and occupied her mind with her morning opening routine, she was feeling much stronger.

Until Nikki walked in an hour later. She didn't recognize her at first. She was bundled up in a black parka with violet piping, a matching purple scarf, and a stocking cap with a huge pom-pom on top. This cold spell must have finally knocked some sense into her to dress for the season.

Drew smiled in reflex at how cute she looked. Nikki smiled back as she pulled off the cap and smoothed down her sleek hair.

"Good morning." Nikki's perfect teeth accentuated her smile, but the way it reached her dark eyes was even more enticing.

"Good morning. I wasn't expecting you until next week." Drew felt her resolve melting like a Hershey bar left on a dashboard in July. It didn't help that Nikki had untied the scarf and was unzipping her coat to reveal a skintight red sweater beneath it. And she was still smiling that killer smile.

"You're not returning the cello, are you?"

"Not a chance."

She needed to stay behind the counter. Keep a safe distance. That was key. *Treat Nikki only as a customer. Stay behind the counter.*

"So, what can I do for you today?"

"I'm here to buy a couple more guitars." Nikki flipped up her collar and draped the scarf over her shoulders. "Phew, it's hot in here."

"I can hold on to your jacket while you shop if you'd like." *What am I doing?* She was five steps away from helping her off with her coat. *Stay behind the counter.*

"God, I hate these single-digit days." She peeled off her coat. "You freeze your ass off outside, then roast inside. I'll take you up on that offer to hold on to this. Do you mind?"

Of course she didn't mind. And if she could pry her eyes away from Nikki's chest and slender curves for two seconds, she might curtail the drool that was threatening to spill over her bottom lip. "We have a rack over here just for customers." She pointed to the coat tree at the end of the counter. *No, that didn't sound rude at all. Offer to take her coat and then essentially tell her to hang up the damn thing herself.*

She came around the counter and took the coat from Nikki's outstretched hand. *So much for that strategy.* She took extra care in making sure the coat was secure so she could keep her back to Nikki a few seconds longer. She glanced at the door, praying for another customer to come in so they wouldn't be alone.

"Are you manning the shop by yourself today?"

"Till noon. It's not usually busy for the first two hours, and as you know, we have a small staff."

Nikki looked pensive for a moment, as if she was tucking the information away for future reference. "Is that safe?"

She shrugged. "I don't have much choice. Until we can afford to hire more help, that's how it is."

Nikki twisted and looked out the front windows, just long enough for Drew to step a little farther away from her. It helped slightly, despite the mild waft of Nikki's cologne that tickled her nostrils. Nikki seemed to be considering her next words carefully.

"I have a friend who works for the Portsmouth PD," said Nikki, still gazing outside. "She's a K-9 trainer now, but she used to be a cop. One call and I bet she could arrange a few extra patrol drive-bys on the days any of you are here alone."

She wasn't sure what she'd expected Nikki to say, but it wasn't that. It was sweet. More than sweet. It was a caring gesture. Protective. Selfless.

Nikki turned to her, her expression serious. "You just say the word. I know Randi. She'd make it happen, trust me."

Nikki was putting the ball in her court. Not taking control or disregarding her feelings on the subject. That's what her mother would have done. She would have bragged about having powerful people wrapped around her little finger, willing to do whatever she asked at the drop of a hat. Nikki was just making the offer. It wasn't even Nikki with the pull; it was her friend. A friend that obviously had a strong enough loyalty to Nikki that Nikki was confident in her doing her this favor.

There were more small businesses around here than she could count. She knew most of them were in the same boat, getting by on bare minimum staffing, especially during the winter months when tourism was practically nil. Unless the store offered something unique or hard to find, most people were at the malls shopping the big-name stores.

And last year, there was a serial rapist nabbing local teenagers off the streets. They finally caught the guy, but still, it had really shaken up the otherwise low-crime community. The bank DJ's used was on the next block, so she and her dad walked their deposits there every day. They always took precautions by concealing the bag and varying the time of day, but most of the time, one of them went alone while the other watched the store. Geena also shared that responsibility when necessary.

"Okay. I suppose it can't hurt—as long as it's no trouble. But it's not just me. There are a lot of us in this neighborhood working alone. If you think she can have them keep an eye on all of us, then—"

"Consider it done."

"Thank you." Something was different. Nikki wasn't her usual smug self. Interesting. Should she trust it? "What's the catch?"

Nikki's mouth dropped open. "Catch? There's no catch." Nikki looked hurt. "I happen to care about this community. It's been very supportive and instrumental to Passion Play's success." She walked to the coat tree and yanked off her parka. "But never mind—"

"Wait!" Drew rushed to her side. "I'm sorry. It's just that..."

"That I've been a pushy jerk who kept flirting with you and wouldn't accept no for an answer." Nikki stabbed her arms through the sleeves. "I don't blame you for hating me so much."

She caught Nikki's arm before she could step away. "I don't hate you." She *didn't* hate Nikki. She couldn't even dislike her anymore. She'd tried. She'd failed.

"You sure act like it sometimes," Nikki mumbled. Her shoulders sagged, and she studied her feet. "Why is it so hard for people to believe that I might want to do something nice just for the sake of doing something nice?" She looked up. The rims of her eyes were moist. "I know I come on a little strong, but I'm working on that. I'm so sorry for disrespecting you."

Too bad they weren't standing in the brass horns department. Drew would've gladly inserted her own head into a tuba bell. "I'm sorry, too," she said softly.

A tiny droplet escaped Nikki's eye. Without thinking, Drew wiped it away with her thumb, resting her palm against Nikki's cheek a little longer than necessary. Her skin was even softer than she'd imagined.

Nikki's eyes sharpened with surprise for a nanosecond before they closed, and she leaned into the touch. A content, nearly silent exhalation followed, and Drew's heart quickened at the sensuality of the sound. It would be so easy to kiss her right now.

Whoa.

The bells on the front door jingled, and a whoosh of arctic air parted them like teenagers caught making out in the school's janitorial closet. Before it registered what might have happened—or what she'd wanted to happen—Nikki breezed past the customer and headed to the door.

She stopped and stared sadly at Drew's reflection in the glass. And then, like the air that had just been sucked from her lungs, she was gone.

"Who can I see about signing up for guitar lessons?"

Drew blinked several times before it clicked that she had a customer standing in front of her. "Uh, that would be me."

The young woman followed her to the counter. "Was that who I think it was?"

"Yes."

But it most certainly wasn't who Drew thought it was.

Not anymore.

❖

After driving aimlessly for half an hour trying to clear her head, Nikki realized she hadn't even turned on the heat. Drew's touch had warmed her to the core. A few more seconds and she might have pulled Drew into her arms and kissed her.

They were damn lucky that customer walked in when she did, or Nikki could have blown everything. Her willpower was bordering on nonexistent as it was. She'd walked in determined to check her ego at the door, and as it turned out, it had taken no effort at all. The thought of Drew being there alone and any possible dangers it presented had put her into full-on protective mode. What transpired from that point on came naturally.

She turned into her garage and slumped back in the seat. Without even trying, Drew stripped her of the defenses that usually stopped her from blurting out things that exposed her vulnerabilities. Showing weakness wasn't acceptable in her family. It meant you wouldn't get ahead. Or promoted. Or elected.

Or in my case, loved.

She tried to get her mind off Drew, but she was like an annoying song she couldn't get out of her head. Except there was nothing annoying about Drew. Infuriating at times, but not annoying. She respected Drew for being herself and for standing her ground. Drew didn't give a shit that she was a rock star, and Nikki liked that about her. Even if she was kind of a shit for making assumptions that weren't fair.

She needed to get back to her old foolproof way of dealing with her feelings. She needed her music. She muted her phone and sat down at the piano. She closed her eyes. The smooth keys beneath her fingertips felt like coming home, more so than her uninspiring surroundings. She played without knowing where that first chord would take her, and she let go. After sixteen bars in E minor, the melody shifted to its relative major, G. *Ah, now that's beautiful.* Happier sounding, simultaneously bold and sweet, it would serve as a strong chorus before it moved back into the minor key for the next verse.

After an hour, she scribbled it all down and arched backward into a stretch. She was stiff, and her back cracked as she reached above her head. Her stomach growled, reminding her she hadn't eaten since breakfast, and she needed groceries again. Lyrics would have to wait.

She gobbled down a PB&J to hold her over and headed back out, not even bothering with a list. She already had enough words jumbled in her head, and none of them were making any sense yet. One encounter with Drew and the confidence she used to feel around women was shot to hell. She talked a good game, but what if she was nothing more than what she already was? She'd exceeded her career ambitions, and she'd still fallen short in her father's eyes. She'd thought she was Jaymi's soul mate. *And look at how that turned out*. No matter how many times she'd been with Randi sexually, they would've never amounted to more than friends. Her gut had told her Drew was attracted to her, yet whenever they saw each other, one of them got upset with the other.

As she grabbed her keys and headed to the garage, a common thread wove its way into her mind. No matter who it was she thought about, it came down to one thing: She wanted love. To give it, to receive it, to feel it, to make it, to share it.

Just like her groceries, she needed everything. How in the world did she get it all? How did she become a person someone else could love?

Unlike her groceries, she couldn't just make a list and buy it all.

CHAPTER EIGHTEEN

Drew left Melissa in Geena's capable hands and braced herself for the cold that awaited her outside. She'd finished her hour-long orientation with her new employee, thankful for the distraction, and then couldn't wait to get out of there. Geena beamed with the prospect of training her, as she did with every new hire. Drew needed to pick up a few things at the supermarket, which was another good excuse to leave early.

Nikki's teary expression had torn up her heart all day. The feel of Nikki's cheek against her palm hadn't helped. *Why did I do that?*

Her mouth soured with the taste of regret. She parked her truck and fished a piece of paper from her pants pocket. She added mouthwash to her list and went inside.

She made quick work of shopping. She'd shopped here for so long that she knew exactly where everything was, and her list rarely varied. Cooking for one didn't inspire much on the McNally menu. She suddenly had a vision of having Nikki over for dinner. Not as a date but as a friend. How would that go? Nikki hadn't exactly left on a high note today.

She sighed as she turned down the last aisle and grabbed a tub of butter from a dairy cooler. Maybe it was for the best. Even if Nikki was a sweetheart underneath all that brassy rock star persona, how could she be sure Nikki wasn't playing on her sympathy as a ploy to get her into bed? She rolled her cart toward the frozen desserts. *I need ice cream.* She plucked three pints of Ben & Jerry's off the shelf and headed to the checkouts.

She got in line and rolled her eyes at the absurd headlines and doctored photos on the tabloids and magazines in the racks. She could understand the desire to pursue a career in the performing arts, but why anyone wanted the fame that went along with it was beyond her. Almost as disturbing was the fact that people liked reading this garbage. Who cared who was sleeping with whom? Or about the supposed affairs they were having? Or that someone gained or lost weight or was rumored to be pregnant? *Who gives a shit?*

The thought of people spying on them, taking pictures without their knowledge, spreading rumors about them and their loved ones, invading their privacy at every turn, passing judgment on every little thing they did, holding them to superhuman standards simply because they lived in the public eye—it was disgusting. Her mother was crazy.

Did that mean Nikki was crazy, too?

That's when she heard a familiar voice to her left, coming from the other side of the candy rack between the lanes.

"How much are those boxed Thanksgiving meals you're selling?" Nikki asked.

"Ten dollars each," answered the cashier.

"And they're donated to needy families here in Portsmouth?"

"Yes, and the surrounding community. Would you like to buy one to donate?"

Drew moved forward as her cashier finished with a customer. She strained to see around the woman in front of her, who was placing the last of her items on the belt. Nikki stepped in front of the payment pad. Even with her back turned, Drew could easily hear Nikki's next words.

"Make it one hundred and you have a deal. Do you have that many on hand?"

The cashier's face lit up. "If we don't, we can get more," the girl gushed. Drew guessed she couldn't be more than nineteen or twenty.

"Ma'am?" Drew's cashier was trying to get her attention. "I can ring you up now."

Drew quietly apologized, not wanting Nikki to know she was there. She took her time emptying her carriage, curious to hear the rest of the exchange.

"That's so generous of you," said Nikki's cashier. "Thank you so much, Ms. Razer! Would you mind if I called my manager over? He might like a picture of you with your donations to put on our website or something."

"That's kind of you, but no. I don't want any publicity for this. In fact, promise me you'll say it's an anonymous gift."

Drew's associate was no longer paying attention to Drew's order. She'd obviously overheard what was going on and had turned to see who was making such a large purchase. They both watched as Nikki swiped her card, said "Thank you" for the receipt, and then turned and exited the store with her groceries.

She and her cashier stared at each other.

"Wow," said the woman. "I wish more people were that generous."

Drew looked at her total on the screen. "Will you take back the cartons of ice cream and ring up one of those meal donations instead?"

"Sure thing." She found the ice cream, scanned them off her total, and called over a young bagger and asked him to put them away.

"I wish I could afford to buy more of those meals like she just did."

She smiled warmly at Drew. "If I made her money, I would, too. But every little bit helps. You've just made one family's holiday much better than it might've been otherwise, so thank you."

"You're welcome."

She wheeled her cart through the lot, dodging snow and ice patches as if it was an obstacle course. She retraced her steps and started over when she couldn't remember where she'd parked. The shift taking place within her heart grew clearer with each step. *That* was the real Nikki Razer. Not the bold and alluring rock goddess who strutted across the stage, soaking up the idolization of thousands of women who didn't know her at all.

Not the way I'm starting to know her. And I really like the woman I'm starting to know.

A lot.

❖

Nikki pecked away at the piano keys, working out the kinks of a melody to go with the chord progression she'd written earlier in the day. Maybe Jaymi could add lyrics, since her own words kept getting jumbled with the thoughts and feelings that weren't forming any semblance of fluent language lately.

She put the new song away. No use beating a dead horse. She needed some release. She pounded out a few random chords and then dove into Elton John's "Crocodile Rock," one of her favorite songs to play. She'd had a few beers, which made belting out the chorus even more fun. As fun as it could be singing it alone. In her empty house.

With no one to talk to. Or cuddle on the couch with. Or to hold her as she fell asleep.

This sucks. She stopped halfway through the second verse and slammed both forearms down on the keyboard. The mishmash roar echoed and bounced off the walls for so long it finished the song for her. *Fuck it. I'm going to bed.*

Her phone rang. Or was she hearing things? It was coming from her coat, still splayed across the easy chair where she'd tossed it after she'd hauled in her groceries. She stumbled across the room and pulled it from the pocket.

"'Lo?"

"Um, hi. Nikki? It's Drew."

She couldn't have heard that right. She looked at the screen. Sure enough, Drew's name was on the display.

"Hello?"

"Yeah, Drew. Hi." She plopped down on the couch and nearly slid off onto the floor. *Damn leather. Yep, blame the furniture, not the beer.* "Sorry, I'm just surprised to hear from you." She gripped the arm to regain her balance and then stretched out the full length of the couch.

"Yeah, I'm sure you are."

Nikki waited. After the way Drew had brushed her off this afternoon, she wasn't about to make this any easier for her. *Geez, Jaymi's right. I really am an asshole when I drink.* She couldn't do it. She didn't want to be an asshole to Drew again. "I'm glad you called," she finally said.

"You are?"

"Yeah." She rolled onto her back and draped one arm over her eyes. She was beyond thrilled that Drew had called, but she didn't trust what might come next.

"So, I've been thinking…uh, about your offer for the police escort?"

"And?"

"Are you free to come by DJ's tomorrow so we can talk about it?"

"So, you believe me that there's no catch?"

Drew sighed. "Yes, Nikki, I believe you. I thought maybe you'd like to join me for lunch, so I can make up for being such an ass today?"

"Lunch?" Nikki heard a faint chuckle.

"Yes, lunch. You like Moe's Subs?"

"Does a guitar need strings?"

"Point taken."

She heard a smile in Drew's voice, and the brief silence that followed was a comfortable one. She hesitated, afraid she'd say the wrong thing.

"I know where you can get a good deal on strings."

She smiled. *Is she flirting with me?* "I bet you do."

"Anything for my favorite customer."

Definitely flirting. But why the sudden change of heart? *Don't overthink it. Let this play out and see where it goes.* "So, I'm still your favorite?"

"Why don't you come by tomorrow and find out?"

Chapter Nineteen

Thirty-eight-degree November air stung Nikki's cheeks as she made her way across DJ's parking lot. They had agreed to one o'clock, but Nikki wanted to surprise her by showing up with food in hand. She walked into the store at twelve thirty, and the sounds of a bluegrass jam greeted her. She rounded the corner and caught the last verse of a duel between Jerry on banjo and Drew on guitar. Once again, she was blown away by their amazing talent.

Their obvious love and admiration for each other tugged at Nikki's heart. She'd never had that kind of bond with her father. It took a minute for either of them to notice her. Drew's face lit up with a breathtaking smile that chased away Nikki's bitterness in a heartbeat.

"You're early," Drew said with the enthusiasm of a child.

Nikki wondered if that was from the high of the musical connection she'd just shared with her father or happiness at seeing her. Either way, she was so damn beautiful Nikki didn't know how in the world she was going to keep her hormones in check.

Drew looked at the bags in Nikki's hand. "You already got our food?"

"This way you can enjoy your full lunch break."

Jerry placed the banjo on a stand. "Something she doesn't do nearly enough." He turned to his daughter. "I'll keep an eye on things. You kids go and enjoy yourselves."

Nikki handed Jerry one of the bags. "This one's for you."

"Shucks, you didn't have to do that." Jerry accepted the bag and peeked inside. "How'd you know classic Italian was my favorite?"

"You kiddin' me? It's a Moe's. It's everyone's favorite. I figured I couldn't miss."

Drew gave her a smile that said she'd just scored some major points. She made a mental note to make sure she kept a smile on Jerry's face, too. Not that it would be hard. She adored the man already. Jerry and Drew both offered to reimburse her for the food, and she refused.

She followed Drew to her office. The walls were decorated with a photo of a classical guitar against a black background, a collage painting of orchestral stringed instruments, and a Monet and Van Gogh mixed in. It was definitely a working space, but it looked as if Drew had done some recent tidying by clearing a space on her desk. She excused herself briefly to retrieve sodas from the mini-fridge in the small break room across the hall. Drew closed the door and positioned a metal-framed, vinyl chair in front of the desk. She motioned for Nikki to sit and then sat behind the desk across from her.

Drew avoided eye contact as she emptied the contents of the bags. *Did the temperature just plummet in here, or is Drew nervous to be alone with me?*

Something was off. The longer the silence stretched between them, the less she trusted the situation. *That's it. No more pussyfootin' around.*

"So, why the change of heart, Drew?"

Drew twisted off the bottle cap and took a long swig. "I saw you in the grocery store yesterday."

"And you didn't bother to say hi?"

"No, I was…surprised to see you there."

"Why? Rock stars need to eat, too, you know. Where do you think we get our food? Flown in by helicopter?"

"That's not what I meant—"

"Maybe you were too busy judging me for splurging on exotic, imported, off-season fruit."

"No—"

"What can I say? I like melons." She grinned. She knew she was being a brat, but enough was enough. She needed to get under Drew's skin somehow and get her to lighten up.

The increasing redness on Drew's face was either a blush or simmering anger. "Why do half the things that come out of your mouth have sexual undertones?"

Yep. It's a blush. "They only sound sexual if you have a dirty mind. Which tells me you either have a dirty mind, or it's been a hell of a long time since…" Nikki held up her hands in surrender. *Old habits die hard.* "I'm sorry. I didn't mean that."

Drew sprang from her seat. "You are unbelievable!"

Nikki slouched back and interlaced her fingers behind her head. "And you have yet to throw me out of your office. Why is that?"

She could practically hear Drew's squeaky wheels spinning as she obviously fought to maintain her professional composure. Nikki didn't give two shits about professionalism right now. Even Jaymi's and Randi's proverbial reprimands in her head telling her to "shut the hell up" took a back seat to her persistent curiosity. There had to be a fire in Drew buried deep down somewhere. She just needed someone to light the fuse.

Drew closed her eyes and let out a long breath through her teeth. She lowered herself back into her chair. "Because…I saw a side of you that I…it's because of something else you bought. I wasn't talking about your melons."

Nikki feigned offense. "You don't like my melons?"

"Will you shut up about the melons already?" Now Drew was fighting a smile. And turning red again. "I'm talking about the Thanksgiving dinners you bought for the needy, you jerk."

Nikki dropped her hands and sat forward. "How did you know about that?" *If that cashier said anything after I specifically said to keep it anonymous…*

"I was in line at the register next to yours. I heard the whole thing."

"Oh. Well, it was nothing, really." She shrugged and rubbed her thumb back and forth along the arm of the chair. "It's not like I'm volunteering my time down at the soup kitchen or anything."

"Nikki, how can you say that?" Drew leaned forward and clasped her hands together on the desk. "You gave meals to a hundred families. That's a big deal to those people."

She didn't know what to say. All the times she'd been trying to do something—anything—to change Drew's opinion of her, and she managed to do it without even knowing Drew was there. Maybe the key was to stop trying. Suddenly, the old building didn't feel so cold anymore.

"I'm sorry for being a jerk just now."

"No," Drew said softly, waving her off. "I owe you an apology, too."

As if the room was eavesdropping on her thoughts, the heat kicked on, ticking and clinking as if it was joining the conversation.

"I'm listening."

Drew pried open a bag of chips as if buying a moment to gather courage. "I've been making assumptions and passing judgment on you since we met. Not that you don't get out of line sometimes, but at least you're gracious enough to acknowledge those transgressions and apologize for them. I, on the other hand," she released a long sigh, "have continued to hold them against you based on my own issues. Issues that have to do with you as a celebrity, not with who you are as a person."

The tension seeped from her shoulders. "But you don't really know me as a person."

"Exactly my point."

Drew picked up a pen and rolled it between her fingers. It drew Nikki's attention to the blotter-sized calendar planner on the desk. It was covered in cartoony doodles of animals and musical instruments, many of which would have given Charles Schulz a run for his money. Drew's name was randomly mixed in between the drawings, each one written in a different lettering style.

Looks like Drew has artistic talents, too.

"Drew, are you saying you'd like to get to know me as a person?" Nikki's hopes rose the instant the words left her lips.

Drew raised her head and finally looked her in the eye. "Yeah, I guess I am."

She studied Drew's face, trying to get a read on whether her interest was sincere or if she was only making peace so that she wouldn't rescind her offer. "Why?"

The directness of her question seemed to throw Drew off for a moment. She unwrapped her sandwich and gestured for Nikki to do the same. *Buying time again.* She appreciated Drew's nature to answer thoughtfully, a trait Nikki wished she had. Her temper and unfiltered vocal reflexes had gotten her into trouble more times in her life than she cared to admit.

"To put it simply," Drew looked away shyly, "in spite of my best efforts not to, I like you." She quickly took a swig of her drink.

"Well, it's probably no secret that I like you, too, Drew." Nikki reached for her soda. "What do you propose we do about that?"

"I thought…I was hoping…do you wanna hang out sometime? To be clear, I'm not asking you out. I thought we could get together—"

"As friends?" Nikki's heart soared when they finished the sentence together.

"Yes."

She returned Drew's smile. "I'd like that very much."

They held each other's gazes. Maybe they'd finally reached a cease-fire. A comfortable silence swept Nikki's barriers away like a frozen river freed by the sun's warmth at the end of a harsh winter.

Nikki broke eye contact and swallowed hard. "Other than Randi, I don't have any other friends outside of the band."

Drew looked surprised by her admission. She traced a pattern with her finger over one of the doodles and frowned. "I don't have many friends, either."

Nikki barely heard her, but the lonesome tone in Drew's statement resonated loudly in Nikki's mind. Perhaps she and Drew had more in common than musical interests. She sat forward and smiled. "Okay, so let's hang out. What would you like to do?"

Drew's face lit up, a glint of confidence returning to her eyes. "We've become rather good at eating together. How about dinner?"

"I would love to have dinner with you. I'll take you anywhere you want to go. My treat."

"Oh no. I invited you, and you bought us lunch. How does a home-cooked meal sound?" One corner of Drew's mouth hitched upward in what was probably a touch of anxiety over her response, but to Nikki, it was sexy in an unassuming way.

"After living on the road and eating out for the last six months, that sounds like heaven on earth."

"That's what I was thinking. Are you free Saturday?"

"Saturday's good."

With the awkwardness diminishing, they dug into their sandwiches. Drew said, "There is one thing I need to ask you, though."

Nikki's excitement dimmed. Drew had already expressed concerns about drugs and alcohol. What else was she worried about? "Shoot."

"Do you like cats?"

Nikki chuckled in relief. "Yeah, cats are cool. Unfortunately, my mom had allergies, so the closest thing I ever had to a pet was a small tank of tropical fish when I was a kid. Now I'm never home enough to take on the responsibility, so it wouldn't be fair to them."

"Good. I would've been bummed if you'd said no."

Nikki dramatically swiped the back of her hand across her forehead. "Whew. Me too." She popped the last bite of half her sandwich into her mouth. "So, you have a cat, huh?"

"Three." Drew smiled, as if thinking of them instantly warmed her heart. It was fucking adorable.

"Whoa. You've got your own little family, huh?"

"Yup. Andres, Vinnie, and Fret."

Nikki took a moment to take in the wall décor once again. "Let me guess. You're a fan of Andres Segovia, Van Gogh, and…who's Fret named for?"

"Wow. You're good. Fret named herself. She likes to play guitar with me."

"Can't say as I blame her. With you for a teacher, I bet she's already mastered pull-offs and hammer-ons."

Drew laughed at the reference to fret-hand fingering techniques. "She's a regular Eddie Van Halen. In fact, I think in her next lesson, I'll teach her how to play with her teeth like Jimi Hendrix."

"Now that's something I'd pay to see."

"I wouldn't have to charge much. She'll work for Pounce treats."

"I'll stock up." Nikki emptied her soda. "I'm really excited about taking up a new instrument."

Drew lowered her brows into that serious look that was so unbelievably sexy it nearly unraveled Nikki's composure.

"Oh yeah?"

"Are you sure you're up for the challenge of teaching me the cello?"

Drew leaned back in her chair and grinned. "You bet I am. You know, I would've thought you'd rather learn the banjo or mandolin. How are you going to work a cello into Passion Play's sound?"

"Who says I have to? Maybe I just want to learn for my own enjoyment." Nikki knew the lessons would be as pleasurable as the satisfaction of mastering something new.

Drew stood and gathered the wrappings of their lunch and threw them in the trash. "*That* is the most important reason to learn."

Nikki opened a package of cookies and offered one to Drew.

"You're spoiling me, you know. I've got a wicked sweet tooth," Drew said before crunching off a big bite.

"I'll keep that in mind." Nikki bit into hers. "So, you really want me to ask Randi to play bodyguard for your bank runs?"

A five-minute discussion of that topic turned into more than an hour talking about Drew's numerous ideas for additional teaching programs she wanted to implement at DJ's. Drew's enthusiasm lit up the room. With every one of her animated comments or ideas, Nikki's appreciation for her own music instructors grew exponentially. She'd taken them for granted at the time. In her determination to be the best and her tunnel-vision focus on achieving her goals, she hadn't fully grasped the difference teachers made in the world.

The realization only intensified her attraction to Drew. "I'm sorry I teased you about performing."

Drew wrinkled her eyebrows in question.

"When we first met and I bugged you about getting your dad on a stage or in a studio? You were right. We all have our own dreams, and it's not my place to judge yours."

Drew sat back and smiled contentedly. She searched Nikki's face, and her eyes softened. "Thank you for saying that. It means a lot, coming from you."

"Passion Play wouldn't exist, and I wouldn't be where I am today, without teachers like you. And shop owners like your father."

Drew shrugged. She cleared her throat and stood. "Yeah, well, I wish everyone could appreciate my dad for who he is." Drew frowned, and Nikki caught her glance at a framed photo on the desk she hadn't noticed before. A preteen Drew, Jerry, and a woman she assumed was Drew's mother. Jerry looked much the same, minus the graying hair. Drew stood in front of them, Jerry's arm protectively draped over his daughter's shoulder. Although Drew and Jerry were in modest casual attire, the mother was dressed to the hilt in an expensive, low-cut short dress, her hair done to the nines.

She desperately wanted to ask Drew about the picture, but now wasn't the time or place. "Well, I'd better go so you can get back to work. We still on for dinner Saturday night?"

"Definitely. I'll text you the address."

"What can I bring?"

"How about dessert?"

"Your wish is my command." Nikki released her hand and headed out the door wearing an unabashed smile.

She couldn't wait for the weekend to arrive.

CHAPTER TWENTY

Saturday night couldn't come fast enough. Nikki spent her nervous energy cleaning her condo from top to bottom, practicing a few of Passion Play's new songs, going for a drive to get used to the new vehicle, browsing for over an hour at Bull Moose Music, and spending far more than necessary on used LPs. She resisted the temptation to busy herself with the company of friends, feeling instead that time alone for a little introspection was of higher priority these days.

She headed to the bathroom for a shower. She put extra effort into grooming and shaving and getting the spikes in her hair just right. She walked naked to the bedroom and fingered the outfits in her walk-in closet.

They'd be eating in, so she didn't need anything too dressy. But she didn't want to go too casual either. Regardless of their agreement that this evening was about hanging out as friends, she still wanted to look good. She selected a fitted white cotton button-up shirt and a pair of designer jeans. She pulled on ankle-high black boots and finished off the look with a black leather vest.

She parked the Jeep behind Drew's truck in the driveway of a multifamily town house. She took a minute to steady her hands and ascended the few porch steps to the apartment.

Drew opened the door, and Nikki couldn't move. She was in blue jeans and a royal blue button-down shirt with the sleeves rolled up to the elbows—and a black apron covered in plump mustached chefs and wooden spoons. She looked sexy and adorable as she discreetly scanned Nikki head to toe. The warmth of the oven and scintillating aroma of marinara invited her in before Drew could do so.

She returned Drew's smile. "Hi."

"Hi. Come in."

"Whatcha got cookin'?"

Drew said, "Chicken parmesan. I just need to turn on the garlic bread that's in the toaster oven."

Something brushed against Nikki's leg.

"Hey, who's this?" She looked down and saw a tiger cat scrutinizing her with pale green eyes. It had a white blaze on its nose that flared out around the mouth and chin, and a white chest and feet.

"That's Fret. What've you got there?"

Nikki handed her a bottle of wine and then pulled a carton of gelato from the plastic grocery bag. "And I figured these wouldn't hurt." She removed the Pounce canister from her coat pocket.

Drew chuckled and shook her head. "Are those complimentary, or will Fret have to play for them?"

"First one's on the house."

"Don't give them any until we see how dinner comes out. If I screwed it up, we'll all be dining on cat treats." Drew set the wine on the table and put the dessert in a nearly empty freezer.

"Good thing I bought the gourmet flavor." Nikki caught sight of a giant puffball of an orange cat lounging in a pet bed, making no move to join in. Fret rubbed against her again. "Hey, cutie pie. Can I pick you up?" She petted Fret's head, and she began to purr.

"She's a cuddle bug, so I'm sure she'll let you. I can't promise you'll see Vinnie. He's a bit skeptical around strangers. Andres over there doesn't get excited about much. He's almost fourteen, so he prefers to hang back and supervise."

Nikki hauled Fret into her arms. "You're a little charmer, you know that?" She scratched her cheeks and behind her ears. The purrs grew louder.

Drew folded her arms across her stomach in mock jealousy. "As usual, Fret gets all the attention." She scrubbed Fret's head but kept her gaze glued to Nikki. She lifted the cat's chin and kissed her on the nose. "Don't you, sweetie pie?"

Nikki's heart was melting. She was in dangerous, uncharted waters that she wanted desperately to test. Waters she could drown in if she wasn't careful. She could smell the clean scent of Drew's coconut shampoo, and the overhead light brought out the gold in her hair. She desperately wanted to run her fingers through it. She swallowed hard and released Fret onto the floor. "Maybe I should get a cat. At least then I'd have someone to keep me company when I come home."

Drew gave her a thoughtful look and then nodded as if she

understood. "Living by yourself has its perks, but it can get lonely sometimes."

Drew's vulnerability touched on her own crumbling barriers, and all Nikki could manage was a nod and what she hoped was an understanding smile.

Drew opened the oven and pulled out a large baking dish. "Would you mind grabbing the salads out of the fridge?"

They filled their plates and—after Drew shooed Fret off one of the chairs—sat down at the small round table in the corner of the kitchen.

Nikki sank her teeth into another mouthwatering bite. "It's been a very long time since I've had a home-cooked meal. This is fantastic."

"Thank you. Don't you cook for yourself?"

"Yeah, but nothing this elaborate. It seems silly to cook a big meal for only one person. So I make quick, easy meals or get takeout a lot."

"I don't eat this well when I work a night shift, but when I'm out at five, I cook big meals." Drew suddenly became interested in tearing her slice of garlic bread into chunks. "It gives me leftovers to bring to work for lunches."

"That's a good idea. Saves money, too, I'm sure. Eating out can get expensive."

Drew replied only with a nod.

Nikki had a feeling money was a sensitive subject for her. "You have a nice little place here. It's very homey."

"It's small but affordable and enough room for just me." She popped a piece of bread in her mouth and politely swallowed before continuing. "I'm sure it's nothing compared to what you're used to."

She thought of her barren condo. She already felt more at home in the hour she'd been here. "No, it isn't, but probably not in the way you think. I bought this huge, modern-style condo last year. I went a little over the top after the band started making decent money, and I'm starting to wish I'd put a little more thought into what I was spending it on."

"Such as a sports car that you can't drive in the winter?" Drew teased with a little quirk of her lip.

She pretended to be offended. "For your information, I had the Mustang before we made it big."

"Oh, all right. I'll let that one slide, then."

"How generous of you." She ate the last of her meal and wiped her mouth with a napkin. "That was delicious. Thank you very much."

Drew sat back and rubbed her belly. "You're welcome. That was pretty darn good, if I do say so myself. I'm glad you enjoyed it."

They smiled at each other for a long minute.

"I'm sorry, but I can't help wondering how in the world such a beautiful, talented, intelligent woman who can cook this well is still single?"

Drew took her time considering her answer. Something Nikki was coming to expect. "This will sound totally clichéd, but since I finished college, I've been focused on my career. Romantic relationships haven't been a priority." She paused for a beat, as though she was going to say something else but stopped. "What's your excuse?"

Nikki would've believed her answer had it not been for the slight defensive tone in her voice. The career part might've been accurate, but she knew there had to be more to the second reason. The familiar image of Jaymi and Shawn together invaded her thoughts again and tore at her heart. She couldn't exactly tell her the biggest reason—that she'd wasted years falling for someone she couldn't have. "Same as yours."

Drew looked at her skeptically. "Uh-huh."

"I had a girlfriend in high school. Then I dated a few girls in college, but nothing that stuck." There. She'd come clean. A little, anyway. "Come on, you must've had a girlfriend at some point in your life."

Drew looked down and pushed leftover sauce around her plate with her fork. "I dated a girl for a while at Berklee, but it only lasted a couple months. Not enough time to become anything serious. Her name was Kelly."

"And?"

Drew shrugged. "And a lot of things. Do you really want to spend our evening listening to me drudge up a bunch of unhappy shit?"

Nikki leaned forward. "I want to get to know you. If that includes hearing about your unhappy shit, then so be it. Lord knows I have enough of my own. You can hear about it if you want. Then we'll be even."

Drew chuckled at that. "Okay, but let's stick to the abridged versions for now. I'm having too much fun tonight to waste time on unhappy shit."

Nikki grinned. "Okay, shoot. Give me the abridged version of the tale of Drew and Kelly."

"Okay. She was an incredibly talented singer-songwriter. But we wanted different things. She wanted the big time and everything that goes along with it, including the wild lifestyle, something I had no interest in. She got in with a bad crowd. Next thing I knew, instead of saving her gig money to record a demo and go to LA, she was spending it on partying. Drinking. Drugs. She got high on anything and everything she got her hands on. I can't tell you how many times I got a phone call in the middle of the night to go pick her up at a bar or friend's house because she was too wasted to drive."

"That explains why you asked me if my band uses drugs."

"Exactly."

"Well, I can assure you we've always been clean and intend to keep it that way." Nikki saw a grateful smile play on Drew's lips. Should she tell her about her wilder days when she'd shown up at rehearsals toting a few beers and the fights it caused with Jaymi? Nah, maybe she'd tuck that away for now. "Did you know Passion Play went to LA for a few years?"

"No, I didn't. Is that where you got your big break?"

"Weirdly, no. We came back when Jaymi's mother got sick with cancer." Nikki's stomach wrenched at the memory and the agony Jaymi went through in the year that followed. Her girlfriend cheating on her. Her mother passing away. Jaymi's depression and the way she beat herself up over writer's block when the band finally regrouped and started gigging again. Of course, then Shawn came along and saved the day.

"That's so sad." Drew's brow furrowed in sympathy. "Is that what that tribute song is all about? The one she and Shawn sang at the end of your show?"

Nikki nodded. "Yeah. Anyway, we were all glad to be home, and things took off here. None of us were that crazy about living out there, so it all worked out."

Drew released a shy smile, as if that bit of information pleased her. "I'm glad you're here." She stood. "Let's clean up, and we can move to the living room where it's more comfortable."

"Sounds good to me." She breathed again, glad she didn't have to bare her soul all at once.

They worked easily together, clearing the table and loading the dishwasher. Drew wiped off the counter and turned to face her. Her smile disappeared suddenly.

"Oh no."

"What?" Nikki followed her line of sight downward. There was a quarter-sized blob of marinara sauce on her white dress shirt, just below her breasts. "Shit. That's what I get for wearing white and eating Italian food."

Drew grabbed a clean dishrag and ran it under the sink. "That'll stain. We have to get some cold water on it." She spun back around and took a step. A loud "merow" sounded at their feet, and Drew stumbled forward, landing in Nikki's arms. Fret scampered into the living room.

"You were saying?" Nikki felt the cold damp cloth against her chest. It did nothing to quell the warmth spreading within her.

Drew took a small step back and frantically began wiping at the stain. Nikki held back a laugh when she saw Drew's flushed cheeks.

Drew accidently brushed her breast. "Sorry."

She covered Drew's hands. "No worries."

Drew stilled and looked up into her eyes.

She released Drew's hands and reached for her top button. "This will be easier if I take this off, don't you think?"

"Uh…"

"Don't worry. I have a tank on underneath." She popped another button. "Do you have something I can wear over it?"

"Oh. Yeah. Right." Drew didn't move.

"Drew?"

"Sorry. Is a sweatshirt okay?"

"I'm a bit taller than you, but whatever you have is fine."

Drew nodded and left. Nikki resisted the urge to follow her into the bedroom and sat on the couch. She heard a drawer open and close, and Drew returned with a navy-blue crew sweatshirt. Nikki took off her vest, finished unbuttoning her shirt, and stood up.

"Oh no," Drew said.

"What now?"

Drew poked her in the stomach. "It soaked through. Look."

Nikki reflexively caressed her cheek, and Drew's pupils grew dark.

Shit, I almost crossed the line already. She dropped her hands and took the sweatshirt from Drew. "Maybe we should have that gelato before I put this on. You know, in case I dribble again."

Drew took a step back. "Yeah." She sounded out of breath.

She wondered if Drew's heart was beating as fiercely as hers was.

"But I don't want you to get cold. It's okay if you dribble. Go ahead and put on the sweatshirt. I'll get dessert." She hurried into the kitchen.

Nikki threw on the sweatshirt.

She was too keyed up to sit, so she wandered over to the oversized bookcase in the corner. The top shelf was full of books, all about music and art, from what she could see. The rest was a gold mine of LPs. She had almost every genre imaginable, but most were classical, early blues, and jazz, as well as some easy listening and big band. Many looked to be originals. Nikki was in heaven.

Drew placed two bowls on the coffee table. "Would you believe that's not even close to what I wish I had?"

"This is incredible! I am so jealous. How long have you been collecting vinyl?"

"My whole life. Call me crazy, but it's my obsession. I have CDs, too, but they just don't—"

"Sound the same."

They finished the comment in unison.

Nikki pulled out an Ella Fitzgerald record. "I know what you mean. There's a warmth to the tone you can't duplicate digitally. I love Ella."

Drew's eyes lit up. "You're kidding? She's my all-time favorite. I have an original copy of everything she ever recorded except for one album that I can't find."

She smiled and suddenly had the urge to go to the ends of the earth to find it for her. "Impressive. You have excellent taste. Can we listen to this now?"

"Sure." Drew powered up an old stack stereo and put on the record. As soon as Ella's smooth vibrato filled the air, Drew closed her eyes and smiled. She seemed to relax into a hypnotic state for a moment. Her eyes flew open. "The gelato! It must be melting."

They laughed and sat on the couch to have dessert. They ate without conversation, as if neither wanted to miss a note.

She gestured for Drew's empty bowl. "Let me clean up. You turn the record over. I want to hear the other side." When she returned from the kitchen, she impulsively reached for Drew's hand. "Dance with me." She backpedaled when Drew seemed hesitant. "I'm sorry, you don't have to. You can say no this time without any backlash from hecklers."

Drew gave her a shy smile and took her hand. "We'll have to be careful so we don't make the record skip."

"I'll take it easy with you. No dips or spins." She wrapped her arms around Drew's waist. *How the hell am I going to resist kissing her now?*

"Okay." Drew hooked her hands behind Nikki's neck and stepped closer.

Oh shit. She closed her eyes, and their cheeks came gently together. Drew's warm breath sprang goose bumps on her neck. *Does it count if Drew kisses me first?* They continued to move to the music.

"Nikki?"

"Hmm?"

"We have an audience," she whispered.

"We do?"

Drew gestured to the recliner. Fret was watching them. Andres had awoken from his nap and stared at them from his bed on the floor.

Nikki pulled their bodies together. "I can't blame them. I can't take my eyes off you either."

Nikki's cell phone rang. Her coat pocket muffled the sound, but she knew who it was by the ringtone.

Drew leaned away. "Do you need to get that?"

Three more rings and it would go to voice mail. Her instincts were screaming to answer it. She pried herself from Drew's embrace. "Yeah. I think I do."

She answered just in time. "Jaymz, you okay?"

"Um, I don't know."

She wasn't okay. She was speaking through tears. Nikki was all too familiar with the sound. "What's wrong?"

"We had a fight. Shawn stormed out and took off in her car. I'm worried sick about her. I don't—"

"I'm on my way over." She disconnected and shrugged into her jacket.

Drew stood in the doorway, her brows drawn together with concern. "Everything okay?"

"I gotta go. I'm sorry. Jaymi's…something's wrong. Can I call you tomorrow?"

Drew nodded slightly. "Yeah, sure."

The record ended, and the silence it left chilled Nikki to the bone *She's hurt. Quick, do something.* "I'm so sorry. I promise something special to make up for this, okay?"

She drew back her shoulders and pressed her lips into a straight line. "You don't have to." She sounded defeated.

You're killing me here, Drew. "I really am sorry, but I need to make sure she's okay."

"She's your friend. It's all right."

"Thanks for understanding, and for an amazing evening." She resisted the temptation to give her a quick peck on the lips and left.

Had that call come a minute later, she would have kissed her. She was almost sure of it. *Saved by the bell. But I'm gonna kick Shawn's ass if she hurt Jaymi again.*

She maneuvered the Jeep carefully down the winding road to Jaymi's place. Did she do the right thing by leaving? Maybe, maybe not. At the very least, it would keep her hormones in check for now. Or would it? The good thing was that she couldn't wait to get back to Drew. If, that is, she hadn't fucked it up by running to Jaymi's rescue.

❖

Drew closed the door behind Nikki and fell with her back against it. What just happened? One minute they were sharing a love for Ella, dancing close, on the cusp of their first kiss, and then Jaymi called, and Nikki took off faster than a horse in the Kentucky Derby.

She went to the turntable to put away the album. Their night had gone much smoother than she'd thought it would up to that point. After her initial butterflies, she'd been relieved to find that Nikki was actually easy to talk to. In the privacy of her apartment, without the threat of fan interruptions, without the potential opportunity for her celebrity persona to surface, without the salesperson-customer relationship in the way, Nikki had let her guard down. She was nothing like she'd expected. That scared her a little. She'd expected Nikki to act suave and forward. She'd been just the opposite. If anything, she seemed reluctant to make a move. When Nikki had suggested taking off her shirt to treat the stain, she thought for sure Nikki was going to try something.

It had taken a great deal of willpower not to make her own move at that moment. They'd agreed to get together as friends, but she had to admit she'd started craving more. Nikki's beauty and soft curves were hard to resist. She'd been working up the courage to kiss her when the damn phone rang. What sucky timing.

Or maybe it was perfect timing. If Jaymi hadn't called, who knew what might have happened.

As she brushed her teeth, she saw Nikki's shirt hanging on the garment hook on the door. She'd left in such a hurry, she'd forgotten it. She didn't know what Jaymi's crisis was, but Nikki didn't hesitate to go to her, no questions asked. *Would I have done the same thing for a friend in need?* Yes, she would. If she had friends, that is. She respected Nikki's loyalty.

Or was it something more than loyalty? She slipped on her pajamas and shook her head. She was probably overthinking things again. She'd seen the bond Nikki had with Jaymi and her other bandmates firsthand. They were closer than family.

She gathered her kitties and crawled into bed. She'd let it go for tonight. *Maybe Nikki will confide in me when she calls tomorrow.* If she didn't, then it would only prove that she was protective of Jaymi's privacy. That wasn't a bad thing, either. It was admirable.

As if she needed another reason to like her more.

How many women had she dated who were fans of Ella Fitzgerald? Who had the same appreciation for music on vinyl? How many famous people had she met who'd sworn off drugs? Or who cared more about being there for a friend than the possibility of having sex? None. That was how many. Her disappointment dissipated as she drifted off to sleep.

Until she recalled the love song that was Jaymi's ringtone on Nikki's phone.

CHAPTER TWENTY-ONE

Nikki bolted up the long outdoor stairway along the side of the barn to Jaymi's apartment. She knocked but didn't wait for an answer and let herself in.

Jaymi looked up from the kitchen table and gave her a stern look. "You didn't have to rush over here."

She slung her jacket over a barstool. "The last time you called me upset about a girlfriend, she had cheated on you. I knew this had to be serious." She sat next to her and rubbed Jaymi's shoulder. She pointed to the empty beer bottle on the table. "Is that yours or Shawn's?"

"Mine."

She blew out a breath. "You're drinking? Shit, now I know it's bad. What's going on?"

"I don't know. Ever since we got back from this tour, we've been bickering over every little thing. Stupid stuff, like forgetting to take out the trash or leaving a towel on the floor. I don't understand it. We've never fought."

"Geez, Jaymi, it's not surprising. We've been nonstop for over two years. Writing, recording, rehearsing, touring. At least the rest of us can go home and get away from each other. You and Shawn are around each other twenty-four seven. When do you ever get any time to yourselves? I know you. You need your alone time."

"Yeah, I know. But it's never been a problem before."

"Look, that six-month tour was intense. It's a miracle we aren't all at each other's throats. We all need some time to decompress."

Jaymi shrugged.

"But Shawn didn't storm out of here because of a towel on the floor. Is there something else going on with you guys?"

Jaymi sniffed and swiped her nose. "No, it's…she's going through a hard time, dealing with some unresolved family stuff."

Nikki didn't want to pry, and she knew Jaymi wouldn't tell her anything even if she asked.

Jaymi got up. "You want a drink?"

She fiddled with the corner of the woven placemat. "Sure. What the hell."

Jaymi opened two beers. Nikki followed her into the living room, and they plopped onto the couch together.

"We can go look for her if you want. Any idea where she might have gone?"

Jaymi shook her head. "Usually when she's upset, she goes downstairs to hang out with the horses. I'm nervous about her driving while she's this upset. She'll be back once she's cooled off. She needs the time alone as much as I do; she just doesn't always know it until she's taken it."

Nikki took a long swig. Her head buzzed, and she remembered she'd already had two glasses of wine. Shit. Too late now. She'd pay for mixing the two in the morning. "You want me to kick her butt when she gets back?"

Jaymi laughed and pulled her into a hug. "You always need to be my knight in shining armor, don't you?"

"I prefer to think of myself as your security blanket." She put her beer on the side table and wrapped her arms around Jaymi. God, she felt good. She rested her chin on Jaymi's head and inhaled her clean scent as she stroked her hair. "You sure you're okay?"

Jaymi nodded, burrowing her face between her neck and shoulder. Nikki kissed her forehead.

"I miss hanging out with you." Jaymi withdrew from the embrace. She wrinkled her brow. "What's with the Berklee sweatshirt?"

"It's Drew's. I was at her place when you called." *Shit. I wonder how she'd feel if she knew I was curled up with Jaymi right now?*

Jaymi's eyes widened. "Oh, Nikki. I'm so sorry. Why didn't you tell me?"

"Jaymi, it's okay—"

"No, it's not okay. God, I feel like such a heel."

"Hey, don't worry about it, okay? It wasn't a date." *Not technically, anyway. It sure felt like one.* "And she knows we're friends. She understood."

"But—"

"But nothing." She reached out to stroke Jaymi's cheek and stopped herself. Instead, she squeezed her hand. "I'll always be here for you. You're my best friend, Jaymi. She knows that."

Jaymi looked into her eyes and then down at their joined hands. She wished she knew what Jaymi was thinking right now.

She got her answer when they heard the door open, and Jaymi jumped up and ran into Shawn's arms. "Baby, thank God you're back. Are you okay?"

"Yeah. I'm sorry, Jaymi. I—"

Nikki swiveled just in time to see Shawn glare at her.

"What're you doing here?"

Jaymi placed her hand on Shawn's cheek and turned her head to look at her. "I called her because I was really upset when you left."

"Why didn't you call Devin or one of your other friends?"

Nikki walked over to them. "I'm sure she tried Devin first and couldn't get a hold of her." She had no idea if that was true, but she had to get Jaymi off the hook.

"Devin was working and couldn't talk."

Her lucky guess punched a hole in her gut. She may have been lying to cover for Jaymi, but Jaymi wouldn't lie. Even if it made her look worse to do so. So why did it hurt so much to know she was Jaymi's second call and not her first?

She slipped on her jacket. "I better go." She turned to Shawn, who looked as if she'd been crying for a year. Her heart went out to her. "I'm here for you, too, you know." She meant it, too. Despite everything, she loved Shawn, in a kid-sister kind of way.

Shawn cocked her head and gave her a quizzical look.

Nikki smiled. "Someday, you'll believe me when I say that." She gave Jaymi one more reassuring glance and let herself out.

CHAPTER TWENTY-TWO

Drew couldn't move. There was one cat between her knees, one wedged against her side, and the other was on her chest poking a paw into her cheek. She opened one eye and quickly closed it again. It was too bright in here. The dull ache pulsing through her temples wasn't helping. Vinnie poked her again and meowed.

"Oh, all right." She scratched his head and wrapped her arms around him. He pushed away and hopped onto the floor. He was in no mood for that mushy stuff right now, which she knew, but hey, there had to be some form of payback for waking her up with his demands for breakfast at—she glanced at the clock—six thirty on her day off.

Fret crawled over her leg and slipped out to join Vinnie while Andres yawned and stretched within the crook of her arm. She gave him a tug and kissed his cheek. He would have been content to sleep in as well, but the other two weren't going to let that happen.

Her flannel sleep pants dragged on the floor as she shuffled to the bathroom. She threw a zipped hoodie over an old black T-shirt that boasted "Musicians duet better" in white letters.

Later, she pushed away her half-eaten bowl of cereal. She wasn't sure how much sleep she'd gotten last night, but it wasn't much. Nikki's abrupt departure wasn't quite as confusing as her choice of ringtone. Why would she have a love song ringtone for her best friend?

Maybe it was Nikki's ringtone for everyone. It was her own song, after all. Maybe she was proud of that song—and she had every right to be. It was beautiful.

Whom had she written it for? Drew wasn't a songwriter, but she knew that the sentiment behind the lyrics in love songs didn't usually come out of nowhere. There were genuine emotions and feelings behind them—often from the writer's personal experiences. Nikki had been in love with *someone*.

She took care of the dishes, threw in two loads of laundry, and set to work on her Sunday chores, feeling grateful for what little distraction they provided.

When she was done cleaning, she jumped in the shower. Her musings about Nikki circled back to the love song. It was absurd to think she'd never been in love or had a girlfriend who inspired love songs. She was charming and beautiful. *She still seems interested in me.* Yet Nikki could have easily made a move on her last night, and she didn't. *Maybe I'm just a temporary distraction until the band's break is over.* Then what? Nikki won't have time for anything else but her career. *Including me.*

Just like Mom.

She let out a huge sigh and got dressed. She couldn't let this thing with Nikki lead to something she knew she couldn't handle. By one o'clock, she'd finished her laundry and had eaten lunch. Now what? She growled in frustration. She wasn't going to sit around waiting for a phone call.

She dug out her cello. Nikki would be in tomorrow for her first lesson. Perhaps she should brush up on her own skills. After quickly tuning, she took her position on the stool and drew the bow across the strings. Ah, that sound. She ran through some scales to warm up. Then she closed her eyes. A Mozart piece trickled its way into her brain like a gentle brook and emptied itself out through her hands. The sound wrapped itself around the tiny apartment like a warm blanket, and she was lost. No, not lost. Found. Home. At peace.

Day-to-day worries sloughed off note by note. The heartbreak of her mother's choice of career and fame over parenthood drifted out to sea. Her loneliness crumbled like an avalanche. Her abbreviated evening with Nikki last night…

She ground the bow harder, increasing the volume to a level that could trigger complaints by her neighbors. But she played on. She was hurt. She was frustrated. She hadn't wanted to admit it last night. Admitting it would have meant admitting that she was afraid of whatever it was she was feeling.

After the generous kindheartedness she'd witnessed at the grocery store, she still had no idea if—or how—she wanted Nikki in her life. She'd witnessed enough to know that Nikki was a loyal friend. If that's all they were meant to be, would it be enough? She moved with the phrase she was playing as if she were dancing in Nikki's arms again. She'd almost said no before Nikki gave her an out—not because she didn't want to dance, but because of how badly she wanted to say yes.

Was it wise to give in to her attraction, which was stretching beyond physical now? They were beginning to open up to each other about very personal experiences and feelings whenever they were alone lately. Last night, she'd felt so close to Nikki emotionally, she'd wanted to kiss her. Was Nikki feeling that way, too, despite their agreement to only be friends?

Was it healthy for them to hang out if the attraction was mutual, or would their hormones get the best of them? What then? Could she date Nikki casually as Geena had suggested? What if it turned into something more? None of Nikki's good qualities erased the fact that her career would take her away for months at a time or that she possessed the same type of obsessive career drive that had taken away her mother. It didn't discount her reputation as a player, either.

She catapulted off the stool when a string snapped and whipped a gash in her arm. Her chest heaved, and she dropped the bow. She spewed out a few choice words and sprinted to the bathroom sink. Nikki was more than that, wasn't she? Why was she trying to convince herself that she wasn't?

She jumped again when a song of Passion Play's interrupted her thoughts. *Nikki's calling.* She toweled off and swiped the screen.

"Hello?"

"It's your favorite customer."

"Hi." She watched a red streak trickle down her arm. "Damn."

"I'm no longer your favorite?"

"Uh, no. I mean yes. Sorry, can I call you right back? I'm bleeding all over the place."

"Bleeding? Are you okay?"

"Yes, I'm fine. I just broke a string, and the end caught me in the arm."

"Shit, that sucks. I hate when that happens. You sure you're all right? Want me to come over and administer first aid? Call an ambulance? Perform CPR?"

She laughed. Nikki was a musician and knew it wasn't serious, and the teasing was just what she needed. She went from angry to amused in seconds.

"I don't think I need all that. But I wouldn't turn down a little TLC—if you're so inclined to provide such services, that is." *What the hell am I doing?*

"TLC is my specialty."

She'd never been good at flirting. Yet now she sounded as if she'd been taking lessons from Marilyn Monroe on how to charm someone without even trying.

"Hello? Anyone home?"

She pulled the washcloth away from her arm. "Oh, sorry. I was just checking my arm." *Good save there, Valentino.*

"And?"

"I think I'm gonna live."

"Thank goodness for that. Can I still come over? I was hoping I might be able to make up for taking off last night."

A smile snuck up on her. "Sure. Come on over. It might not hurt to keep me under observation." *Nice one.* She was getting good at this.

"I'm looking forward to it. Do you need me to bring you a new set of strings? I have a few spare sets."

"You have spare cello strings?"

"Cello? Not guitar? Shit, that must sting like a son of a bitch."

"I'm fine, really." She checked the wound again. The bleeding had finally stopped.

"I'll stop at DJ's on my way. I'm in good with the manager. I can get you a good deal."

"Really? I heard she's a hell of a saleswoman." She paced through the tiny apartment, her insides buzzing with excitement. She didn't even try to fight it.

"She is. She's also gorgeous. Oops, I'm sorry; I'm trying to behave, but it's not easy."

Heat swelled into her cheeks.

"Hey, Drew?"

"Yes?"

"You need to learn how to take a compliment, you know that?"

"Maybe you can help me with that, too."

"I'm gonna have to because there are more where that came from."

"Why am I not surprised? Don't worry about the strings. I'll get some when I go into work tomorrow. I can buy them at cost."

"In that case, I'll be there in twenty minutes." Nikki hung up before she could reply.

She danced back to the bathroom and put a Band-Aid on the pesky cut. She looked at what she was wearing. Yucky old jeans and a hoodie. No good. She rifled through her miniscule selection of clothes and cursed.

Why didn't she ever invest in her wardrobe? Other than work clothes, she rarely had the funds to spend on such frivolous things. Her paychecks went to food, rent, and utilities. Well, and cat food and litter—she couldn't very well neglect her kids. The only indulgence she ever treated herself to was records—on those rare occasions when she found one on her wish list.

She changed into a newer pair of jeans and swapped the sweatshirt for a fairly decent long-sleeved pullover. It would have to do until she had a few extra bucks to upgrade.

She smiled. It felt good to have a reason to shop for new things to wear. It had been too long since she'd felt this way. Far too long.

CHAPTER TWENTY-THREE

When Drew opened the door, Nikki knew she was in trouble. Drew looked so adorable, she wanted nothing more than to scoop her up on the spot and kiss her. Not that she didn't appreciate the sexy, skimpy attire most women wore to impress her, but she'd always thought a woman in jeans was the sexiest thing going.

The rust-colored pullover complemented Drew's fair hair beautifully. And those caramel eyes, *oh God…*

"Would you like to come in?"

"Yes, of course." She smiled. "I was admiring the view."

Drew gave her a confused look. "I have a view?"

"Honey, *you* are the view."

Drew stepped aside so she could walk in. "You need to get your eyes checked. I look like a total bum. Shopping for clothes isn't—"

"You look beautiful, Drew."

Drew looked at her as if she had three heads. "Yeah, right." She walked away and headed toward the kitchen. "Would you like something to drink?"

She gently caught Drew's arm as she reached for the refrigerator door. "Those aren't just empty words. I don't waste my time saying things I don't mean."

Drew shook her head slightly. "I'm sorry. You're right. I do need to learn how to take a compliment. It's just that…you always look so great, and with business being slow, buying clothes hasn't been high on the priority list."

"First of all, thank you for saying I look great. See what I did there? I accepted your compliment. Easy. Second, we're not competing in a fashion show. For the record, I'm a sucker for a woman in blue jeans."

Drew still looked skeptical.

"When you grow up with parents who invest all their energy into appearances and making an impression, you learn to appreciate people who are down-to-earth. I care more about what's on the inside."

Drew's lips twitched upward. "Thank you."

"For what?"

"For the compliment."

She grinned. "Now that's more like it." She took Drew's hands in hers. "Which arm?"

"Huh? Oh, that. The right. It's fine."

Nikki carefully slid up Drew's sleeve. Though she'd put a Band-Aid on the cut itself, there was a noticeable red stripe on her inner forearm where the string had struck the flesh.

"Yikes. What were you doing, Pete Townshend windmills?"

Drew chuckled. "On the cello? Hardly. A Mozart piece."

"Shit, girl. I'd hate to see what'd happen if you played speed metal."

"No chance of that happening. That's one style of music I can't stomach."

"That makes two of us." She looked at Drew's arm again, realizing she was still holding her hand. She lifted it and placed a light kiss just below the mark. She snuck a peek at Drew and saw slight pink rise in her cheeks. She kissed the crook of her elbow. She heard Drew take an uneven breath. "Better?"

Drew nodded.

Stop. You need to stop now before you cross a line and scare her off again. She released her and stepped back. "Let's go out."

"Out?"

"Yes. Out."

"And do what?"

"I don't know. Anything. I'll take you to dinner. Or…you want some new clothes? I'll take you shopping—and please, don't worry about money. I'll buy you whatever you want—"

"No." Drew pursed her lips. "I wouldn't feel right about that."

"What if I say it's an early Christmas present?"

Drew seemed to consider this for a moment. She shook her head. "That's very generous of you, but I can't promise I'll be able to reciprocate." She brushed past her into the living room.

She followed her and stopped in the archway. "I don't need anything in return."

"Nikki, that's not the point. I can't afford it. I'd feel guilty."

She spotted the cello in the corner. "Then give me a gift that you don't have to buy. Play me something on your cello." She waggled her eyebrows. "When you have all four strings, that is."

Drew took in a long breath and released it. "I'll think about it."

"Good. In the meantime, I'm going to take you out, and we'll do something that doesn't cost anything. How about that for a compromise?"

"You drive a hard bargain. Did you learn that skill from your father?"

Nikki flinched. Was she like her father? His ability to take charge of a situation had contributed to his success, but at what expense? Had he bullied people to get what he wanted? She'd always seen him as pushy and controlling. The possibility that she might do the same…

"I'm sorry," said Drew. "I meant that as a compliment. You made a very convincing argument. I think it's sweet that you're taking my feelings into consideration."

She looked at the big orange cat napping in his bed, surrounded by old furniture and things that mattered to Drew. Family photos on the tables. Artwork on the walls. Music books in a bookcase. Records in a cabinet. Her cello by the outdated stereo. Drew didn't have a lot, but what she did have mattered. Her modest belongings were things that were dear to her heart. Not a shitload of meaningless material things that were the best money could buy. Here she was thinking she was an asshole for being like her father, and Drew saw her as strong yet considerate. She was liking Drew more by the minute.

"Put your boots on and grab your coat. And bring a hat and mittens, too. You're going to need them."

Drew gave her a sideways glance, shrugged, and got what she needed from the closet. "Let's go."

"Don't you want to know where I'm taking you?"

"Surprise me." She grinned and shrugged into her coat.

❖

Nikki maneuvered the Jeep down and around several back roads. They were out in the boonies somewhere, surrounded by trees and occasional farmhouses. They slowed and pulled into a driveway lined with vehicles. They parked behind the last car.

"Bundle up. We're going to be outside for a while."

Drew zipped her jacket and pulled her stocking cap onto her head. She had to admit, Nikki had piqued her curiosity. "What is this?"

"You'll see." She jumped out. "Hurry up before everything melts."

Melts? She got out, and they walked up the gravel driveway until they reached a huge farmhouse, a barn, and several outbuildings.

Nikki offered her arm. "This way."

Drew looped her arm through Nikki's, enjoying the closeness, and followed her lead onto a wooded path. Despite her assumptions about Nikki when they'd first met, she was surprised at how much trust in her she felt now. There was a protectiveness about her, something that spoke of a deep loyalty to those she cared about.

The walkway ended in a wide-open field. There were people everywhere, in scattered groups. As they got closer, Drew saw what the attraction was.

"Snow sculptures?"

"Yes. They do this every year—well, as long as we get enough snow."

They made their way to the closest sculpture. A three-foot high curved wall of snow had a G-clef and a measure of music carved into its side. "Wow! That's gorgeous."

"This year's theme is music." Nikki stepped closer to it. "Holy shit, I can't believe the details. It's in C-minor. Beethoven's Fifth!"

Drew looked at the notes on the staff. "Hey, you're right!"

She looked at the childlike excitement in Nikki's eyes and melted. The pom-pom on her bright blue cap was huge. Her hair stuck out the sides like a kid's would, as if she couldn't care less how she looked. She looked huggable in her puffy black and purple parka. God, she was even more beautiful when she let her guard down.

"Come on!" Nikki reached for her hand. "Let's see what's next!"

About twenty feet away was a life-size double bass. It looked real enough to play. The sunlight sparkled on the snow. They were surrounded by coniferous trees dappled with snowy white patches. They were completely shielded from the outside world. Other than the quiet comments by the few people there, it was completely silent. "How did you even know about this?"

"Jaymi lives right up the street. Her landlords know the people that own this place. They just started doing this for fun, and word got out."

Her stomach soured at the mention of Jaymi's name. *Strange that she'd say, "Jaymi lives up the street" rather than "Jaymi and Shawn."* She wondered if Nikki and Jaymi had ever come to this together.

There were seven sculptures in all. They took their time appreciating each one. A saxophone. Electric guitars. A full drum set. And a Mount Rushmore–inspired representation of four classical composers. They got to the last one, and Drew noticed everyone else had left. This one was the most magnificent.

Nikki held her arms out as if bowing to a master. "I surrender to you and humbly request that your combined genius continue to inspire me." She knelt and bowed her head. "John. Paul. George. Ringo." She spoke with reverence. "I am forever devoted to your legacy." She smiled and caught Drew's eye.

Drew burst out laughing.

"Ah, you dare laugh, and you have yet to pay your respects."

She swiftly mimicked Nikki's ritual, and before she knew it, they were both sitting on the ground, giggling like children. Nikki dropped spread-eagle on her back and started making a snow angel.

Drew made her own angel. When they finished, they both lay motionless, looking up at the cloudless, electric blue sky.

Drew said, "You're a total nut."

"Thank you."

"I'm glad you took that as a compliment." She rolled over and propped her head on her hand.

Nikki did the same. "Can I ask you something, Drew?" Her soft tone suggested it was something serious.

"Sure." Her stomach fluttered as she waited out Nikki's long pause.

"Are you hungry?"

She laughed again. Nikki was totally unpredictable, and the pleasant surprise of never knowing what she'd say or do next made her feel more alive than she had in ages. "Starving. What did you have in mind?"

Nikki stood and pulled her up and into her arms. Her chest pounded. Shivers ran up and down the length of her body. She recognized the burning look in Nikki's eyes and was sure it matched her own.

"How about a snow cone!" Nikki smooshed a handful of snow into her face and took off.

She brushed the icy wet stuff off with her sleeve. "You brat!"

Scooping up a handful of her own, she let it fly and nailed Nikki in the back.

Nikki's next shot hit her in the thigh before Nikki took cover behind the Beethoven sculpture.

"Hey, that's not fair. You know I won't risk damaging that!"

A snowball sailed out and hit her in the torso. She kept her eyes on the snow wall and formed three more snowballs. She cocked her arm, ready to throw, and jumped beside Nikki's hiding space. She wasn't there.

"What the…where'd y—"

Nikki pounced out from behind the trees and wrestled her to the ground. The thick padding of their winter garb did little to diminish the wonderful friction between their bodies. She lay helpless beneath Nikki's weight and returned her grin. This was fun. Maybe she could do casual after all. "Resorting to hand-to-hand combat now, are you?"

Nikki's smile widened. "I'm out of ammo."

"Oh, I doubt you're ever out of ammo."

"True. But I still need to know one thing." Nikki shifted her hips and moved her knee dangerously close to Drew's center.

"What?" Drew tried to focus on the words, rather than the feel of Nikki's body against her.

"Would it offend you if I offered to treat you to dinner?"

"I could be convinced."

"And what, may I ask, do I have to do to convince you?" Nikki's soft tone was sexy as hell.

She let her gaze drop to Nikki's full lips. She knew they were probably even softer than they looked.

"Hey! Look at this one!" A child's high-pitched voice pierced her ears, and they instinctively jumped apart.

Nikki discreetly diverted a glare that could have set the kid's hair on fire. The family of five that had wandered into the display couldn't have had worse timing. Or better timing, whichever way she decided to look at it. Despite the obvious attraction between them, she still wasn't sure how much she was willing to let herself be swept away by Nikki's charm. Geena's urging to go for it and keep it casual kept playing through her head, but it still went against her nature. *Maybe that's exactly why I should take Geena's advice. Playing it safe hasn't exactly worked out for me in the past.*

The mother gave them an odd look as they emerged from behind the sculpture. Nikki flashed an exaggerated smile. "Lovely day, isn't it?"

They walked past them, and Nikki boldly threw her arm around her shoulders. Drew suppressed a laugh, nearly doubling over in her efforts to keep quiet.

Nikki pointed downward. "Hey, better tie your—"

Drew's right leg jerked to a stop, and she face-planted onto the ground as she got tangled up in her loose laces.

"Shit!" Nikki knelt beside her. "Are you okay?"

She let out the belly laugh she'd been holding in, and Nikki joined her. "Thanks for the warning."

"Lot of good it did."

She pushed herself up. "Great. Now I'm really soaked through."

Nikki grinned.

"Shut up."

"How do you know what I'm thinking?"

"I have a pretty good idea."

"Oh really? Care to indulge me?"

Drew brushed herself off and started walking to the driveway. "Not in front of the children."

Nikki laughed and waited until they were out of earshot. "You assumed I was going to offer to help you out of your wet clothes?"

She answered with a smile. They climbed into the Jeep.

"You're a scoundrel, Nikki Razer." She loved this flirty banter. It came so easily with Nikki that she couldn't stop herself.

"Scoundrel?"

Drew nodded.

"You ain't seen nothin' yet, honey." Nikki fired up the engine and blasted the heat. "Still hungry?"

She refrained from asking if they were still talking about food. "Yes. But I don't want to sit in a restaurant in damp clothes."

"I'm kinda wet myself." Nikki smiled seductively. "But don't worry. My melons are dry."

Oh, dear God, help me.

Nikki grinned. "Let's get takeout."

"Probably a good idea."

They were quiet for a few minutes until Nikki commented on the sculptures, which turned into a conversation about music and various artists who'd inspired them. Nikki pulled off the main drag, and Drew noticed where they were going.

"Taco Bell? You're treating me to Taco Bell?"

"Don't tell me you don't like Taco Bell."

"Are you kidding? I love it. I just didn't expect—"

"Good. The drive-thru it is. What do you want?" She drove forward to the menu board. "Well?"

"You're something else."

"Are you disappointed? I hope not. I really feel like a taco."

She squeezed Nikki's arm. "Wow. You do feel like a taco! A soft taco, though. Not a crunchy shell."

Nikki rolled her eyes. "Thank you. I think."

"You're welcome."

"Okay then. You ready to order?"

Nikki declined Drew's suggestion to stop at her condo to change her pants, claiming that the Jeep's heat had dried her enough, and she didn't want their food to get cold. They hurried into Drew's apartment. Nikki unpacked the food as Drew fed the cats and excused herself to change. She cursed again at her wardrobe as she pulled on a ragged pair of old jeans. *Oh well. At least they're dry, and we're staying in.* If Nikki liked her, she'd like her for who she was, not what she wore, right?

CHAPTER TWENTY-FOUR

Nikki set up a spread of soft and hard-shell tacos, a Mexican pizza, nachos, and two soft drinks on Drew's coffee table. She was having a blast with Drew. It was great to see her loosening up and revealing more of her personality. Damn, she was funny, too. *And not at all afraid to put me in my place. I like that.*

Drew cooed over her cats before joining her on the couch. "Hi."

"Hi. Feel better? Because you look like a million bucks."

She'd put on old ripped jeans and a denim button-down shirt. Nikki nearly drooled. How could she be this dressed down and still be so fucking sexy?

Drew chuckled. "If I look like a million bucks, then you must not be a millionaire yet to know what a million bucks looks like."

"It doesn't matter either way. A million bucks ain't got nothin' on you, honey."

She loved Drew's lack of pretense. It made her that much more irresistible. No way was she leaving here without a kiss tonight.

They ate and chatted in between bites. After they cleaned up, Drew asked if she wanted to stay for a while and watch a movie.

"Sure."

Drew pointed the remote at the modest 32-inch flat screen TV. "Ooh! *Amadeus*! My favorite movie!"

Drew's excitement made her smile. "I love this movie, too."

They launched into a back-and-forth reenactment of one of its scenes, and then Drew swiveled on the couch and faced her.

She was sure they hadn't quoted it word for word, but it didn't matter. She caught the look in Drew's eyes and held her gaze. "For God's sake, can I kiss you now?"

"You'd better."

Nikki dipped her head and softly kissed her, tasting the sweetness of the soda with hints of their dinner. Drew moaned and opened her mouth, allowing better access as their tongues met. *Worth the wait. Definitely worth the wait. God, she feels good.* Nikki's center throbbed already, but she couldn't let things move too quickly.

Drew seemed to have other ideas as she climbed onto her and deepened the kiss. Drew's need surprised her. Even more surprising was the argument in Nikki's head telling her to slow things down. She'd had enough of women jumping her and wanting only sex. She knew Drew was nothing like those other women, but the overwhelming sensations were too much.

She pulled away for air and ran her thumb across Drew's bottom lip. "Wow."

"Sorry. I got a little crazy there."

"Don't be sorry. It's…wow."

Drew propped herself up on her elbows. "Are you okay?"

"Yeah. This is…you surprised me, that's all."

"Oh. I'm sorry."

Nikki stroked her cheek. "Will you stop apologizing? I like what you're doing. I'm just trying to take things slowly, and you caught me off guard."

Drew sat up, looking puzzled. "Me too. You're not what I… expected."

"What did you expect?"

Drew shook her head.

"Come on. Tell me."

"You'll think I'm a total jerk."

Nikki felt bad for pressing her for an answer, but she had to know. Just how bad was her reputation anyway?

"I was afraid of being another one of your one-night stands."

She knew it. But hearing it from Drew stung. Bad. She couldn't be upset with her. She had only herself to blame.

She lifted Drew's chin and looked her in the eye. "You're not a jerk for thinking that. But if that's all I wanted with you, I would've made a move on you the day we met, and you wouldn't have seen me since."

Drew's shoulders slumped, and she sighed heavily.

Nikki shifted away from her and leaned against the arm of the sofa. She'd hit another sore spot. "What's wrong?"

"I don't want to get into this now."

"Why not? Get into it. I want to know everything about you. You know, in addition to your exceptional kissing talents."

Drew tried to hide a blush by turning away. She shook her head slightly as if fighting to regain an air of seriousness.

"Hey. If you really don't want to talk about it, that's okay. I just want you to know that I'm interested, and in case you haven't noticed, I've kind of taken a liking to you."

Drew stroked her cheek. "You're sweet."

The soft touch and sentiment sent wondrous shivers through her core.

"I guess we've blown the attempt to just be friends, huh?" Drew smiled, but her tone suggested regret.

"Are you sorry about that?"

Drew looked away. "I'm…not sure yet. Friendship is one thing, but I have to confess I have reservations about getting involved with you romantically."

That's just great. I screwed around so much that now I've screwed myself. "Whatever you've heard about me, and my reputation with women, it's probably true. I'm not proud of it."

"So, what does that make me? Your flavor of the week?"

Nikki's heart rate accelerated. "What? No!"

"Well, if the rumors are true, how do I know I'm not just some winter break fling?"

Nikki shot up off the couch. "I told you that if I was only interested in sex, I would've been long gone by now." Shit. She wasn't ready for this. She closed her eyes for a moment and shoved her fingers through her hair. She needed to calm down. She returned to the couch. "I won't blame you if you don't believe me when I say I'm done with that shit."

"Really? What's changed?"

She took a deep breath and let it out slowly. She could at least be honest about some of the reasons. "What's changed is I hate falling asleep next to a stranger in a hotel room in a different city night after night. I hate myself for letting women fuck me who don't give a shit about who I am as a person. I hate coming home to my empty house and aching to know what it would be like to have someone I love there to greet me. Someone who missed me. Someone who knows how I like my coffee and what I like to eat and how I like to spend my free time and what I like to watch on TV. I'm tired of feeling alone and ashamed and unsatisfied." She wiped her eyes, surprised to find them moist. *What the fuck is this?*

Drew rubbed her thigh. "Hey. You okay?"

She straightened and cleared her throat. "Yeah." She looked into Drew's eyes. "You want to know something?"

"What?"

"I feel like you see me."

Drew's mouth twitched into a smile that sent a jolt straight to Nikki's heart. Drew wrapped an arm around her shoulder and tugged her into her arms. She snuggled up to her and tucked her head beneath Drew's chin. *John and George could come back to life and do a Beatles reunion, and it wouldn't make me feel happier than I am right now. Is this all it takes? Being in her arms like this?*

Drew combed her fingers through her hair. God, she loved her touch. She shifted and cupped Drew's face in her hand. Drew looked at her with tenderness and swiped the wetness from beneath her eyes with her thumbs. Nikki kissed her again, gently, teasing with her tongue, savoring the softness of Drew's lips and the taste of her mouth. She pressed a bit harder. The sensuous moan she elicited almost sent her over the edge. *She's not even touching me, and I'm so ready...*

Drew slipped her hand beneath Nikki's shirt and urged her closer. The soft feel of her palm on her bare skin was incredible. If she didn't slow things down soon, she'd be helpless. She didn't want to fuck things up so soon by sleeping with her, or she'd only be discrediting her confessions of only a few minutes ago.

She broke the kiss and pulled back. "We'd better slow this down."

Drew was breathing heavily. She closed her eyes and nodded. "Yeah. That might be a good idea."

"Not that I want to stop, but...you know—"

"I know. I understand. Let's not get carried away too soon."

"Yeah."

She straightened out her shirt and steadied her breathing. Drew followed suit. She saw movement on the floor behind a table lamp next to a glider. A black and white cat with yellow eyes was checking her out. Drew turned to where she was looking.

"Vinnie," Drew said quietly. She extended her hand toward the floor. "It's okay, Vinnie. Come say hi."

Vinnie approached Drew slowly, keeping an eye on Nikki, before butting his head at Drew's hand. After she gave him some affection, he cautiously walked alongside the couch toward Nikki. She let him sniff her hand, and when he leaned against her leg, she took that as acceptance and stroked him. He then sauntered away and jumped onto the recliner. He curled up and twitched his tail in contentment.

Drew turned to her. "You've passed all three inspections. I think that's a good sign."

"And what about your inspection?" She pulled Drew into her arms again. "Did I pass that?"

Drew kissed her lightly. "Most definitely. But since you don't want me to use you for sex, and I don't want to be a one-night stand, I think we should call it a night."

"Yeah, I guess I should go. I don't want to wear out my welcome."

She put on her jacket, and Drew walked her to the door.

"You haven't." She released a smile. "Thank you for today. I had a great time."

"Me too." She gave Drew a chaste kiss on the lips. "I'll see you tomorrow."

"Tomorrow?"

"My first cello lesson, remember? I want to be well rested so I can concentrate."

"Don't be late."

She gave Drew a soft poke in the ribs. "What happens if I am? Detention?"

Drew put her hands on her hips. "Definitely detention. And I won't go easy on you."

"Promise?"

Drew laughed and playfully shoved her out the door. "Get outta here."

"Good night, Drew."

"Good night."

Chapter Twenty-Five

Drew made sure the lesson room was ready for the twenty-eighth time and checked the clock. Nikki was almost ten minutes late. Maybe she'd scared her off. She'd given Nikki so many mixed signals that it was no wonder. *She must think I'm a total tease.* She knew she'd done the right thing, though. After Nikki shared her feelings about wanting someone to come home to, bringing her to the brink of tears, she had to put on the brakes. It wouldn't be fair to either one of them to let this thing get serious.

She didn't want to be alone for months on end, missing her partner, rarely having someone to come home to herself. She'd always wonder if another woman was taking care of Nikki's needs. Sure, Nikki said she was tired of it, but could she trust that it was really out of her system? Would she resort to her old ways when she got lonely?

Or horny. Her center started throbbing at the memory of what almost happened last night. Within an hour after Nikki had left, she'd had to strip naked on the bed and take care of her own needs.

"Penny for your thoughts?"

She jumped at Nikki's voice. *Better keep your penny, or you might be sorry.* "You're late, Razer."

"Ooh, last-namin' me." Nikki closed the door, walked up beside her, and grinned. "Gonna give me detention, McNally?"

"That's Ms. McNally to you." She sat and motioned for Nikki to do the same in the seat diagonally from her. She positioned her instrument between her knees. "And I'll think about it."

"I'm bound to get into more trouble. You might as well give it to me."

She ignored the double entendre and picked up her bow. "Get into position like this." Nikki's grin grew wider. She was more adorable by the minute. She needed to get her focused on the lesson.

"Make sure it's comfortable and fairly close to you. But allow enough clearance for the bow, so you're not striking your knees when you stroke."

Nikki burst out laughing.

"Will you be serious? Get your mind out of the gutter."

Nikki laughed harder. She loudly cleared her throat. "Be aware of proximity between stroke and knees. Got it."

It was no use. Drew joined her. When the laughter finally subsided, they got back into position. Their giggle fits out of their systems, they settled in for the lesson. She was impressed with how seamlessly Nikki transitioned into student mode. Her determination was dead serious, and she hung on her every word. She was a quick learner but was having difficulty holding her bow at the correct angle for simple notes.

Drew got up and stood behind her. She draped her arms over Nikki's shoulders. They were cheek to cheek, and she felt Nikki's smile. "Like this." She placed her hand over Nikki's right hand and gently squeezed, rotating it slightly forward. "Relax your wrist. Now, across this way." They slowly dragged the bow across the strings. "Nice and easy." It made a smooth, even sound. "Yeah, that's it."

It felt so good having Nikki's body wrapped in her arms. They moved the bow back and forth several times, and then she let Nikki make the movements on her own with Drew's hand simply resting over hers.

As soon as she released her, Nikki swiveled within her embrace. Nikki dropped the bow and grabbed the back of her head, pulling her in for a kiss that buckled her knees. She moaned into Nikki's mouth. Nikki slid her tongue inside, and she had to stifle another, much louder moan. She was at work, for God's sake. They had soundproofed the lesson room walls but not the doors.

They stood together, lips still locked, and Nikki awkwardly discarded the cello into its stand. She snaked her arm around Drew's waist, squeezing their bodies together. "God, Drew, you taste good." She kissed her hard and then began kissing her way across her jawline and neck.

Drew's breath disappeared. She struggled to speak; the sensations taking over her body with the feel of Nikki's lips were almost too much to bear. She imagined how electric making love to her would be.

Nikki came back up her throat and caught her lips again. She finally withdrew and rested her forehead on hers. "I think I have a little crush on my teacher," she whispered.

"Just a little one?"

"No. A big, huge, gargantuan, out-of-this-fucking-world crush."

The temperature spiked in her face. "I think that stunt just bought you detention."

Nikki kissed her cheek. "Mission accomplished."

She play-slapped Nikki's arm. "You're such a delinquent."

Nikki grinned.

"I'll have to give you some menial task to do for punishment."

"Oh yeah?" They started to put away their instruments and pick up. "Like what? Need me to clap your erasers? Clean your chalkboards? Organize the art supplies?"

"Get with the twenty-first century, woman. Schools don't use chalkboards anymore."

Nikki followed her out the door. "So, what then?"

She had to get away from her before her hormones got the best of her. She went behind the checkout and retrieved a stack of 8x10 photos of Passion Play. She slapped them on the counter. "Sign these, and then get the rest of the band to do the same. I'm already running out of the ones you guys signed last week."

"You're giving me homework?"

"Yes. And it's due by Wednesday. You also need to practice your lesson."

"I guess that's not so bad. I was afraid you were going to make me scrub floors with a toothbrush or something."

She nodded. "That's a good idea. I'll keep that in mind for next time you misbehave."

Nikki put her hand to her chest. "I'm hurt! You're already assuming I'll get in trouble again."

"Hey, you warned me this would happen. I'm just planning ahead. Just in case."

"You sure do come up with a lot of excuses to see me."

Yeah, I do, don't I?

Geena stepped in beside her and rang out a customer. "Hey, do I need to give you two a time-out?"

"Just me," said Nikki. "Apparently, I'm a troublemaker, and I'm not to be trusted."

"Says the woman who blindsided me in the face with a fistful of snow."

Geena burst out laughing and gawked at Drew. "She seriously did that to you?"

Nikki said, "Not seriously, no. It was not at all serious."

"That's awesome!" Geena high-fived Nikki. "She's too serious too much of the time. Good for you."

Drew sensed a gang-up and reined in her defenses. "Fine. Go ahead and poke fun, you guys."

They continued laughing as Nikki filled Geena in on the snowball fight.

"I need to prep for my next student. Nikki, don't forget your cello."

Nikki grinned and stopped her before she headed back down the hall. "And my homework. Due tomorrow."

"Wednesday."

"We'll see." She kissed her on the cheek and winked as she turned to leave. She waved to Geena. "See ya."

As soon as Nikki was gone, Geena was on her tail. "Spill."

"I'm not spilling anything. I have a lesson in ten minutes. I need to get ready."

"There's nothing to get ready. I already prepped it. Spill."

Drew unnecessarily straightened and rearranged the stools and music stands.

"Come on, Drew! I'm dyin' here. She is some kind of crazy for you."

"You said yourself I need to keep this casual. I can't—"

"Ms. McNally?" Her nine-year-old pupil stood in the doorway, his guitar case propped on the floor and almost as tall as he was.

"Hi, Zac. Come on in."

Geena smirked as she slipped out of the room. "This isn't over."

No, it wasn't. It was far from over.

What happens when the next tour starts? What happens if Nikki grows tired of me? Or…what if Nikki was falling for her? Then what? *I break it off because I won't be able to handle it?*

She sighed and turned her attention to Zac, who was still waiting patiently to start his lesson.

Chapter Twenty-Six

"You can invite Nikki, too. If you'd like."

Drew smiled at her dad's suggestion, then caught herself. Joining them for Thanksgiving dinner would be considered more of a steady girlfriend kind of thing, wouldn't it? Not exactly casual dating territory.

As tempting as it was, she didn't want to give Nikki the wrong impression. "That's sweet of you, Dad, but I'm sure Nikki already has plans with her own family." She walked away to assist a customer looking at bass guitars. She turned toward the door when the bells chimed again. Nikki.

Her dad gave her a wink and smiled. "Speak of the devil."

"Hey, I don't know what she's told you, but Drew threw her share of snowballs."

"Then I taught her well." He hustled over to Drew. "Why don't you see what Nikki needs, and I'll look after our bass player." He walked away before she could object.

Nikki handed her a manila envelope. "I finished my homework."

Drew slid out the photos. "That was fast."

"I lucked out that everyone was home except for Jaymi. And she showed up before I left, so there you go."

"And if she hadn't been home?"

"Jaymi isn't hard to find if you know where to look, so I still would've had these to you today."

She filed the photos with the others behind the register, buying time with the awkward feeling she always got when Nikki talked about Jaymi.

"I practiced my lesson this morning, too."

"Oh. Good for you."

"I'm getting better with positioning my bow." She smiled wider. "Thanks for the extra help with that, by the way."

"Just doing my job."

Nikki pouted. "You mean that wasn't special treatment?"

Once again, she fought to keep her feelings in check. "I believe it was you administering the special treatment, not me." *Sure. Flirt back.*

"I can't wait for my next lesson." Nikki shoved her hands in her coat pockets. "Well, then. I don't want to keep you from your work. I need to call my mother to see what time I have to show my mug for dinner next week, so I best be going."

So, she does have plans with her family. Good. *That will help cool things down between us. And she didn't invite me, either, so she's respecting my wishes.* Even better.

Nikki walked to the door and blew her a kiss. "Cheerio."

Drew barely had, "See you later," out of her mouth, and Nikki was gone. What the hell? She should be glad, right?

So why was she so irked that she'd only gotten to spend ten minutes with Nikki before she rushed off? Why was she disappointed that she didn't even have the option to invite her to Thanksgiving dinner now?

Because maybe she wanted more than casual after all.

Damn it. *This wasn't supposed to happen.* Now what? *No, don't go there. Let there be a little distance between us, and the feelings will fade.* They'd only grow if they were reciprocated anyway, right? Right. Okay, then. *Get back to work, and forget about Nikki for a while.* They'd made no plans to get together again before her lesson next Monday. Perfect.

The store was exceptionally busy for a Tuesday. She'd definitely seen an increase in sales since they'd started the promotions and additional advertising. Still, her workday dragged, or maybe it just seemed that way because as hard as she tried, she couldn't get her mind off wondering when she'd see Nikki again.

"Hey, boss."

Geena's voice made her jump. Drew was in the acoustics room indulging herself on the newest addition to their classical guitar inventory.

"Hi, Geena. Is it three o'clock already?"

"Yep, I just clocked in. Anything you need me to do?"

"I left you the accessories order to work on. It's been busy in here today, but you've got Jerry till six, and Mario just came in, too, so I might take off early."

"Not a bad idea. You should rest up now before the Black Friday rushes start next week. I'm sure we can handle it. No lessons tonight?"

"Just yours at four and five," she said. "So, check on the drums room first."

"Okay. Hey, speaking of lessons, I need you to get in touch with Nikki. You've got all their numbers under lock and key."

She hung up the guitar. "What are you talking about?"

"We just drew a name for our 'lessons with Passion Play' winner. She wants a vocal lesson with Nikki."

The day just got a whole lot brighter. "Oh yeah?"

"She gave me some times she's available. We need to call Nikki to see what works for her." Geena smiled. "I'm sure you won't mind calling her."

"Don't start with that."

"Start what?"

"Getting all wound up about me and Nikki. I'm trying to keep things casual, which in case you've forgotten, was your idea, thank you very much."

"Uh, you're welcome." They walked out of the room together. "Hey, my girl's got one last game tomorrow night before the break. You wanna go? All of my friends are heading home, and I hate sitting by myself."

They stopped at the sheet music racks and began organizing the few things that were out of place. "Oh sure, wait to invite me when you're desperate."

Geena gave her a shove. "I am. Very desperate. I wouldn't want to be seen with you otherwise."

She gave Geena's ponytail a tug. "Thanks for the ego boost. You really know how to turn on the charm."

"That's what she said. And not that I want to be a third wheel, but if you want to bring a date, that's fine with me, too."

They rounded the corner to work the other side of the book rack. "Aha! The truth comes out. You want me to bring Nikki to ratchet up your popularity on campus. As if you need it."

"Hey, I resemble that remark!" Geena slapped another misplaced book into the crook of her arm. "For your information, I'd be just as happy hanging with you. I know you're my boss and all, but I happen to consider you a friend. So, bring Nikki or don't. Either way, I think it'll be good for you to get out."

Drew's heart warmed. She knew Geena was fond of her, but this was the first time she'd ever been so candid about their relationship. She was right. They had become friends. Maybe it was crossing a line seeing each other socially, but what the hell. She'd already broken the rule of not getting involved with a student. Besides, she had no other friends to speak of. Since college, she'd devoted her life to her career. She hadn't kept in touch with her college friends and hadn't felt close enough to any of them to care. Now her career was stable, but other than her solitary life with her cats, things had grown benign.

"Drew, listen. You want the truth? I think it's great that you're dating Nikki. But you gotta have friends, too."

"You're right." Drew sighed heavily. "I've become a total bore. I'm even bored with myself. You sure you want to hang out with me?"

Geena gripped Drew's upper arm. "Yes. I will make it my personal mission to exorcise the boring right out of you. Starting with a hockey game where you can hoot and holler to your heart's delight and chow down on junk food and all in the company of dykes of all ages. How's that sound?"

"It definitely does *not* sound boring."

"Good." She released her. "I'll even drive since I have a parking pass. I'll pick you up at six. Game starts at seven."

Drew nodded. "I'm excited."

"And by nine o'clock tomorrow night, you'll also *be* exciting. That is, if you can stay awake that late."

"Ha ha, very funny."

"Hey, if you fall asleep on the ride home, I'm never taking you out again."

"I won't fall asleep." She headed down the hall.

"I'll believe it when I see it."

"Get back to work, ya lazy bum," she said in her best gangster voice.

Geena hollered after her. "You know, I might just resemble that remark, too."

Drew laughed and slipped into her office to grab her coat. Describing Geena as lazy couldn't be further from the truth, and the banter lifted her spirits. Life was changing, and it felt good.

❖

Drew hit Send on Nikki's number and buzzed with the excitement that was becoming a regular occurrence whenever she contacted her. She found that she missed her when she wasn't around.

"Drew McNally's favorite customer, at your service."

Drew chuckled. "Do you ever just say 'hello'?"

"I like to keep people on their toes."

"You don't say. I hadn't noticed, Snow Queen."

"Oh, please don't flatter me with such titles. It might go to my head, and then I might be tempted to anoint you as my round-the-clock personal attendant."

She dropped onto the couch and knew her face had just lit up like a firefly. "Do I dare ask what that would entail?"

"Oh, you never know. You'd have to be at my beck and call to tend to my every whim, need, and desire."

"So, basically, I'd be your slave."

"Hey, don't go putting a negative connotation on it. You don't know what I'd ask for. It could be something fun and exciting. For both of us."

Funny she'd used the word "exciting," considering her conversation with Geena an hour ago. "What makes you think I'm qualified for such duties?"

"Shit. You're right. I should think this through. I'll have to put you through some sort of test or initiation."

Drew's center tingled as she imagined various initiations she would enjoy, all of which involved them being naked together. She cleared her throat. She'd better change the subject before she said something too provocative and embarrassed herself. "I'll keep it in mind. Anyway, I called because this week's contest winner requested a vocal lesson with you."

"No kidding? When do I report for duty?"

She listed a few days and times the winner provided.

"Nothing tomorrow or Thursday?"

"No. Why? You aren't free Friday or Saturday?" Fret jumped onto the couch next to her and started kneading her thigh. She scratched her head, and she started to purr.

"Anytime is fine. It's just that…"

Drew stretched her legs out on the couch, and Fret settled on her chest. "What?"

"Well…" Nikki actually sounded insecure. Was that possible?

Drew shook her head. "Well what?"

"I was hoping to see you before then. Can I interest you in dinner tomorrow night?" Her words sounded rushed.

Dinner with Nikki sounded wonderful. But tomorrow night was the hockey game with Geena. She opened her mouth to invite Nikki to come along and stopped. Geena was right. Even though she and Nikki weren't a couple, she needed to make time just for friends. As much as she hated to turn her down, she knew it was an opportunity to do the right thing.

"I'd love to, but I already have plans with a friend."

"Oh." Nikki sounded deflated.

It felt a bit empowering, if she were to be perfectly honest with herself. Women threw themselves at Nikki, and she had her choice of any of them. *And she's choosing me.*

"And I have to work the closing shift on Thursday. How about we schedule the lesson for Friday afternoon, say at four, and we go out afterward?"

"Okay. Yeah, that'll work."

She heard the sound of a refrigerator door opening and closing. "So, have you been practicing?" She heard Nikki pouring herself a drink.

"Huh?"

"Your cello lesson."

"Oh, right. Yes. Over an hour today. I just wish I could get that clear tone like you're able to get."

"You've only had one lesson. It takes time and practice. You'll get it."

"I want to get it now."

Drew laughed. "You don't have much patience, do you?"

"I like to be good at what I do, that's all."

"You have millions of fans that can vouch that you are very good at what you do." *And I can personally vouch for you being a fantastic kisser.* Suddenly, the thought of not seeing—or kissing—Nikki again for another three days seemed like forever.

"If you say so."

Vinnie hopped onto the arm of the couch behind her head. He dangled his tail so that it tickled her cheek. "Would you like to arrive an hour early so I can help you prepare?"

"That's a good idea. That way if there's anything in particular you think I should go over, I'll be ready."

"Okay then. I'll see you Friday around three?"

"You got it, Professor."

Drew smiled and shook her head. Nikki had her heart dancing again. She was in trouble here. Serious trouble.

CHAPTER TWENTY-SEVEN

Nikki arched and rubbed the crick in her neck before she cursed and shut down the laptop. She'd been on the computer for hours searching for an original copy of the Ella Fitzgerald record Drew so desperately wanted and had come up with zilch. She'd scoured every antique shop within forty miles earlier today with the same results.

She pushed away from the desk and stretched to get out the kinks. It was only four o'clock, but thanks to the end of daylight saving time a couple of weeks ago, it was as dark as night. She hated this time of year. The holidays were supposed to be a joyful time filled with love and family and giving. Humbug.

Not *her* family. No, for *her* family it was all about making impressions and decorating the house to look like the perfect home, suitable for a Christmas card photo. Holiday parties for business associates and politicians and their perfect, wax-faced wives. Or the rare female government representative and her clean-cut husband, who usually overcompensated for his lesser position by loudly bragging about whatever shmucky white-collar job he had. *Fuck Hallmark and its fucking good cheer.*

She and her mother would end up in a fight before every gathering because she'd resist "putting on a good dress" and making nice with the phonies. She'd complied until she was sixteen. That year, before the guests had arrived, she'd snuck into the kitchen, loaded a plate of food, and then disappeared into her room. Earlier in the week, she'd emptied her closet of every dress she had and given them to the charity shop, a move her mother had hated, but at least it had made her feel as if she had some semblance of control over her life. It hadn't lasted, but it had been a start.

Her phone rang. *Drew.* Her spirits lifted immediately.

She answered in her sexiest voice. "Hey there, anointed one. Are you ready for your first initiation?"

"Nikki?" It wasn't Drew's voice.

She sat up straight. "Who's this?"

"It's Geena. From DJ's?"

Her stomach soured. Something was wrong. "Yeah. I remember."

"Drew's in the hospital. She's all right, but she asked me to call you."

She shot to her feet and headed to the closet. "Which hospital? What happened?" She yanked her leather jacket from a hanger and stabbed one arm through a sleeve.

"Portsmouth Regional. She got hit in the head with a hockey puck."

Drew plays hockey? "She what?"

"She's fine. She's got a minor concussion, and she has one hell of a goose egg on her forehead. They're releasing her in a few minutes, but I don't think she should be alone tonight. She wouldn't let me call Jerry because she doesn't want to worry him."

"I'll look after her. Should I meet you there or at Drew's place?"

"You might as well go to her place. We'll be leaving here shortly."

The ten-minute drive felt like an hour. She vaulted up the stairs and gave a cursory knock to announce her arrival and went right in. As she rounded the corner to the living room, Vinnie scooted off toward the bedroom.

Geena was kneeling in front of the couch beside Drew. "Hey. You got here quick."

"I don't live far."

Drew was lying on her back, one leg bent and resting against the back of the couch, and she held a giant cold pack on her head. Fret was curled up between her knees. Andres was in his usual spot on his bed in the corner of the room.

Nikki crouched down next to Geena. "What the hell happened? Are you okay?"

"Yeah, I'm fine. You guys are making too much fuss over this."

"Shut the hell up, and let us take care of you," said Geena. "The puck flew over the barrier. She was lucky. A couple of people put their hands up to catch it, and that slowed it down. But hotshot here was busy loading cheese onto a nacho and wasn't paying attention—"

"I stuck my arm up just in time, but it ricocheted into my forehead."

Nikki placed her palm on Drew's cheek. "Let me see."

Drew lifted the pack. Geena was right. She had a large purplish lump about an inch above her right eye. She leaned over and kissed it.

Drew managed a smile. "Thank you for coming."

"Of course I came."

Her eyes drooped and then closed. "Sorry. Headache."

Geena stood and backed away. "They already gave her some pain meds. The hospital ran tests and said it's just a mild concussion. Nothing to worry about."

"Good. That's good. Geena, thanks for taking care of her. If you need to get going, I can take it from here."

"Okay. Thanks, Nikki." She showed Nikki the discharge instructions from the hospital and went over what to do if she saw any signs of trouble.

Drew called out from the couch. "Hey, are you sure you're all set with covering the store while I'm out?"

Geena rolled her eyes and shook her head. "Will you stop worrying about work? Jerry and I will figure it out. I don't want to see you again until Saturday. And you'd better not come in then either if you're not up to it. Don't you have any faith in me?"

Nikki held back a laugh at the indignation in Geena's eyes. She was a spitfire, this one.

"Of course I do." Drew sighed, her voice slightly muffled with her arm draped over her face.

Geena touched her knee. "Then stop worrying. We'll handle it."

Nikki pushed the door closed behind Geena and returned to Drew's side. She looked pitiful. Nikki wrapped her hands around Drew's hand that lay along her side. "Is there anything I can get you? A drink of water? Change of clothes?"

"Water sounds good." Drew's lip twitched upward, and she lifted the ice pack and gave her a mischievous look. "Are you offering to help me into something more comfortable?"

She leaned over and pecked her cheek. "I'm offering whatever you need." She retreated to the kitchen for the water.

Drew sat up and took a long drink. "Thank you. Would you mind helping me to the bedroom? I just wanna go to bed and sleep this off, but I'm not feeling very steady on my feet."

"At your service." She wrapped one arm around Drew's shoulders and helped her up. While Drew stopped in the bathroom, she turned down the bed and tried not to think about the fact that she was in Drew's bedroom.

Drew shuffled in and sat down heavily. "Could you grab me a T-shirt and a pair of sleep pants out of my dresser? Second drawer down."

She handed Drew the clothes. "I'll be right outside the door if you need me." She scooted out before she was tempted to help her change. As much as she'd love to see her naked, now was not the time. She stepped around Fret and wandered into the kitchen to pour a glass of water for herself and refilled Drew's as well.

She stopped short in the doorway and caught her breath at the cutest sight ever. Drew was curled up under the covers and surrounded by all three cats. Her hair stuck out in all directions, squashed down on one side from the ice pack, and she appeared to be asleep. She set one glass on the nightstand and gently sat on the side of the bed, careful not to disturb the little family.

She couldn't get over how beautiful Drew was as she slept. She tucked a lock of hair behind Drew's ear and kissed her cheek.

She whispered, "Good night," and started to get up.

Drew caught her wrist. "Stay with me?"

"Yes, of course. I'll be on the couch—"

"No. I mean here. Will you stay and hold me while I sleep?"

She looked into Drew's eyes. She couldn't have said no if she tried. "If that's what you need, I'll stay with you."

"It's more than that." Drew squeezed her hand. "It's what I want."

Nikki nodded. She went into the bathroom and stripped down to her T-shirt and underwear. She slipped under the covers and relished feeling the entire length of Drew's body next to her own as she pulled her close.

It was surprisingly easy to push away her physical desires. All that mattered right now was that Drew felt safe and cared for.

It didn't take long to fall asleep.

CHAPTER TWENTY-EIGHT

The lingering dull ache in her forehead was the second sensation Drew was aware of as the remnants of sleep wore off. The first was the soft body wrapped around hers and the warm breath on the back of her neck. Familiar, yet…not. A cat pressed a paw to her cheek, and she forced her eyes open. Vinnie's whiskers tickled her face as he sniffed her nose.

She looked at the hand that covered hers, adorned with silver and turquoise rings. *I'm in bed with Nikki. And it feels wonderful.* She brought Nikki's hand to her lips and burrowed back into her embrace.

"Good morning," Nikki whispered and tightened her hold.

"Morning."

"You feel so good in my arms."

"Mmm," was all she could manage. She didn't dare admit just *how* good she felt being in them. She shouldn't get used to this. Or should she? *Should I stop overthinking this and simply enjoy it while I can?*

"How're you feeling?" Nikki scratched Vinnie's head—it was a good sign that he was even staying within arm's reach of her—and then lightly brushed hair off Drew's face.

"Better. The headache's still there."

"You'll feel better after breakfast and a shower."

She shifted onto her back and looked up into Nikki's serious eyes. Her black hair stuck up at odd angles. It was adorable. "You're probably right."

"Did you sleep okay?"

"Yeah. You?"

"Better than I have in ages."

Drew took a moment to ponder why that was the case and shoved aside a fleeting hope that being with her was the reason. Andres and

Vinnie hopped off the bed. Fret, who'd been sleeping at their feet, stretched and then walked across on top of them and began kneading her stomach. She giggled.

"Hey, my little sweetums. You heard 'breakfast,' didn't you?" Drew kissed Fret's head. Fret answered with a meek "meow" and headed off to the kitchen to join her feline friends.

"Tell you what. You get in the shower, and I'll fix breakfast."

"You don't have to do that. You don't have to babysit me." She sat up, and the walls seemed to shift.

Nikki was in front of her in an instant.

"Whoa."

"Are you all right? You're white as a ghost."

"I felt a little dizzy, that's all." She closed her eyes and took a deep breath. The feeling in her brain subsided, but now her stomach was rebelling.

"Lie back down. You need fluids." Nikki yanked on her jeans and disappeared. She returned within a minute with a glass of water.

Drew drank the entire glass in several long gulps. "Thank you."

"Better?"

"Yes, much. I'm okay, Nikki. Really. You don't have to stay." She didn't want her to go but hated for her to feel obligated.

Nikki frowned. "I'm not leaving if you're still woozy."

She held out her hand. "Help me up and we'll find out."

Nikki pulled her to her feet and into her arms.

Drew released a smile. "See? I'm fine. Who knew you were such a softie?"

"Shh, don't tell anyone. My fans think I'm a rough 'n' tough rocker."

"Your secret's safe with me. Along with your phone number."

"I better be good to you so you don't sell me out."

"Never."

Nikki kissed her forehead. "You've got quite a shiner, but the swelling's gone down a bit." She snapped her fingers. "Darn. I was looking forward to calling you 'Lumpy.' How do you feel?"

"Still lumpy." She rubbed her head. It felt huge. "I need a hot bath and a big breakfast."

She gathered clothes, and Nikki walked her to the bathroom and started the water.

"Holler if you need me. I'll see what I can scrounge up for breakfast." She turned to leave and stopped. "Oh, and your kids are going to climb my legs and scratch out my eyeballs if I don't feed them soon."

She chuckled and explained the wheres and whats and hows to feed the trio. Once she was alone, she inspected her bruise and concluded that Nikki was right. It wasn't as bad as it had been last night. She sank into the tub. *God, this feels good.* Not just the way the hot water soothed her body but the way Nikki took charge and took care of her. *And my kitties.* She really was a softie.

A light knock on the door interrupted her dreamy thoughts. "Hey, you okay? You've been in there a while, and you're awfully quiet."

"Uh, yeah. I'm getting out now."

"Good. You stay in much longer, and you'll prune. Besides, breakfast will be ready in a few minutes."

When she walked into the kitchen, she couldn't suppress her smile. Nikki was at the stove scrambling eggs. She was barefoot and looked right at home. Drew's heart melted just a little, and she did her best to avoid looking at the perfect shape of her braless breasts pressed against her T-shirt.

Nikki turned and rewarded her with a slow smile. "Feel better?"

"In more ways than one."

"Good."

Nikki let her off the hook by not asking her to elaborate. Neither said a word as they finished preparing the food and sat down to eat. The domesticity of the simple activity was soothing. They didn't even have to talk to relax into sharing something as normal as getting up together and having breakfast as if they'd done it a hundred times before. The image of a kiss good-bye at the door as one of them left for work followed.

But if Nikki left for work, how long would she be gone? Just for the day or for months at a stretch? Was Nikki even interested in a serious relationship? There were so many things they'd never talked about. So many things they still didn't know about each other. They'd spent a month flirting and had gone out a couple times. They hadn't even had their first kiss until a few days ago. Their conversations had touched on a few personal subjects here and there, but they had yet to go deeper. Why was that?

Because you've been so hell-bent on keeping your distance because you're afraid she'll abandon you the way Mother did.

She finished her toast. Nikki had her elbow on the table with her chin in her hand. She stared at Drew with an unreadable expression.

"Care to share?" Nikki asked quietly.

"Huh?"

"You're thinking pretty hard on something. Any chance you'll let me in on what's going on in that head of yours?" Nikki held her position and kept her eyes glued to hers. "I've got all day. Don't forget, I'm a musician. I'm a trained professional when it comes to listening." She smiled.

And just like that, Nikki gave her the opening she needed to open up. So why was she hesitating? Was Nikki's interest in her thoughts a sign that maybe she *was* looking for a relationship? If so, would Nikki be as devoted to her as she was to her career?

Nikki narrowed her eyes. "You're not answering. Are you okay? Is it your head?"

"No, I'm fine. Breakfast was great. Thank you." The deeper thoughts stayed put.

Nikki sat back and looked relieved. "You're welcome." She drained her coffee and began clearing the table. "You're a thinker, aren't you?"

"Excuse me?"

"You're an introvert. Rather than talk out things with other people, you spend time alone processing your thoughts."

Drew stood and gathered the dishes. "Huh. You're right. I never really thought about it that way, but yes, that's exactly what I do."

"Jaymi's the same way. She's an open book when it comes to being there for other people, but if something's bothering her, I've learned to let her be. She'll talk when she's ready." She looked away and smiled. "Whatever she's mulling over usually shows up in her song lyrics, which makes me laugh. All those private thoughts end up out there in the world for everyone to hear anyway."

The far-off look on Nikki's face spoke volumes of her affection for Jaymi. It was a bit unnerving, but again, she reminded herself that Nikki and Jaymi had been friends since college and probably knew each other like the backs of their hands.

"You two are very close, aren't you?"

Nikki finished loading the dishwasher and wiped her hands on a towel. "She's my best friend."

"And what about Shawn? Are you close to her?"

Nikki let out a long breath, but not without a smile. "She's a pain in my butt." She shook her head and let out a silent chuckle.

"You two aren't friends?"

"Let's just say it's complicated but getting simpler."

"I don't understand."

Nikki hung the towel on a cabinet door. "Shawn and I have kind of a love-hate relationship. Although it's been more on the love side lately. She's like the sister I never had, and I'm probably the same to her."

"Is she an only child, too?"

"Yeah. The band is her family." Nikki dropped into her chair and fingered the corner of the place mat. "In fact, I'd say Shawn and I are both closer to the band than we are to our own families."

She joined her at the table. "And that creates a bond between you."

"I guess. I see it more than she does. She…hey, how did we end up talking about me again?"

"You started comparing me to Jaymi, that's how."

Nikki pursed her lips and rubbed her hand over her eyes. "Take it as a compliment. You're both amazing people. You know, I could really use a shower." She stood and pushed in her chair. "Are you okay for about an hour if I run home to clean up and change?"

"Sure. I feel fine. I told you, I don't need a babysitter."

"I don't feel right leaving you alone. Do you…would you like it if I hung out with you for the day? Because I really do want to know what's on your mind. If you want to share it with me, that is."

It always floored her when Nikki acted insecure. It made her more human, more endearing.

She had to admit there was nothing she'd rather do than spend the day with Nikki. If she could get her to keep opening up, maybe she could finally calculate the risks of dating her.

And if she was worth the risk.

CHAPTER TWENTY-NINE

Nikki pulled on an old pair of jeans and a crewneck sweater. Casual and comfortable. Just like Drew. She loved that they were finally getting to know each other better. The more they talked, the more she liked her. Was Drew feeling the same way? She still seemed hesitant to open up. Would Drew give her a chance? *Only one way to find out.* She needed to know what Drew was thinking, and she was bound and determined to find out today.

She got back to Drew's in less than an hour. Drew welcomed her with a smile and a kiss on the cheek. Nikki's heart skipped a beat once again at the sight of her. Her blond hair was tousled from lounging on the couch. Her sweet caramel eyes danced when Nikki opened a grocery bag full of fixings she'd gathered from home to make them soup and grilled cheese sandwiches for lunch. When Drew carried on a conversation with her cats about the food being for her, not them, Nikki's heart swelled even more. Drew was cute, beautiful, playful, and sexy all at the same time. Perhaps Drew's most loveable quality was that she was genuine and didn't try to impress anyone. She was nothing like anyone she'd ever been with, and the desire to share something deeper grew stronger every time she was in her company.

"I love how you're always thinking of your next meal," Drew said as she put the perishables in the fridge.

"It's the little things in life that make me happy." She pulled Drew into her arms and kissed her. "Eating. Sleeping. Spending time with people I care about."

Drew leaned back within the embrace and scrutinized her. "Your career doesn't make you happy?"

"Of course it does, but that's a different kind of happy. It's not the same kind of happy I feel when I'm holding you." She leaned in for another kiss. God, those lips were dangerous. She pried herself away. "This is a much better kind of happy." She took Drew's hand and led her to the couch before she was tempted to take her to the bedroom. "What else do you love, Drew? What makes you happy? I have all day."

She kicked off her shoes and curled up on one end of the couch facing Drew, who looked at her as if she couldn't tell if she was serious or not. Either that, or she didn't know the answers.

"You've seen what makes me happy. My dad. Music. My cats. My job. I don't need much."

Nikki studied her. How Drew ordered her list didn't surprise her. The length of it did. "So, what's missing?"

"Nothing. I have everything I need."

"Uh-huh." What about love? Didn't she need someone to love? *I know I do.* She didn't dare bring up the L-word yet, so she took a different approach. "What about what you want?"

A shadow seemed to fall across Drew's face, and she stared at her lap. "It isn't realistic to think I'll ever have everything I want, so there's no sense talking about it." She crossed her arms. "I have what I need, and that's what matters."

Nikki again got the impression Drew was repeating an argument she'd had before, but it sounded as if she was trying to convince herself, too. "Having what you need is important. But there's more to life than that." She jabbed her in the shoulder. "Come on, lighten up. Let's just say, hypothetically, you could have anything you wanted. What's the first thing that pops into your head?"

"Nikki, I don't see the point. To be honest, I'm broke. Even though our profits are going up, I won't make much more than I'm making now. I don't want to sound like I'm whining or hinting that I want you to buy me things—because obviously you're in a much better financial situation than I am." She raked her fingers through her hair, wincing when she accidently brushed the lump on her forehead. "Damn it, Nikki. I can't even take you out on a real date because I can't afford it. Do you know how embarrassing that is?"

"That's nothing to be embarrassed about, Drew. I understand your situation, so I don't mind paying when we go out. That's never mattered to me—"

"But it matters to *me*. I'm not a freeloader, Nikki. I've busted my ass for everything I have, and I'm proud of that. But I don't feel right letting you pay all the time."

Nikki reached over and took her hand. "Hey," she said quietly. "If I thought you were a gold digger, I would've burned rubber a long time ago. Why shouldn't I spend money on you if I have it? I hope you're not going to let your pride get in the way of what we have going here."

Drew laced her fingers through Nikki's. "It's not just that." She spoke in a near whisper. Nikki waited patiently for her to continue.

"I'm afraid."

"Afraid of what?"

Drew sucked in a big breath and let it out slowly. "I'm afraid that I'm not exciting enough for you. Admit it, you're not gonna settle for someone like me and my boring life in this little town, not with everything you've got out there waiting for you—"

"Whoa, back up the train there, missy. First off, after months on the road and waking up in a different city every stinking day, I crave this 'boring' little town like a junkie craves his next fix. It's my town, too, you know." She slid closer and stroked Drew's cheek. "Secondly, I'm more excited to see you than I am right before I hit the stage. No one has ever made my heart pound like that before." She kissed her lightly. "I find you fascinating, Drew McNally."

Drew's eyes darkened with desire. Her gaze dropped to Nikki's lips. Nikki's pulse accelerated in anticipation.

But Drew didn't move, and then her eyes closed. Shit. Maybe her injury was worse than they thought. If so, she needed to get her to the hospital. Panic rushed through her, but Drew opened her eyes and sighed.

"What happens when you go back on the road? How does that work?"

Whew. Okay, she's okay. Nikki's heart rate quickened again. *Afraid you'll miss me?* She tamped down the instinct to crack a joke. Drew was serious, and she deserved a serious answer. She hadn't given this enough thought. It was inevitable they'd be separated for long stretches while she toured. She'd have to leave Drew behind at home while she spent endless nights alone in hotel rooms and on the bus.

Could she stand going months without seeing her? Without kissing those soft lips? Without enjoying even the simplest things together like going to the Taco Bell drive-thru? Or enjoying lunch breaks together at DJ's? They hadn't even made love yet, but just sleeping with Drew in her arms last night had been glorious. Would Drew wait for her? Shit, she hadn't even thought about that. What if she didn't? What if Drew met someone else? *What if I do? Now that I'm over Jaymi and ready for a relationship...am I putting all my eggs in one basket?*

The thought of Drew with another woman coiled her stomach.

Drew got up. "That's what I thought. Once you get that adrenaline rush of being 'Nikki the rock star' again, I'll be the furthest thing from your mind."

Nikki stood and held Drew at arm's length. "No! You've got it all wrong." She looked her in the eye. "Don't go assuming things about me again. That couldn't be further from the truth."

"Then why's it taking you so long to answer my question?"

"Because I'm afraid, too. I'm afraid I'll lose you."

Drew's eyebrows shot up. "Lose *me*? I'm just a nobody in a dead-end job in—"

"Will you stop? God, Drew. You aren't a nobody. Do you have any idea how hard it is to meet someone like you with the job I have?"

Drew looked at the ceiling. "'Someone like me.' That's exactly my point."

Did Drew really think so little of herself? Or was she just sabotaging a potential relationship by assuming they couldn't maintain it over the long run?

"Don't you know how special you are?"

Drew stared her down. "If I'm so special, then explain to me how someone who supposedly loves me chooses a career over me?" She freed herself from Nikki's hold and stepped back. "Or why they can't accept me for what I am? I'm a teacher. That's what feeds my soul. Why do people think I'm wasting my talent just because I don't want fame and fortune? Does that make my dreams any less important? Why would I think you're any different?"

The questions she threw hammered Nikki's heart, and when tears began streaming down Drew's cheeks, she fought the urge to take Drew into her arms. She didn't want to disrespect her space.

"Try me."

Drew rubbed her wet face with the heel of her hand. She set her jaw in a hard line and looked away.

"Drew," she said softly. "Let me in." She lifted Drew's chin. "Tell me who you're talking about. Please?"

"Why do you care? Why do you want to know so bad?"

"Because if I have any chance with you at all, I want to make sure

I don't make the same mistakes as whoever it was that hurt you this much."

Drew took in a deep breath. "You can't. No one can hurt me as much as she has because no one is supposed to love me as much as she's supposed to."

She was talking in circles, but Nikki held back the many questions she had. She wanted Drew to continue, so she kept it simple. "Who?" She had a feeling she knew the answer, but they'd promised each other to not make assumptions anymore.

"My mother." Drew looked relieved that she'd said it.

She'd guessed correctly. "Tell me."

Drew's eyes grew dark. "Margo Hollister cares about one thing and one thing only. Her acting career." She spat out her words. "Not me or my dad or any of her other husbands. She tossed all of us aside like we were inconveniences. If you don't serve a purpose in her pursuit of fame and fortune, she has no use for you."

No wonder Drew had been reluctant to go out with her. She wasn't in the habit of following the Hollywood scene the way she paid attention to the music business, but she'd heard of Margo Hollister. Which meant her mother had achieved the fame she'd so desperately desired. Still, Drew must know by now that she wasn't like her mother. She looked back on her own career path. She couldn't say she'd ever "tossed" people aside, as Drew had put it. After one-night stands, maybe, but to advance her career? Never.

"You don't think I'm the same way, do you?"

"I don't know you well enough to come to that conclusion."

"But you're already assuming I am. You've assumed that since we met."

Drew's eyes searched hers as if questioning her own instincts. It hurt that Drew wasn't denying the assumptions. She was either afraid they were right, or she knew they were wrong and was struggling with letting them go and taking a chance.

Nikki was sick of assumptions. She only cared about the truth. Her truth.

"I can only speak for myself. I've already made my dreams come true. When I was chasing that dream, I made sacrifices, too—"

"So, you can't blame me for having doubts, Nikki. I saw firsthand what it did to their marriage and how she hurt my dad. She never gave a shit about *his* dreams. He was happy doing what he was doing—

playing gigs with his band and sitting in as a studio musician. But all she could do was criticize him and treat him as if he was in the way of her own ambitions. And then she did the same thing to me—when she could be bothered to pay attention to me, that is."

Nikki could relate to having parents who dismissed their child's dreams, but at least hers were there for her in almost every other way. Poor Drew. Amazing, beautiful Drew. Who loved to teach and pass on her love of music to others. Who showed her father love and devotion on a daily basis. Whose heart was tortured with bitterness and fear because of her mother's neglect. *Bitterness she's projecting onto me.*

"Okay, now I understand you a little better, but you didn't let me finish. I'll admit I sacrificed a lot of things." She sighed. "But never people, Drew. In fact, other than the one I had in high school, I've never had a steady girlfriend. When I went to college and we put the band together, I swore off relationships. You want to know why? Because I didn't want to have to choose between the band and a lover. Back then, the band would've won every time." She dropped onto the couch and began flipping the corner of the armrest cover up and down. "If I'd had a girlfriend, it wouldn't have been fair to her."

Drew's features softened, and she joined her on the couch. "Don't you see? You did the same thing my mother did. You sacrificed love, too."

Nikki shook her head. "No." *I sacrificed Jaymi's love.* Except Jaymi's love was never hers to sacrifice. It was her own needs she'd sacrificed. *For the band.* Maybe Drew was right. She couldn't admit it to her, though. It would only feed her doubts. Drew was finally opening up, and she felt herself shutting down.

If she was finally being honest with herself, she needed to be honest with Drew, too. "Maybe."

"Maybe?"

"Once."

"Once what?"

"I loved someone."

Drew turned and tucked one leg beneath her. "And?"

"And I put the band first. Things were taking off, and I couldn't pass up my break. I made the mistake of assuming she'd still be available, that I had time to…wait."

The corner of Drew's lip quirked up. "Us and our damned assumptions."

"Ironic, isn't it?" They chuckled. "I'm glad things turned out the way they did, or I might not be here with you now." She never thought she'd ever say that and mean it, but it was true. She looked at Drew, and her heart filled with a desire she'd never felt before. Not even for Jaymi.

Drew said, "Sometimes, irony plays to your advantage."

"I'm glad you feel that way."

Drew smiled, but it didn't last. "You asked me earlier what I want. It's not that I don't *know* what I want, Nikki. I'm afraid of wanting what I can't have. So, asking me to voice it…it feels as though I'm setting myself up to get hurt. Saying it out loud makes it real."

"I know the feeling." Nikki reached for Drew's hand and gave it a squeeze. "I share one part of who I am with our fans—my talent. I won't lie, having them love me back for that talent is an amazing feeling. I love being a performer. But once I walk off that stage, that's as far as the love goes. It's just adoration from strangers, nothing more." She choked down the lump crawling up her throat. For the second time in Drew's presence, her eyes watered. "It used to be enough."

Drew moved closer and cupped her cheek. "And now?"

"It's not even close."

"Why is that?"

A plethora of reasons ping-ponged around in her brain. How could she even begin to answer that question? She searched Drew's eyes as she awaited her response, and before she could stop herself she blurted, "I want someone to love me for who I am off the stage."

They both fell silent. She wasn't ready to open that can of worms, and she was fairly certain Drew wasn't either.

CHAPTER THIRTY

Drew sensed that Nikki wanted to say more. She dared not guess what it was. Doing so would stir feelings she wasn't ready to face. This conversation was the closest they'd gotten to discussing their relationship and where it might or might not be going. She'd had no idea Nikki longed for something serious.

Nikki was looking down at their joined hands. Though she was silent, it felt as if she was wrestling with what she wanted to say. Or *if* she wanted to say it. She'd finally opened up about someone she'd loved. Though she didn't go into much detail or say who it was, it didn't matter. Considering what she'd told Nikki about her mother, it had taken guts for Nikki to admit as much as she had. *What matters is that she's glad to be here with me now.*

Drew lifted Nikki's chin to look her in the eye. Her expression was soft and sad. Then her stomach growled loudly, and they smiled at each other.

"I guess that means it's lunch time." Drew kissed her cheek, the moment broken. "If you get the soup on the stove, I'll make the grilled cheeses." She headed toward the kitchen with Fret at her heels.

"I'm supposed to be taking care of *you*," Nikki said as Drew handed her the pans.

"You've been taking care of me since last night. The headache is gone. I feel fine." She grabbed the butter and cheese out of the fridge and set to work on assembling the sandwiches. "In fact, I feel well enough to go back to work tomorrow."

Nikki gave her a stern look. "No dice, sweetheart. You have doctor's orders to stay home and rest. Take advantage of it."

Drew's heart danced a little jig at the term of endearment, even if it wasn't meant as such.

"Your father and Geena both said you never take vacations, so here's your chance." She poured two cans of soup into the pot and flipped on the burner.

"And who's gonna stop me?"

Nikki squared her shoulders. "I am. I'll hide your keys and whisk you off to a place far, far away if I have to."

Drew grinned. "Oh really?" She liked the sound of that. A vacation trip would be wonderful. If it wasn't the week before Thanksgiving, that is.

"Hey. Where'd that smile go?"

"I'll admit that's very tempting, but you know it's not possible this time of year."

Nikki took out bowls and plates from a cupboard. Amazing how quickly and easily she'd learned her way around Drew's kitchen. "Looks like I have more work to do in the 'boosting your confidence' department. You've finally learned how to take a compliment, but," she held Drew's face in her hands, "I might have to make it my mission to show you that anything is possible if you want it bad enough."

They were back to talking about *wants*. Maybe Nikki was right. She'd grown cynical and pessimistic. Working within the safety net of her father's business and the pain of her mother's neglect had derailed some of her own ambitions. Maybe those ambitions weren't as lofty as becoming a rock star, but they were no less important. *Didn't I just say that an hour ago? That my dreams were important, too?*

She flipped over the sandwiches. "You're right."

"Of course I am." Nikki poured milk in two glasses and added spoons and crackers to the table. "I may not be a professional teacher like you, but I'm damned good at bringing out the best in people. Just ask my coworkers."

They sat down to eat. Coworkers? *The band.* Right. She hadn't really thought of them that way before, but that's exactly what they were. Before she could comment, Nikki continued.

"Would you believe when we first met, Jaymi was scared shitless to get on a stage?" She spooned soup into her mouth. "Once she got up there and got going, she wasn't bad. She'd do okay playing and singing, but that was it. She played. She sang. She was…I guess technically competent is the best way to describe it. But *I* helped transform her into a *performer*." She tore off a bite of her grilled cheese. "Now look at her. She's incredible. And Shawn…well, her confidence—musically speaking, anyway—was in the toilet when she came back from

California." She grinned. "Shawn had no problem putting me in my place when it came to other matters, though."

Nikki's love for Jaymi and Shawn was sweet and evidence of her devotion to those she cared about. She was beginning to believe that Nikki would probably be equally devoted to a lover. *Maybe even more so.* "With that kind of passion, it's no wonder the band is so successful."

"Passion is what it's all about. It's also about fun. Why do you think we named the band Passion Play?" Nikki slurped her soup. "Kay used to hide in the shadows next to Brian's drum set. She knew she could play circles around any bass player out there, but she hated the spotlight. Then she started writing songs with us. Next thing you know, she had the itch to sing lead on a few of them."

Drew couldn't contain her smile. She knew where this story was heading, and the pride in Nikki's voice was inspiring. "Let me guess. You helped her overcome her anxieties."

Nikki's eyes sparkled. "Damn right I did. Now she plays and sings right up on the front line with the rest of us. She's one fucking talented woman, I tell you. Bassists don't get enough credit and neither do drummers, but we'd be nothing without her and Brian, who also, by the way, is one of the most rock steady drummers I've ever heard."

They cleared the table and got comfortable on the couch again. "You can't have a tight sound without a strong rhythm section."

Nikki nodded as she stretched her legs out in front of her with her ankles crossed. Drew sat next to her and tucked her legs beneath her. Fret took the empty end, and to her surprise, Vinnie cautiously entered the room and hopped up on his favorite spot on the back of the couch behind her head. Andres stretched, yawned widely, and sauntered out of the room. She heard him crunching on kibble in the kitchen.

A comfortable silence grew between them. It was sinking in that she rarely had the luxury of a few days off in a row with no obligations, and it felt good. Nikki looked at her with hooded eyes and a small smile. It occurred to her that Nikki might not have gotten a good night's sleep last night as she had claimed, being in a strange place and most likely worrying about her. *Had* Nikki worried about her? Having someone around who worried about her felt good, too.

"Why don't you put on some music?" Nikki asked, discounting Drew's assumption that she might want a nap.

"What do you want to hear?" Drew got up and powered on the stereo.

"Something on vinyl." The corners of her mouth curled up slightly. God, she was sexy. "Surprise me."

She ran her fingers over the spines until she saw what she wanted. She put on the album, set the volume on low, and settled back in next to Nikki—a little closer this time.

"Ah. Nat King Cole. One of the most beautiful voices to ever grace the planet." Nikki draped her arm across Drew's shoulders.

She relished how safe she felt with Nikki holding her. She grew warm against her body. It was barely two in the afternoon, yet she struggled to keep her eyes open. She didn't want to succumb to sleep. Her desire to keep talking and getting to know each other niggled at her mind.

Drew said, "Dad almost named me after him, but Mother wouldn't hear of it. She wanted something more unconventional. Typical Hollywood diva." Her last sentence tasted as sour as it sounded.

"You don't like your name?"

"Oh, I like it all right. It suits me better, especially since it's unisex, and I turned out to be a lesbian. Not that lesbians don't have typically girlie names. You know what I mean."

"I love your name." Nikki shifted and gave her a quick kiss. "I think it's sexy."

Drew's face grew warm.

"You're so cute when you blush." Nikki rubbed their noses together. "Now, be a good girl and thank me for the compliment."

"Thank you."

"You're welcome."

She cuddled a little closer, resting her arm across Nikki's stomach. "I envy your confidence."

Nikki's belly bounced in silent laughter. "Don't. Sometimes I think it would've been better if I'd had to work harder for it than to eat all the humble pie I've swallowed from being overconfident. I'm sorry your mother didn't do more to boost yours. You're a good person, Drew, and very talented, too. Teaching is a gift that should never go unappreciated."

"You're sweet."

"I mean it. I've taken my confidence for granted because it's in my blood. I have to give my parents most of the credit, really. My father was the perfect role model, as far as how to channel your energies to make your own success. My mother's loyalty to him was unyielding. She made sure he never had to worry about anything so he could focus on his work.

"They paired me with the best music teachers. They praised my progress every step of the way, pushed me to always give one hundred percent, supported me in everything—well, until I got older and ditched the classical music path they had set out for me." She chuckled with a hint of bitterness.

"I'd say you've done okay with the path you chose. They must be proud of you."

Nikki let out a long breath. "If they are, they've never said so."

Drew was astounded. How could her parents not be proud of her? Nikki was a huge success. She was a gifted musician with millions of adoring fans. The support she gave her bandmates and her drive to succeed were two of the biggest reasons Passion Play was as good as they were and most likely key to them garnering the attention that got them signed to a record deal in the first place.

"Nikki?"

"Yeah?"

"Just because they don't say it doesn't mean they aren't proud of you."

Nikki shrugged. "My father hates to admit when he's wrong. I think it has more to do with that than anything."

Drew didn't want to stereotype, but she thought that sounded typical of politicians. Side One ended, adding a convenient pause to their conversation. She reluctantly slipped out from beneath Nikki's arm and turned the record over. When she turned around, Nikki was right behind her, holding her arms out as an invitation.

She melted into the embrace, and they danced, Nikki singing along to "The Very Thought of You." Drew lost herself in the awesome combination of music and the gorgeous woman in her arms. Nikki was so much more than the cocky, flirtatious celebrity that swaggered into her shop almost a month ago. She was selfless, caring, and loyal. She was confident and strong, yet she'd also chosen to show Drew a side of herself that was sweet, funny, and vulnerable.

Nikki was working her way into her heart. She couldn't deny it, and she wasn't sure if she wanted to. How many relationships had she missed out on because she assumed they'd all turn out like her parents' marriage?

Story of my life, isn't it? I've always played it safe, and where has it gotten me? A job that I enjoy but barely puts food on the table and—aside from the gratification of teaching—leaves me feeling frustrated much of the time. A tepid existence of "work-eat-sleep" and then do it all over again. A nearly nonexistent social life. No dates. No romance. No sex life. She laughed inwardly. Outside of work, she interacted with her cats more than people.

Maybe she needed to push aside her resentments and fears and past failures and stop using them as excuses for settling for less. Her heart had been dormant for ages. Maybe it was time to break out of her comfort zone, which had gone from safe to suffocating.

The song ended, and Nikki gently lifted her hair away from her forehead. She examined the bruise. "How are you feeling?" Nikki spoke gently, completely unaware of the epiphanies forging a path through Drew's subconscious walls.

"Okay." She needed to add a few thousand words to her reply, but assembling them into a single sentence that made sense was impossible at the moment.

"You sure? You look…I don't know. Like you're either in pain or you're trying very hard to make up your mind about something."

She shook her head. *How does Nikki do that?* "I'm fine, really. A little overwhelmed, that's all, with…this." She motioned back and forth between them.

Nikki smiled sleepily. "Me too." She stroked Drew's cheek. "I understand why you have reservations about dating me." Her gaze wandered momentarily before settling on Drew's eyes again. "I really like you, Drew, but I won't lie. I'm gone for half the year. I worry that you'd rather be with someone who's around all the time. I worry that I won't be enough." She inhaled deeply and slowly released it. "I want to be worth waiting for," she nearly whispered.

Drew's heart threatened to burst through her chest. She put one hand behind Nikki's head and pulled her down into a kiss. To let the moment go without kissing her would have been a crime. Nikki enfolded her, deepening the kiss, solidifying the connection as their tongues found each other, stroking softly and sweetly, as she pulled Drew closer.

Drew moaned when Nikki's hand slid under her shirt and caressed her back with a touch that raised goose bumps over her entire body. Drew moved her other hand across Nikki's bare stomach. She swore she could feel Nikki's heartbeat speed up, and Drew hastily cupped one breast and ran her thumb across the nipple protruding through the silk bra.

"Oh God," Nikki gasped, breaking the kiss just long enough to catch her breath before claiming Drew's lips again, this time with a possessive force.

Nikki seemed to collapse in her arms as Drew rolled the firm nub between her finger and thumb and then yanked at Nikki's waist with her other hand. Their centers crashed together, and Drew could feel her own wetness.

"God, Drew. Your kisses set me on fire."

Drew couldn't explain the powerful need pulling at her. Nikki's vulnerability today—and her willingness to share it with her—had chipped away at some of her fears. The confidence Nikki had in her and the gentle way she'd managed to get her to open up had touched on a need she'd been suppressing for far too long.

They made out in the middle of the living room until the turntable was once again silent. Drew pulled back. "Wow."

Nikki took a moment, her chest heaving. "Yeah."

"Can I ask you something?"

"Anything."

"Do you wanna hang out with me till I have to go back to work Saturday?"

Nikki beamed. "I thought you'd never ask." She grabbed her coat. "My bag's already packed. I just have to run out to the Jeep and get it." She yanked open the door. "I wanted to be prepared. You know, just in case you couldn't be left alone."

Had she planned to spend the night with me all along? She returned minutes later with a duffel bag slung over her shoulder and lugging her cello.

"You brought your cello?"

Nikki let the bag slide off onto the floor and set down the case. "I need to practice. I still have a lesson on Monday, don't I?"

"You're something else, Nikki Razer."

"I wouldn't want to disappoint my teacher." Nikki kissed her, long and slow. "You should meet her. She's hot."

"Oh really?"

Nikki nodded. "Really, *really* hot. And she's one hell of a kisser, too." She kissed her again. "She's also smart. And sweet." Another scorching kiss. "And she makes the best grilled cheese sandwiches."

"Now that takes talent."

"Oh, I could go on and on about how talented she is." Nikki kissed her way down her neck.

Drew's breath caught when Nikki dragged her tongue across her collarbone.

"And God, she's beautiful."

Nikki's hot breath nearly caused her legs to crumple beneath her. If she kept this up, they'd never leave the apartment again. "Nikki."

"Hmm?"

"Don't you have to practice?"

Nikki straightened up and pouted. "Is my kissing that bad?"

Drew laughed. "The cello, babe. I thought you wanted to practice your lesson?" She placed a soft kiss on Nikki's lips. "Trust me, you don't need any practice in the kissing department."

Nikki grinned from ear to ear. "You called me 'babe.' I like that."

Drew withdrew before she was tempted to kiss her again. They still needed to take things slowly, but it sure felt good to have made a decision about making changes in her life. Now all she had to do was figure out how. Letting go of her fear of dating someone in showbiz might be a good start.

CHAPTER THIRTY-ONE

Nikki was enjoying one of the best days of her life. She'd take a day like this over a meaningless quickie with a fan any day. Simply being with Drew, doing nothing in particular with no place to go and no other commitments, talking, getting to know each other, and all in the comfort of Drew's modest apartment. It all created a sense of peace within her she'd never experienced before. She didn't want the day to end.

She also wondered what tonight would bring. Another night of cuddling? Or would the feelings they'd shared so far lead to sex? It still felt too soon. She knew Drew wouldn't take the decision lightly either.

It was better to wait. Drew was too special to move too fast. Passion Play wouldn't go out on the road again until early next summer when their next album was released. That gave them plenty of time to make sure they were on the same page.

After cello practice, they browsed Drew's DVD collection and selected some movies to watch. Once they settled on the couch again, however, the TV was soon forgotten, and they ended up talking again, this time swapping childhood stories. Then coming out stories. Teenage heartbreaks, crushes on straight girls, college years, and beyond. Everything, in one way or another, revolved around music.

It was after midnight before they were talked out and too tired to delve into any new subjects. Drew clicked off the TV. They unfolded their legs and sat forward. After endless conversation, the awkward silence filling the room now seemed foreign.

"I won't assume last night's invitation was a standing one, so I'm fine sleeping on the couch tonight." She brushed Drew's bangs back and lightly kissed the bump on her head. "You should really get some rest."

"Yeah." Drew nodded and sighed heavily. "Yeah, you're probably right." She got up and left the room, taking Nikki's oxygen with her.

Oh God. What have I gotten myself into? She shook her head vigorously. She could do this. She would respect Drew's space and take things slowly.

Drew came out of the bathroom with an armload of bedding and a pillow. "I'll make up the couch if you'd like to use the bathroom."

Nikki's expression must have shown her disappointment.

"Don't get me wrong, I…"

"We shouldn't move too fast." Nikki kissed her cheek. "I agree. It's okay, Drew. Today was amazing. Let's just leave it at that for tonight, okay?"

"Okay."

"I'll take those. I don't mind putting my bed together." Nikki accepted the bundle, which Drew seemed to have forgotten she was holding.

"Do you have everything you need?"

Everything but you. But I'm working on that. "Yes, thank you."

"Good night, then."

"Good night."

Drew retreated to her room, closing the door behind her but without latching it. Nikki didn't want to read too much into that, so before her starving libido could overtake her brain and lead her to Drew's room, she zipped through her nightly routine and wrapped herself into a cocoon on the couch.

Her mind buzzed with replays of the day, but soon, the gravity of what it all might mean weighed in. It should have scared her shitless. Instead, it lulled her into a dreamless sleep.

It started out dreamless, anyway. She awoke to the memory of Drew sleeping in her arms the night before. The image was so intense it pierced the pitch-black darkness she saw when she opened her eyes. The vision gave way to the fierce throbbing between her thighs. She reached down, tempted to relieve it, but knowing the woman who could satisfy her craving was only yards away seemed like a betrayal to her own body. She withdrew her hand. *Go back to sleep.*

She did need to pee, however. She stifled a growl and disentangled herself from the covers she'd wrapped too tightly. She refused to look toward Drew's bedroom directly across from the bathroom and quickly shut the door behind her. After relieving herself, she stared long and hard into the mirror. A few months ago, she'd disliked what she saw. At least now, she could respect the person in the reflection. She leaned on the vanity and dropped her head, closing her eyes. She'd stay at home tomorrow night. This was too hard, and Drew was well enough to be on her own now.

She flipped off the light before opening the door—she didn't want the light to wake up Drew. She carefully opened the door and stepped right into Drew.

Drew let out a surprised gasp as they collided, and Nikki grabbed her arms to keep from knocking her over.

"Oh! Nikki. Sorry, I didn't see you."

"Are you all right?"

"Yeah. You?"

"Yes. What're you doing up?"

"I went to the kitchen for a drink of water."

"You need night-lights in this place." She loosened her grip on Drew's arms but didn't let go. They were standing so close she could feel the heat radiating from Drew's body. Or maybe it was her own. Her eyes finally adjusted, and she could make out Drew's shadowy form. The pulse down below she'd just dispelled was back. "Well. Uh…I'll let you get back to bed."

She moved away, but Drew grabbed her hand. Nikki stilled. Drew rested her palm against her face and stepped closer. Drew's breath was warm against her throat. Nikki's heart raced faster and faster, like the crazy, sped-up string orchestra at the end of the Beatles song, "A Day In the Life," charging through the last few measures, and then, like the final chord slammed down on the piano keys, Drew's lips suddenly claimed hers.

Nikki stumbled backward, pressed against the wall as Drew fell against her. The initial shock wore off, and Nikki kissed her back ferociously, without apology. She snaked her arms around Drew's waist, her hands easily finding their way under her T-shirt to caress the softest skin ever. She barely had time to register how good Drew felt before Drew returned the favor.

Drew's touch turned her insides to lava. She lowered one hand to Drew's ass and pulled their centers together. She needed to feel Drew against her. Now. Drew moaned into her mouth and rocked with her. Shit, if they kept this up, she'd come within minutes.

Drew broke the kiss. "Take me to bed." Her words came out in a hard whisper, not a command as much as a plea.

"You sure?"

"Oh yeah." Drew kissed her hard. "Are you?"

Nikki's thoughts fast-forwarded to morning. For the first time ever, she knew she'd wake up without regrets. "I'm sure."

In the dim light from the window, she watched in awe as Drew lifted her shirt over her head, and then dropped her sleep pants to the floor and kicked them off. She was gorgeous. Her breasts were perfect and round, not too small or too big. Her flat stomach, the enticing curve of her hips, her legs firm and strong—an invitation for worship if she ever saw one. Nikki took in every inch of her beauty, thinking of the closeness they'd shared earlier, talking about their lives and their losses. She couldn't believe Drew had asked her into her bed as well as into her heart.

Drew grabbed fistfuls of Nikki's shirt and looked at her with a devilish little smile. "This needs to come off."

Nikki raised her arms and let Drew undress her. Drew sat on the bed, and Nikki bent over and kissed her. Their lips stayed locked as Drew crab-walked backward across the bed and Nikki walked on all fours above her. She brushed her breasts back and forth across Drew's. The sensation of skin-to-skin contact nearly sent her over the edge. She sat back, straddling her and running her hands over Drew's torso. She could feel their combined wetness as she gently rocked against her.

"Oh God, Nikki. Oh God, you feel so good."

"We're only getting started," she whispered.

She gave Drew a brief, soft thrust and lowered herself over her, taking a breast in one hand and the other into her mouth. Drew let out a growl. Nikki took her time, indulging herself with the sweet taste of each nipple before kissing every exposed part of Drew's body she could reach. Drew squirmed and moaned in pleasure, and Nikki knew she couldn't tease her much longer.

She came back up and placed a lingering kiss on her mouth. "Are you ready, baby?"

Drew answered with a scorching kiss. Nikki reached between them, and Drew opened to her touch, meeting each stroke as Nikki lost herself in the feel of her, her scent, her sounds, her every move. She held back her own orgasm as Drew closed around her fingers. Nikki opened her eyes just in time to see Drew throw back her head and vocalize the most wonderful sound. Drew's angelic face shone in the thin veil of moonlight that stretched across the room. She mentally burned the image into her mind, thinking that nothing would ever rival it for as long as she lived.

Drew's shudders finally subsided. Nikki gently settled on top of her, still inside her, and Drew's arms came around her. Nikki slowly withdrew her fingers, missing the connection immediately.

She kissed Drew's cheek and waited for her to open her eyes. "I've never experienced anything so beautiful."

"That was amazing. *You* are amazing."

"If I am, it's because of you." She kissed her lightly. "You do things to me, Drew. I've never felt like this with anyone."

"Like what?"

"Safe. Myself. Real." Nikki looked away, feeling exposed but in a healthy way. If that even made sense. "Like I matter."

Drew touched her cheek. "You matter to me," she whispered. "More than I expected."

"Is that a bad thing?"

Drew scrunched up her brows. She seemed to be considering her answer carefully. "I hope not."

Nikki's confidence faltered. "You still have doubts."

"Don't you?"

She thought for a moment. "I'd think there was something wrong with me if I didn't." Nikki rolled off onto her side and propped herself up on one elbow. "Not doubts about whether you matter to me. Because you do. A lot. I have doubts that I'll be any good at relationship stuff—if that's what this is—if that's what you want it to be."

"You mind if I confess something?"

Uh-oh. She didn't like the sound of this, but she couldn't exactly say, *"Yes, I do mind,"* and then be left wondering what it was she needed to confess. "Should I call the cops?" *Yeah, make a joke. That'll make things easier.*

In the dim lighting, she saw Drew smile. "That won't be necessary."

"Phew."

"When we first met, I was hell-bent against getting involved with you."

No surprise there. "Yeah, that was pretty clear. It's okay. I'm glad that's changed."

"It changed because I decided that as long as we kept it casual, then I was safe. We could be friends or date and have fun, and then when you left again, it would be no big deal. No strings."

Casual. No strings. Drew didn't want a relationship. She wanted a fling. They weren't on the same page after all. The hurt bubbled up before she could stop it. "Did you ask me to stay because you were hoping to seduce me?"

"No!" Drew rolled onto her side and faced her. "No! God, no, Nikki. Just the opposite. Please, let me finish. What I'm trying to say is that I've grown to care about you, and I wasn't prepared for any of this. I didn't expect to…" Drew's eyes widened as if she almost said something she'd regret.

"To what?"

"Nothing. I mean, argh, I don't know what I'm saying, and I'm making no sense. None of this makes any sense." Drew lowered her gaze and pursed her lips together.

Nikki grazed her fingers across her cheek. "Hey," she said softly. "Maybe we're putting too much pressure on ourselves. We haven't known each other very long."

"So, can we just play it by ear for now?"

"We're musicians. We're supposed to be good at playing by ear. That gives us an advantage, don't you think?"

"Nikki, I'm not talking about improvising a guitar solo here. I'm talking about our hearts. There's a much bigger risk involved."

Good point. A valid point. But taking risks had never deterred her before. If anything, they made her more determined to succeed. She wasn't about to change that now.

"Then I guess there's only one thing to do."

"What's that?"

"Make that two things." She caressed Drew's cheek.

"Okay…"

"First, let's play it by ear and see how it goes. I'm willing to take that risk if you are."

"If I'm being completely honest, I think my heart's already made the decision for me."

"So that's a yes?"

"Yes, it's a yes."

It was encouraging that Drew answered so quickly, but she gave Nikki a sideways glance.

"What's the second thing?"

She ran her hand across Drew's stomach. "We need to make love again. At least one or two or three more times. Maybe more. You know, make sure it's worth the risk."

"I like the way you think."

Nikki peppered kisses across Drew's neck. "I like the way I think, too."

Drew sandwiched her face in her hands. "Know what else I like?"

"What?"

"I like the way you kiss." Drew pulled her down for a kiss. "And I like the way you touch me."

Nikki cupped Drew's breast and swiped her thumb back and forth over the nipple. "I like the way you respond when I touch you." She gave her a long, languid kiss.

Without warning, Drew flipped her over and covered her body with her own. "Not so fast, hot shot. You've already had your way with me once. This is a duet, not a solo. My turn." Drew reached down between them and dragged her fingers across her labia.

Nikki's breath hitched. Drew began a steady stroke as Nikki took her breasts into her hands and gave them the attention they deserved. Drew bent down and exhaled into her ear before kissing and sucking her neck. She quivered all over, overwhelmed by the sensations, and then Drew slipped inside her, and she cried out.

Drew moved her mouth to her areolas, alternating between licks and sucks, making them almost as wet as she was down below, pushing her into a frenzy. She was going to explode.

Drew brought her lips to hers again. "I need to taste you." She withdrew and expertly separated her with two fingers before taking her into her mouth.

She was already so close that it didn't take long for her to climax.

Oh yes. Definitely worth the risk.

Chapter Thirty-Two

Drew awoke with an acute awareness of Nikki's naked body tangled with hers. Muscles she'd forgotten she had were sore from hours of lovemaking. She wasn't surprised at how easily she'd given in to her carnal desires. It was the ease with which she'd divulged her fears—and then how eagerly she'd agreed to Nikki's request—that had her questioning her judgment.

Had she just set them up to get hurt? In the heat of the moment, she'd said she could handle dating Nikki, but what if she couldn't? She couldn't predict the future any more than Nikki could.

She almost laughed out loud. If Nikki had turned out to be the person she'd assumed she was when they first met, then maybe she could have had a casual fling with her because she wouldn't have liked her so much. *How screwed up is that?* Did she really think she'd rather have a couple of months of meaningless sex with someone she didn't care for than this? Or would she rather take a chance on a relationship with a woman who was sweet, loyal, caring, sensitive, funny, and actually very down-to-earth? *Not to mention an amazing lover.*

Was she really willing to risk her heart for Nikki?

There was that word again. *Risk.*

Air. She needed air. The room seemed to have sucked it out of her, and panic flooded her body. Wasn't everything in life a risk? *What are you going to do? Lock yourself up in your room like a hermit and avoid every damn risk for the rest of your life?*

Nikki shifted and wrapped her body tightly around her. "Hey," she whispered. "What's wrong?"

At the sound of Nikki's voice, she burrowed backward into the embrace. Her breathing slowed. Nikki's warmth soothed her almost immediately; she'd sensed Drew's discomfort. Nikki enveloped her hand in hers and squeezed.

"Drew? You're scaring me. Are you okay? You're not sorry about last night, are you?"

She rotated within Nikki's arms and hugged her. She hated the insecurity she'd put in Nikki's eyes. "No. I'm not sorry. A little overwhelmed but not sorry."

She kissed her bruise. "If it makes you feel any better," she whispered, "I'm a little overwhelmed, too."

"You are?"

"More than a little." Nikki kissed her lightly. "Last night was incredible." Another kiss. "I can't believe I'm here with you." She teased her with her tongue and deepened the kiss. "See how much fun taking risks can be?"

Drew chuckled.

"I wasn't trying to be funny."

"I know," said Drew. "Turns out in addition to your other talents, you're also a mind-reader."

"You mean you're thinking of spending the whole day in bed ravishing my body, too?"

Drew laughed harder. "Close. I was thinking about my aversion to taking risks."

She could tell Nikki had a wisecrack response on her lips, but Fret pounced on top of them and kept her from saying it.

"All right, cutie pie, I'll get you your breakfast." She gave Nikki a peck on the lips. "As for you, breakfast will have to wait."

"Aww. No fair."

"Sorry. Kitties reign supreme in this household." She crawled out of bed, collected her jammies, made a pit stop in the bathroom, and set about preparing her kids' morning meals.

Nikki joined them a few minutes later. "Any chance I can talk you into taking one more day off?"

She interlocked her fingers behind Nikki's neck and gave her a proper good morning kiss. "After last night, that is *very* tempting—which only proves you're a bad influence on me. Or a good one. I'm still determining which.

She poured juices and handed one to Nikki. "I can't take any more time off—"

"You can't or you won't?"

"Well, I…I suppose it's a little of both. I guess I could. We just hired Melissa to help out during the holidays. I can see if she's available to work Saturday, and Geena could take care of the cats, but it's the weekend before Thanksgiving—"

"Which means it's probably your last chance to take a little time off before the rush."

She cracked eggs into a skillet as Nikki started the coffee. This routine was growing on her. "It's also probably going to be really busy, hopefully. Why do you want me to take it off?"

"I think you need a lesson in spontaneity." Nikki grabbed mugs from the cupboard and put bread in the toaster.

"What are you up to?"

Nikki grinned. "Oh no, you don't. If I tell you, it'll take away the risk factor, and hence spoil your feeling of accomplishment."

The panic was back. "You're not going to make me do something crazy like jump out of an airplane, are you?"

Nikki gave her a sly smile. "Now you're reading *my* mind."

"Nikki Razer, if you think for one minute…stop laughing at me! Are you out of your freakin' mind?"

Nikki took her by the hands. "I'm kidding, I'm kidding! We'll stay on the ground, I promise. Unless," she winked, "you're walking on air like I am right now."

"Really?" Drew's heart danced.

Nikki brushed her cheek and smiled so widely that Drew thought the corners of her mouth would reach the back of her head. "You'd better believe it, baby."

The instant heat flooding Drew's face told her she was blushing like crazy.

"Can you at least tolerate another long ride in a limo?"

Now she'd really piqued her curiosity. "How long?"

"It'll be farther than Boston this time, but I'll have you back on Sunday."

They filled their plates and sat down to eat.

"And when will we be leaving?"

"We can go tonight after I do the vocal lesson with your prize winner or tomorrow morning. Your choice."

"How am I supposed to know how long I want to be away if I don't even know where we're going or what we'll be doing?" She tore her toast apart into quarters and dipped a piece in her yolk.

"Hey, spontaneous, remember? Don't you trust me?"

"I might regret saying this, but for some ridiculous reason I can't explain, I do."

"Then tonight it is."

❖

"Can't you at least give me a hint?" Even if she didn't know what they were going to do, Drew at least wanted to know where they were doing it.

"You'll see when we get there."

Nikki grinned that deadly grin that always turned her insides to goo. Drew wanted to simultaneously strangle her and kiss her all over. Nikki's secretiveness was maddening, but it was such a turn-on, she didn't know how she was going to tamp down her excitement and sit still, no matter how comfortable the limo's leather seats were.

She'd gone insane all afternoon waiting for Nikki and speculating on what she had planned. Now, after an hour on I-95 South, Nikki still hadn't revealed anything. Nikki was animated about their upcoming adventure but seemed preoccupied otherwise. She was quiet right now, her face serious with what looked like worry.

"Everything okay?"

"Huh? Oh, yeah. Everything's fine." Nikki slid to the other end and turned sideways, facing her with one leg bent on the seat. "I'm a little nervous about all this. It's…I want everything to be perfect."

Drew patted her knee. "When are you going to realize that you don't have to be perfect?"

Nikki shrugged, and Drew's heart softened again with Nikki's rare display of vulnerability.

"It's a big step, though, isn't it? Traveling together?"

"You travel with the group all the time."

"That's different. They're my friends. I mean, you're my friend, too, but—"

"Nikki, relax. Even though I have no idea where you're taking me or what we're going to do, I know we'll have fun no matter what." She lifted Nikki's chin and locked eyes with her. "I get the feeling you need this little vacation as much as I do."

Nikki gave her a quick kiss. "I think maybe I do. Don't take this the wrong way, but it feels strange to travel without the band."

Drew swiveled to face her. "You really do care about your friends, don't you?"

Nikki held her gaze, her mouth a firm straight line. "I'd protect any one of them with my life. I'm closer to them than my own family. Maybe that's because I'm an only child, but even so, I can't imagine my life without my family."

Drew had no siblings, either, yet she felt closer to her dad than anyone else. "I guess what I have with my dad is special. He's everything to me."

Nikki smiled. "He's a great guy. And he adores you." Her smile faded. "I never had that kind of bond with my parents."

She leaned over and took Nikki's hand. "You felt neglected because of it, didn't you?"

Nikki looked at their joined hands. "I wasn't neglected if you're talking about pushing me to succeed or spoiling me with material things. But…" Nikki looked up at her. "It felt more like they were my career managers, not my mom and dad. They cared more about me representing their public image and reputation by making something of myself according to how it fit into *their* lives, not mine. Don't get me wrong; I'm grateful for the musical training I had and for never having to worry about money or anything like that. But I resented them for not caring about what *I* wanted or anything else I was interested in. They saw my talent and decided *for* me that I was going to be a professional musician."

"No matter how old we get or how they treat us, we never stop wanting our parents' love and approval, do we?" Drew swiped a tear off Nikki's cheek and gave her a smile. "The musician part worked out okay, though."

"I know. It's getting better. At least they've come around with accepting me as a lesbian." She chuckled under her breath. "But they still wish I had become an opera singer instead."

"There's still time to do that, too. If you wanted to."

"No, thanks. I'm a rocker, through and through. I don't think that'd go over well with my fans, either."

"They'd flock to every show just to drool over you, even if they hated opera."

Nikki kissed her. "You're the only one I want drooling over me."

Her insides went gooey again. "Sorry, but I don't think your fans are going to stop drooling over you anytime soon."

Nikki cocked her head and smiled. "Well, as long as it sells records and concert tickets, I guess I can live with that." She held out her arms. "Come 'ere, drooler."

She shuffled across the smooth leather seat. Nikki tugged her against her side and dropped an arm across her shoulders. "This is nice."

"Mmm." Nikki kissed the top of her head. "Since we're swapping parent stories, tell me more about your mother."

Drew tensed for a moment, but Nikki had opened up about her folks, so it was only fair that she do the same. "Well, you know she's an actress. She's like your father, obsessed with her career. My dad virtually raised me on his own. My mother was hardly ever around, and when she was, it was always all about her. I don't think I was planned, so I always felt like she saw me as a nuisance who interfered with her plans."

Nikki played with Drew's hair as she talked. It was a simple gesture that made her feel cared for and special. It lulled her into a safe and content sleepiness.

"I can see why you have a hard time with people in show business." Nikki kissed her on the forehead. "It's not exactly conducive to raising kids or having a 'normal' life. But I believe that if you have kids, they should be your number one priority."

Now they were in some serious territory. Did Nikki want kids? *Do I?* The thought hadn't crossed her mind before, since she'd never been involved with a woman long enough for the subject to come up. "Why don't you take a nap?" Nikki jarred her out of her thoughts. "It's a long ride, and we have a big day ahead of us tomorrow. I want you well rested, considering we didn't get much sleep last night." She added a mischievous smile to her last sentence.

"How long a ride?"

"Go to sleep, and it'll go by faster. I'm going to snooze, too."

So much for getting any more information out of her. She snuggled into Nikki's warm body and closed her eyes. Maybe she was right. The time would pass easier if she slept through the ride.

She awoke when she sensed they'd stopped moving. They were in a city and parked in front of a fancy hotel. She blinked until she could focus on the name.

"Welcome to New York City, sweet thang."

"Oh my God. New York? The Park Hyatt?"

Nikki shifted away and pointed out the window on her side. "Yes. And even better, look what's across the street."

Carnegie Hall. "Nikki! What have you done? Is Passion Play playing at Carnegie Hall?"

Nikki chuckled as the driver unloaded the trunk and met the

bellhop at the curb. "No, we're not *that* big yet. However, I would be most honored if you would accompany me to a concert there tomorrow night."

"I, uh…what?" She shook her head. This was not possible.

"So? You interested?"

Drew's door opened, and the driver offered his hand to help her out. The smog mixed with the crisp November air and assaulted her nostrils. It was awful and wonderful. "You're taking me to a symphony? At Carnegie Hall?"

Nikki joined her by the side of the car. "Mozart's Twentieth Piano Concerto, actually. Is that okay with you?"

"Is it okay? This is unbelievable. I can't believe you did this! How did you do this?"

Nikki looped her arm in hers, and they headed into the hotel. "It's called the internet. You should try it sometime."

They walked into a humongous, elegant hotel lobby, the kind she'd only seen in the movies. She wasn't surprised when the concierge greeted Nikki by name before they'd even checked in. She was in such a daze that she hardly remembered the elevator ride to the umpteenth floor. The bellhop was waiting patiently.

Nikki opened the door, and Drew's jaw dropped. "You could fit my apartment in this room!"

"It's a suite."

Nikki tipped the man after he unloaded their bags.

"Nikki, this is too much. I can't afford—"

"Oh no, you don't. This is my treat, and you're not going to stop me from spoiling you this weekend."

"But I don't even have anything to wear tomorrow night!"

Nikki slipped her arms around her waist and smiled. "You will. I'm taking us shopping."

"I can't let you do that."

Nikki shrugged. "Okay, fine. I plan on buying myself a new outfit, but if you'd rather wear something you brought, suit yourself."

For crying out loud. Nikki knew she couldn't wear jeans or khakis to Carnegie Hall. They probably wouldn't even let her in. "Why didn't you tell me I'd have to dress up? I could have gone to the mall this afternoon. At least there I know I can afford something halfway decent."

"Didn't I just say this weekend is my treat?"

"You know how I feel about paying my own way."

Nikki grabbed her hand and led her across the room. She pulled open the drapes, revealing a full view of the cityscape *and* of Carnegie Hall. She turned to Drew. "This view doesn't hold a candle to the excitement on your face." She kissed her. "You're beautiful, Drew. And the truth is, I'm crazy about you, and I want to spoil you rotten this weekend."

"I don't know what to say. I feel guilty."

"Don't. Please don't. It doesn't matter to me how much money you have. The point is, *I* can afford to do this. I *want* to do this. Not because I want to show off, but because you deserve this, and I want to make you happy. So, please, let me."

The hopeful expression on Nikki's face was doing a number on her stubbornness. She had to admit she was ecstatic. When would she ever get a chance like this again? Two nights in a luxury hotel? Shopping in downtown Manhattan? Mozart at Carnegie Hall? With Nikki?

It was perfect.

She took Nikki's hands. "Okay, I'll let you, but on one condition."

"Anything."

"You have to let me pay for at least one thing while we're here."

Nikki's shoulders relaxed. "You have yourself a deal." She kissed Drew lightly on the lips. "Now, I suggest we begin this adventure by taking advantage of the garden tub with a long, hot bubble bath, and then we get a good night's sleep on that king-sized bed. What do you say?"

"I say I like the way you think."

"It seems I've heard that before."

"It's worth repeating."

Nikki gathered her in her arms and placed several kisses on her neck and along her jawline. "Know what else is worth repeating?"

She struggled for breath. "Last night's bedtime activities?"

Nikki drew back and smiled. "Now I like the way *you* think."

CHAPTER THIRTY-THREE

Drew had never had sex in a bubble bath before, but she quickly added it to her list of favorite things—especially with the way Nikki had sent her over the edge twice. The second time, they came together. They dried each other off with towels that were thicker than her winter parka. Then they took turns putting body lotion on each other and fell naked onto a bed that was so comfortable, Drew thought she'd died and gone to heaven.

By then, they were too tired to make love again. It was just as well, considering they wanted to get up early to fit in as much fun as they could before the 7:30 curtain call. Despite her excitement, Drew slept soundly. How could she not in a bed this soft and curled up next to Nikki's just-as-soft skin?

She awoke with the remnants of a dream in which she was playing her cello on the stage of the Weill Recital Hall. Even through the blinding spotlight, she saw everyone she knew in the audience: her parents—surprisingly seated together—Geena, Melissa, Nikki, and the other members of Passion Play. Even her cats were lounging on the seats.

She opened her eyes. Nikki was still asleep next to her, looking gorgeous and content. Despite her early reservations, she loved the way things were going. She was exciting and sweet and generous and fun. She loved the easiness of their conversations. She loved how in tune Nikki was with her needs. She loved their shared appreciation for all styles of music.

Maybe she really was ready to take a shot at a relationship. *"I'm crazy about you."* Nikki's words prompted a huge, shit-eating grin. *I'm in New York City with one of the sexiest, most beautiful, most sought-after rock stars on today's music scene. Me. Lowly music store manager Drew McNally.* She carefully slipped out of bed and went to the bathroom. She helped herself to one of the plush robes, tugged a knot in the belt, and swung open the bathroom door.

Nikki rolled over onto her side and propped up on her elbow. "Well, good morning, beautiful," she said with a sexy smile.

Drew caught a glimpse of Nikki's naked form beneath the sheet.

"I know that look." She got out of bed and walked over in all her naked glory. "Too bad we don't have time to act on it at the moment." She gave Drew a knee-buckling kiss and closed the bathroom door behind her.

Nikki reemerged a moment later. "Would you like breakfast out, or shall I order room service? If I order now, we'll have time to shower and dress before it arrives."

Drew quickly ran calculations in her head. She'd offered to pay for one thing. Could she afford breakfast here?

"Well, while you're making up your mind, I'll jump in first. If you want to eat here in the room, go ahead and order. We have two hours before our first stop, so don't take too long to decide."

"Our first stop?" It was hard to concentrate on making decisions with Nikki rummaging through drawers in the nude.

"Yes. We don't have to go far, but it starts at eleven. Wear the best outfit you brought with you, and then our second mission will be finding us each something smashing to wear tonight. Sound good?"

She scanned the menu while Nikki was in the shower. Paying for breakfast was out. If she couldn't even afford breakfast, how was she going to treat them to anything else? Her stupid pride was going to set her back at least half a week's worth of groceries.

Oh well. So, she'd live off cereal and peanut butter sandwiches for a few days. It'd be worth it. What were credit cards for, anyway? She called in the order, happy that she would be keeping her end of the deal *and* that she knew what Nikki liked to eat.

She hurried through her shower and dressed in tan khakis and a green and beige pinstriped dress shirt. She took extra care to get her hair just right, feeling anxious and excited for their mysterious "first stop."

She stepped out of the bathroom. Breakfast had already arrived. "Hey, I was going to pay for breakfast."

"Don't worry about it, babe. It's charged to the room."

She felt her face flush. Of course it was. How stupid of her. No problem. The day was young. She'd have more opportunities to pay for something.

Their first stop turned out to be a tour of Carnegie Hall. Nikki admitted that although she'd been to a few concerts there with her parents, this was her first tour. Sharing a "first" together only made it more special. They were like kids in a candy store, and the hour went by way too fast.

They stepped out into the brisk November air, and she squinted in the bright sunlight. She hooked her elbow through Nikki's offered arm, and they walked on with purpose. Drew would have been nervous walking the streets of big cities alone, but Nikki's confidence filled her with a sense of security.

"Are you ready for a light lunch?" Nikki asked.

"Sure." A light lunch sounded like something she could afford.

"What are you hungry for? I say we do something that's totally New Yorky."

Drew laughed. "New Yorky?"

"Yes. I'm dorky in New Yorky." Nikki flashed her a huge goofy smile. "What's your pleasure, my treasure?"

"Pizza, my dear. They say it's the best here."

"You're right. It's a delight."

"We should totally write lyrics together. Do your fans know what a goofball you are?"

"No. And don't tell them, either. My cool factor might slip a few notches."

Drew yanked her away from the teeming sidewalk crowd and under a storefront awning. She grabbed Nikki's lapels and kissed her. "Not a chance. You are the definition of cool *and* hot. You cover the full spectrum, babe."

Nikki kissed her back softly. "I love that I can let my guard down and be myself with you."

"You mean you're not a goofball with other people?"

Nikki shook her head. "Just Jaymi, but only after we have a few beers in us."

We. Us. Interesting. Nikki told her they only drank socially.

Nikki's look turned somber as she continued, "We haven't done that in a long time."

That was a relief, but what was with the mood change?

Nikki looked at her and smiled. "I'm glad my partying days are over."

Drew relaxed. *Me too.*

Nikki hailed a taxi and instructed the driver to take them to the best pizza place in the neighborhood.

"Can we go to one of those parlors where they have those little round tables and you stand up to eat?" Drew asked. They only had one day. She wanted as much of the Big Apple experience as she could squeeze in.

The driver dropped them at a place that matched their request exactly. Nikki agreed to let her pay for the fare and lunch, although compared to all the other activities they were doing, she felt a little cheap that those were her only contributions so far. She didn't rule out charging something later, too, should the opportunity present itself.

She sank her teeth into the most mouthwatering pizza she'd ever eaten. It was so good, she almost felt guilty that she hadn't paid more for it. After lunch, Nikki led the way in and out of clothing stores along Fifth Avenue. They had just enough time to get back to the room and change into their new outfits before heading to dinner.

A Broadway-sized butterfly dance took over her insides as she shrugged into the blazer and straightened the collar of her white tuxedo shirt. She'd decided to be pseudo-mod stylish by going without a tie. She topped off the fitted suit with the fedora Nikki had suggested to conceal the bruise above her eye. She checked her look in the mirror and liked what she saw. She felt classy. She shoved away the guilty budget-brain nag and delighted in the joyful perfect fit of her new attire.

Nikki was certainly accomplishing her goal of spoiling her. Drew beamed at her reflection. *I look damn good with this smile on my face, too.*

Nikki turned around when she heard Drew come out of the bathroom. "Wow."

"What do you think?"

"Wow."

Drew did a little spin, her confident smile filling the room with a glow that could put Broadway spotlights to shame. Then Drew turned that smile on her, and Nikki knew that Drew also liked what she saw.

She smoothed down the front of her white coat with tails and stepped into Drew's arms. "Wow."

"Is that all you can say?"

"Drew, you're absolutely stunning. How do you expect me to pay attention to the orchestra with you sitting next to me wearing this?"

Drew's smile widened, if that was even possible, and said, "I guess we'll both suffer, then, because you look gorgeous and dashing and downright delicious in that tux."

"Delicious, huh?"

Drew cleared her throat. "Scrumptious." She gave Nikki a soft, sensuous kiss that promised of things to come.

Things that had to wait. Drew's kiss chased away coherent thought and tempted her to say to hell with dinner and concertos. Drew finally pulled away, leaving Nikki's feet struggling for purchase and her heart threatening to escape her chest.

"You kiss as good as you look. Which is why we need to go."

Drew caressed her with her eyes. "I already know what I want for dessert."

"That makes two of us." She led them to the door before she completely crumbled.

She checked her pockets, making sure she had everything, and offered Drew her arm. "Are you ready for the night of your life?"

"Lead the way."

CHAPTER THIRTY-FOUR

As hard as it was to leave the hotel suite earlier, Nikki wouldn't have traded Drew's obvious enjoyment of their evening out together for anything. It began with a divine Tuscan meal at Trattoria Dell'Arte on Seventh Avenue. After the spill incident during her first meal at Drew's apartment, she avoided ordering a dish with red sauce. Nikki guessed Drew's hesitation in ordering was a reaction to the prices, but she convinced her to pay no attention to them. A deal was a deal. She'd let Drew pay for a few things today, which meant the rest of the weekend was her treat. It was worth it when Drew couldn't stop raving about the food and the vintage white wine Nikki had chosen.

If that weren't enough, the concert was perfection. Drew seemed spellbound by the sights and unmatched sound quality of Stern Auditorium. During the second movement, appropriately entitled "Romanze," Drew's eyes closed as if the delicate piano melody was flowing through her veins and filling her with peace. She was angelic. Nikki gently took Drew's hand, prompting a contented sigh and sweet upward twitch of Drew's lips.

Nikki lost the ability to breathe. Everything shifted. Every defining "before and after" moment in her life and every significant event that was burned in her memory galloped through her inner vision. The day she acknowledged she was a lesbian. The first time she kissed a girl. The 9/11 terrorist attacks. The day she signed Passion Play's recording contract. The night she crossed the line with Jaymi. And now…*the day I knew I was in love with Drew.* As sure as she'd been able to visualize her musical dreams coming true, she could now picture Drew in every dream she wanted to come true from this point on.

The movement ended, and Drew met her gaze. "How did you know?" Drew said softly.

"Know what?"

"How'd you know that's my favorite piece of music ever written?"

"I didn't. I remembered how much you enjoyed it when we watched *Amadeus*. It's played at the end when they roll the credits, right?"

Drew kissed her cheek. "You are beyond sweet."

They quieted as the third movement began. Nikki was swept up in the music and Drew's beautiful face, but her new mission in life challenged her focus. She wanted nothing more than to spend her remaining days making Drew happy.

And nothing was going to stop her.

After perusing the gift shop for souvenirs, they walked to Times Square. She happily tagged along as Drew marveled at the neon signs and flashing lights and led her into shops that captured her interest. They popped into a café and warmed themselves with piping hot chocolate.

It was after one when they finally got back to their room. Drew's cheeks were pink from the cold as she hung their overcoats in the closet.

She slinked her arms around Nikki's waist. "That was the most fun I've ever had in my whole life."

Nikki felt her smile reach her ears. "Yeah? Which part?"

"All of it."

"So…I did a good thing bringing you here?"

"Yes. Nikki, thank you so much. I had such a blast. The symphony alone would have been more than enough. But dinner and Times Square, too? And this outfit! I don't think I've ever worn anything so fancy before. I don't know how I'll ever thank you."

Nikki cupped Drew's face in her hands. Drew's eyes darkened. "Kiss me, and we'll be even."

She closed the gap and lost herself in Drew's lips. *Your happiness is all the thanks I need.*

❖

Skip the bubble bath tonight. She was taking Nikki straight to bed. Their cheeks were chilled, but Nikki's full lips were hot against hers. They'd kissed many times by now, but there was something different this time. Despite the long day and late hour, she lost all sense of time. She wanted to savor every minute of this glorious night. Nikki seemed to be in no hurry, either.

She reluctantly pried her lips away. "Nikki."

Nikki didn't stop. She just kissed her elsewhere. Her face. Her jawline.

"Baby."

Her neck.

"Oh, God. Baby, I don't want to sleep standing up."

Nikki traced the shell of her ear with her tongue. "Who said anything about sleeping?"

The warm breath sent shivers straight through to her pulsing center. "Then take me to bed and make love to me."

Nikki kissed her lips. "You're reading my mind again."

Drew sat on the bed, and Nikki kissed her again, pushing the blazer off her shoulders. She worked two buttons open on her shirt and kissed her bare shoulder. She unbuttoned two more and placed kisses along her collarbone.

Drew closed her eyes and dropped her head back, reveling in the torturously slow process. Nikki took care of the last button. She waited for her to remove the shirt, but Nikki surprised her by unbuttoning her pants instead. Nikki knelt and kissed her stomach as her hands reached behind her and unhooked her bra. Her kisses traveled downward to just above the waistband of her underwear. She teased one finger along the edge.

She combed her fingers through Nikki's hair, tempted to urge her head between her legs. Instead, she let the anticipation build for whatever Nikki had in store for her. All thoughts drifted from her consciousness, and her physical senses took over.

Nikki kept kissing her stomach as she removed Drew's shoes and socks. Drew caressed her back and shoulders and then braced her weight on her palms behind her. The throb between her legs grew stronger. Nikki came back up and placed a firm kiss on her lips. She slipped off Drew's shirt and then her bra. She scooted Drew back and straddled her before their lips connected again.

"Take off my shirt." Nikki's voice was hoarse with desire. She held Drew's gaze and removed her tie.

She took her time with the shirt, as Nikki had, and kissed her body as she did so. God, her skin was like silk. She brushed her hands across Nikki's abs, her back, and in a few easy moves, Nikki was topless. They came together again in a more urgent kiss, breasts pressed together and their centers growing hotter with building friction.

"Drew." Nikki's breath was ragged. "God, Drew, you're so beautiful. I want to show you how special you are to me, baby."

They finished undressing and got under the covers. Nikki lowered herself on top of her and gave her another round of kisses all over her lips, her face, and her neck. She was so achingly beautiful; Drew couldn't believe Nikki was with *her* when she could have any woman she wanted.

Nikki stroked her cheek with the backs of her fingers, triggering another response below. "I wanna get lost in you."

Nikki's dark eyes caressed her soul with a longing look that said this wasn't just sex to her. Before she could register what that meant, Nikki claimed her lips again and began an easy stroke between her legs. She lost interest in analyzing anything. Nikki moved to her breasts and alternated between nipples, licking and sucking and nibbling to her heart's content. At the same time, Nikki's fingers teased her into a need so fierce she couldn't think if she wanted to.

She arched into Nikki's movements, craving release yet never wanting it to end. "Baby, oh God, this feels so good."

Nikki kissed her. "I could make love to you all night, and I still wouldn't get enough of you."

Her heart pounded and swelled with emotion. Their connection was so intense, and she still wanted more. "Nikki. Come to me, baby. I want to taste you when I come."

"Oh God." Nikki exhaled deeply against her skin, sending another jolt through her system. Nikki swung her body around and lowered herself onto Drew's mouth.

Drew almost lost control when Nikki brought her lips against her. Nikki slowed her pace, giving her own body time to catch up to Drew's, until they matched each other's rhythms. Drew exploded seconds before Nikki. They fell apart, gasping for air and moaning in shared pleasure.

Moments later, Nikki wrapped her body into hers and kissed her gently. "I have never experienced anything more beautiful. Thank you for sharing yourself with me."

Her words touched Drew's heart. "What a beautiful thing to say."

"I mean it, Drew. This…what I feel for you when we're together like this…it's like nothing I've ever known."

Drew swallowed hard. Was Nikki falling in love with her? It was too soon for that, wasn't it? She'd heard of people falling fast. They'd discussed being in a relationship, but she needed to be careful to take things slowly now for exactly that reason. She needed to make sure this was right before throwing around the L-word.

Nikki was too wound up to sleep. As far as she could tell, Drew was dead to the world, totally oblivious to her inner war of words. Words that almost slipped out last night on more than one occasion. *I'm falling in love with you, Drew.* Did she even have to speak the words for Drew to know? Could Drew feel it when she touched her? When she kissed her? When she was making love to her?

Drew rolled over and hugged her from behind. A lock of Drew's hair and warm breath caressed her bare shoulder. She never wanted this night to end. She peeked at the clock. She needed to get to sleep. They had to check out by eleven, and then she planned to surprise Drew with a tour of the Met before they headed home. It was crazy to cram in so much in only two days, but she had no idea if and when they'd ever get this chance again.

Their lives were going to get busy again after the holidays, and they wouldn't have much time together. Drew might find that she couldn't handle it. She was used to a simple, routine life in one place. If Drew didn't feel the same way about her, she probably wouldn't stick around.

The last time she'd fallen in love, she'd waited too long to act on it, and she lost out to another woman. That was different. She'd known Jaymi for a few years, not a few weeks. She'd buried her feelings because of the band's "no dating each other" rule. There were no such rules with Drew.

She didn't like waiting to go after what she wanted. She wasn't a rock star by accident. Still, singing her heart out wasn't the same as putting it out on her sleeve to be stomped on. She might get her heart broken again. Or scare Drew off. Why couldn't she have as much courage in the love game as she did in the music business?

She needed advice. Maybe she'd call Randi next week. Right now, she needed to sleep. She brought Drew's hand to her lips and drifted off, too exhausted to think about it anymore.

CHAPTER THIRTY-FIVE

For the first time in a long time, Drew had no gumption to go to work. She was exhausted, but it was a good tired. She floated into DJ's with a newfound energy and sense of adventure. She buzzed around the store all morning, rearranging instruments, setting up new displays with Geena, talking her dad's ear off with ideas for boosting sales, and basking in the afterglow of everything she'd shared with Nikki in the last few days.

She caught herself fantasizing about playing with a symphony orchestra. She'd never had such lofty ambitions before. Maybe she'd allowed the anger toward her mother to squelch her dreams. Now it felt as if dreams were just waiting for her to reach out and grab them.

"My God, woman. You're on fire!" Geena said as they finished the last grouping of Black Friday package deals.

"You wouldn't believe the sound in that hall, Geena. It was inspiring."

"I'm talking about you and Nikki. You are so lucky."

"Hello?" She gently wrapped her knuckles on Geena's head. "Are you forgetting you have a girlfriend?"

"Of course not! I'm just saying, we all knew she was gorgeous and exciting, but who knew she was such a romantic?"

Drew sighed and smiled. "She has such a good heart, Geena. I don't think she shows that side of herself very often."

"Look at you, totally smitten." Geena waved her hand in front of Drew's face. "You're a goner, girlfriend."

"What? I am not."

Geena huffed. "Yeah, right. So much for casual. You're falling for her. You should see your face right now, all dreamy and smiley."

"Stop it!" Drew knew Geena was right.

Geena's mouth suddenly dropped open, and she began to laugh.

"What?"

"Who's dreamy and smiley?" It was Nikki's voice behind her.

Oh no. How much did she hear of their conversation?

Geena grinned. "We were just discussing the eighth and ninth dwarfs, Dreamy and Smiley. You know, the ones in the original draft of *Snow White*, before the editor cut them out."

"Ah. That's why we've never heard of them." Nikki winked at Geena and kissed Drew's cheek. "I'm ready when you are."

"Ready for what?"

"My cello lesson. It's Monday, remember? *And* I'm on time this week. Aren't you proud of me? I have to confess, I didn't have time to practice this weekend."

Geena discreetly slipped away, laughing under her breath. "I wonder why?"

"Get back to work, you slacker."

"I will if you will."

Nikki followed her to the lesson room and set up. "Dreamy and smiley, huh?"

"Shut up."

Nikki secured her cello in a stand and wrapped her arms around Drew's waist. "I've been feeling a bit dreamy and smiley myself. You know why?"

She suppressed a grin. "Why?"

Nikki kissed her, long and slow, pulling their bodies together. Drew's body temperature rose in an instant. "That's why. Well, that's one reason."

"You're trouble."

Nikki gave her a sly smile. "I know."

She cleared her throat and stepped away. "We should get started."

"I thought that's what I was doing."

"On your *lesson*."

"Right. I have so much to learn." Nikki peeled off her jacket, revealing a tight maroon sweater. Drew was hit with the memory of the beautiful body beneath it.

Considering she'd only had one lesson, Nikki played surprisingly well. She seemed to be a natural in all things musical. They wrapped up in just under an hour. "We have five minutes to spare."

Nikki looked at the wall clock and grinned. She pinned Drew

against the wall, and they locked lips. "I don't know how I'm going to get through the rest of the day without you." Before Drew could answer, Nikki kissed her again, hard, pressing her groin into her already starving center.

"I know what you mean."

"Come over after work? Please? I'll make dinner this time."

It was the first time Nikki had invited her to her place. She didn't want to make a habit of spending every night together, but she was curious to see where Nikki lived. "That sounds great. I'll have to go home first to feed the cats and spend a little time with them. They haven't forgiven me yet for going away for two days."

Nikki backed away. "I suppose I can last that long."

"Are you telling me you can't find something to occupy your time for a couple of hours?"

"Actually, I was thinking I'd go visit my friend, Randi."

"Randi? Oh right, your friend at the police department. And then dinner at your place?"

"Yes. I'll text you the address. I trust you won't sell it in a Black Friday deal with my phone number?"

"Ooh, what a great idea!" She cupped her hands around her mouth and announced, "On sale now: celebrity tours of the rich and famous!"

"Shh!" Nikki covered her mouth with her own.

She caught her breath. "You know just how to shut me up."

Nikki swung open the door. "There's plenty more where that came from, too, *Dreamy*."

"I hope so, *Smiley*."

"Let me know when you're on your way over so I can start getting dinner ready."

She walked her out and caught sight of Melissa at the counter chatting with Geena. Nikki greeted Melissa with a fist bump before she left.

Drew said, "Hey, Melissa. How are you today?"

Melissa cocked her chin and smiled. "Not as good as you, from what I hear."

"Geena, what did you tell her?"

"Nothing she hadn't already figured out on her own." Geena played a drum roll with her fingers on the counter and finished with a vocalized cymbal crash.

"Duh. It's obvious you guys are hot for each other." Melissa picked up her guitar case.

Geena reached across the counter and nudged Melissa in the arm. "You've got news of your own there, stud muffin."

Melissa's face reddened.

"What news?" Drew dipped her head to catch her eye. "Something good?"

Melissa smiled shyly. "Well…" She blushed even more. "I kinda have a girlfriend."

Drew filled with pride. Though she'd suspected Melissa was gay for years, the teen had just come out to her. "That's awesome." Melissa shrugged, and Drew hugged her. "Does your mom know?"

She nodded.

"And she's okay with it?"

"Yeah."

"You have the coolest mom."

"Yeah, I do."

They made their way to the lesson room. Drew closed the door and placed her hands on Melissa's shoulders. "I have never been more proud of you. It takes guts to come out to people."

"You're telling me. I was scared sh—sorry. I was really scared."

"I'm glad you felt safe to share that with me. And with Geena."

"Well, I knew you guys wouldn't care. You're gay, too." She pulled off her coat and tossed it on top of her guitar case. She sat down with her guitar and picked at the threads at the hole in the knee of her jeans. "But my mom…"

Drew sat across from her and waited while Melissa set her lesson book on the music stand and found the right page. "Coming out to the people who mean the most to you is always the hardest. We're both lucky to have parents that are okay with it."

"My girlfriend wasn't as lucky. Her parents didn't reject her or anything, but they're trying to convince her it's just a phase."

"They're in denial. It's common. Hopefully, in time, they'll see that she's the same person she's always been."

"That's what I told her."

Smart kid. "Besides, once they get to know you and see how awesome you are, they'll come around."

She blushed and gave another "aw, shucks" shrug before changing the subject by suggesting they get started on her lesson.

"Before we start, there are two things you need to know. One, as long as you're working here at DJ's, your lessons are on the house."

"Really? My lessons are free?"

"You bet. It's included in your employee discount."

"Sweet. Thanks! What's the other thing?"

"I want you to know that Geena and I are always here for you if you ever need someone to talk to about coming out or about anything else you're dealing with. And that goes for your girlfriend, too. Okay?"

Melissa nodded. "Okay." She beamed. "She's really cool. You'll like her. I'm wicked lucky."

"You both are. I can't wait to meet her."

Drew's earlier musings of performing professionally dissipated. She could never give up teaching. It was more than just bonding with students like Melissa on a personal level as well as musically. It was knowing that she was making a difference in people's lives.

That was the only motivation she needed.

CHAPTER THIRTY-SIX

Nikki's thoughts swirled between Jaymi's advice and hopes that her first turn as dinner host went off without a hitch. She'd stopped by Jaymi's and talked about her feelings for Drew since Randi was working a lot lately. The discussion had been easy and comfortable, and there was no question that anything romantic she'd felt for Jaymi was truly gone. It was a relief, and she found that she had a true friend to lean on, which was a massive bonus.

She didn't think she'd ever been so nervous in all her life. She lit two tapered ivory candles on the black dining table that fit the space perfectly but was larger than she'd ever needed. She adjusted the silverware again. She did a quick double-check of the vegetable steamer and the pot of boiling potatoes on the stove and snuck a peek at the steaks and the clock. Drew would be arriving any minute.

She rubbed her temples and willed her heart rate to slow down. She took a deep breath. It was only dinner. It wasn't their first date.

It was, however, the first time she'd ever cooked dinner for someone. She wanted to make an impression that Drew would never forget. Not only with a good meal but with making her feel welcome and at home.

Ironic. She barely felt at home here herself.

The doorbell rang. She slid across the hardwood floor in her sock feet and swung it open. "Hi!"

Drew broke into a smile and thrust a half dozen carnations out in front of her. "Hi yourself. These are for you."

Nikki melted. Drew brought her flowers. Simple. Romantic. Genuine. Not flowers thrown onstage from fans. Not flowers sent to her dressing room or hotel room in hopes of getting laid. Flowers because they were dating. Flowers because Drew liked her. Maybe even loved her—at least a little. She could only hope.

"Drew…" It was all she could get out.

"And I brought dessert, too." She held up a covered round tin. "Chocolate cream pie. I picked it up after work at that little bakery on Penhallow Street."

Nikki stepped between the bouquet and pie and kissed her fully on the lips. The sweet aroma of the carnations mixed with the scent of Drew's coconut shampoo summoned memories of their lovemaking in New York. She pulled her closer, and their bodies melded together. Drew's arm came around her waist, and she felt the flowers against her back. She smiled into the kiss because she knew Drew's attention was also on keeping the pie plate level.

Drew let out a breath and shook her head. "What a greeting."

"I couldn't wait another minute to kiss you." She gestured for the flowers. "Thank you for these. That was very sweet." She headed for the kitchen. "Come on in. I don't think I have a vase, but I'll find something to put those in."

"Nice place." Drew put the pie in the refrigerator without hesitation.

Did she already feel at home?

It wasn't just the oven raising the temperature in the room. Nikki watched Drew wander into the living room and wished she could read her mind. The lighting seemed to shift as if she were watching a sunrise. Drew's presence in her home breathed life into the walls, the air, and the furnishings. The vastness that used to feel cold and distant now moved inward like a blanket wrapping around her shoulders. Drew stopped at the baby grand piano. Its black finish, stark against the white walls, gleamed beneath her fingertips as she ran them reverently along the edge.

She looked at Nikki with a questioning look.

"Go ahead. Play something."

"Really?"

"It's not a decoration." She returned Drew's smile. "Why don't you serenade me while I tend to dinner?"

She turned and went back to the kitchen. The open concept lent its acoustics beautifully to the sounds that followed. As she plated their meals, time seemed to move in slow motion. She wasn't surprised that Drew's skills on the keys were no less impressive than they were on the other instruments she'd heard her play.

Drew could probably audition for anything she wanted and be a shoo-in. Shit, she bet she had what it took to teach at a college level, too. What was she doing here? Did this little New Hampshire town have any clue of the treasure in its midst? Was she really happy, or was she settling? And if she was settling, for what reason? Didn't she believe in herself? Was she afraid of failing? Of success? Or did she really have no idea how talented she was?

They sat down for dinner, and Nikki couldn't look away from the way the warm glow of the candlelight shimmered in Drew's eyes. She was stunning. In blue jeans and a simple hunter green button-up shirt, she was as beautiful as she'd been on the night they dressed up for the symphony.

They ate in relative silence, commenting on the meal, but otherwise, Nikki felt little need to fill the spaces with conversation. She was content to savor the uniqueness of the situation, and by the time they'd finished, Nikki realized she had barely taken her eyes off Drew.

"What?" Drew dipped her head, shyly.

"I…"

"What is it? Did I dribble gravy on my shirt or something?"

"Huh? Uh, no. You…" Drew had done the impossible. She'd rendered her speechless.

"You seem to be having a hard time finishing sentences tonight. Is it me?"

"Yes."

Drew frowned. She'd misunderstood.

Nikki took a long sip of wine. "You're in my house."

Drew covered her hand. "I know. You invited me, remember?" She smiled and looked around her. "You do live here, don't you?"

"Yes, of course." She turned her hand over and interlaced their fingers. *It never felt like home until…now.* It was too soon to say *that. Rein it in, Razer. You'll scare her off.* "I've never had anyone over for dinner before."

"Are you kidding me? All this space and the fancy appliances and furniture? I figured you must host dinner parties for all your famous friends on a regular basis." Drew finished her salad.

"The closest I've had to that is takeout pizza with Jaymi." She smiled wryly. "And she'll deny that she's famous, so I don't recommend bringing it up."

"What about you?"

"I don't see the point of denying it."

The smile left Drew's eyes.

Me and my big mouth. She swallowed and sipped her wine. "What I mean is, it's reality, and I have to accept that. It has its perks, but it also means I can't let my guard down a hundred percent. I hate that side of it."

Drew pulled a face and set down her utensils. Her hands dipped to the cloth napkin in her lap. "So, despite that, you'll take advantage of your fame when the opportunity arises?"

"Yes. Sometimes—"

"Unbelievable. All this time, I thought you were different."

She tried to suppress her ire but no dice. "Different than whom? Your mother? Based on what you've told me so far, I *am* different. Why do you always put a negative spin on fame? Do you think I would've had the same leverage to establish scholarships if I wasn't famous? Do you think I'd have the money to make the donations I make? I'm not just talking about those Thanksgiving dinners you saw me buy. You don't even know about other ways I've used my notoriety to help others." She stood and threw her napkin onto the table. "*Including* you and your store."

She crossed the room and stormed onto the balcony. The gust of wind that needled her flesh through the fabric of her sweater was no match for her burning tears. *Fuck it. No one will ever get me.* She braced her palms on the rail and hung her head. *I thought* Drew *was different, and she thinks* I'm *not.* She huffed out staccato breaths and watched each exhalation form a transient cloud in the air.

She barely felt Drew's hand on her shoulder.

Drew's other hand reached around and turned her head. "I'm sorry. Nikki, I'm so sorry."

"Sorry for what?" Nikki backed away. "Forgetting that I'm a human being with real feelings? Well I've got news for you, sweetheart." She punched a fist to her heart twice. "This is real. It loves and beats and breaks just like everybody else's." She wiped her soaked cheek, and her arms fell limp at her sides.

Drew looked down, shoved her hands in her jeans pockets, and then clenched her arms against her sides as another biting wind blew snow off the rail and assaulted them. "I'm such an ass. You must think I'm as cold as this weather. God, Nikki, I promise you, that's not who I am."

Nikki hugged herself and caught Drew's eye. "I only wish you would see me for who *I* am, Drew. I can't change that I'm famous, and I won't apologize for it."

"You're right." Drew let out a long sigh and stepped toward her. She rubbed Nikki's arm. "Come on. Let's go inside before we look like the next round of snow sculptures."

Nikki slid open the glass door. "After you." Once inside, she ducked into the bathroom. She took a few minutes to freshen up, but the mirror revealed she still looked like shit. Her hair was spiked from wind instead of pomade, and her cheeks were crimson. She grabbed a blanket out of the linen closet and found Drew on the couch with her legs tucked beneath her. She looked small and helpless. It was impossible to stay angry when all she wanted to do was hold and protect her.

"I'm sorry, too." She draped the blanket over Drew. "Better?"

Drew nodded. "Thank you."

"Be right back." She cleared the table and stacked the dishes on the counter. Cleaning up could wait. A few minutes later, she carried two steaming mugs of hot cocoa into the living room.

"You read my mind." Drew curled her hands around the cup. She blew on it and carefully took a sip.

Nikki tucked herself in beside her beneath the blanket. It was toasty from Drew's body heat. If she weren't so wound up, she could easily nod off.

"When I was seven or eight, my mother was up for a part as a single mom," Drew said. "At that age, I didn't know much about the roles she usually got, but I knew this one was different." She took a drink. "You wanna know why?"

"Why?"

"Because all of a sudden, she started taking me with her everywhere she went. It was the happiest I'd ever felt. She took me to the zoo. She took me to Disneyland. She made a big deal of going out for ice cream or to McDonald's for a Happy Meal. I remember people kept taking pictures of us no matter what we were doing or where we were. She showed me off and bragged about how beautiful and talented I was and that I was the light of her life." Drew's smile faded, as did the light in her eyes.

They sipped their drinks, and she waited for Drew to continue.

"I'll never forget the day she got the news that she didn't get the part. It was as if someone had flipped a switch. Just like that, our 'special time' ended. She never came right out and said so, but she made me feel as though it was my fault. I was crushed. It was all for show. She was just getting ready for a role, one she didn't want in real life."

"Oh, Drew." She took Drew's cup from her and set it on the coffee table with her own. "She never should have done that to you. Using you to further her career…I can't imagine how painful that must have been for you."

"Do you see why I snap the way I do? It's like an emotional reflex—things are out of my mouth before I can stop myself. Then I hate myself for it because I'm taking it out on other people. I don't mean to, Nikki. Honestly, I don't." She began crying.

Nikki put an arm around Drew's shoulder and pulled them together. "I know you don't. I guess we're alike in that way. My temper gets the best of me and my filter goes—" She made a Frisbee-toss gesture with her hand and whistled. "Right out the window."

Drew snuggled her head between Nikki's chin and collarbone. "When you're hurt, it can be hard to control your feelings."

"Yeah." She played with Drew's hair. "Maybe that's what we're doing wrong. We need to let our feelings out rather than hold in our pain."

"It helps to have someone to share them with." Drew pulled back and held her gaze. "I've never told anyone about that before."

Her eyes shone, and Nikki swiped a thumb beneath each one before cupping her jaw. Nikki touched her lips to hers, tasting the salt from their shared tears. "I'm glad you told me." She kissed her again, softly and then lifted her chin. "You can tell me anything, okay? I want you to know that. I want you to feel safe with me."

"I can't believe you'd feel that way after the way I've treated you. I keep passing judgment on you, and still, you forgive me."

"I see a lot of myself in you. I can relate to that bitterness because of my dad." She took Drew's hand in her own. "You think she'll ever come around?"

"It'd be a miracle if she did. Everything was always all about her. 'Does my hair look all right? Is my makeup okay? How does this dress look on me? Do I look thin enough? Should I get a nose job?' She never paid any attention to what I was wearing—unless I was going to be seen in public with her, which was almost never.

"When I came out to her, she was okay with it. She'd figured it out before I did. She said, 'Oh, darling, everyone's gay in this town. Don't sweat it.' She acted like it was no big deal. Well, maybe it wasn't a big deal for her, but I'd just done the most terrifying thing I'd ever had to do. Maybe it was old news for a Hollywood celebrity to come out of the closet, but middle school is a whole different world. Don't get me wrong—I was relieved she and Dad didn't reject me, but I was terrified when it came to my peers. I thought telling her first might make it easier to tell other people. I wanted her emotional support. I wanted her advice. Instead of acknowledging the magnitude of what I'd just done, within minutes she was saying, 'Well, that explains why you never wanted to play dress-up with me or had any fashion sense whatsoever.' And just like that, she had something else to do or somewhere to go."

Nikki squeezed Drew's hand. "I had the opposite problem. My father was afraid my being gay would cost him votes. My mom didn't reject me outright, but she pressured me to hide who I was for my father's sake." She stroked Drew's thigh and toyed with the hem of Drew's shirttail. "This might sound twisted, but your mother makes me feel better about myself. I guess I'm not as self-absorbed and obsessed with my career as I thought I was."

She chuckled lightly, and Drew did the same.

"We're both lucky we're not more screwed up than we are."

Nikki leaned back and cocked an eyebrow. "Speak for yourself, McNally."

Drew laughed. "Shut up. You know it's true. For the record, I don't think you're self-absorbed. Vain, maybe, and a bit overconfident at times, but from what I've seen, you're quite the opposite of self-absorbed."

"You think so?"

Drew's eyes twinkled as her lips twitched upward. She kissed Nikki's cheek. "I know so."

"Thank you for saying that. It always feels like people only look at the outside. I guess I'm so used to it that I assume I have to play the part to keep everyone happy."

"Says the child of a politician." Drew tapped Nikki on the nose. "It's no surprise you'd feel that way. You don't have to do that with me. I like you better when you're like this. Warm. Open. Caring."

Nikki could actually feel herself blush. "I don't think there are many people who would describe me that way."

Drew furrowed her brow. "Then they don't know the real you. You run to Jaymi's rescue when she's upset. You support your bandmates. You drop everything to put gas in Melissa's car. And you offer me advice on my mom."

She shrugged. "Yeah. So?"

"You're always there for people you care about, aren't you?"

"I don't know about *always*, but I try."

"So, who's there for you, Nikki?"

She rested her cheek on the top of Drew's head. She loved the silky feel of Drew's hair. "My parents gave me everything I needed to succeed, but when it comes to my emotional well-being, the band is my extended family. They're the ones who keep me going."

"You've already told me about all that." Drew traced a light pattern with her fingertip on Nikki's stomach. "What I want to know is, who sees you cry? Who do you open up to when you're upset or need a friend to talk to?"

"Jaymi, most of the time. Or Randi. They're my closest friends."

Drew pushed herself up and looked at her. "I met Randi today."

"You did?"

"She came by the store to introduce herself, and she offered to escort us to the bank." Drew studied her for a second. "I thought you were going to visit her?"

Shit. Did Drew think she'd lied to her? How would she feel about her seeing Jaymi instead? *Stupid guilty conscience. That's all this is.* It wasn't as though Drew would have a reason to distrust her. *Calm down and just tell her the truth.*

"Yeah, I planned to, but she was working. I hung out with Jaymi instead."

"Oh." Drew settled back onto her shoulder and resumed her finger doodles on her belly. If not for the tension she sensed, she'd be getting aroused by the touch. "So, how'd you and Randi meet?"

Fuck. She let out a long breath. How could she possibly answer that question without making both herself and Randi look bad?

"Did you used to date her?"

"Ay-ay-ay, Drew. Are you sure you want to know?"

"Is it really that bad? Is she one of the fans that you slept with?"

"No. I mean, yes, she's a fan now. We met before anyone knew who Passion Play was."

Drew's body stiffened. "So…I'm confused. Did you sleep with her or not?"

What would Drew think of her if she knew the truth? After looking like a saint compared to Drew's mother a few minutes ago, now she was going to come off as a total whore. On the flip side, it felt good to think that Drew might be a wee bit jealous.

"Nikki? Oh God, you're not involved with her, are you?"

She is *jealous*. "No. Not anymore."

"Oh." Drew pulled her knees into her chest and hugged herself. "So, she's an ex."

"No, she's not an ex but…shit, Drew. If you must know, yes, we've slept together. More than once. Randi's a good friend, to both me and Shawn. I don't want you to think badly of her. She's got a heart of gold, and she's very happily in a relationship with a wonderful woman now."

"And how many other 'friends' have you slept with, Nikki?"

"Nobody! Geez, Drew, if I didn't know any better, I'd think you were jealous." She nudged her and flashed her a big smile. She didn't want to fight again.

Drew pursed her lips. "I am *not* jealous."

"You are, too!" She tickled Drew's stomach.

Drew shrieked and wiggled away, but she was already wedged up against the end of the sofa and couldn't get far.

Nikki persisted despite Drew's attempts to push her away. "Admit it!"

She gasped.

"And now you're turning green!"

"That's because you're making me nauseous, you jerk! Stop tickling me!"

"You are such a liar." She eased off. She pulled off the blanket and let it drop to the floor.

Drew pounced toward her. Surprised, Nikki slid off the couch on her butt, taking Drew with her.

"Ow!" said Nikki.

"Hey, I'm not that heavy."

"No, but the floor is hard. At least you had me to cushion your landing."

Drew straddled her lap and hooked her hands behind Nikki's neck. "How gracious of you."

Nikki grinned and waggled her eyebrows. "There is a fee, however."

Drew leaned closer. "I don't have any money." She shifted her body and their centers met. "Will you take other forms of payment?"

"I can think of several."

"Such as?" Drew's lip quirked upward.

"Admit you're jealous first. Then we'll negotiate." She ground into her.

Drew's breath hitched. "Oh. No fair."

She slid one arm around Drew's waist and pulled them together. "Admit it." She moved her hand higher beneath Drew's shirt. She caressed the soft skin along Drew's side and teased a finger beneath the bottom band of her bra.

Drew dropped her head onto Nikki's shoulder. "You're such a jerk," she whispered.

She nuzzled Drew's ear. "Ready to confess yet?" She ran her tongue along the lobe and exhaled.

"No." Drew shivered.

She ran her fingers across Drew's breast and circled the hard nipple. "Now?"

"Oh God." Drew moaned. "Yes."

"Yes, you like what I'm doing, or yes, you're jealous?"

Drew sandwiched her face between her hands. "Yes, I love what you're doing, and yes, I'm jealous. You win, all right?" She caught Nikki's lips in a hard, demanding kiss.

Nikki started to lie back, but rather than join her, Drew backed away, stood, and pulled Nikki into her arms, locking them into another scorching kiss. "Now take me to bed and give all those other women reasons to be jealous of *me*."

CHAPTER THIRTY-SEVEN

Drew took Nikki's hand and chased her up the carpeted stairs. Nikki stopped on the landing halfway up and crushed her mouth to hers. They fell against the wall, hands grabbing at clothing, gasping for breath between kisses. Nikki started backward up the next flight, their lips still locked as she fingered the button of Drew's jeans. As turned on as she was, Drew knew that if they continued disrobing here, her two left feet might send them tumbling to the bottom—and to the emergency room.

Drew pried herself away. "To bed, baby. Please."

Nikki gave her an understanding look. Without a word, she led her to the bedroom. More light-colored walls, scantily decorated, and a king-sized bed with a black and burgundy comforter awaited them. Drew didn't bother taking in the rest of her surroundings. That could wait. She removed what clothing remained on her body as Nikki did the same. Nikki yanked down the covers, and they fell into each other.

She kissed Nikki with a hunger she'd never felt before. She wanted her so badly it scared her. She knew she was falling hard for her. Fame or no fame, she wanted her as much as she wanted to breathe. She kissed her way down Nikki's neck. An hour ago, they were freezing on the deck. Now the heat between them was undeniable. She tasted the salty sheen of sweat on Nikki's collarbone and then sucked in her nipple, already hard and ready for her.

Nikki moaned and moved beneath her. "Drew…oh baby…touch me. Please, touch me." She squeezed Drew's breast and pinched her taut nub, nearly making her scream in pleasure. "I need…fuck, Drew, please. I want you inside me."

She slid two fingers within her. Nikki raised her hips to meet her, and they rocked and moved as one. She grew acutely aware of every sound Nikki made, to every movement and response to her touches, and she soaked it all in as if each fulfilled sense had come together in a perfectly composed symphony. Nikki closed around her and cried out. She continued light strokes as she rode out the waves and then became still.

Nikki caressed her back. "Drew. Come up here and let me hold you, but…stay inside me. I need you, baby. I need this connection."

She had no intention of withdrawing. She kissed Nikki's stomach, between her breasts, her neck, and then tenderly touched her lips to hers. "Me too." She looked into Nikki's eyes. The vulnerability and love she saw in them took her breath away. She wondered if her own eyes were as revealing.

Did she dare admit how strong her feelings were? She nestled into Nikki's shoulder. Nikki's arms came around her, emanating warmth that was both physical and emotional. She wanted to stay there forever.

Forever? For real? Could Nikki be feeling the same way?

"I feel so close to you right now it scares me," Nikki whispered.

Drew kissed her. "I feel it, too."

She wanted her again. She captured Nikki's lips and removed her hand from Nikki's warmth. Nikki whimpered in protest. Drew continued kissing her, savoring the combined sweetness of Nikki's lips and tongue. She hovered over her for a moment and then slowly grazed her breasts across Nikki's several times. Nikki's skin was as soft as the silk sheets beneath them. Their combined wetness sent tingles through her veins. She sat back on her heels and ground into her, arching back, reveling in the feel of her own hair tickling her back, amazed that she could ever feel this free and unbridled while making love.

"Oh, Drew, baby, you're gonna make me come again."

She increased her tempo and pressed harder with each thrust. They crested within seconds of each other and screamed in unison as they went over the edge together. She collapsed into Nikki's arms, writhing and shaking as the high slowly subsided.

They fell silent. She wrapped herself into the length of Nikki's beautiful body, their limbs entangled and misty. She was still throbbing with desire. She wanted her again. God, how could she still be this aroused? It had been years since she'd been with another woman, but she'd never wanted anyone so much in her life.

"How about dessert?" Nikki asked.

She wanted dessert, all right. And it came in the form of Nikki's wet—

"I want some pie." Nikki propped up on one elbow. She gave Drew a mischievous smile and ran her tongue along her jawline. "And I want to eat it off your body."

Holy shit. "That's the sexiest thing anyone's ever said to me."

Nikki walked out of the room in all her glorious nakedness. Drew's clit pulsed in anticipation. She closed her eyes and lay spread-eagle on the crimson sheet. She heard Nikki come back in, but she remained as she was.

"Perfect. You're perfect, Drew. God you're beautiful."

Drew smiled and opened her eyes when she felt Nikki's weight beside her. "You're the one who's beautiful. I could drink in the sight of you all night and never get enough."

"And you, baby, are delicious." She held up the pie and scooped a generous dollop of whipped cream onto her finger. She smeared it onto each of Drew's nipples, which responded immediately to the cold. "And I'm going to devour you." She flicked at the cream with her tongue, varying the length and pressure of the strokes in between swallows until it was gone. She then sucked in the nipple and massaged it with a sensuous kiss before repeating the process on the other side.

The sensations were beyond anything Drew had experienced before. They were soon taking turns as they took full advantage of the spacious bed to play and touch and taste. She lapped a line of chocolate down Nikki's stomach and stopped at her neatly trimmed mound.

"Don't stop, baby. Take me, all of me, and I want you at the same time."

Drew swung one leg over her body and took Nikki into her mouth. Her knees almost buckled when Nikki pulled her down by the hips. Nikki spread her tongue over her aching labia and worked her lips, sending her into such oblivion that she nearly stopped her own lavishing of Nikki's soft folds.

In a matter of minutes, she came so hard she almost stopped breathing. She moaned loudly, exhaling heavily, wanting desperately to send Nikki over the edge. She slipped a finger inside her and stroked frantically. Nikki released a deep, guttural scream. Drew pulled the covers over them as she kissed a trail to Nikki's face.

"Nikki, baby. That was…"

"I think the term you're looking for is un-fucking-believable."

She smiled into Nikki's hair. "You have such a way with words." She kissed her. "But I have to agree."

"From now on, when we go out to eat, we're ordering dessert to go."

"I like the way you think."

"I like the way I think, too." Nikki lightly ran her fingers down Drew's arm and then kissed her sweetly.

"I like the way you do…everything."

She slid her hand around Drew's waist, drawing their hips together. "Oh yeah?"

She kissed her long and slow. "You know what I like the most?" She stroked Nikki's cheek and looked her in the eye.

"Tell me."

"I like the way you make me feel." She took Nikki's hand and held it to her heart. "Here."

Nikki stared at her, her expression unreadable. What was she thinking? Did she feel the same way?

She wanted to tell Nikki she was falling for her. That it was more than a physical connection they were sharing. That if she had the guts to completely let go, she could see them together, in a real relationship, in it for the long haul. Forever.

"Me too," Nikki said. "Listen, Drew. I'm no saint, and you know that. I know you have your doubts about me. Hell, I have my doubts about me." She moved their joined hands to her own heart. "But you make me want to be a better person. You inspire me, Drew. I admire you so much. You're a remarkable woman—"

"Geez, Nikki, come on. I'm just a small-town music teacher who can barely afford to take you out to dinner. What is it you see in me?" Her eyes stung with threatening tears. Who was she kidding? There was no way she could hold Nikki's interest forever.

Nikki lifted her chin. "The fact that you have no idea how special you are is exactly one of the things that *makes* you special. Don't you get it? I don't give a shit about how much money you have or what you do for a living. You make a difference in the lives of those who know you. I see the joy in your father's face whenever you're around. I see the way Melissa looks up to you. I can tell Geena thinks the world of you, too. And Christ, where else can someone go around here to take cello lessons? Or any other orchestral instrument? This community needs you." Nikki kissed her tenderly. "I need you." She kissed her again. "I can't talk to anyone else the way I talk to you. I can't explain it. I can let my guard down with you and still feel…safe."

She pulled Nikki closer. Her heart pummeled her chest. Its rhythm sounded in her ears like a mantra. *She loves me. She loves me. She loves me.*

And I love her, too.

Chapter Thirty-Eight

Nikki kissed her mother's cheek as she stepped inside. She was giddy and miserable. If she'd known things would end up going so well with Drew, she would've made plans to spend Thanksgiving dinner with her and Jerry. She smiled. At least they'd be having dessert together later. *Dessert has a whole new meaning now.*

"Nikki, darling, your cheeks are redder than Rudolph's nose. Did you drive here with the top down?"

"Of course not, Mom. It's a hard top, not a convertible."

Her father puffed on his pipe. He looked out the window. "With the money you're making, you should've invested in a Lincoln Navigator or a Land Rover if you wanted an SUV."

Nothing's ever good enough, for you, is it? "I happen to love that Jeep. Besides, I have better things to do with my money."

She followed them into the kitchen. Her mother was prepping the feast, most of which she'd had delivered from a local five-star restaurant. She was still slim and shapely in her beige dress slacks and white silk blouse beneath a rose-colored cashmere sweater. Her sleek straight hair was almost as dark as Nikki's, thanks to professional coloring to hide the gray.

"I hope you took my advice on those investments I told you about. Did you meet with Floyd?" He snuffed out his pipe—her mother forbade him to smoke in the kitchen or dining room.

"I have my own financial advisor, Dad. Don't worry. I'm doing okay."

He harrumphed and began carving the bird with an electric knife.

The three of them worked together in silence to put the food on the table and sat down. They filled their plates, quiet as they buttered and salted, poured gravy, and sliced turkey.

She took her first bite and waited for the other shoe to drop.

"You should be doing better than just okay."

And there it was. "Dad, don't start. I'm doing very well. I'm successful. I'm happy. What more do you want from me?"

He stared at her for a moment. Nikki knew he was struggling to let it go. She hoped to God he would. He went back to eating, and she did the same.

"I've been thinking."

Here we go.

"Now that you've made a name for yourself with this rock group, maybe it's a good time for you to capitalize on it and make an opera album. You know, show 'em you're not just a flash-in-the-pan pop star."

"Are you serious? Opera?"

Her mother purposely concentrated on her food, caught in the middle again without showing any inclination to stand up for her daughter.

"Sure. Why not?" He set down his knife and put a hand on her forearm. "You are a classically trained musician, sweetheart. You've made your point. Now, don't you think it's time you grew up and started earning a real return on our investment? Pop groups these days are a dime a dozen. Opera, on the other hand…"

"*Our* investment? What about my investment? *I* put the work and practice into my career, not you. And flash in the pan? Is that all you think of my band?"

"Come on, you know as well as I do that the rock music scene is no more than an excuse to extend adolescence. You'll be thirty next year. You can't keep living like a teenager. With your training, opera is a much more respectable career path." He gestured at her arm with his fork. "Of course, if you perform live, you'll have to wear something that'll cover up those tattoos. No one's going to take you seriously with that nonsense."

"You're unbelievable." How many insults was she supposed to take?

"I want the best for you, Nikki. Why can't you understand that?"

"I do understand it, but that doesn't mean you get to control my life. I'm your goddamn daughter, not a business deal."

"Nikki, language, please!"

Sure. *Now* her mother had something to say.

"Why can't you be happy for me? Why can't you be proud of me?"

"Why can't you be grateful for the opportunities I provided for you?"

"I am grateful, Dad. Every day. And guess what? I'm not just saying that because it's Thanksgiving. I was just telling my girlfriend that the other day—"

"Girlfriend?"

Her mother lit up, but Nikki knew she was jumping at the chance to change the subject.

"Why didn't you tell us you have a girlfriend?"

"So he can spout off his disapproval of that aspect of my life, too?" She stood and threw her linen napkin onto the table. "No thanks." She turned to leave.

"Honey, don't go." Her mother touched her arm. "Not like this. At least stay for some pie."

"Let her go." Her father scooped a generous bite of mashed potatoes onto his fork. "She's only proving my point—acting like a spoiled teenager instead of engaging in an adult conversation." He shoved the food into his mouth. "I thought we could have a mature discussion, but—"

"Telling me what to do without giving a shit about what I want or what I have to say is *not* a discussion." Nikki took a step toward him. "Nothing I do is ever going to be good enough for you anyway, so what's the point?"

Her mother followed her frantically to the door. "Nikki. Honey, don't leave like this. He doesn't mean any harm. He's just trying to help."

"He's insulting me and trying to run my life. As usual."

Her mother smiled. "He doesn't want you to rest on your laurels, that's all. And you won't. I know you. You love a challenge. Whether you admit it or not, you two are alike in that way."

"I don't want to be his challenge. I just want to be his daughter." She hugged her mother. "Thank you for dinner, Mom."

She headed down the walkway toward her Jeep—the vehicle she was so proud to buy—and sped away from the estate. She swiped the tears from her cheeks.

She'd had high hopes of enjoying a peaceful holiday and telling her parents all about Drew. *I called her my girlfriend.* Was Drew her girlfriend? Hell, she was the closest thing she'd had to a girlfriend since high school. She was sure Drew's dinner was going better than hers. Maybe Jerry could give her father lessons in parenthood.

She downshifted as she looped around the on-ramp. The roads were clear, but she waited until she hit the straightaway on the highway before she opened the throttle. She was ready for pie now. At Drew's place.

❖

"Hey, you're earlier than I expected." Drew closed the door behind Nikki.

Nikki engulfed her in a bear hug. "God, I missed you."

"It's only been two days." Nikki's parka muffled Drew's voice.

Nikki held her fiercely.

"Are you okay?"

"I'm fabulous!" Nikki loosened her grip and kissed her urgently. Something was off. Nikki seemed far from fabulous. Despite her efforts to avoid eye contact, Nikki couldn't hide the red rims around her eyes.

Fret wound herself between their legs and mewed. Nikki shoved a bottle of wine into Drew's hand, then scooped up Fret and covered her face with kisses. "I love this little furball!" Fret stiff-armed her in the cheek. "Where are the other two munchkins?" She put Fret on the floor and looked around.

"We saved you some pie, Nikki."

"Jerry!" Nikki opened her arms and bounced across the room. "You handsome devil, you. Gimme a hug!" She wrapped herself around him before he could answer.

Either her visit with her parents hadn't gone well, or she'd had a few too many glasses of wine with dinner. If that were the case, she shouldn't have driven here. Nikki let her dad go and crouched next to Andres's bed. She petted him and cooed over his high-decibel purrs. Vinnie scampered into the bedroom, wary of becoming Nikki's next victim of overzealous affection.

Drew exchanged a look with her dad, who also looked concerned.

"Maybe I'd better go," he said quietly as he lifted his coat from the back of a chair.

Nikki sprung to her feet. "You can't leave! I just got here. It's family time. Drew, pour the wine. Let's have a toast for all we're thankful for, shall we?"

Drew placed her hand on Nikki's shoulder. "Are you sure you haven't done enough toasting already today?"

Nikki's smile faltered. "You think I'm drunk?"

"You are acting a bit…odd."

"What're you talking about? I'm just full of holiday cheer. At least I am *now*. I can assure you, there was nothing worth toasting where I just came from."

"Oh, Nikki."

"Hey. No pity parties allowed. Jerry, don't you dare go anywhere. I need to be around you two. Maybe I'll take notes. See if I can teach my dear ol' dad a thing or two about what real fatherhood means, huh?"

"Nikki—"

"Let me ask you, Jerry, are you proud of Drew? Do you tell her how amazing she is at her job? Or do you tell her that what she's doing with her life isn't good enough for you every chance you get?" Nikki's voice faded, and her arms drooped to her sides as if the air had been let out of her.

Drew stood helplessly.

Nikki looked up at her dad as her tears spilled over. "Do you hug her and tell her you love her?"

She stepped toward Nikki, but her dad beat her to it. He enveloped Nikki and motioned for Drew to join them. Nikki was probably embarrassed by her outburst, and maybe even more so by the group hug, but it didn't matter now. They were giving her what she needed, whether she was too proud to admit it or not.

"Pride is a terrible thing if you let it get in the way of what's really important." Her dad's soft baritone always soothed her, and she hoped it had the same effect on Nikki now.

"Some men aren't so good at expressing their feelings." He stepped back and held Nikki at arm's length. "It doesn't mean he doesn't love you, kiddo. Which I'm sure he does."

Nikki backed off and turned away. She wiped her face. "I'm sorry." Her voice sounded little in the small space. "I've spoiled your day."

Drew put an arm around her. "No, you haven't. Besides, what's a holiday without a little family drama?" She gave her shoulder two quick tugs. "Come on. I know how much you love dessert." She discreetly gave Nikki a sly smile.

To her delight, Nikki blushed and then smiled.

"No fair," Nikki whispered.

"You can pay me back later."

Nikki glanced Jerry's way. Seemingly satisfied that he was out of earshot, she replied, "Don't think I won't."

She smiled. She added something else to her list of things she was thankful for—that extra can of whipped cream she'd put in the shopping carriage two days ago.

"So, what'll it be, Doodlebug?" Her dad snapped them out of their private moment. "Pumpkin or chocolate cream?"

They burst out laughing and answered in unison. "Pumpkin."

"We'll save the chocolate cream for later," Drew added.

"Doodlebug?" Nikki asked.

"He's called me that since I was a kid."

Jerry cut the pie and distributed three slices onto plates. "Haven't you noticed Drew's habit of doodling all over everything?"

"You know, now that you've mentioned it, I did notice an assortment of drawings on the desk calendar in her office."

No sooner had they sat down to eat than Fret showed up at their feet again, hoping for a bite. She sat up and stretched out her neck so that her chin was level with the table. She poked a paw into Drew's thigh. She gave the kitty a stern look and told her to be good.

"Thank you, Dad, for sharing my dirty little secret."

"What, that you have artistic talent, too? It's hardly a secret." He chugged a glass of milk. "I'm sure if you hadn't decided on music, you'd have become an artist of some sort."

"I have noticed her affinity for fine arts." Nikki smiled at them both.

She'd finally relaxed outwardly, although Drew was sure she was still shaken over whatever had transpired with her family earlier.

He proceeded to indulge Nikki's requests for more dirt on her childhood antics, which could have been embarrassing had they not all ended up laughing their butts off. Her father really knew how to put an entertaining spin on otherwise boring anecdotes. Her own memories of such events were less pleasant, but she was grateful for their character-building lessons.

They finished cleaning up, and Nikki easily persuaded Jerry to put on some music and dance with the two of them. It was silly and spontaneous and more fun than Drew could ever remember having on a holiday. Drew's phone rang. She answered blindly.

"Oh! You answered! I expected I'd get your voice mail."

"Mom?"

"Don't act so surprised, doll. I'm just calling to wish you Happy Thanksgiving."

"You don't even call me on my birthday most years. Why wouldn't I be surprised to hear from you today?"

The music filling her apartment seemed to exaggerate the eerie silence on the other end of the line. Was her mother alone? It was hard to feel sorry for her. This was the life she'd chosen. Career above family, with no grasp on how to balance the two. She looked at Nikki, who seemed to have less trouble in that department—at least when it came to her chosen family.

"Well. You know how hectic my schedule can be. I'm at the producer's mercy sometimes. You know that. And it's not like you ever go out anywhere, so I knew I'd likely catch you alone so we can talk."

She simmered at the assumption—even though the odds were likely it would be accurate. *Not this year.* Her father spun Nikki around and dipped her. Nikki giggled.

"Turn the TV down, dear. I can hardly hear you."

"It's not the TV."

"Oh. Don't tell me you're actually out at a party? Well, now I'm the one who's surprised."

Thanks for the vote of confidence, Mother. "Actually, I'm at home, but I have company."

"Really? Who?"

"Dad and…and a woman I'm seeing."

She grunted. "I should've known you'd be with your father."

Drew ignored the usual dig.

"Did you say you're seeing someone? I hope it's not that girl from college."

"Of course not, Mom. That was ages ago."

"Well, it's not like you keep me up to date on your life. What's her name? What does she do?"

How would her mother feel about her dating a rock star? Then again, she might not even know who Nikki was. They didn't exactly run in the same circles.

"Her name is Nikki. She's a singer."

"Oh, Drew. Not another coffeehouse wannabe. When are you going to raise your standards? I swear, you're just like your father."

Thank God for that. "She happens to be a member of a very successful rock band. And what's wrong with me being like my father? He's a wonderful—"

"Which band?"

"She's the lead singer of Passion Play."

Her mother let out a small gasp. "Nikki Razer? You're dating Nikki Razer? Oh, this is big. This is really big. She could be your ticket, baby! You can finally get out of that dead-end job at your father's. Have you talked to her about career possibilities? She could probably get you in with one of the major labels as a producer or—"

"Are you serious? That's what you care about? How she can further my career?"

A hand fell softly on her shoulder. "Talking to your mother, I presume?"

"How'd you guess?"

"Is that your father? Put him on. Maybe I can convince him to talk some sense into you."

She saw Nikki in the shadows of the living room, thumbing through albums, probably trying to respect her privacy and not overhear her end of the conversation. Without the music playing, it would be hard to do.

Her dad chuckled and spoke in the direction of her cell. "Maggie, we both know she's got more sense than the two of us put together and then some. Leave her alone." He winked and said under his breath, "Good thing we already ate."

Yes. Good thing because her appetite would've been lost.

"Oh, you tell him to shush." Her mother wasn't budging. "Listen, I'll send you some money. You come back out here to LA, and I'll make some calls. Which label are they with? If we both put in a word for you—"

"Forget it, Mom! I'm happy where I am, doing what I do, and I am *not* going to use my girlfriend to get me a job as a music producer!"

If she'd had it in her, she would disconnect now, but she couldn't bring herself to hang up on her own mother.

"Fine." She heard a shuffling sound, as if she were changing positions on the sofa. "I was only trying to help, you know."

"I know."

"I have to say, I'm surprised you'd be with someone so famous. That doesn't sound like you at all."

"Yeah, well, it surprised me, too." She stole a glance at Nikki, who was now pondering the next music selection with her father. "But she's special."

"She'd have to be to win you over."

"What's that supposed to mean?"

"It's a compliment, dear. You're very choosy. I just hope she appreciates you and treats you well. You deserve it."

She smiled. It was probably the sweetest thing her mother had ever said to her. "She does. And thank you."

"Despite my shortfalls as a mother, I do love you, Drew. I hope you know that."

She hated that she questioned whether the sentiment was sincere or if her mother's acting skills had simply gotten better. Either way, she was touched that she'd said it. "You have a weird way of showing it sometimes, but I know you do. I love you, too, Mom."

They said their good-byes, and Nikki came to her side. "Did I hear what I thought I heard?"

Great. *Nikki thinks I want her to get me a job as a record producer.*

Nikki interlocked her fingers behind Drew's waist. "Did you just call me your girlfriend?" She grinned widely.

"That's my cue to leave." Her dad looked pointedly at Drew. "You get a good night's sleep. Big day tomorrow." He gave them each a kiss on the cheek and gathered the generous amount of leftovers she was sending home with him.

"So?" Nikki planted light kisses along her jawline. "Are you going to answer my question? Or do I have to kiss it out of you?"

"Yes."

"Yes, you called me your girlfriend? Or yes, I have to kiss it out of you?"

"Both."

"I was hoping you'd say that." Nikki smothered her face with kisses. "Now, before we do anything else, I'm going to take *my* girlfriend to bed and kiss every inch of her. If we need to vent about our nutty parents, it'll have to wait until after I've made you come at least twice."

She gave Drew no chance to object as she claimed her mouth in a lip-lock and pulled her into the bedroom. They stripped frantically. She pulled Nikki down on top of her, the sensations of Nikki's tongue and lips on her body almost too much to bear. Nikki plunged her fingers inside, taking her hard and fast to a mind-shattering orgasm.

Nikki withdrew and resumed her kisses, down one leg and back up the other, while she worked Drew's nipples between her fingertips. Just as her body began its descent, Nikki dragged her tongue across her center and sucked in her clit. *Fuck!* She was climbing again, into an out-of-control pulse that she never wanted to end, contradicting the craving for release; she clutched handfuls of Nikki's hair as she raised her hips to maximize contact with Nikki's mouth. She wrapped her legs around her and exploded.

And still, Nikki wasn't done. She continued licking and kissing her and then, without warning, she slipped a finger inside and stroked her in a smooth and deliberate rhythm. Her body's throbs soon matched Nikki's tempo. It was torturous and glorious and erotic, and her head swam as she finally let go.

"Oh, dear God. Tomorrow's Black Friday, and I'm not going to be able to move," she said once she caught her breath. Nikki's head was on her shoulder, their arms wrapped around each other.

"Which is why I'm not staying."

"Oh, you're cruel. So cruel."

"Cruel? I'm making sure you're rested for the busiest shopping day of the year. You should be thanking me. It is Thanksgiving, you know."

"Thank you."

"Oh no. Thank you." She kissed one cheek. "And thank you." She kissed her other cheek. "And thank you." She placed a lingering kiss on her nipple. "And you." She sucked in the other one before returning to Drew's neck.

"No. Thank you." Drew shut her up with a kiss and then sank her fingers deep inside her over and over until she'd thanked her properly. Twice.

They cuddled for another hour as they vented about their parents.

"Can you imagine me in an opera?" Nikki huffed.

"You do have the voice for it, but I'm not sure the opera world can handle you. How many out lesbian opera stars are there?"

"No idea."

"You know." Drew propped up on an elbow and caressed Nikki's cheek. "If anyone can pave the way, it would be you. Your father might be on to something." What was she saying? Nikki would become even more famous if she took on such a groundbreaking endeavor. She'd have two careers and even less time for a relationship. Was she sabotaging this already so she wouldn't get hurt?

"I'm not interested. Maybe it would be something to consider later on in my career, but not now. I love what I'm doing. I love my band. I love my rock 'n' roll. And I love…" Nikki bit her lip.

She cursed the dim lighting. Was Nikki blushing? *Please finish that sentence with "you"…*

"The idea of you producing music."

"You…what?"

"Drew, you have an amazing ear, and your musical knowledge covers the whole spectrum. I can't believe I hadn't thought of it before."

Nikki sat up, and her speech became more animated. "Jaymi and I have talked about adding real strings to some of our songs. It's very expensive, but we can afford it now. Don't worry, I wouldn't ask you to produce the whole album, but you could help with the arrangements. I can make one call to our manager and make it happen—"

"Wait just a minute. Haven't we been over this before? Dad needs me at the store, and I thought you understood what teaching means to me."

"We could work around that. A couple of months of rehearsals, then a month or so in the studio, and boom. Done. What do you think?"

Where would she possibly find the time to run the store, keep up with her students, go out with Nikki, take care of her cats, and be there for her dad, much less have any time to herself? "You know I don't have the time to make that kind of commitment."

"Okay, so take a short leave of absence. Give Geena some more hours or something."

"Geena's a senior in college. I can't ask her to sacrifice her studies when she's already working more than she should be as it is. What if sales drop off after the holidays, and your promotions end, and Dad can't afford to hire someone in my place, even if it is temporary? Not to mention he takes a vacation every spring to go play golf with his brother at Myrtle Beach. He needs me to run the business while he's gone."

"Drew, just think about it—"

"You don't get it, do you?" She was going to hyperventilate. "Don't dangle a carrot in front of my face when you know damn well it's not possible." She put on the light, shot out of bed, and gathered her clothes.

She ducked into the bathroom. She stabbed her hands under the faucet and cupped cold water onto her face. Her heart was racing. She couldn't believe Nikki would side with her mother. She wanted to be angry, damn it. The way she'd been angry with Mother.

Except the only person she was angry with was herself. She'd gotten good at making excuses, hadn't she? Or was she just realistic? If DJ's started struggling again, how would it survive without her? How would her dad feel if she left when he needed her the most?

But…what if they were right? There was a time she'd dreamed bigger and wanted more. If she didn't chase her dreams now, what did that mean for her future?

CHAPTER THIRTY-NINE

Nikki knew she'd set Drew's creative wheels spinning. Not that Drew would admit it. Over the next couple of weeks, they danced around the subject, though it was a thorn between them. There was a definite increase in shoppers due to the holidays, and Drew cited the boom in business as proof of how badly DJ's needed her. She did her best to avoid adding to Drew's stress and didn't bring up anything to do with family or career goals. She bought her meals when she could, rubbed her feet after long shifts, and even stopped by Drew's apartment to tend to the cats when she got stuck late at work.

She filled her own time with Christmas shopping and writing songs. She knew it wasn't a coincidence that she heard strings in all three of them as she worked out the arrangements in her head. When she played them for Jaymi, she agreed they would sound great with violins and cellos. She mentioned nothing of her suggestion to Drew. She didn't want to jump the gun in case it never happened.

It was the second week of December, and she was still no closer to finding the Ella Fitzgerald album. She was searching the internet for the millionth time when her phone rang. Lance, Passion Play's manager, shared news that made her bounce around the living room. She couldn't believe it. She called DJ's, knowing Drew wouldn't answer her cell at work.

"Are you up for another ride to the Big Apple?"

"It'll have to wait until after the new year, Nikki. You know I'm swamped."

"One day, Drew. Take one day off. Please?"

"Why? What's going on?"

"Passion Play's been nominated for two Grammys! We're invited to do a TV interview and a performance for one of those daily morning shows at Times Square."

"Nikki, that's awesome! Wow. Congratulations. When's the show?"

"Friday. We're heading down tomorrow night."

"Tomorrow? I can't get away on such short notice. Not now. We're running on a skeleton crew as it is, you know that. Geena has finals this week, so I can't ask her to cover."

Her heart sank. Drew was right. It was selfish of her to ask, but she wanted her there so badly. She supposed this was going to happen from time to time. "Jaymi's so lucky."

"I'm sorry, what was that?"

"I said Jaymi's lucky. She gets to have her girlfriend by her side for everything. It's not fair." She wondered if Drew could picture her pouting.

"I would love to go, baby, but I just can't. I'm sorry. I'll be able to watch you on TV, right?"

"Sure. Yes, of course."

"Sorry, Nikki. I have customers, I have to go."

They hung up, and she sank into the sofa. She was about to get the first taste of her job taking her away from Drew. They had rehearsal tonight, then a meeting tomorrow at Lance's office before the long ride to New York. A night alone in a hotel room, the show, then another five-hour trek home. And that was nothing compared to a tour schedule.

She sighed. She could deal with this, right? Drew would be working anyway. Maybe she'd stay in New York for the whole weekend. Catch a show. Do some shopping. She pouted again. It wouldn't be the same without Drew.

She wandered from room to room, restless and unable to focus. Finally, she hauled out her suitcase and packed, paying less attention than usual to her outfit choices. She only needed something decent for the show itself. Otherwise, she couldn't care less. If Drew wasn't there to impress, what was the point?

Her phone chimed with a text. Drew.

I'm so proud of you. I really wish I could go. I hope you understand.

She smiled and sent a reply.

Of course I understand. But don't think you're getting out of going to the Grammy Awards with me in Feb.

The phone rang. "Really?" Drew's excitement was palpable.

"I was going to take your dad, but it might spoil my reputation as a lesbian."

"Don't you dare. And impossible. Your reputation there is firmly established."

"Good. Because you're going. I'll triple Geena's pay to cover for you if I have to."

"You might have to pay more than that to make up for how jealous she's going to be."

"I'd bring the whole lot of you if I could get enough tickets. Melissa, too."

"Now you're talkin'. But my dad can't cover the store by himself for that long."

"I don't think they allow that many guests, anyway. I'll have to settle for just you."

"Settle?"

"You know what I mean."

"I'm just teasing you. Maybe I'll even visit my mother while I'm out there—if she can spare the time."

She heard the sadness in Drew's voice. As far as she knew, Drew hadn't spoken to her mother since Thanksgiving. Nikki hadn't spoken to her father, either. She wondered what he'd think of her band's nominations. Maybe, just maybe, he'd finally be convinced that they were the real deal and that she'd made the right career choice.

She sighed heavily. Drew and the band would be there—the people who loved her for who she was, and that's all that mattered.

She spent the night at Drew's. It was bittersweet, knowing she'd be away for the next four days. The thought that she'd never worried about being away from someone else for any length of time before made her smile. They agreed that having some time apart would be good practice. Their relationship would have to endure these tests if it was going to survive. Better to find out earlier rather than later if they had what it took, right? They talked and laughed and had sex, and Nikki slept with Drew in her arms. It was perfect.

Drew headed off to work, and Nikki drove to Lance's office where they were all meeting to take the limo to New York.

Lance splayed his hand over his heart and exaggerated a shocked expression. "Well, slap my ass and wake me from my wet dream! I am marking my calendar: the first time in Passion Play history that Nikki Razer is ready to go before everyone else."

"And I think this is the first time in history you've ever looked better than me before nine a.m."

Lance looked over his electric blue suit, white dress shirt, and hot pink tie. He slicked back his blond pompadour and buttoned his black leather overcoat. His metrosexual style would blend in well in the city, but his ultra-modern fashion sense drew stares in the small towns of New Hampshire. "Pshaw! I always look better than you, honey. You're damn lucky we play for opposite teams."

Nikki ducked into the car. "I've seen you throw a ball. I'm not worried."

"Ouch! What's got your lady boxers in a bunch this morning? Missing your Drewie pooh-bear already, are you?"

She received additional teasing about her unusual punctuality from her bandmates, but she simply claimed that Drew was a good influence on her. It was true, after all.

The gang was quiet for the first half hour or so until Jaymi caught her eye and broke the silence. "I don't know about the rest of you, but I'm psyched to get back in the studio."

Lance jumped right in. "We need to really focus on getting this next album out pronto. Even if you don't win a Grammy, sales will skyrocket if we release an album on the coattails of two nominations."

The conversation continued with plans to start putting songs together at rehearsals. Nikki felt a little guilty for only having three new songs to contribute, but just talking about playing together again fired her up. As much as she'd needed the break, she had to admit she was itching to get back onstage. Having new songs to add to the repertoire kept her job fresh and challenging. She couldn't wait to hear what everyone had written.

"So, Nikki, how are the cello lessons going? I'd like to add some strings this time." Jaymi grinned. "*Real* strings—not synthesizers."

"There's no way in hell I'll be ready to play on this album, unless you enjoy the sounds of sick birds."

Everyone chuckled. Jaymi flapped her arms like a chicken, and Shawn provided sound effects.

Kay asked, "What about Drew? Would she be interested in playing on the record? I popped into DJ's last week and heard her playing a violin. I was blown away. She should charge admission just to walk into the store."

"I've told her that, too." Nikki sat up straighter. *So, I'm not the only one who thinks so.* "She says she's happy just teaching, but I'm telling you, when I took her to that Mozart concert, I saw something in her eyes. If she got a taste of performing, I bet she'd love it."

Shawn asked, "So, what's holding her back?"

"Opportunity." Lance was practically bouncing in his seat. "She needs an offer she can't refuse. Is she really that good?"

"She can play the hell out of anything you put in her hands." Nikki's excitement bubbled up as she imagined all the ways Drew could enhance their sound, yet she had a nagging feeling Drew would turn them down flat.

"So, the question remains." Jaymi sat forward and clasped her hands together. "Would she be interested? I like the idea of adding another local undiscovered talent to our lineup." She stole a loving glance at Shawn, the undiscovered talent added a few short years ago.

"I don't know…"

"It can't hurt to ask her, Nikki," said Shawn. "Jaymi and I already blew the no-dating rule to bits, so what the hell."

"I don't think I'd be so lucky, Shawn. Anytime I've brought up anything like this, it's caused a problem between us—"

"I'll talk to her, then," Lance stated. "This is a business decision. I'll ask her to audition, play a few tracks for her, ask her what she'd add for arrangements, you know, the works. She doesn't have to commit to anything."

"Yeah. Maybe if she has a chance to tap into her own potential, she'll change her tune." Jaymi chuckled. Intended or not, Jaymi loved puns.

Maybe they were right. Drew might take an offer from their manager seriously. She'd have plenty of time to think about it. The holiday rush would be over, so she wouldn't have to feel guilty about taking some time off work. The question was, would she feel as if Nikki hadn't listened to her? She'd been pretty clear about where her passion was and how much she detested fame. The last thing Nikki wanted was for her to feel as if she'd been snuck up on. But then…she'd said she didn't want to talk about it because it was a dangling carrot she couldn't have. What if she could?

❖

Weary from the endless ride and a meeting with the show's producers, Nikki exited the elevator Thursday night and walked down the corridor to her hotel room. Shit. The leggy blonde in the long fur coat standing at the end of the hall looked familiar. She stopped short. *No. Please no.*

"I've been waiting for you."

"You wasted your time. Go away, Amy."

"Oh, Nikki," Amy purred. "I'm touched. You remembered my name this time." She opened the coat to reveal a scarlet teddy underneath.

"I'm not interested." She turned away and swiped her key card.

Amy wedged herself between the door and jam, blocking Nikki's entry. She draped her arm over Nikki's shoulder, pried open the coat farther, and rubbed her thigh alongside Nikki's leg. "I find that hard to believe, considering what we shared the last time you were in town."

Nikki pulled the door shut and moved Amy's arm as she stepped away from her. "I said I'm not interested. Now move out of the way, or I'll call security." She took out her phone.

"Oh, come on, now. You don't want another taste of this? A night of no-strings fucking? Remember how good it was last time? I'm wet right now just thinking about it." She grabbed Nikki's hand and tried forcing it between her legs. "Wanna see?"

Nikki yanked her arm back and headed back toward the elevator. "Get lost." She pressed the button. She'd have her forcibly removed if she had to.

Amy's stare turned cold. "You'll be sorry. You wait, Nikki. You'll be sorry."

The elevator doors parted. "Good-bye, Amy." She stepped inside and immediately hit the lobby button. "Christ, woman. Take a goddamn hint already!" She blew out a breath. Maybe it was a good thing Drew hadn't come along after all.

She walked swiftly to the piano bar, where she found a hidden booth and nursed a drink for an hour. She hoped she'd waited long enough. It was closing in on ten, and they needed to be at the gig by seven the next morning. After bidding Drew good night with a text, she headed back to her room.

She sighed with relief when she rounded the corner and saw no one. Still, she approached her room with caution. *Who knows where that loony could be hiding?* She stole a peek in the vending room as she crept by. Empty. Taking one last look around, she slipped into her room and flipped the extra locks in place for good measure. She took a quick, hot shower and crawled into bed, glad she'd brought pajamas. It was going to be a long, cold night without Drew by her side.

She couldn't believe how much she missed her. They'd only parted that morning—she looked at the clock—sixteen hours ago. How was she going to survive month-long tours? What was she thinking? This falling in love shit was fucking harder than she'd imagined. If she thought being around Jaymi all the time was tough before, being away from Drew was going to kick her ass into the next decade.

If she called this late, would she wake her up? Would Drew mind if she did?

Fuck it. She swiped her phone and tapped Drew's picture.

"Hey, baby." Drew sounded half asleep.

"Hi. Did I wake you?"

"Yes, but it's okay. I'm glad you called."

"Are you sure?"

"Of course. Everything all right? Why are you up so late? Don't those morning shows start wicked early?"

"They do. I don't care." No way was she going to tell Drew why she'd stayed up later than planned. "I missed you. I couldn't sleep without hearing your voice." It wasn't a lie.

"I miss you, too." Drew's voice was muffled, as though her face was half buried in her pillow.

She heard one of the cats purring. The image of Drew curled up with her three furry friends was cuteness overload.

"I miss the kids, too."

"If I didn't know any better, I'd think you were trying to charm your way into my bed again."

Nikki burrowed into the covers and grinned. "Is it working?"

"I think you know the answer to that."

"Shall I bring dessert?"

"Nikki Razer, you do not play fair."

"Is that a yes?"

Someone knocked on her door. Shit. *If that bitch is back...*

She missed hearing Drew's reply as she slid out of bed as silently as she could. She looked through the peephole. "Jaymi," she murmured.

"What?" said Drew.

She swung open the door.

Jaymi was wearing a shit-eating grin. "Are you alone?" She playfully punched Nikki in the arm. "Ah, just kidding! I know those days are over." She gestured to the phone Nikki was now holding away from her ear. "I'm sorry," she whispered. "I didn't realize you were on the phone. I can come back."

"No. It's okay," she said to Jaymi. "Hey, Drew? I gotta go."

"Everything all right?"

"Yeah, everything's fine. I should let you get back to sleep. I'll call you tomorrow." They bid each other good night, and she turned her attention back to Jaymi. "You want to come in?"

"Thanks, but I actually came by to see if you wanted to join the rest of us. We're going for a nightcap at a blues club down the street."

"At this hour?"

Jaymi stepped back, looked Nikki up and down, and broke into an even bigger smile. "You're already in your jammies?" She ducked her head into the room and looked around. "Who are you, and what have you done with my best friend?"

She folded her arms. "I could ask you the same thing. Since when do you head out this late when we have an early-morning commitment?"

"I'm too keyed up to sleep." She tugged on Nikki's sleeve. "Come on, how often do we have the chance to hang out in New York and have some fun?"

Jaymi had a point, but she didn't trust that Amy wouldn't resurface and cause more trouble. It'd be best to lay low for the rest of their stay. "Maybe next time, Jaymz. I'm not really up for it tonight."

"Wow. I've gotta hand it to Drew. I never thought I'd see the day we'd reverse roles as the responsible adult."

"Shut up."

"It's not an insult, you knucklehead." Jaymi sighed. "I still say you're missing out, but okay." She bounced on the balls of her feet and shot both arms in the air as if she'd just launched a game-winning home run over the left field wall. "We're going to the Grammys!" She engulfed Nikki in a bear hug and kissed her several times on the cheek.

She grinned at Jaymi, and her heart swelled with their shared joy. "Get out of here, and go have some fun, you goofball."

"Takes one to know one!" She hugged her again. "But I love you anyway."

"I love you too, Jaymi." It felt good to exchange those words aloud.

They looked at each other for a long moment, and Nikki's heart pounded as the full force of their bond enveloped her soul. She'd never felt more at peace with their relationship. She knew she'd never again feel pain associated with her love for Jaymi. *I'm in love with Drew.*

"Tell the gang I said hi, and I'll see you all in the morning."

"I will. Later, tater!" Jaymi bounded down the hall to the elevator in her barely contained excitement.

She sighed contentedly. Damn, it was good to have friends.

Chapter Forty

Drew awoke in plenty of time to watch Nikki and the band on the early morning show. Nikki was charming, but she looked tired, as did the rest of the band, but their excitement was evident.

She tried hard not to feel jealous and insecure, but she knew Jaymi was in Nikki's room last night. Late last night. She'd very clearly heard Jaymi ask if she was alone, and she was unable to make out what was said after that. That felt wrong for two reasons. Either Jaymi expected Nikki to have company, or she was hoping to be alone with Nikki for her own reasons.

She shook her head and finished dressing for work. She was being ridiculous. Jaymi would never cheat on Shawn. She'd never seen two people more in love. *And Nikki wouldn't cheat on me, would she?* They'd just started referring to each other as "girlfriend." That was pretty darned close to meaning they wanted to be exclusive, even though they hadn't actually used the word. Was Nikki so weak that she couldn't last one weekend away without satisfying her carnal desires?

Was she going to feel this insecure every time Nikki had to go away? She rolled her eyes. If she couldn't trust Nikki with her best friend, she really was pathetic.

Her phone rang just as she headed outside. She answered immediately, both relieved and nervous. "Good morning, baby." At least she didn't sound pathetic.

"Good morning, beautiful. God, it's good to hear your voice. I miss you so much."

"You do?" Drew turned the key to her dead bolt and descended the stairs to the driveway.

"More than you could possibly imagine."

"I miss you, too." She climbed into her truck and turned the key, cranking the heat dial all the way up. "I saw the show. You did great."

"Yeah? I felt like shit, though."

"You looked tired." She wedged the phone between her ear and shoulder. She rubbed her hands together. It took too long for this old beater to warm up.

"Yeah. We all are. Look, I'm sorry about last night. Jaymi came by to invite me for a nightcap with the group. I didn't mean to cut you off so abruptly."

"Oh. Hey, it's all right. You have every right to celebrate with your friends."

"It doesn't mean you're not important to me, too. I hope you know that."

See? You were being stupid. Her heartbeat slowed noticeably. "Well, I'm glad the show went well."

"We were a little out of our element, but I thought we did all right. Live TV is much different than doing a concert, let me tell you. I'd rather stick to singing."

She shoved aside a familiar association with her mother's TV exposure and reminded herself this was a different situation. "So… you're staying down there for the weekend, right?"

"Yeah. I'm going to get some shopping done while I'm here."

She heard a smile in Nikki's voice, which made her smile, too.

"For me?"

"What do you think?"

"Don't go too crazy. You know I can't afford much for you." She frowned. She hadn't even begun her Christmas shopping.

"If I find you beneath my tree wearing nothing but a big red ribbon, that would be fine with me."

She burst out laughing. "That can be arranged."

Nikki let out a long, sexy sigh. "Now who's being cruel?"

"You started it."

"I did, didn't I?"

"I hate to cut this short, but I need to get to work." The truck was finally warm.

"Oh, all right. Have a good day, babe."

"You too."

Her commute was so much better than she'd anticipated. Now if she could just get through the next two days, she'd be golden. Maybe she'd get some of her own shopping done. She grinned as she mentally added a large red ribbon to her shopping list.

❖

Her mood considerably brighter after talking with Drew, Nikki finished her brunch and hit the stores. Thanks to a tip from one of the morning show's producers, she finally found what she was looking for. She smiled as she imagined the look on Drew's face when she opened it. She couldn't slow her pace back to her room if she'd wanted to.

The holidays this year were going to be beyond amazing. She could feel it. Cuddling with Drew, sipping hot chocolate on Christmas Eve. Making breakfast together the next morning in their new pajamas and fuzzy slippers after a beautiful night of lovemaking. Maybe she'd bring her here, to New York, to enjoy the festivities at Times Square on New Year's Eve. They'd dance and blow noisemakers and shout the countdown together with the crowd as they watched the ball drop. And then, they'd kiss at the stroke of midnight.

She safely tucked her package under her arm and opened the door to her room. The sound of crinkling paper sounded beneath her foot. She gently placed the bag on the table, picked up the manila envelope she'd stepped on, and looked it over. It was blank, and sealed only with a metal clasp. Weird.

She shrugged out of her coat and opened it. Photos. She slid the contents out onto the table. Photos of Jaymi in her arms. Jaymi kissing her cheek.

Me, naked, in bed with Jaymi. Obviously, this one was doctored. Her memory flashed to Amy taking her picture in the hotel a few months ago, covered only to the waist. She must've taken the others last night from around the corner in the hallway.

"What the fuck are you playing at, you bitch?"

She flipped over the bedroom picture and got her answer.

Unless you want these plastered all over the tabloids and social media, you will pay me $500,000 cash. I gave Jaymi her own set of pictures. You can tell her yourself why you call out her name while you fuck other women.

Below the message were instructions on how she was to package the money, a place and time she was to deliver it, along with a threat that she would make things much worse for her if she went to the authorities.

Ice ran through her veins. Her legs turned to rubber. She was tempted to sit and collect herself, but she had to get to Jaymi. With any luck, she hadn't been back to her room to find the package. *It's one thing to fuck with me, but to mess with Jaymi…*

She shot out of the room and bypassed the elevator, electing to run up the four flights of stairs. She needed to burn off her fury. She reached the landing of Jaymi's floor. Leaning against the wall, she gasped for breath and willed her pulse to decelerate. She pulled in a lungful of air and hissed it out as slowly as she could manage. *Steady now. You need a clear head.*

She knocked on Jaymi's door.

Her stomach lurched when the door swung open. Shawn's red, hardened face told her all she needed to know.

"I trusted you," Shawn said through gritted teeth.

"I know about the package."

"And?"

"Shawn, there's nothing going on between me and Jaymi. You know that."

"Do I?" Shawn thrust the photos in front of her face.

"What's going on?" Jaymi approached from the other end of the corridor.

"Why don't you tell me?" Shawn shoved the pictures into Jaymi's hand and turned her back on them both. She raked her hands through her hair as she walked back into the room.

Nikki and Jaymi stepped inside and closed the door.

Jaymi's eyes bugged as she looked at the photos. "What the hell?"

"Extortion, Jaymi. I know who it is. She came to my room last night, and I told her to get lost. Now she's demanding money from me, or she'll release the photos."

"Oh, who gives a shit about your damn money, Nikki." Shawn then turned to Jaymi. "How could you do this to me?"

"Shawn." Nikki softened her tone, knowing Shawn had every right to be angry and confused based on the evidence. "Jaymi came to see me last night to invite me to join you guys, and she hugged me because she was excited about all the good things happening for the band right now, but that other picture is a fake. Look at it. Jaymi's Photoshopped into it. She would never cheat on you."

"She's right, baby." Jaymi put a hand on Shawn's shoulder. "Hey, come on. Look at me. I love you, Shawn. I wouldn't trade what we have for anything."

Shawn let out a long breath and closed her eyes for a moment. She shot Nikki a furtive glance and then looked at Jaymi. "I'm overreacting again, aren't I?"

"Yes, you are." Jaymi hugged her. "You have nothing to worry about, baby. I promise."

"I'm sorry, guys," Shawn said, her voice muffled in Jaymi's shirt.

Nikki rocked back and forth on the balls of her feet. She cleared her throat. "I hate to break up your little moment here, but we need to figure out how we're going to deal with this situation."

"We?" Shawn pulled away from Jaymi. "You created this mess, not us. Pay her off and make it go away."

"It's not that simple, babe," said Jaymi. "Even if Nikki pays her the money, the woman still has the photos. There's no guarantee she won't still sell them or post them."

"She's right," Nikki added. "Not to mention this could have a negative impact on the whole band and Jaymi's reputation."

Jaymi turned to Nikki. "What about Drew, Nikki? How's she going to feel when she hears about this?"

A knife twisted in her heart. Drew was going to flip. This was exactly the type of thing that had made her hesitant to get involved with her in the first place. *This wouldn't have happened if I wasn't famous.* What about the pictures of her and Jaymi? Would Drew be jealous? She laughed inwardly. Drew had no reason to be jealous, but could she convince Drew of that?

"Nikki?" Jaymi's voice brought her back. "Hey. Talk to me."

"I don't think she's going to take this well. What am I going to do?"

Jaymi said, "We need to call Lance. Let's start there, okay? He'll call the band's attorney. They'll know what to do."

"Yeah. Right." She collapsed into a chair. "I do know one thing. I'm not sticking around till Sunday and risking running into her again. I'm coming home with you guys tomorrow."

"And then you're going to talk to Drew. You don't want her finding out about this from someone else."

A dull ache traveled up her neck to the base of her skull. What if they couldn't resolve this before they went home tomorrow? Should she call Drew and warn her? Then again, if they could pull the plug before it hit the fan, maybe she could spare her from the whole thing. She didn't want to have this conversation over the phone. *What a mess.*

Chapter Forty-One

The influx of Saturday afternoon holiday shoppers had DJ's employees hopping. Drew's adrenaline was wearing off since she hadn't slept well the last few nights. It had been harder to adjust to Nikki's absence than she'd expected, and the more she noticed it, the harder it had been to fall asleep.

Melissa handled herself adeptly at the register as she, Geena, and Jerry managed the sales floor. Drew's heart swelled at the sparkle in her dad's eyes as he helped a couple select their child's first guitar. He shared the story of Drew's reaction when she'd found hers beneath the Christmas tree when she was six. He told that story to everyone, and she never grew tired of hearing it.

If their revenues equated his enthusiasm, they'd be golden. That wasn't the reality of business, though. As she checked the sales reading at five, she was pleased that it was higher than usual, but after the holidays, they'd likely be back to squeezing out every dime they could muster.

"Go ahead and take your break, Melissa."

Melissa blew out a breath and thanked her before scooting off to the break room. Drew straightened out some bills in the till and jumped when a single red rose appeared in her line of sight.

Nikki stood in front of her wearing a huge smile. "I wanna buy a kiss. Will you accept a rose as payment?"

She grinned. "Only if it includes a hug." She bolted around the counter and threw her arms around Nikki. "God, I missed you."

Nikki squeezed her tight. "I should have brought more roses."

"No need. You're home a day early!"

"I couldn't stand to be away from you another day." Nikki gave her a quick kiss. "Or another night."

She led Nikki by the hand to the office and shut the door behind them. She gave her a long, slow kiss as she slid her hands beneath Nikki's sweater. Nikki's flesh responded with goose bumps, and she cursed her confounded retail schedule and the commercialization of Christmas.

"Babe, I'm so sorry, but Melissa's on her break, and I can't stay off the floor for long."

"Yeah, I know." Nikki's shoulders slumped and she dropped into a chair. "I'm so fucking glad to be home."

Drew sat next to her and took her hand. "Something wrong?"

"Yeah. Maybe. I hope not." Her smile was forced. "I'll fill you in tonight at home, okay?"

Her heart crumpled. Maybe Nikki couldn't handle the separation and had changed her mind about having a relationship. She knew this might happen. Yet the sudden mood change was a far cry from her greeting a few minutes ago.

Nikki leaned over and rested her head on Drew's shoulder. "Don't worry, Drew. Everything's gonna be all right."

"Nikki, what's going on?"

Nikki sat up. "Nothing I can't handle." She smiled again, and this time it reached her eyes. "So, you missed me, huh?"

Okay, she obviously didn't want to talk about it, so Drew didn't push. "I'm not sure I dare admit to you how much." She returned Nikki's smile and kissed her cheek. "On the one hand, I'm glad you're back early, but you screwed up my plans for going Christmas shopping tomorrow."

Nikki suddenly broke into a grin.

"What?"

"Nothing."

"You liar. What are you up to?"

Nikki shook a finger at her. "Didn't your parents ever tell you not to ask questions at Christmastime?"

She grabbed Nikki's finger and kissed the tip of it. "What'd ya get me?"

"Nothing."

"You're full of shit."

"I thought you had to get back to work?"

Drew sighed loudly. "Spoilsport." She yanked open the door. "I'll call you when I get home."

Nikki gave her another knee-buckling kiss that reassured her that she had no plans of breaking things off.

"On second thought, meet me at my place."

"Oh yeah? Does that mean the cats missed me, too?"

"I swear when Fret meows, she sounds like she's singing one of your songs."

"She's one smart pussycat."

Nikki blew her a kiss just before she left. Drew checked her watch. Only three hours to go until they'd be together again.

If she could barely stand three hours without her, how was she going to handle three-month tours?

She was both relieved and disappointed to see that the crowd had thinned considerably. She began making the rounds, straightening up the store. Geena rushed to her side with an odd look on her face.

"Geena, what's wrong?"

Geena pursed her lips and tilted her head as if considering whether or not to tell her something.

"What is it? Did someone steal something? Is the till short?"

Geena shook her head. "No, nothing like that. It's...well, it's about something Melissa just showed me on her phone."

"I don't understand."

Geena pulled her cell from her back pocket. She held it to her chest. "Now, these might be old, in which case it's probably not a big deal, but if they're recent, then I'm gonna kick some ass."

"Geena, what are you talking about?"

She sighed deeply. "Okay, I'll show you, but brace yourself. You're not going to like what you see."

She rotated the phone outward and showed Drew the screen. It was logged on to a Facebook post displaying photos of Nikki with Jaymi. Two photos were taken in what looked like the doorway of a hotel room. Nikki was holding her in one picture, and in the other, Jaymi was kissing her cheek. Geena scrolled to the third photo.

Acid swept through her stomach and crawled up her throat. Nikki was lying in bed on her side, naked and covered only to her waist with a sheet. Jaymi was in the bed with her, her body blocked by Nikki's, so that only her head was exposed. She took the phone from Geena and scrolled to the top. It was an unofficial public page created exclusively for Nikki Razer fans.

Her gut feeling had been right. There *was* something between

Nikki and Jaymi. But how long ago? If it *was* in the past, then Geena was right, it was no big deal. Though she wasn't happy Nikki hadn't told her about it. Still, she didn't think Nikki, Jaymi, or any of the band members would be happy with someone posting these pictures on social media.

Who took them? What if they weren't old? Were they having an affair? Her heart seized her from the inside out. Was this what Nikki needed to talk to her about? *Nikki wouldn't do this to me, would she? Dear God, poor Shawn. She'll be crushed.* And what about the bad publicity this would bring to the band?

"Drew?" Geena gripped her shoulder. "You all right? Come on, talk to me, boss."

There was nothing to say. Nothing good could come from this. She handed Geena her phone and walked away. Her dad took one look at her and sent her home without her even having to ask. He could always tell when she wasn't feeling well. Little did he know it wasn't her body she was worried about—it was her heart.

She gathered her cats in her arms, curled up on the couch, and waited for Nikki to arrive.

❖

"Son of a bitch, she didn't waste any time, did she?"

Drew held out her phone in front of Nikki's face. "You told me you and Jaymi were never romantically involved."

"We weren't!"

"You weren't? So, these are recent?"

"Yes. I mean no."

"Which is it?"

"Shit, Drew." She ran a hand through her hair and let out an exasperated breath. "Lance and our attorneys are taking care of it."

"What do they have to do with you and Jaymi having an affair? Does Shawn know?"

"We're not having an affair!" Nikki took the phone from Drew and pointed to the doctored picture. "This is a fake, Drew." She needed to calm her down and explain. Even the cats had left the room.

"I don't understand. Who took these? And why?"

She gave the phone back to Drew and tried to lead her to the couch. Drew didn't budge.

"They were taken by a woman I slept with—*once*. A fan. Months ago, in New York, before I met you." She told Drew about the photo taken that day—of her alone in bed and explained that she must have Photoshopped Jaymi into the picture. "She showed up at my hotel room again this past Friday night. I told her to get lost. The next day, I found the photos shoved under my door with an extortion threat."

"I take it you didn't pay up." Drew's arms were wrapped around herself as she kept her distance.

"Of course not. The lawyers advised me not to. Can you blame me? It's not like it would've stopped her. Now she doesn't have any ammunition or anything to sell. She's got no power."

"Don't you see? Either way, this lunatic is screwing with your life. Why? Because you're famous, and she knows she can fuck with you. This is the same kind of shit I had to be around with my mother. It made my dad crazy. Even if it's not true, the rumors are going to fly, and just like that, yours and Jaymi's reputations will be shot to hell. Shawn gets hurt. I get hurt. The band loses the respect of its fans—"

"Hey." Nikki hardened. "The band will be fine. No one fucks with my band and gets away with it."

Drew's shoulders dropped, and she walked into the kitchen. She leaned on the counter and dropped her head. "Of course. The band. It's always going to come first, isn't it?"

Nikki stepped toward her. "The band's my life, Drew. You know that." She softened her tone and stroked Drew's arm. "That doesn't mean you're any less important."

Drew's lip quivered. "I feel like I have to get in line to be a priority for you, Nikki. You stop by DJ's, and fans swarm to you. You can't turn them away any more than you can deny your bandmates anything. I see how you are with them. Jaymi calls or stops by, and you drop everything for her. Shawn or Kay or Brian need you, and boom. You're there."

"Drew, they're my family. I love them. You knew this about me going in. I thought you admired that about me?"

"I do."

"Have you forgotten that I rushed to your side when you were injured? I stayed with you and took care of you for days. Doesn't that count for anything?"

Drew turned and looked at her, the pain and longing clear in her eyes. "Of course it does. But—"

"But what?"

Drew stood motionless. "There will be times when you can't be here for me. I know that's nobody's fault. It's just the reality of your job."

She shook her head in frustration. "What do you want from me?"

"I don't know. Nothing. Everything." Drew's voice was tight with emotion. "I want things I have no right to ask for."

"You haven't asked."

"I don't need to, Nikki. I already know the answer."

Nikki reached for her only to have her step away. The physical distance was nothing compared to the emotional gulf that she feared was about to grow larger. Quietly, she said, "Ask me."

"I want to be number one for a change," Drew said bitterly. "For once, I want to be the most important person in someone's life, the one who comes first. I want someone who will love me above everyone and everything else. I know that sounds selfish, but I deserve that. I think everyone deserves to be loved that much."

"You do, and you're right." She knew she was treading on thin ice, but she had to challenge Drew's anger. "But I think you're confusing me with someone else." If Drew wanted to question her loyalty to their relationship, then she had a right to put a mirror in front of Drew's face, too. "I'm not your mother who wouldn't give you the time of day when you were growing up. I'm not your father who won't loosen his purse strings so you can achieve your dreams. But I can give you the love you deserve *and* the resources you need for your ambitions—if you'll let me."

Drew let out a long sigh and pulled her gaze away. "You don't understand." She shoved past her and went into the living room.

Nikki gave her a minute before following. She found her in front of the window, looking out into the night.

"I *do* understand, and that's what you can't handle." Nikki's motivational instincts kicked in, and she gambled her remaining chips with one more challenge. "You're afraid."

Drew spun around, her arms folded in protection mode. "You're damned right I'm afraid."

"I'm talking about more than our relationship, Drew. You don't even realize it, but you're afraid of success. Yours and everyone else's, and instead of letting that fear motivate you, you project that fear onto everyone around you."

"What the hell are you talking about?"

"You want an example? Melissa."

Drew screwed up her face. "What?"

"You're squashing her dreams. If you don't encourage your best student to go after her dreams, then what kind of teacher are you?"

"How dare you! I'm trying to *protect* Melissa."

"From what? Being successful? Being happy?"

"From turning into a puppet who's sentenced to a life at the mercy of money-hungry music industry executives and obsessed fans who won't let her have any peace or privacy."

"Is that how you see my life? I have more control over it than you give me credit for."

"Oh yes. I see that in the photos of you that were so easily put out there for everyone to see."

"A small hiccup that will be swiftly taken care of by our attorneys. Melissa's not as stupid as I have been. And plenty of non-famous people have this happen, too. It happens."

Drew blew out a breath and shook her head. "How you can be so blasé? My God, you're arrogant."

Nikki's pulse quickened, and heat flooded her neck. "It's called faith, Drew. I've surrounded myself with people I have faith in. They won't let me down."

"That may be true, but you've let *them* down. Can't you see that? They're all going to get hurt in one way or another by those stupid pictures. The difference between them and me is that they knew the risks of fame when they pursued this career path with you. They did so willingly. I'm not willing to be collateral damage. It was tough enough going through it with my mother. I don't want to go through it again."

Was she serious? Drew couldn't really believe she'd treat her the way her mother had. Hadn't she already shown Drew how much she cared about her? "Baby, come on. This will all blow over before you know it."

"Will it?"

"It's just a stupid Facebook post."

"What happens if it ends up in the tabloids? How many other fans have you slept with that might jump on the bandwagon? I've seen what happens. One person sells a story, and next thing you know, there are a dozen copycats who want to sell theirs."

Nikki hadn't considered that and winced internally at the possibility. "Christ, Drew. I'm not *that* famous."

Drew bit her lower lip and squeezed her eyes shut for a moment.

"I'm just a singer in a band that's only put out two albums." Nikki hoped her response to Drew's silence would ease her mind.

"You're more than that, baby. It's not just the scandal I'm worried about." Drew's voice was drastically quieter than it had been a moment ago. "Passion Play's up for two Grammy awards. That's huge, Nikki. If you win, you'll be more famous and in even higher demand. I'll never see you. I'll never come first."

Nikki's eyes filled with tears. She steeled herself and asked the question she didn't want Drew to answer. She needed to know. "What are you saying, Drew?"

"I've seen you onstage. I know what your career means to you. I've seen what the band means to you. No matter how much you care about me, I'm always going to play second fiddle to your career." Drew's eyes shone with moisture. "I don't want to play second fiddle when I know I'm good enough for first violin."

This couldn't be happening. Her insides ripped in half. She could handle a fight, but losing Drew was unthinkable. "Baby, you can't honestly expect me to give up my career?"

Drew stepped toward her. She looked into Nikki's eyes, and as always, Nikki was lost in the sheer beauty of them. She gasped when Drew tenderly stroked her cheek. One touch and she nearly came undone.

Drew gave her a light kiss. "I told you I had no right to ask."

Nikki rested her forehead against hers. "Please, baby. We can make this work," she whispered. "We have to try."

Drew took a shuddered breath and pulled out of their embrace. Tears betrayed her attempt to look stone cold. "I'm sorry." She shook her head slightly. "I can't. I won't."

She walked away and closed the door behind her as she disappeared into the bedroom. Nikki couldn't move, paralyzed by grief over what she'd just lost.

And for the first time in her life, she knew how it felt to have no music in her soul.

Chapter Forty-Two

Drew burrowed her head in her pillow and waited for Nikki to either leave or barge in. She wasn't sure which she was hoping for, which only made the passing minutes more torturous. She knew this day would come. She should have kept this casual. Why hadn't she listened to her gut? Or to Geena? This pain was even more wretched than she'd imagined it could be.

She hadn't expected to fall in love with her. She winced, the truth of the realization hitting her like a mallet striking a gong. She'd lived and worked in this area for years. Of all the women she'd met while working with the public, why in the world couldn't she have fallen for one of them instead of Nikki? *Because no one captured your attention—or your heart—the way Nikki has, that's why.*

A noise at her bedroom door made her heart jump. Scratching, followed by a meow. Fret. Then the distant click of the front door closing. *She's gone.*

Careful not to disturb Vinnie, who had curled up next to her, she slid off the bed and let Fret into the room. She hopped onto the bed and began her evening grooming ritual as Drew walked through the empty apartment. The only evidence of Nikki's earlier presence was the faint remnant of her cologne lingering in the air. She inhaled deeply, longing for one last sensory souvenir of Nikki Razer.

It wasn't enough, and that was proof she'd made the right decision by ending things now. In time, Nikki would fade into another painful memory of lost love. After what had happened with Kelly, she should have known better than to get involved with another musician. Especially a famous one. There would always be another scandal, another performance, another TV appearance, another album to record, another tour, and…another reason to leave. *Another crazy fan to create chaos in our lives.*

Andres brushed against her leg. She gently scooped up the old duffer and hugged him. His rumbling purr and plump body comforted her aching soul. She crawled under the covers, surrounded by her fur babies, and cried.

At least her kitties thought she was the most important person on earth. Even though she hated herself for what she'd done. *Did I just make the biggest mistake of my life?*

❖

Nikki sank into the couch and stared at the flames dancing in her fireplace. The time passed in a blur. She looked at the corner of the room where she'd planned to put a Christmas tree. She imagined Drew lying nearby on the fur rug in front of the hearth, wearing only a red ribbon.

She closed her eyes, which still stung from tears she thought would never run out. She should go to bed, but she didn't know how she was going to sleep, knowing she'd never again hold Drew in her arms. She leaned forward and picked up the Ella Fitzgerald album that lay on the coffee table.

Maybe she could give it to Jerry to pass along, though she'd give anything to see the look on Drew's face when she opened it. Then again, would it bring Drew joy or sorrow? Would she look upon it as a farewell gift and be satisfied with the brief time they'd had together? Or would she regret her decision and long for what could have been?

She selfishly hoped for the latter. *Was* she being selfish? No. She'd given Drew her heart. She'd treated her well. *I would give her the world if I could.*

Except Drew didn't want the world. Drew wanted her to be something she wasn't. She wanted the impossible. *If Drew can't accept my life as it is, then she must not love me enough to give us a chance.*

She shoved off the couch with a frustrated huff. A fleeting image of Drew's cats napping by the warmth of the fire teased her imagination before she snuffed out the flames. Having Drew and her beloved kitties living here with her was a fantasy she no longer had the right to indulge in. The four of them would have brought life to the place, that was for sure.

She wandered through the rooms, one by one. Without Drew, nothing held any meaning. Once again, this was merely a place to sleep and keep her stuff. One step up from a hotel suite. She ended her trek and picked up the album she'd moved heaven and earth to find. A year ago, she might have smashed it to bits in a fit of pain this unbearable. Instead, she hugged it to her chest. Drew would cherish it, and she cherished Drew so fiercely that she made a snap decision.

She threw on her leather jacket and chased her own shadow out of the house. She was giving the album to Drew *now*. Not because she expected it to change Drew's mind. Not because she wanted to prove her love to her. Not because she wanted Drew to feel guilty. But because she wanted Drew to have something she wanted and thought she'd never have. *I know all too well how that feels.*

She zipped through the empty streets in her trusty Jeep. Everyone was either in bed or catching last-minute deals at the malls. Patches of crusty snow lined the curbs, blackened with car exhaust and the salt-and-sand mix from city plows. Snow that, just like her heart, had fallen hard and fast, only to be shoved aside, unwanted. She scrubbed away tears as she fought off the images of the snow sculptures, the snowball fight, the feel of Drew's body pressed against hers when their first kiss was postponed by nearby voices.

She reached Drew's house with no memory of how she got there. The route had already become automatic. She peered up through the windshield. The apartment was dark. Maybe this was a bad idea. She shook her head and grabbed the album off the seat as she stepped out. *Just do it and get it over with. You might not get another chance.*

She quietly climbed the stairs, let out a deep breath, and knocked. And knocked again. And again. Tipping her head back, she took in the overcast sky, the light of the moon diffused by the streetlamps. She sucked in a lungful of cold air. She knew Drew was home. She rapped sharply again. *I'm not leaving here until I give this to you.*

Finally, there was noise from within. The door opened slowly.

Drew looked at her with bloodshot eyes. "Nikki, please. Don't make me say good-bye to you again. It was hard enough the first time."

"I'm not here to pressure you." She gripped the album at her side. Handing it to Drew unwrapped in the doorway was so far removed from how she'd planned to present it to her that it felt sacrilegious. She held it out to her. "I wanted to give you this."

Drew's mouth dropped open, and she looked at her with wide eyes. "Oh my God."

"Merry Christmas, Drew. I was thinking of you, even while I was gone. I just wanted you to know."

She ran down the stairs. She heard Drew say something, but she knew if she turned around, she wouldn't be able to handle looking into Drew's eyes for one more second without wanting her.

She sped home, the reflection of the wet streets competing with her soaked eyes. She needed release but had no desire for any of her usual crutches. Singing. *Nah.* Drinking. *No thanks.* Sex. *Yeah, right.*

After a lingering stare at her cello, she readied herself for bed. Sleep was the best escape at her disposal tonight.

Gooseflesh sprung across her bare skin as she pulled the satin sheets over her body. Her bed provided no warmth, no comfort, no rest. She imagined what her life would be like without the band or her career. What purpose would she have? Her need to sing and perform came as naturally to her as breathing.

This is who I am. If Drew couldn't accept her as she was, then she had to imagine her life without Drew.

Her eyes filled again. Life without Drew would be as painful as life without her music. It was becoming excruciatingly clear that having both was too much to ask.

CHAPTER FORTY-THREE

Are you crazy?" Geena said for the third time as Drew tried to explain why she'd ended things with Nikki.

"I'm not crazy. I'm realistic."

Geena followed her down the hall to the office. "No. You're crazy. I can't believe you broke up with her over a stupid picture."

Drew plopped into her chair. "That's not the only reason. I needed to nip it in the bud before it got too serious."

"Too serious? You're too late, Drew, can't you see she's in love with you? It's so flipping obvious you feel the same way."

"We've only known each other a couple of months. No one falls in love that fast, Geena."

"Bullshit. I fell in love with Jen the moment I saw her. And look at us—together almost two years already."

"Totally different situation."

Geena threw her hands in the air. "I give up. You are officially the most stubborn person I've ever met. And I think you're lying to yourself if you think this is the right thing to do."

"And you need to get back on the floor before someone robs us blind."

"There's no one in here."

"Sure. Twist the knife even more, why don't you? It's almost Christmas, and our sales still aren't where they need to be. I don't know why I even bother to work here anymore. If it weren't my father's…" Shit. She shouldn't be saying this in front of Geena.

"Hello? Excuse me?"

Geena jumped at the sound of a man's voice behind her. She turned and asked, "How can I help you, sir?"

"I'm looking for Drew McNally. Is she here?" The lilting voice sounded vaguely familiar.

"That depends," Geena responded protectively.

"It's okay, Geena." She moved out from behind her desk. "Lance, is it?"

"Yes!" Lance extended his hand for her to shake. "We met briefly a couple months ago. You may recall that I'm Passion Play's manager?"

"Yes, I know. Nikki speaks very highly of you."

Lance dropped his mouth wide open in mock surprise and slapped his cheek. "*Does* she now?" He then gestured dismissively. "Oh, you're just being polite."

Drew wasn't sure if she should take him seriously or not. What was he doing here, anyway? She asked him to have a seat, and she returned to the safety of her desk. Geena discreetly closed the door behind them and headed back to work.

"What can I do for you? I know you had to replace quite a bit of your equipment recently. I'd be happy to work out a deal with you if there's anything else the band needs."

Lance crossed his legs and brushed nonexistent lint off his perfectly pressed slacks. "Actually, I'm here to offer *you* a deal."

"I don't understand."

"How would you like to work on Passion Play's next album?"

The heat flooded her neck and face as quickly as she stood. So, this was how Nikki wanted to play? She thought she could use her leverage in the music biz as a ploy to get her back? Well, it wasn't going to work.

"No thanks."

Lance frowned. "You haven't even heard the offer."

She sat back down. "Fine. Let's hear it." She could at least appease the poor man.

Lance cocked his head and blinked rapidly, probably confused by her dismissive demeanor. "Well, anyway," he continued, seemingly regaining his composure. He took a deep breath and looked her in the eye. "I'm here to ask if you'd like to arrange and play strings on our new album, with the possibility of co-producing a handful of songs. We'll pay you quite well, and you'll be entitled to a small percentage of royalties from record sales. Of course, we would arrange a meeting with the band and our attorney to discuss the details—all of which are negotiable—but I wanted to run it by you first to feel out your interest. What do you think?"

Dollar signs flashed across her mind. No more scrounging for spending money. No more canned soup for supper. No more…time for teaching. She'd be selling out and leaving her dad high and dry.

"Look, if this is Nikki's underhanded way of getting me to change my mind, you can tell her to forget it."

"I assure you, Nikki didn't send me. The band believes you'd be a good fit after one of them heard you playing one day. Change your mind about what?"

"About—" *Nice try playing dumb.* Nikki had obviously put him up to this, and she wasn't falling for it. She knew how Nikki worked now. Nikki always leapt before she looked, assuming Drew couldn't say no if she'd already bought tickets or made travel arrangements or whatever. She'd signed up for cello lessons as a way to force her to spend time with her. When Nikki hadn't shown up for this week's lesson, her motivations became clearer. "Nothing."

Lance studied her for a moment. He withdrew a business card from his breast pocket and wrote something on the back of it. He slid it across the desk toward her. "This is a ballpark figure of what we're prepared to pay you to work on the album. It's negotiable, of course. We'll pay you twenty percent of the agreed fee up front when we sign the contract." He stood and put on his overcoat. "If you decide to tour with us, too, the potential to earn more is…I'm sorry, I'm getting ahead of myself. At least give it some thought. Call me if you change your mind, but I will need an answer soon. We head into the studio next month."

She pocketed the card without looking at it and then thanked him as she walked him out. He paused before stepping outside and took an appraising look around. "You have a wonderful store here, Drew. Think of what you could do with the place with a little extra cash flow, hmm?" He smiled hopefully and let himself out before she could reply.

She didn't bother correcting him that it was her father's store, not hers.

Two seconds later, Geena was on her heels. "What was that all about? Who was that guy?"

Drew filled her in on what had transpired.

"Oh my God, Drew! What an opportunity!"

"I said no."

Geena shook her head. "You *what*? Okay, that's it. I'm taking you to a doctor. That hockey puck must've hit you harder than we thought. What is wrong with you?"

"Geena, don't you see what's going on here? Nikki's using this to get me back. Why would Lance show up *now* to offer me this? He doesn't even know me."

"Maybe she talked you up. Hell, your reputation speaks for itself. Everyone knows what an incredible musician you are."

"Now you're the one who's crazy. What reputation? Nobody knows who I am."

"Uh, hello?" Geena wrapped her knuckles on Drew's head and yanked her cell phone from her pants pocket. "Look at this." She tapped away on the screen. "*Yelp* reviews. Five stars. 'I'm so glad I brought my son to DJ's for lessons. I checked out every teacher in the area, and there's no one more qualified than Drew McNally. She's also kind, patient, and her enthusiasm is contagious.' Here's another one: 'I won't take lessons anywhere else. I learned more about music in one month than I did in a year of music theory class in high school. Drew's the bomb.' And this: 'I can't believe Drew doesn't perform anywhere. She plays every instrument under the sun like she was born with it in her hands.'

"Shall I go on? If you Google DJ's, the ratings and reviews are all like this. People love the store and most of all, they love *you*, Drew. Can you imagine the business it would bring in if people knew you worked for Passion Play?"

How did she not know this? *Because you've been wallowing in self-pity. Because you've allowed yourself to be influenced by your dad's stubborn ways. Because you didn't have the courage to stand up to him.*

She was learning all too well that although social media could be your best friend, it could also be your worst enemy. A business association with Nikki Razer now wouldn't put DJ's in a positive light.

"My decision stands, Geena. Now, if you'll excuse me, I have work to do."

But instead of covering the sales floor, she ducked back into her office. With shaky hands, she reached for the card. She should just toss it in the trash bin. Did Nikki really think she could bribe her way back into her life? Although she doubted the band's manager would make her this offer if he didn't think she was qualified. She assumed she'd still have to audition to prove her credibility.

No problem. She knew she was good enough. She knew she could play whatever they threw at her.

The problem was how would Dad manage the store without her

while she took time off for this type of commitment? Geena couldn't cover her hours due to her class schedule. They could hire a temporary replacement, but she didn't want her father burdened with working any additional hours. He was overdoing it as it was. If she worried about him now, she hated to think of the stress he'd be under if she wasn't around as much to alleviate it.

Maybe the others hadn't noticed the signs of fatigue, but she had. He'd been slowing down over the last few months. She wondered if he could even afford to retire if he wanted to.

Either way, he needed her more than Passion Play needed her. Did Lance say they might want her to tour with them, too?

She thought of the reviews Geena quoted. She thought of her students. They needed her, too. Abandoning them would be as bad as abandoning her father.

She flipped over the card. *Oh my God.* She fell into the chair Lance had just vacated. *Twenty percent of this would cover my rent for a year!* Her mind raced with what she could do with the balance.

But at what cost? If the offer came from an impartial person, she might consider it. But it hadn't. It came from Nikki. An offer from Nikki had strings attached. Strings that played on her heart and her conscience.

She was beginning to understand how her father felt all those years ago when her mother kept pressuring him to be something he wasn't. Pressure that ultimately led to his decision to file for divorce. *I just want to teach, damn it.* There was no way she was going to let fame and fortune seduce her as it had Mother. There was no way she was going back to Nikki when it would only lead to heartbreak. Nikki's words came back to her. *You're afraid.* Was that what this was? Was she throwing up obstacles because of fear of success?

She tore the card in half and then in half again. She fisted the pieces into a ball and threw them across the room. She went back to work where she belonged.

CHAPTER FORTY-FOUR

Nikki barged into Lance's office. "What the hell is taking so long?"

Lance glared at her and wrapped up his phone call. "And hello to you, too, your highness," he said after he'd hung up. "I'm sorry your throne isn't here. I've sent it off for its weekly polishing."

"Very funny. How long can it take to trace a stupid Facebook page and arrest that bitch?" She took two steps and had to turn around. A fuckin' hamster wouldn't have room to pace in here.

"Would you untwist your bloomers for two minutes and calm down? It's only been a week. Celebrity extortion isn't exactly high priority on the NYPD's docket, you know. We're doing everything we can. If she'd shown up to get the bag of fake money at the drop, it would have been over. But she obviously knew she was being set up."

She slumped into the high-backed vinyl chair that faced his desk. "I should just hire a private detective."

"Well, that is an option. Although they don't come cheap. I think if we're patient, we'll find that this whole thing will go away on its own, and everyone will forget about it before we know it."

"It's the principle of it, Lance. It bugs the shit out of me that she's getting away with this."

"I know, honey." He leaned back and interlocked his fingers. "I would think you'd be more upset over Drew turning down our offer."

She shot forward in her seat. "What offer?"

"The offer we discussed on our way to New York, remember? I asked her if she wanted to work on the album. Didn't she tell you?"

With everything going on, she'd completely forgotten about that. "We broke up." A lump caught in her throat as soon as the words left her lips.

"Oh, honey." Lance was up immediately. He rubbed her back. "I'm so sorry. When did this happen?"

"Last weekend, when we came back."

"Why didn't you tell us?"

"Don't you think I've suffered enough humiliation this week?" She slid down into a slouch. "You think I wanted everyone to know I also got dumped over this bullshit?"

"Well, now it makes sense why she said…uh, why she turned me down."

"Said what?"

"I don't remember."

She straightened up. "Bullshit, Lance. What did she say?"

Lance backed away as if he didn't trust her temper and returned to his seat. He cleared his throat. "Um, I don't remember exactly, but something along the lines that if this was your, um, 'underhanded way of getting me to change my mind, then she can forget it.'" He tipped his head in sympathy. "I'm sorry."

Nikki rubbed her temples. "I wish you hadn't approached her so soon."

"You know me. No time like the present. And I didn't know things had gone south between you." Lance's timing for clichés and attempt at making light of this only made it worse.

"You don't understand," she mumbled. "On top of everything else, now she thinks I'm trying to buy her forgiveness with a job offer."

"I didn't know, darling." He softened his voice. "I never would have done this without your blessing. You know that. But after that conversation we had, I thought the band was in agreement—"

"It's okay, Lance. It's not your fault." She stood and turned for the door. "As usual, I've fucked up everything. With the band. With Drew. With everything. I'm surprised you all haven't kicked me out by now."

Drew's decided she's better off without me. Maybe Passion Play is, too.

An opera album didn't sound like such a bad idea now.

❖

Nikki opened the refrigerator door. Empty. Not that she was hungry, but she figured she needed to eat *something*. Since the meeting with Lance, the attorney, and the band's public relations manager four days ago, she hadn't left the house. She glared at the cello propped up in the corner of the living room. It taunted her, begged her to practice, but why bother now? She'd prepaid for three months of lessons, but she'd have to eat that money now, along with the thousands of dollars she'd paid for the instrument itself.

Oh well. Maybe someday she'd be inspired to take lessons again. With another teacher, no doubt. Studying with Drew would only be torture. It surely wouldn't be comfortable for Drew, either, because Nikki wouldn't be able to look at her without wanting her. Without needing her touch. Without missing their talks, their laughs, their closeness.

The doorbell rang. *Please be Drew.* She headed toward the door and skidded to a stop. She caught her reflection in a window. *I haven't showered, my hair's a mess, and I'm wearing a concert tee from the last century. Splendid.*

The incessant bell sounded for a third time. She looked at herself again. *Drew's finally here, and I look like shit.* If she wanted Drew to accept her as she was, then she was getting her money's worth today. She let out a huge breath, braced herself, and swung open the door.

She'd never been disappointed to see Jaymi in her life. Until now.

"Well, at least you're dressed." Jaymi held up two bags. "I have food, beer, and a stack of movies. Now let me in."

Nikki stepped aside. "Am *I* this annoying when I pull my tough love act?"

Jaymi loaded the beer in the fridge and unpacked cartons of Chinese food onto the counter. "You're annoying all the time." She tweaked Nikki's chin. "But I love you anyway." She grabbed two plates from a cupboard, distributed the food between them, and carried them to the living room. "Let's go, you bum. Pick a movie and open the beers, will you?"

"Jaymi—"

"We're celebrating."

Nikki pried off the beer caps and followed her. "Celebrating what?"

"If you had answered your phone today, you'd know what." Jaymi sat on the couch.

"I haven't exactly been in the mood to talk to anyone lately." She waited. "Well? Are you going to tell me, or do we have to play twenty questions? I'm not in the mood for that, either."

Jaymi accepted the beer and took a sip. "They arrested Amy. They tracked her down through her IP address."

Jaymi patted the seat, and Nikki sat beside her.

"They've taken down the Facebook page, Lance released a statement today, and voilà, crisis over."

Nikki closed her eyes and let out a huge breath of relief. She tipped her beer back and enjoyed the cold liquid traveling down her throat. "One crisis, anyway." She stared at the plate of food in front of her, willing her appetite to return. "I still lost Drew."

"I have only one thing to say to you where that's concerned." Jaymi bit into a crab Rangoon and then waited until she'd swallowed before continuing. "I have never known you to give up on something you want. You had one setback. So what? If you love her, then fight for her, Nikki."

"Fight for her? I don't know how to do that, Jaymi. She's a person, not a record deal. Drew doesn't want me or the life I have to offer, so what's the point?"

"Wow. You really do love her, don't you?"

Damn it, Jaymi was going to make her cry. She stifled the urge and sighed. "More than I imagined was possible."

Jaymi squeezed her shoulder. "I need to say something, Nikki, and please hear me out before you flip out on me, okay?"

She braced herself. "I'm listening."

"If I were you, I'd be having second thoughts about staying with someone who'd ask you to give up your career to be with her."

"She didn't ask."

"She may as well have." Jaymi placed a hand over hers. "Look at me." The look in Jaymi's eyes was as warm as her touch. "If you love someone, you find a way to make it work."

Jaymi's words, though spoken softly, twisted painfully through her heart. She choked down another sob. "So, you're…you're saying she doesn't love me?"

"I'm saying that if you love each other, you'll find a way to make it work. Do you think it's easy for Kay to be away from LaKeisha for weeks at a time? And look at Lance. He's engaged, for Pete's sake. Do you think that if Shawn hadn't joined Passion Play that I wouldn't miss her like crazy every single night we'd be apart? Right now, Drew's just scared of losing you. Give her time. She'll figure out that it works both ways." She smiled and squeezed her hand. "And she'll realize that you're worth it."

She wished she felt as optimistic as Jaymi did. "I hope you're right."

"So do I. And if not, it's her loss."

She pulled Jaymi into a tight hug. "I don't know what I did to deserve a friend like you."

"I could say the same about you." Jaymi smiled against her shoulder. "I love you, you knucklehead."

She drew back and chuckled. "Right back at ya, Jaymz." She guzzled her beer and pressed "play" on the remote. "*Miss Congeniality*? Again?"

Jaymi grinned. "I can't crush on Sandra Bullock when I watch it with Shawn, but with you…"

"She's jealous of a movie star, but she's okay with you hanging out with me?"

Jaymi's smile widened, and she shrugged. "There's no accounting for the logic of the heart, my friend."

"Crush away, my friend. Crush away."

"I knew you'd understand."

Nikki smiled for the first time in a week. "I'm the one who needs cheering up, and yet here we are, catering to *your* needs."

"You're very giving, you know." Jaymi motioned with her chopsticks. "It's one of your best qualities. Drew must have seen that by now."

"Lot of good it did."

"Give it time." Jaymi took a swig and then tore off a bite of her egg roll. "Are you going to help me eat this food or what?"

Nikki fumbled with her chopsticks and sat back with her plate on her lap. She shoveled in several bites, finally acknowledging how famished she was. Maybe Jaymi was right. She'd give Drew a little time to cool off and then try again. She was worth it, after all.

CHAPTER FORTY-FIVE

January rolled in with a series of blizzards that killed DJ's sales for two consecutive weeks. Thank goodness their holiday numbers had surpassed their year-end goals. Despite the fact that Nikki's pictures had been taken off social media, enough people had seen them to drive even people not interested in the band into DJ's for a possible glimpse of them. She wasn't thrilled with the reason, but she couldn't deny being happy with the sales.

She'd enjoyed Christmas with her dad, despite the lonely curiosity of how Nikki was spending hers. She hadn't gone into detail about her breakup with Nikki with her father; she'd simply said they wanted different things, and it didn't work out. She mentioned nothing of Lance's offer, either. After ignoring several of Lance's messages, she finally responded with a polite, "Thanks, but no thanks" voice mail of her own.

She spent New Year's Eve eating takeout Chinese food. The cats wanted her to share her sweet and sour chicken—which, of course, she did—and then she curled up under a fleece throw with them and watched movies. She shut off the TV just before midnight, resisting the urge to switch over to regular broadcasting. She couldn't bear to watch the ball drop and subject her sorry self to raucous celebrations and kissing couples. She started her year just like she'd started the one before, alone with her cats. But this year, it felt like a slap in the face when she let herself consider what it might have been like instead.

One by one, seasonal colds attacked the entire DJ's staff, herself included. Without Melissa, they were back to single coverage much of the time, so she wasn't able to call out sick. When the bug hit her father at the beginning of February, she fought tooth and nail to get him to stay home and let her take on the extra shifts. He refused. *I definitely know where I get my stubborn streak.*

She was grateful that Nikki's friend Randi had held true to her word. She had continued to escort them to the bank whenever they asked. She was reserved and professional whenever she came in and gave no indication of whether or not Nikki had told her they had split up.

Randi walked in on a Friday afternoon, and Drew breathed a sigh of relief. She and her dad were both on, but he was still so ill that she called Randi to drive him to the bank. Otherwise, she would have had to leave him alone while she went, or he would have insisted on walking there himself.

"Hey, Drew." Randi greeted her with a smile. "Jerry, you ready?"

Her father replied with effort as he moved slowly from around the counter. "I still don't think this…is necessary." His breathing was labored and rapid.

"Look at it this way, Dad. You're getting your money's worth out of your tax dollars."

He managed a small smile and took two short steps. Drew watched in horror as one of his knees buckled, and he grabbed his chest and fell forward onto the floor.

"Dad!" She bolted to his side, and Randi knelt on his other.

"I can't…breathe," he puffed.

"Drew, call 9-1-1." Randi pulled open his jacket and put her ear to his chest. "Irregular heartbeat. Lungs don't sound good, either. Jerry, try to stay calm and listen to my voice, okay?"

Drew yanked her cell from her hip and dialed. One ring was too long. "Come on! Answer!" The call finally connected.

"9-1-1. What's your emergency?"

"It's my father. He collapsed—"

"Gimme the phone." Randi held out her hand. "This is Hartwell. Get an ambulance down here pronto. We have a possible heart attack and symptoms of pneumonia."

"Oh God, he's losing consciousness!"

Randi barked out the address and handed the phone back to Drew. "Give the dispatcher all the information you can on your father." She yanked open Jerry's shirt. "I need to prep for CPR, just in case. Stay with me, Jerry! Can you hear me?"

Her father mumbled, and his head lolled back and forth.

"Drew, do you have any aspirin?"

"Yes, I think so. In the break room."

"Go get it. Here. Take this with you." Randi handed her the bank bag that he'd had tucked under his arm.

She ran down the hall, tossed the moneybag in her desk drawer, and fled across the hall to the break room. The EMTs came through the front door as she handed Randi the pills and a bottle of water.

She was barely aware of her actions for several minutes, but somehow, she'd managed to lock the store and was now in the front passenger seat of Randi's police car, following the ambulance at a frightening speed. Her inner voice drowned out the sound of the sirens. *Dad, please, you have to be okay. Dear God, please, he's too young and too stubborn. You can't take him yet.*

Randi deftly maneuvered through town, taking shortcuts Drew never knew existed, and despite the longest ride of her life, she knew they'd arrived at the hospital in record time. Randi left her alone to give her privacy as she filled out forms in a daze. When she finished, she looked up to see Randi on her cell phone but keeping an eye on her. Drew handed over the clipboard and was told they would come for her as soon as they had any news.

Randi came to her side as Drew reclaimed her seat in the waiting room. "Is there anyone you'd like me to call? Any family? Friends?" Randi leaned forward on her knees and locked eyes with her. "Nikki?"

"Nikki and I broke up a couple months ago. I haven't seen or heard from her since." She was angry about that even though she had no right to be. She'd been clear, and Nikki had respected her wishes. It sucked.

"I know," she said quietly, holding eye contact. "I'm sorry."

"I was surprised, really. I expected her to show up every day trying to charm me into changing my mind."

Randi smiled. "She can be very persuasive."

"That's an understatement. She's a woman who's used to always getting what she wants."

Her smile vanished. "Not when it comes to her heart," she said solemnly.

"You must think I'm an asshole."

"No. I don't." Randi seemed to be wrestling with something. "Nikki doesn't think that either. Look, I probably shouldn't tell you this, but maybe it'll help you understand what Nikki's going through right now. For years, Nikki was in love with someone she couldn't have—someone who didn't love her in return—not in that way, I mean." She rested a hand on Drew's knee. "She's keeping her distance because she doesn't want to endure that kind of pain again."

Like the smoothest modulation in a classical composition, the pieces slid into place. "It's Jaymi, isn't it? She's in love with Jaymi."

Randi's long pause suggested she was reluctant to betray Nikki's confidence. "*Was,* Drew, *was.* That all changed when she met you."

Wow. Her gut had been right all along. Somehow, knowing the truth didn't make her feel much better. "I don't want to be Jaymi's stand-in."

"Whoa, wait a minute. You're not. Trust me. I know more of Nikki's secrets than anybody. You are no rebound. She loves you."

"She told you that?"

Randi shook her head. "She didn't have to."

"Even if that's true, she'll never love me as much as she loves her career."

Randi narrowed her eyes. "Why does it have to be a competition?" When Drew had no answer, she stood. "You sure you don't want me to call anyone for you?"

"No, thank you, Randi. I can call them. You've done more than enough. Thank you for, well, taking charge and…everything." The tears slipped out before she could stop them.

Randi handed her a box of tissues from a side table.

She accepted it gratefully and blew her nose. "You don't have to wait around if you have to get back to work." Drew tossed her tissue in a small trash bin Randi held out for her.

"I'm not going to leave you here alone. And aren't you forgetting something?"

Drew cocked her head, confused. "What?"

"I'm your ride."

Oh, yeah. She could call Geena to pick her up. *Shit!* Melissa had a lesson scheduled today, too. She'd worry if she showed up to a closed store. She'd have to call them both since Geena was supposed to come in at four to work the closing shift. *I suppose I should call Mom, too.*

"I need to make a few calls. Really, Randi, you don't have to stay unless you want to."

Randi stood. "I'll stick around a bit, but I'm not leaving until someone can wait here with you and I know you have a ride. I'm willing to do both, okay? Deal?"

She nodded and managed a small smile. "Okay."

Randi gently patted her shoulder and gave it a squeeze. "Okay, then." She made sure Drew had her number saved in her phone and left her alone so she could make her calls.

She sent Geena a text and received a prompt reply confirming that she would head right out to reopen the store. She dialed her mother's number and fought back tears. The frightened child within desperately wanted her mom, and she was crushed when she got her voice mail. The seconds ticked by as she took a moment to gather her wits and then left what she hoped was a coherent message.

The minutes stretched into an hour. She'd doodled in the margins of a *People* magazine and added facial hair and other exaggerated modifications to photos of celebrities before painful tightness in her body prompted her to get up and stretch. She stood, arching backward and reaching toward the ceiling until her spine loosened slightly. Randi had kept a respectful distance, checking in periodically with a look or a few encouraging words. It was simultaneously comforting and uncomfortable. *It should be Nikki here with me, caring for me, staying by my side.*

Finally, a nurse came for her and brought her into a room to meet with the doctor. She focused on her words as she reeled off a bunch of medical mumbo jumbo and then calmly explained his condition in layman's terms.

As she absorbed the information, questions of how she was going to handle the unforeseeable future weaved their way in and out of her mind. Insurance claims and impending medical bills. Covering the store. Finding someone to take care of her cats.

How utterly alone she was.

She nodded and thanked the doctor. She became acutely aware of an empty chair beside hers. She wished so badly that Nikki was in it.

Randi reluctantly agreed to leave once Drew filled her in and explained that she was spending the night. She stepped into an empty elevator and headed to the intensive care unit. A kind-faced older woman at the nurses' station told her they were getting him settled, and she could see him soon.

She found a vacant corner at the end of the hall by a window. Before she could change her mind, she took out her phone and tapped *My Favorite Customer* on the contacts screen. *As it turns out, Nikki, you're still my favorite.* It took three rings before Nikki answered, sounding a bit out of breath in a noisy background.

"Drew?"

"Yeah, it's me."

"Are you crying? What's wrong?"

"I'm at the hospital. It's my dad. They just moved him into intensive care."

"What happened? Is he okay? Are you okay?"

She spilled out an abbreviated version of the earlier events. "I was so scared, Nikki. I thought…he grabbed his chest and just fell over. I thought I was going to lose him." She started crying again. "They said he has walking pneumonia and serious blockages in two arteries."

"Oh, man. Are you okay? Is Randi still there with you?"

"I sent her home. I'm staying the night. There wasn't any reason for her to stay. He's stable, but he needs bypass surgery as soon as possible. They have him on blood thinners and some meds to clear out his lungs. As long as he responds well, they'll operate on Monday."

"Damn it."

Drew heard an overhead page and shuffling noise in the background. "Where are you?"

"O'Hare. We're on a ninety-minute layover to LA."

"The Grammys," she said absently. "That's this weekend, isn't it?"

"Yes. Sunday. I should be there with you, Drew."

But you're not. That was the point, wasn't it? Nikki should be here, but she couldn't be. *If we get together again, this is how it will always be. Nikki will be torn between me and her band's commitments, and I'll be torn between either accepting that or asking her to choose.*

"You can't miss the Grammys, Nikki. You've worked your whole life for this."

"But…Drew, I—"

"No, Nikki. This is exactly what I didn't want to happen. Please, listen to me. You need to go. This is a once-in-a-lifetime opportunity, and I know what it means to you, and I…" *I care about you too much, Nikki, but you'll grow to resent me, and I won't be able to handle that.* "I'd never be able to live with myself if I knew you were only here because you felt obligated to be here."

"Drew, you don't understand—"

"I just…I just wanted you to know what was going on." She disconnected before Nikki could weaken her defenses. She wandered back to the waiting room and shut off her phone. She needed to conserve the battery—or so she told herself. *I need to let her go before this gets any harder.* It had taken every ounce of strength not to stop Nikki as she'd run away from her the night she'd brought her the Ella Fitzgerald album. She still hadn't been able to listen to it.

It was going to be a long night.

❖

Nikki stared at her phone. She squeezed it so hard she feared it might shatter in her hand. *Drew doesn't want me there. She's in crisis, and still, she doesn't want me there. But she called. What does that mean?*

"Nik, we need to go. They're about to board." Jaymi tugged at her sleeve. When she didn't budge, Jaymi tipped her head and forced eye contact. "What's wrong?"

She snapped out of her funk and looked around her. Five questioning faces stared back at her. Jaymi. Shawn. Kay. Brian. Lance. People she loved more than life itself. People who counted on her every day. For strength. For encouragement. For love. For friendship. For livelihood.

"I love each of you more than you'll ever know."

Jaymi rubbed her arm. The concern on her face was palpable. "Hey, tell me what's going on."

She looked into Jaymi's beautiful blue eyes—eyes that used to break her heart into a million pieces every time she looked at them. Eyes that used to ignite painful longing and useless desires that she thought she'd suffer with forever. Now all she wanted to do was cry on her best friend's shoulder.

She'd stayed away from Drew for two months because she'd had enough of wanting someone she couldn't have. She'd learned the hard way with Jaymi that it was no way to live.

Except it was different with Drew. *Drew loves me. I'm sure of it.*

"Jaymi, can I talk to you a minute?"

"Yeah, of course." Jaymi turned to the rest of the band. "Go ahead, guys. We'll be along in a minute."

As she filled Jaymi in on the situation back home, it became crystal clear what she needed to do.

❖

Drew checked the time. Again. *Whoever invented the clock was a sadistic bastard.* The people working there also needed to look up the definition of "soon" because according to her dictionary, she should have been able to see her dad hours ago.

Stiff and hungry, she checked in with the nurses' station again only to learn they still had no idea when she could see him, and she headed to the cafeteria. As she slid into a remote corner booth with food she hoped she could keep down, she stared at the empty seat across from her. As badly as she wanted Nikki here by her side, she knew she'd done the right thing by insisting she go to the Grammys.

Maybe it was selfish of me to call. She should be on cloud nine right now, and instead, I might have ruined it for her. She took a tentative bite of her sandwich. Despite her hunger, she tasted nothing, the flavors on her tongue benign and unsatisfying. She forced down the food out of sheer necessity and willpower.

Why does it have to be a competition? Randi's words echoed through her mind.

God, Nikki must think I'm a horrible person. She sucked on her straw, but she couldn't rid her mouth of its cottony coating fast enough. She ripped off the plastic cover and took huge gulps until the cold liquid provided a small semblance of relief.

Nikki's never asked me for a single thing except for a chance to get to know each other and to be appreciated for who she really is.

And time and time again, Nikki had selflessly done things for her without even being asked. Every gesture had been something in Drew's best interest. She was even willing to miss the Grammys to be with her now. What did that say about her?

Maybe she *was* projecting her feelings toward her mother onto Nikki. Her self-absorbed, emotionally unavailable, sorry excuse for a mother, whose only response to her message was a succinct text telling her not to worry, that her father was a strong man, and to keep her posted. Drew had asked Nikki to make an unfair and uncalled for choice. She'd selfishly made it an ultimatum when there didn't need to be one at all. She'd ruined everything.

How *was* Nikki spending her weekend? Was she rubbing elbows with other music stars? Was the band rehearsing like crazy? Was she accepting invitations to after-parties?

Is she missing me?

I hope so. Her insides twisted. *Because I miss you.*

"If you're having the time of your life, then I'm happy for you because you deserve it," she whispered, surprised at her own sincerity with how much Nikki's happiness meant to her.

All Nikki ever wanted was to love me and for me to love her. She dropped her fork onto her plate and fell back against the unforgiving plastic seat. *I love her. I do. My God, I* love *her.* Her heart beat wildly in her chest. *If she loves me too…if I know she'll always come home to me, isn't that better than not being with her at all?*

Her phone chimed. She sighed with relief at the text message and quickly scooped up her food tray. Everything else would have to wait.

She was going to see her dad.

CHAPTER FORTY-SIX

Nikki couldn't deny the atmosphere at the Grammys was electric. There had even been a few moments so far when she hadn't thought about Drew. Yet even when she'd gotten caught up in the thrill of meeting some of her musical idols or posing for group photos or answering questions from red carpet correspondents, there was something missing—everyone else had dates on their arms.

They'd just been ushered to their seats. Sandwiched between Jaymi and Kay, Nikki's peripheral vision caught Shawn's leg bouncing nervously. She fought back her jealousy. Jaymi had her lover by her side for the biggest night of their lives when the woman she loved was three thousand miles away. It hurt even worse knowing that it was Drew's choice to not be here, although with what had happened with Jerry, it was probably a damn good thing she hadn't come after all.

Jaymi swiveled in her seat to look behind them and then stood abruptly. "You made it!"

Nikki turned to see Jaymi hugging her father as he found his seat next to Brian's parents—Jaymi's aunt and uncle—in the row behind them. *Sometimes, Jaymi, I wish I could be you.*

After greeting Jaymi and Brian's family, she turned to Shawn and saw sadness in her eyes. Shawn's parents weren't there either; she'd lost one to death and the other to estrangement. She gestured to herself and the rest of the group. "You've got us, Shawn."

Shawn smiled. "I know."

Everyone settled into their seats as the audience lights dimmed, and Sierra Sparks took the stage to perform the opening number. Nikki's insides fluttered, and she peeked at her watch. Passion Play would be making their Grammy debut in a little over an hour, right before the commercial break prior to their first category nomination. She wanted to savor every minute of this experience, and she was itching to grab the mike again. Rehearsals yesterday had been a rush. She could only imagine how energized she was going to feel in front of an audience of her peers and heroes.

As the show continued, her feelings ebbed and flowed between enjoying the show and worrying about Drew and Jerry. If there had ever been a time in her life she needed to be in two places at once, it was now. Regardless of what Drew had told her, she couldn't help thinking that Drew wanted her there, or she wouldn't have called.

Drew's right. There will be times like this when we'll both have to make sacrifices. Time apart that couldn't be avoided. Long distances between them that couldn't be traveled quickly. Commitments that had to be honored. Was it all worth it?

Is Drew worth it?

Yes. Most definitely. Her stomach lurched. *Does Drew think I am?*

The audience suddenly rose into a standing ovation as the latest pop sensation concluded their performance. The emcee announced a commercial break, and Nikki jumped at the opportunity to escape to the restroom.

She grabbed Shawn's arm on her way by. "Hey. Come with me. I want to ask you something."

Shawn gave her a questioning look, then shrugged. "Okay."

Once in the safety of the lobby, she pulled Shawn aside. "If you hadn't joined Passion Play and you were still back home getting your own career off the ground, do you think you and Jaymi would've stayed together?"

Shawn looked at her as if she was nuts. "Of course we would have. Look at how happy she is in there. It's awesome."

"What if you couldn't have come with her tonight?"

Shawn beamed. "Dude, so what? That would've sucked, but I wouldn't've wanted her to miss this for anything."

"Even if you were having a crisis?"

She studied her feet for a moment and rocked side to side as if considering her response carefully. She looked up and nodded. "Yeah. Yeah, it wouldn't matter what the hell I was going through; I'd suck it up and insist she go. I couldn't live with myself if she missed something this important. Her happiness is everything to me." Her expression turned more serious. "Nikki, what's going on?"

"Jerry's in the hospital."

"Drew's father? Shit. Is he okay?"

"I don't know. But Drew told me not to come. She said roughly the same thing you just did about me not missing this."

"Man. No wonder you're distracted." She nudged Nikki's shoulder with her fist. "She must really care about you."

An inkling of comprehension dawned on her. "You think so?"

"Well, yeah. She's gotta know how much this means to you. Come on, I've seen how tight she is with her dad. If she didn't want you to miss this…"

Theme music emitted from the theater, their cue that the break was about to end, and she still needed to use the ladies' room. "Thanks, Shawn. You've been a big help. You better get back in there."

"Yeah, I guess so." Shawn stared at her for a moment. "You coming?"

"In a minute."

Shawn headed back inside, and Nikki fell against the wall. It was reassuring that Shawn's feelings on the subject agreed with her own gut. *Drew's pushing me away out of fear but also, just maybe, out of love.*

The next segment of the show dragged on. Nerves wiggled their way in as their turn to perform drew nearer, and she channeled all her energy into finding her focus. The band scurried behind a young man wearing a headset, and she nestled into her home behind the mike stand.

She closed her eyes and silenced her mind. She opened them to a wide black curtain rising in front of them, slowly revealing the sea of high-fashioned, designer-clad audience members. The crowd roared as Brian clacked his sticks together above his head and then banged out one measure on the drums. Jaymi, Shawn, and Kay dove into the intro, and they were off.

She stood motionless, one hand on the stand to steady herself and the other wrapped around the microphone, wishing it was Drew's hand, and poured out her soul. They came to the chorus, and she grabbed the mike, stand and all, and took it with her back and forth across the stage as she made love to the audience with her voice. The crowd's response ignited her further.

Jaymi launched into a guitar solo, and they grinned at each other. Shawn strummed wildly away on her acoustic. Nikki reversed direction and caught Kay's eyes glimmering with excitement even though her expression was one of concentration. She rounded on Brian, whose face reflected pure joy. *God, I love this.*

The song ended much too soon. She patted her heart and blew a kiss to the crowd in thanks. Two guests about halfway back were the first to stand. Even from this distance, she recognized them. *It can't be.* The surrounding spectators rose and obscured her line of sight.

"Let's go!" The stagehand waved his hand at them frantically. There was a blur of activity as they handed off their instruments and came together to an area near the main stage to await their fate.

Amidst her mates' chatter, she tried wrapping her mind around what she just saw. Or *thought* she saw.

Jaymi touched her arm. "Nik, what is it?"

"My parents are here."

"They are?"

"How…I didn't give them tickets."

Jaymi chuckled quietly and smiled. "Something tells me your father could score Grammys tickets if he wanted them bad enough."

"But—"

The theme music cut her off, and they all turned their attention to the host, who introduced the presenters for the category of Best Rock Performance by a Duo or Group. After exchanging lame, scripted banter, they named off the nominees one by one.

A drum roll erupted in her chest. *This is it.* Winners or not, she couldn't be prouder of the four people standing with her now.

"And the Grammy goes to…" The woman peeled open the envelope.

Nikki nearly jumped out of her skin at the excruciatingly long pause. *Come on, just say it already.*

"Passion Play!"

They screamed and engulfed each other in a group hug. She floated up the steps and accepted the award handed to her. It would have weighed her down had she not been so high. They walked together to the podium. Jaymi nodded to her to speak first.

She cradled the Grammy securely in one hand and adjusted the microphone. "Wow. I…I'm stunned."

She took a moment to breathe and, without even trying, spotted her parents sporting expressions of pride and happiness that she'd never seen before. *I'm stunned all right—in more ways than one.*

"Whew, so many people to thank. Our fans, first and foremost, for their support from day one. My bandmates, whom I love with all my heart. Our manager, Lance, who's a big pain in the ass, but then again, so am I." She smiled and relaxed slightly when the audience chuckled.

She blew out a big breath. She looked directly at her parents.

"But none of us would be up here right now if it weren't for our music teachers. So, thank you, Mom and Dad, for getting me into lessons and supporting my passion to play. And lastly, to one very special teacher, the woman I love, who couldn't be here tonight." She held up the Grammy. "No matter what the future brings, baby, I salute you." She stepped away as Jaymi took over.

Her entire body tingled, and her mind spun. *I just told the world that I love her.* She didn't even know if Drew was watching the show. She followed the group back to their seats in a daze, but she was intercepted in the aisle by her mom and dad. They were all smiles. It was weird.

Her mom pulled her into a bone-crushing hug. "Oh, Nikki. This is so wonderful! I'm so happy for you!" She released Nikki, and her father took her place.

He held her at arm's length. "That was one hell of a performance. And I'm not talking about your speech, although what you said means a lot." His smile was genuine, the sparkle in his eyes reminiscent of her own. "Even if you hadn't won, I want you to know I'm proud of you. All of you."

She tried to swallow, but her throat restricted with a threat of tears. "You are?" Her voice sounded squeaky.

He nodded and rested his hand on her shoulder. "I promise I'll never hound you about switching to opera again."

She hugged him tightly. "Now, that would be something." She leaned back and couldn't resist teasing him. "A politician keeping a promise."

They grinned at each other, and he chuckled. "Can I count on your vote?"

She cocked her chin in his direction. "Put it in writing, and I'll think about it."

He grasped his jaw in mock contemplation. "You drive a hard bargain, but you got it."

She hugged them both again and rejoined the others. She was now anxious for it all to be over, but they had to stick around for the other nomination.

She needed to get home to Drew, so she could tell her, face-to-face, that she was in love with her.

CHAPTER FORTY-SEVEN

"There's my Doodlebug."

For once, Drew didn't mind her dad calling her that in front of other people. She was so relieved that he was alive that she wouldn't have cared what he called her. He had bounced back well over the weekend. Now they needed to get over the hurdle of the surgery, scheduled only two hours from now.

"Come here." He motioned her closer with his hand. "I want to talk to you about something."

"Okay…" She didn't like the seriousness of his tone.

"I know about the job offer from Passion Play."

She couldn't look at him. She hadn't wanted him to know. "Who told you?"

"Nobody. I overheard Melissa and Geena talking about it."

Troublemakers. She might have to consider scheduling those two on opposite shifts.

"Honey, I don't understand. Why did you turn it down?"

"You know why, Dad. You need me at the store—even more so now."

"Drew." He sighed and shook his head. "I love working with you at the store, and you're very good at what you do, but I never expected you to devote your entire life to the place. That was never the deal. If you want the job, take it. You never know if or when you'll have another opportunity like this. You can't put your dreams on hold, Drew, and I never wanted you to."

She got up and stared out the window, not seeing anything beyond it. It wasn't her father who had trapped her in her job. She'd done it to herself, convincing herself he couldn't do it without her. Nikki was right. She was afraid. Had she thrown away a chance of a lifetime? She hadn't even met with Lance to find out any details. For all she knew, she might have been able to juggle both commitments. Now she'd never know.

"Look at me, Drew."

She turned to face her father.

"Your life is your own. Make it what you want. Don't base your decisions on me, okay? Or the store. If it's truly in your heart to have a lifelong career at DJ's, then by all means, you know you have a job as long as you want. But don't make the mistake of thinking the store means more to me than your happiness."

Her throat caught. She didn't want to cry in front of him. He needed her to be strong right now. "I'm afraid you'll feel like I'm abandoning you." *Like Mom did.*

"Aw, sweetheart, I can take care of myself. Besides, I've been kicking around the idea of retiring and just staying on part-time. If you want to take over the business, it's yours. If not, I'll promote Geena."

"Dad! Don't talk like that. You're going to get through this just fine and be back on your feet before you know it."

He waved at her dismissively. "I know that. I'd already planned to talk to you about it before all this happened." He continued before she could process the decisions she now needed to make. "I know you've been itchin' to try out some new things. DJ's will be in good hands with you gals."

Drew stepped back and dropped into a chair. "I don't know what to say." Would this be a blessing or a curse? If she was able to implement some of her ideas and increase profits, would it be enough to make her happy, or would the burden of ownership interfere with the time she needed to teach? *Or work on Passion Play's album?* Her dad's blessing had suddenly put the offer in a new light. Was it too late to reconsider? According to Lance, they would have gone into the studio last month. And she still needed to consider whether or not she could handle being around Nikki again.

"Think about it, okay? Whatever you decide, you have my blessing. But life can turn on a dime, honey. Don't waste what time we're given."

She nodded. He closed his eyes and drifted to sleep. He shouldn't be thinking about this stuff now. She sighed heavily. She could use some sleep, too. She'd been at the hospital nearly round the clock for three days, going home only to shower and change. Melissa and Geena were taking turns caring for the cats. Geena had stepped up like a true professional by rearranging the schedule to make sure the store would be covered for a week. Geena would definitely be the right choice to take over the business if she didn't want to.

She started to doze, and her father's voice woke her. "Tell me, what happened with you and Nikki?"

Nikki. She'd thought she could handle watching the Grammys last night, but in the end, she decided not to torture herself. How could she enjoy watching Nikki living out a dream come true while she nursed an aching heart and worried herself sick over her dad's upcoming surgery?

"You can tell me it's none of my business," he continued. "But I'm only going to tell you this once. If you're going to let one silly little picture keep you away from the woman you love, then I've failed you as a father."

She looked at him in disbelief. "You're the best father anyone could ask for! And how do you know about the pictures?"

He smiled. "You think I don't hear you girls talking?"

"But, Dad, look what happened to you and Mom. Her career destroyed our family."

His eyes sharpened. "No, it didn't. We were two very different people who wanted different things. It wasn't her fame that came between us; it was who she was and how she handled it. People handle that kind of stuff differently. Simple as that."

She couldn't believe her ears. Simple? It was far from simple.

"You know what's not simple? Love." He reached for her hand and gave it a squeeze. "Whatever it is that's keeping you apart, find a way to work it out," he said earnestly.

"I wish it was that simple, Dad."

"Do you love her?"

She couldn't lie. Not to him. "Yes."

"I know you do."

"You do?"

He just smiled. "If she loves you, too, then stop being so gosh-darned stubborn and find a way." He closed his eyes again, a little smirk on his lips. "Find a way, Doodlebug. You deserve to be happy, and it's time you stop making excuses that keep you from doing what you need to do."

She stretched over the bed and hugged him. "I love you, Dad."

"I love you, too. Don't worry." He mussed her hair. "I'm going to be fine, and so are you."

Hearing the words from her dad made them so much easier to believe.

CHAPTER FORTY-EIGHT

Nikki pulled her Mustang into a space with a screech and ran into the hospital. She stopped at the front desk and dashed off again. She spotted Drew in the waiting room, hunched over, a pen scurrying over a piece of paper on the small table in front of her. *Doodling.* She approached quietly, trepidation quickly descending upon her as she braced herself for whatever reception Drew was about to give her.

When her shadow fell across the artwork, Drew looked up. Nikki saw shock in her eyes, then something that looked like gratitude.

Nikki didn't hesitate. She pulled Drew into her arms. "It's going to be okay, baby. He's strong. He's in good hands here, and he's going to be okay."

"I can't believe you came."

She swiped Drew's tears away with her thumbs. Drew looked as if she hadn't slept for a week, and she was still the most beautiful thing she'd ever seen. God, she'd missed her. Before she was tempted to kiss away the next round of tears, she reluctantly stepped back and got her a tissue. "Why wouldn't I?"

"But the Grammys—"

"Are over. I left right after we said thank you at the podium, and I took the first red-eye flight home I could find."

"You…you won?"

Nikki returned Drew's smile. "Yeah. We won. Both categories."

"Nikki, that's wonderful. I'm so happy for you guys. This'll open up some great opportunities for the band."

She shrugged. "It'll be good for them." They sat down in an awkward silence. "Any news on how the surgery is going?"

"Nothing yet. They took him in about an hour ago."

"How are you holding up? Have you eaten? I can go get you something from the cafeteria."

She started to stand, but Drew caught her by the arm.

She looked at Nikki with wide eyes. "You said 'them.'"

"Yes."

"Not 'us.'"

"That's right."

"Nikki, what are you saying?"

Nikki looked around. There were two people sitting together on the other side of the room. "Can we go somewhere a little more private?"

Drew nodded. "Yeah. They said they'd text me if I wasn't here or if they needed me."

"Care for some fresh air?"

"That sounds good. I need to stretch."

Drew stopped at the desk to let them know she was stepping out. She shrugged into her parka, and they walked in silence. Surrounded by nothing but a concrete parking lot and assaulted by frigid February temperatures, Nikki suggested they talk in her Mustang.

She started the car and cranked up the heat. "I'm taking a break from Passion Play. A temporary hiatus, if you will." She watched Drew's face carefully, gauging her reaction to this unexpected news.

"But…why?"

She swiveled in her seat and cupped Drew's hands in her own. "Because I'm in love with you, Drew. I went from the happiest I've ever been in my life to the most miserable, and the difference was you. A thousand awards can't give me what I had with you." She wondered if her heartbeat drowned out the sound of her voice. "If I have to choose between touring with Passion Play and being with you, I choose you."

Drew's eyes shot wide open. "Nikki, you can't…I can't let you do this. Not for me, not for anyone. You'll regret it, and you'll resent me, and don't say you won't because we both know it's the truth." She turned to look out a window.

Nikki's heart pounded. "Then tell me you don't love me." She gently turned Drew's chin and met her eyes. "Tell me you don't love me, and I will walk away right now."

Drew took a deep, shuddering breath. "I can't."

Her heart leapt inside her chest. She dared not succumb to her excitement yet. She needed to hear Drew say the words. "Tell me."

"I've done nothing but push you away since we met. I've been selfish. I don't deserve the sacrifice you're making."

She lightly stroked Drew's cheek. "Tell me."

"I've let my fears make my decisions for me instead of my heart." Drew lifted Nikki's hand and kissed her palm. "I'm so sorry."

Nikki leaned in until their faces were only inches apart. "Tell me," she whispered.

"I can't tell you I don't love you." Drew met her eyes. "Because I do love you. I didn't want to. I tried not to. But no matter how hard I tried, I couldn't stop falling in love with you."

She covered Drew's lips with her own. Drew wrapped her arms around her as they melted together.

"God, Drew, I missed you so much. I love you, and I promise I will do whatever it takes to make you happy."

Drew kissed her and ran her fingers through Nikki's hair. She shivered with the comfort of Drew's touch.

"Then you need to make two promises to me right now," said Drew.

"Anything, my love. Anything."

"You need to promise me you'll call Lance today and tell him you're not leaving the band."

She tucked back her chin and raised an eyebrow. "But what about me having to be away on tour? And what about me being in the spotlight or getting screwed over with another scandal? I thought you couldn't handle all that?"

"Hell, we've already dealt with that already, and I still love you. We'll make it work, baby, one way or another. Besides, you wouldn't be the woman I fell in love with if you weren't who you are."

She grinned. "Are you sure?"

Drew nodded and gave her a quick peck on the lips. "I hated being apart from you the last two months, too. The holidays sucked, and now I'm really pissed that I missed being with you at the Grammys. And it's all because I was too stubborn and too afraid to let go."

"I can't believe you didn't at least watch it on TV."

"It would've been too painful. I wanted to be there more than anything."

"Well, you're in luck. I recorded it."

Drew smiled that beautiful smile, her caramel eyes twinkling with mischief. "Why am I not surprised?"

"The most amazing thing that happened didn't happen on camera, though."

"What was that?"

"My parents were there."

"Nikki, that's great!"

"That's not the best part. My father said he'd never been prouder of me and that he'd been wrong to try to steer me away from what made me happy."

"Oh, baby, that's wonderful."

Hearing Drew call her baby was such a sweet sound. "I think he finally sees that we're the real deal. Maybe my mom worked on him, too. I don't know, but it was awesome."

"I'm so happy for you."

They kissed for several minutes before making their way back to the cafeteria for lunch. In the hours that followed, she brought Drew up to date with the news of Amy's arrest, and she managed to convince her that Lance had made the job offer without her knowledge. Drew, in turn, told her about her talk with Jerry and that, depending on his health needs, she would consider her career options carefully—including an interest in meeting with Lance to discuss working on the album.

The surgeon showed up and interrupted their conversation. "Everything went very well. We're moving him to recovery in a few minutes." He smiled kindly. "We'll keep him here under observation for three to five days, depending on how he's doing, but it looks like he's going to be just fine. I'll have a nurse come get you when he's settled."

"So, I can see him soon?"

He nodded. "He'll sleep for a while longer, but yes, we'll bring you to his room in about fifteen minutes. That way you'll be there when he wakes up."

"Thank you so much."

While Drew met with the nurse, Nikki excused herself to grab a coffee and to call Randi and Jaymi to give them the news. She smiled. She had lots of good news to report.

For the first time in her life, she felt whole. She had her band. She had success. She had her father's blessing. She had love.

Everything had finally fallen into place.

She rejoined Drew in Jerry's room, and they sat together quietly as he slept. Drew thought out loud, hashing out all the possibilities of the many decisions she had before her.

Exhaustion took over, and Drew dozed on Nikki's shoulder.

Nikki remained silent so as not to awaken either of them. *Silent.* "That's it!"

"That's what?" Drew mumbled.

"What if DJ's had a silent partner who could cover the cost of adding to your team so you'd be able to devote all of your time to teaching when you wanted to?"

Drew sat up. "You want to buy DJ's?"

"No, not buy it. *Invest* in it. You and Jerry would still call all the shots. I'll just put up the dough so you can do what you want with it."

She could see Drew's wheels spinning already.

"That's a great idea."

They both turned at the sound of Jerry's voice.

"Dad! You're awake!"

Nikki stood and headed for the door. "I'll let them know at the nurses' station."

Drew joined Nikki in the hallway a few minutes later. "The nurse asked me to step out so the doctor could check in on him." She smiled. "I don't think he's in any condition to make any legal decisions right now, but you should know he loves your idea."

"And what about you?"

"If it means I'll have time for all my teaching programs *and* work on your album, then I say we go for it."

Nikki's heart raced at the possibility of it coming together so perfectly. "Are you sure?"

"Yeah." Drew hugged her. "I'm sure. But don't think that means you can boss me around."

She grinned. "I wouldn't want to step on your cats' toes. Hey, you never told me what the other promise was."

"Huh?"

"You said I had to promise you two things. I promised I wouldn't quit the band. What's the other thing?"

Drew kissed her softly. "You have to show up for all your cello lessons. You've missed about eight in a row, and you're way behind."

"Oh, really? Is there some kind of punishment for that?"

"There most certainly is."

Nikki grinned. "Excellent. What, may I ask, is my punishment?"

"You need to stay after class and cater to my every need."

"I like the way you think, Professor."

"I like the way I think, too."

"Hey, that's my line."

Drew kissed her long and slow. "Not anymore, partner."

"Partner. I like the sound of that." She caressed Drew's cheek. "So, does that mean you're willing to give this thing a shot?"

"Yes. As it turns out, I've grown very attached to you."

"Ah, the ties that bind."

Drew interlaced their fingers and smiled. "Or in our case, cello strings."

She slid her arms around Drew's waist. "Cello strings can break, you know."

"Then you'll have to play on my heartstrings instead—because I love you, Nikki, and *those* strings are unbreakable."

"Your words are music to my ears, my love. Music to my ears." Nikki kissed her tenderly. "I love you too, Professor."

They went back into Jerry's room, and as Drew and her dad spoke about options, Nikki relaxed into the feeling of being so fully and truly alive. Life was more beautiful than she could ever have imagined, and it was only the beginning.

About the Author

Holly Stratimore discovered a love for writing in high school when she wrote seven humorous stories—just for fun—featuring herself and her friends as the characters. Since her foremost passion was music, she focused her creative energies on writing songs and playing guitar. That all changed in 2007 when a story came to her in a dream. She was compelled to write it down, and her love for writing lesbian romance was born.

In addition to writing and music, Holly is passionate about animals, being kind to others, and making people laugh—and groan—with her quick wit and puns. She is a huge Snoopy fan and finds ways to include Peanuts references in all of her writing endeavors. She is also a self-proclaimed "Potterhead" and loves anything and everything Harry Potter.

Holly resides in New Hampshire, where she enjoys cheering for the Boston Red Sox, attending concerts, walks on the beach and exploring old New England towns with her wife, and spending time with friends and family.

To keep up with Holly's events and shenanigans, visit:
www.hollystratimore.com
Facebook: Holly Stratimore-Author
Twitter: @HollyStratimore
www.boldstrokesbooks.com

Books Available From Bold Strokes Books

Emily's Art and Soul by Joy Argento. When Emily meets Andi Marino she thinks she's found a new best friend, but Emily doesn't know that Andi is fast falling in love with her. Caught up in exploring her sexuality, will Emily see the only woman she needs is right in front of her? (978-1-163555-355-0)

Escape to Pleasure: Lesbian Travel Erotica, edited by Sandy Lowe and Victoria Villaseñor. Join these award-winning authors as they explore the sensual side of erotic lesbian travel. (978-1-163555-339-0)

Music City Dreamers by Robyn Nyx. Music can bring lovers together. In Music City, it can tear them apart. (978-1-163555-207-2)

Ordinary is Perfect by D. Jackson Leigh. Atlanta marketing superstar Autumn Swan's life derails when she inherits a country home, a child, and a very interesting neighbor. (978-1-163555-280-5)

Royal Court by Jenny Frame. When royal dresser Holly Weaver's passionate personality begins to melt Royal Marine Captain Quincy's icy heart, will Holly be ready for what she exposes beneath? (978-1-163555-290-4)

Strings Attached by Holly Stratimore. Rock star Nikki Razer always gets what she wants, but when she falls for Drew McNally, a music teacher who won't date celebrities, can she convince Drew she's worth the risk? (978-1-163555-347-5)

The Ashford Place by Jean Copeland. When Isabelle Ashford inherits an old house in small-town Connecticut, family secrets, a shocking discovery, and an unexpected romance complicate her plan for a fast profit and a temporary stay. (978-1-163555-316-1)

Treason by Gun Brooke. Zoem Malderyn's existence is a deadly threat to everyone on Gemocon, and Commander Neenja KahSandra must find a way to save the woman she loves from having to make the ultimate sacrifice. (978-1-163555-244-7)

A Wish Upon a Star by Jeannie Levig. Erica Cooper has learned to depend on only herself, but when her new neighbor, Leslie Raymond, befriends Erica's special needs daughter, the walls protecting Erica's heart threaten to crumble. (978-1-163555-274-4)

Answering the Call by Ali Vali. Detective Sept Savoie returns to the streets of New Orleans, as do the dead bodies from ritualistic killings, and she does everything in her power to bring their killers to justice while trying to keep her partner, Keegan Blanchard, safe. (978-1-163555-050-4)

Friends Without Benefits by Dena Blake. When Dex Putman gets the woman she thought she always wanted, she soon wonders if it's really love after all. (978-1-163555-349-9)

Invalid Evidence by Stevie Mikayne. Private Investigator Jil Kidd is called away to investigate a possible killer whale, just when her partner Jess needs her most. (978-1-163555-307-9)

Pursuit of Happiness by Carsen Taite. When attorney Stevie Palmer's client reveals a scandal that could derail Senator Meredith Mitchell's presidential bid, their chance at love may be collateral damage. (978-1-163555-044-3)

Seascape by Karis Walsh. Marine biologist Tess Hansen returns to Washington's isolated northern coast, where she struggles to adjust to small-town living while courting an endowment from Brittany James for her orca research center. (978-1-163555-079-5)

Second In Command by VK Powell. Jazz Perry's life is disrupted and her career jeopardized when she becomes personally involved with the case of an abandoned child and the child's competent but strict social worker, Emory Blake. (978-1-163555-185-3)

Taking Chances by Erin McKenzie. When Valerie Cruz and Paige Wellington clash over what's in the best interest of the children in Valerie's care, the children may be the ones who teach them it's worth taking chances for love. (978-1-163555-209-6)

BOLD STROKES BOOKS
Bold Strokes Books
Quality and Diversity in LGBTQ Literature